R. A. Padmos

Ravages

Manifold Press

Published by Manifold Press

ISBN: 978-1-908312-95-2

Proof–reading and line editing: Thalia Communications | thaliacomm.net

Editor: Fiona Pickles

For further details of Manifold Press titles both in print and forthcoming: manifoldpress.co.uk

Other titles by R. A. Padmos:
    Unspoken

Acknowledgements

To my wife, but she's probably going to say something like: "I didn't do anything."

So many individuals deserve to be thanked for their encouragement, their willingness to put up with my doubt if I was the right person to write this story and their patience in what was at times a very slow process. I don't want to hurt anyone by accidentally forgetting a name, so: you know who you are.

A very special thank you goes out to Joanne Morris for her generous sharing of her knowledge of all things football, her red pen before I even dared to present the manuscript to a publisher, and for giving me the Steve Gavan song.

And thank you, people at Manifold Press for taking a chance with this story.

Chapter 1

Steve knows he looks like an idiot. A very, very happy idiot, with a smile that stretches from one ear to the other and eyes that probably shine much too brightly. There's a spring in his step like he won a competition he doesn't remember having entered. He thinks he even smells differently, like he's two men at the same time. He wears the heady richness of Daniël's scent like an exclusive fragrance.

People stare at him while he's walking from the pub where he had shared a pint with a couple of mates, and that's not because they recognise him from the matches on TV or because he's one of the faces on the poster above the bed of their ten-year-old-son. No, the reason is that silly smile on his face. He's absolutely certain of it.

To be past his thirtieth birthday and for the first time having felt a man inside him makes his head reel. There had been no rational reason for him to make such a fuss about it, more so because Daniël has been enjoying the experience several times a week for the past six months and it's not like Steve has to beg for it, either. But what can you do?

Daniël hadn't pressured him for it, reassuring him time and again that sex was great between them. And it is great, every aspect of it. Of course, they have to be careful when they're in the public's eye, the world of professional football and its fans not being known for its open and generous outlook towards gay men, but as soon as they're alone, they shake off all restraint. On occasion they allow themselves a sleep-over and there's no better way to start the day than having a sexy Dutchman to take care of Steve's morning erection by using that talented mouth of his. Or to be invited to Dan's apartment and have a quickie while dinner is keeping warm in the oven. Best of all are the long hours that seem so fleetingly short, they spend in bed doing just about anything that's physically possible and wanted by the both of them. The sheer beauty of looking into Daniël's eyes while fucking him with such intensity – it feels like he's losing his self wholly, only to come back even more complete.

This one thing however he had never allowed, even when Daniël asked it in such a seductive voice he had felt his heart turn and all he could have said was a clear yes. But he hadn't said yes. Not until last night.

A certain someone got really lucky last night, he thinks, and it's our little secret. He's not even sure why he changed his mind, what gave him the courage to turn on his stomach, his legs wide and inviting, to say: "Please, Danny."

Daniël, being the tall boy that he is, and being in proportion in all aspects, had been somewhat intimidating even though Steve had taken that beautiful monster more times in his hand and mouth than he's able to count. Despite Daniël's endearing care and patience, there had been pain, but not nearly as much as he had anticipated, and all of it had been due to his inability to surrender to his own need. The eight-year age difference was not just a number in some aspects of their relationship.

It made him admire his lover even more for being so free and open with his desire to be taken by his man. The easy honesty of it all. Trusting Daniël had come naturally to him. Trusting himself to just let it all happen and see what comes next was a different story. He had been overwhelmed by the force his own emotions, still never doubting he was safe. Daniël had, with no words spoken about it during or after, guided him through the storm, to finally let him rest at the welcoming shore of his body.

It will take time before he can enjoy being fucked even remotely as much as Daniël does, who begs for Steve's fingers when his dick is too exhausted to be coaxed into action yet again, but he is looking forward to the next time. Most importantly, it hasn't changed how he thinks about himself. He's able to look in the mirror and be happy with the man he has become.

It's theirs, the excitement and the sweetness of it all, the short looks during the match and the shared smiles during training. They're still learning to find a way to deal with the reality of playing for a Premier League club while being lovers, six months being such a short time. Their relationship has no public face, it doesn't know about romantic dinners at that nice little Italian place and it doesn't flirt in the dressing room. They always arrive at Three Graces Park for training in separate cars. They never isolate themselves from the others during parties and celebrations. No one needs to know. And no one's going to know.

It hadn't been love, or even lust at first sight, nearly a year ago. Before that, there was appreciation for the young talent, the newly acquired fellow defender. The boy, for what Steve saw was a boy and all the word implies, had simply been one of the items on manager Arnaud Degaré's shopping list. Daniël Borghart, Francesco Moreschi, Dag Jensen, Ray Portland and Neil Miller: the young dogs had found each other instinctively. Impatient, eager, loud, and with a surplus of energy. Fast friends, but also learning there is the starting Eleven, there's the bench and there's everyone else. Steve had noticed pretty soon that Daniël was ready to fight for his spot. He wanted to play matches and right from the first minute too, whenever possible. He hadn't come over all the way from his Dutch town to this city in the North of England to watch the game from the side line.

Soon Steve also saw intelligence, a feeling for the game that couldn't yet compensate for obvious lack of experience that comes with playing dozens of matches at a certain level, but it made him pay attention when the boy got into action. It had pleased him when Daniël started to ask questions. Why Steve had done what he had done during the most recent match. How he managed to see things seconds before they actually happened. How he, not being a fast player, ended up at the right place at the right moment more often than could be explained by statistical chances. The gaffer gave him a place with the starting Eleven in a majority of the games, which must mean he was doing something right. He wanted to learn that too. And although Steve had never been one to use three words if two were enough, Daniël got him talking all right; about the skills of their trade and about keeping the long hours on the training pitch and in the gym. About how defenders learn a different language than those whose whole job it is to recognise that one defining chance to score. "We not only have to see them, we also have to anticipate what they're going to see." And at Dan's thoughtful frown: "When in doubt: go full in and hope for the best."

During the friendly against Sparta Rotterdam, two weeks before the start of the season, Steve had been directed to the bench halfway the second half because of potential problems with his left hamstring and for Daniël, it meant his first chance to prove himself during a match. That's when it happened. And it happened so calmly, so gently he was surprised he even recognised it for what it was. But it also prevented panic. It was simply an emotion among so many others. He could deal with it and still do his job to the full.

He recognised and ignored it, concentrating on the team's performance on the pitch. Or at least he made a brave effort not to give Daniël more attention than the others. With limited success, but who is strong enough to go against his own, all too human heart?

He's grateful for what is happening to him, although he is the first to admit he doesn't understand it to the full. He knows he's a good team-mate, proud to know his work for Kinbridge Town hasn't gone unnoticed during the past five years. He's thankful for his matches with the Irish national team. It all proves he's not without some talent. He tries to be a decent human being, blemishes on his soul and all, knowing that he has to share some of his prosperity, time and modest fame for other reasons than because it looks good in the local media. But why this tall, good-looking, freckled, eight-years-younger guy from Holland insists on specifically having him, will remain a riddle for the time being.

Steve knows he isn't one to turn heads. He doesn't have the appeal of youth, not even when he was young. But then, he was never really young to begin with. Just a regular guy who happens to be fairly good at a certain game; more of a hard worker than anything else, is how he assesses himself. 'Dependable' is the main word they use in the Kinbridge Chronicle when they mention him in reviews about the match, and perhaps not without reason. But he doesn't think there are a lot of teenage girls writing their undying devotion to him in whatever teenage girls are writing in nowadays. That gushing of affection is reserved for the cute ones, like Francesco Moreschi and Daniël Borghart.

He saw them once, Moreschi and Borghart, sitting on a bench in the changing room, heads close together, listening to some, without a doubt, awful heavy metal band on Daniël's iPod. So young and heart-wrenchingly beautiful they had looked. He had already been attracted to Daniël at that time. Who was he fooling … He was so much in lust with the boy he used him as inspiration to his daily jerk-off session, no matter how embarrassed it made him feel, and so much in love it broke his heart to realise that if Daniël would go for another man, it would likely be Francesco. Their striker, who scores simply because he sees no reason not to. The boy, who makes family men on the stands blush by simply waving at them, and who looks like he could easily break, but still returned from his vacation in Spain with a tattooed angel that covers most of his back. Youth for youth. Beauty for beauty.

It didn't prevent him from having one of the most intense orgasms of his life that same night, while fantasizing in great detail about Danny fucking 'Cesco. Sliding his long, fat cock in and out of the tight arse, while grasping the girlish pretty hair. Sweat-slick, perfect bodies. Freckles and ink.

One day, he'll tell Daniël about that fantasy. Even being absolutely sure he doesn't want it to happen in reality, it could make for some nice inspiration.

Only two days later, Daniël kissed him for the first time. He tasted like boy turning into man, like sweets and beer. It was a good kiss, one he eagerly received and happily returned. But it did leave one question.

"What about Moreschi?"

"Francesco?"

"That one, yes. Unless there are other members of the Moreschi family contracted to play for Kinbridge Town when I wasn't paying attention." The uncertainty about where he stood with Daniël made him using far too many words to ask a simple question.

"I'm trying to get into your pants. Why should we talk about Francesco Moreschi?" Suddenly a realisation seemed to dawn upon the boy, and it made him look lost and vulnerable. "I wish he wouldn't keep that hair so long. It makes people want him." He sighed in defeat. "It makes you want him."

"I don't want Francesco Moreschi. I want you, Daniël Borghart." Steve still remembers how he began to smile at that moment, because it had become so blindingly clear then. "And you want me."

Thinking about their first time is like remembering the dozen goals he has scored in his nearly thirteen years as a professional player. Or, better even, it makes him feel like when he prevents an opposing player from finishing an attack in a spectacular manner and without being booked, the crowd singing his praise in a thundering song of affection and admiration. He can't imagine he will ever get tired of the feeling of Daniël stretching out on top of him, covering him with inches and inches of perfect skin, holding him with strong arms, being heavy with muscle and bone, but he can easily take it. And there's just as much chance of him not wanting Danny to kneel before him, opening the jeans to get Steve's cock out and take it between those sinful lips, as him not wanting to be part of the starting Eleven against one of the big clubs.

He's good company too, more so than Steve perhaps had expected. His taste in music leaves a lot to be desired and still Steve easily spends hours watching him dance to a tune that really isn't danceable at all. Just as easily he sits quietly, pretending not to watch how Daniël reads, his face betraying a deep concentration, then, suddenly, there's a smile, because he becomes aware of Steve observing him. Food tastes so much better if eaten in the company of someone who digs in with such enthusiasm it makes Steve laugh out loud. He even likes it when Daniël goes out to a nightclub or a rock concert with the other young guys, because when the boy returns, he's always, literally always, greeted by him with a smile that tells Steve everything he could possibly want to know.

Daniël doesn't expect him to talk when he doesn't feel up to it; he never asks what Steve is thinking when he's quiet and withdrawn. Like he understands that sometimes it's easier to pull Daniël close and kiss him in a way that, for the moment at least, expresses more about what he wants to say than any number of words. Sometimes they watch football on TV, Daniël's head on his lap, his fingers playing with the boy's hair, as happy as …

If there's anything happier than him and Daniël watching a footy match, he'd like to hear about it, so they could try it too. It's a quiet sort of happiness, but it makes him think beyond the moment. He's not ready yet to dismiss himself as ultimately irrelevant, a nice experience at best, in comparison with the much more important career that lies ahead for a player as talented and dedicated to the sport as Daniël Borghart. He thinks he can still manage a couple of good years with those legs of his. Although when it comes to staying with Kinbridge Town, he acknowledges some of it is likely wishful thinking on his part. By the end of the season, he'll be thirty-two, with young guys like Miller and Borghart breathing down his neck. And there's more on the way, with the owners allowing manager

Degaré a very healthy budget. Still, every club, no matter how much in love they are with their new stars, need the dependable players; the older guys who can be overlooked all too easily and still make the difference between a team and eleven high earning guys who just happen to be on the same pitch at the same time. But it's becoming less the alpha and omega of his existence. He wouldn't go as far as saying it's just a game, and things like privacy and what the papers would write or the songs the Kinbridge Kings would sing don't matter, but something is shifting.

And whatever that something is, it makes him smile and swagger a bit like he's drunk, although he's almost never drunk, and think about his future in a way that's new to him. He's no longer young enough to have any grand illusions; the world is what it is and people are what they are, but that doesn't mean nothing's ever going to change. If one day Daniël looks him in the eye and tells him it's all over, that he's no longer as important as the beautiful game, he will bow his head and try to keep his dignity while walking away. Until that day, he will keep on searching for a solution to reconcile the irreconcilables. He's not the one to start the revolution, but he's willing to try and jump over his own shadow to prevent Daniël from being unhappy.

He walks and walks to get rid of the abundance of energy. Dan is getting his parents from the airport and as much as he understands that Mr and Mrs Borghart want to spend some time with their son, he almost wishes they could welcome them in their home together. But no matter how many hours of the day they're spending with each other, there is no *their* home. Daniël had shown him pictures of his parents and his younger sister Naomi, and Steve in return had shown pictures of his mother and grandmother, or nan, as he would always remember her. He guesses Daniël's parents wouldn't be too bad about it, but something shared between a few is likely to become something shared between many. And they are not ready yet to share this with others.

So he keeps on walking, Daniël in his head, with a smile and a swagger and the knowledge that within a few days he'll have his arms full of one sexy Dutchman starving for attention of the non-parental kind. He's almost certain that by that time, he'll be ready to invite Daniël to top him again. If not out of curiosity, he wants to know if the second time will be easier, then because much of the pleasure he had felt the first time came from the absolute joy Danny had radiated. He has to see that look in his lover's eyes again. Perhaps they could try out another position and see how that works out for both of them. He loves it when Daniël straddles him, showing him that having a cock up your arse doesn't mean you can't be dominant, even aggressively so. Once or twice, things like that should be savoured like exclusive delicacies, he had been ordered to grip the headboard of his bed and let them stay there unless ordered otherwise. It had been an extremely educational way of learning that yes, you could be milked dry and still beg for more of the same.

The city is quiet and at rest, the streets all but deserted. Not that he's paying much attention, being happy with the thoughts in his head. He doesn't think he's ever been in this particular part of the city before, but he's sure he'll see something recognisable when he turns the next corner, and there's always a taxi if not.

A taxi to bring him to the nearest place where he can pee with some dignity would be nice, but after waiting a few more minutes he's ready to admit defeat: he's lost. It's obvious he's in one of the city parks and while he's not unfamiliar with many parts of Kinbridge's greener areas, this is definitely a place he has never visited before. It can't be helped: a tree is getting watered one extra time. He opens the zipper of his jeans and for a few seconds stares, oh sweet release, into nothingness.

But no, the eyes that stare right back at him, and then at his penis, couldn't be called nothingness. They have that *is that, no it couldn't be, yes it is him*, look. The look changes into a blatant stare, and the stare into sexual invitation.

Steve feels uncertain of how he's supposed to react. It's not that he's even remotely interested in the man, who must be somewhere in his forties, with an attractive face and, from what Steve can see, an acceptable enough body, he just doesn't know how to end this awkward situation without looking the spoiled and overpaid football star who can't be bothered to exchange a few friendly words with a fan.

Perhaps he should start with putting his penis back again. It feels a lot less silly now Daniël's favourite toy is safely tucked away, even though he can appreciate the great story it will make on the next birthday party the man visits. Not that they're going to believe he saw Steve Gavan, yes, the

Kinbridge Town right-back, I'm not pulling your leg, with his you-know-what in his hand.

The man smiles reassuringly while he stretches his hand out to touch Steve's crotch; his fingers starting to stroke. For a few seconds Steve's too flabbergasted to slap the hand away.

"Your secret is safe with me." The voice is soft and reassuring, like the man tries to calm a frightened animal.

Steve knows how to react to the tricks of a striker during a match. He can handle just about any kind of prank in the dressing room. Losing an important game is just as much part of his trade as the ecstatic feeling of having assisted in a brilliant goal. The sadness of knowing that hard work will not be enough to prevent him from being sent away from the place where he wants to stay until his bones become brittle. He simply deals with it. But this leaves him with his mouth open and his brain working overtime. It should be simple, really: no one touches this part of his body unless he's called Daniël Borghart, central defender at KTFC.

But it's not that straightforward. It's easy enough to slap the hand away, tell the man he's not interested, and none of it would be a lie. That man takes too many liberties, but he's also the first human being who sees Steve in a different light. He wants to say: "Hey, you look a nice enough bloke. I'm not keen on having sex with a stranger in a park, but if things were different we could perhaps grab a pint and see what happens. But you know, there's this wonderful, funny, talented, kind hearted, sexy guy and I love him so much I sometimes feel like I'm going to burst if I can't say it loud enough for the whole world to hear. But I can't say it, because it would destroy his career, and that's so much more than having money and being famous."

He's more than willing to subscribe to the idea of *whatever I do in bed is private*. He certainly has no intention of sharing the intimate details of his sexual relationship with Daniël with others, but why does that mean he has to hide everything that exists between them, unless it's called *being good mates* or *having taken the young talent under his wing*? Even the most tight-lipped players in any professional football competition in any part of the world don't actively hide the fact that they are with a woman. However exciting and, as he knows from wonderful experience, beautiful secret love can be, marriage has limited meaning without being witnessed by other people.

And now there's this insolent bloke who assumes, not incorrectly, that Steve isn't blind to the sexual appeal of men and he can't decide between telling half a lie and taking all of a risk.

"I understand you completely. Okay, almost completely." The man is tenacious; Steve has to give him that. "If I go public on you, I stand the chance of losing my wife, my family even. Please, you don't have to do anything. Just let me touch you. I'll make it really good for you."

There's movement around them, the shuffling of feet coming closer. There are excited whispers he can't understand but can guess the meaning of easily enough.

He refrains from vanity searches on the internet, even if it's about Daniël, with the exception of the articles from a handful of sharp and to the point football analysts. But he's aware of the speculations: which player is one of us? Which player is doing it with which player? Most if it will be motivated by wishful thinking. He can imagine they almost all have their fantasies about the pretty boys, preferably the ones who play in the first teams of one of the major clubs, being one of them, but from the surprised sounds he hears around him he doesn't think his own name has been mentioned very often. That, however, doesn't prevent the rustling of clothes and the collective breathing from going faster; the men trying their best for a fantasy to last them a lifetime. No one will believe them when they post their messages on the online communities, no matter how much they'll stick to what they claim to have seen. Even if their eyes deceived them in a way that's too ridiculous to be true, and saw the truth in a way they would never have come up with. Quiet, nearly invisible Gavan with that fit hot number from Holland? Yeah, right.

His life hasn't prepared him for this. Why don't they ask for autographs for their eight year old nephews? What is this place? Why is this? He doesn't feel the need to be in someone else's dream, when he's already perfectly happy with the one he and Daniël are dreaming. He will never blame people for what happens in the privacy of their own minds, because whoever has real control over that? He can just about live with the idea that some of them share those thoughts on the internet about his Daniël doing it with who knows which pretty player (they'll never guess the truth), but he doesn't want to be confronted with it just because he happens to take a nice long stroll and can't find a loo.

Why doesn't he just open his mouth to tell them, in a nice way, to get lost? He can already hear Dan's laughter when he's going to tell him about it. It can't be that difficult to speak one's mind. He appreciates his behaviour in public reflects on the club, but that doesn't mean he has to accept this kind of … he isn't even sure how to call this. Don't these people have homes to go to? Lovers? Families? He takes a deep breath, preparing himself for the right tone: friendly, but firm.

Before he can even say the first words, they're scattered like a flock of frightened birds. The rustling of clothes has been replaced by the stamping and scraping of nailed boots, and the excited whispers by harsh curses.

The man who couldn't keep his hands to himself is gone with the rest. He must be pretty proficient in the vanishing act because Steve doesn't see it happening. Probably back to wife and kids, saving the story of his big adventure for when he's alone with his computer and the friends whose real names he'll never know.

Chapter 2

"Fucking hell, tell me you're not him."

"Okay, I'm not him." Steve smiles because the look on the face of the man is genuinely funny. If this night is going to stay oddly surreal, he might just as well accept it with a smile and a joke. He guesses the autograph moment will be just about now, together with the more recent standing next to the famous person and ask your mate to make a photo with his mobile phone.

Only then he sees the absolute horror on the face of the man, and on the faces of the others around him. The shattered admiration. He doesn't count them; guesses there might be half a dozen pairs of staring eyes and gaping mouths. No, definitely none of them is thinking: I can't believe my luck today.

"My little boy has his poster above his bed. Plays the same position with his school team. Has his number on his kit. The nipper worships this fucking, bloody ... can't even say it ..."

"If you can't even trust the boys of your own club ..."

"Just now we're finally getting somewhere, with a gaffer who knows what he's doing and owners who give a shit and some new boys with real talent ..."

"It wasn't easy to get airtime for his bleedin' song ..."

"Away games are going to be hell if they ever find out ..."

"In a park, where there's families and all ..."

"Good thing we're here to put things right, because the police have gone all politically correct. Protecting the queers instead of the decent people."

"He didn't even try to get away, like they always do. Saw them running? Won't see them any more tonight. Thinks he's something better. Thinks he's one of us."

What's he supposed to say? That what the men thought they saw was a misunderstanding? That he simply needed to take a leak? That his private life is exactly that, private? That he would never risk the last years of his career as a professional player at this level to seek some cheap thrill in a park, when he has the genuine article in his own bed? That love is love? That no father should teach his child to hate?

Something tells him the men gaping at him are not of the polite conversation kind. And most likely a statement, however truthful, that he just happened to walk in the park, with no greater crime than having his fly open to take a pee, unaware of the kind of place this seemed to be for some, will prove to be useless. They saw what they saw and whatever comes from his mouth cannot be the truth. Above all, he doesn't want any more of this kind of attention, if only because of Daniël's position at Kinbridge Town. Thus far no one has made the connection, but what does that guarantee? Guilt by association can be just as devastating.

"Nice meeting you too. Now boys, it's getting late, so if you'd be so kind as to let me pass …"

They howl with laughter.

"Now boys, it's getting late, so if you'd be so kind as to let me pass …"

"Makes you wonder why we didn't see it sooner."

"They can pretend whatever they want but in the end, it always shows."

Since when is it unmanly to ask a polite question in a civilized manner? No one can accuse him justifiably of having a posh accent. He doesn't sound all that different from them, he knows that all too well. He might have been born in Ireland, but talking he learned in the housing estate in north-west England where he grew up. What's he supposed to say? Get out of my face, mother-fucking sons of just as many bitches, or I'll make sure none of you will ever see Chestnut Road Stadium from less than two miles again?

He has to get away. No way is he staying there with a bunch of bigots, reeking of stale beer and chips fried in oil that's become syrupy. If simple English words are not enough, a modest use of physical force might be the answer. Even with trees and bushes blocking one escape route and those men the other, it shouldn't be too much of a problem. If he can dive between them, something he has done countless times during equally countless matches and training sessions, he should be able to run away. There isn't a single cell in his brain doubting he can outrun any of this unfit lot without even breaking a sweat.

A wall of muscle and fat is enough to stop any rational thought for a few precious seconds. If this is a game to them, it is played by rules he isn't familiar with. And there isn't a referee in sight. If this is a team sport, he's still alone. He misses his team-mates. They would stick up for him, and only later ask him how the hell he got into this bloody mess.

At first, the attack is indiscriminate. The men simply kick and punch and shove whatever they can hit. There's even some hesitation in their action, like they are still not 100 % sure of what they're doing. Perhaps it's the remnants of human decency refusing to give up resistance this early. Six against one can hardly be called fair. Even more than that, he is one of the men who helped in changing their barely hanging on in the lowest regions of the Premier League club into something they can proud of because there's actually something to be proud of. He is a name on a shirt, a name called by the announcer at their home games almost every match, a name in the Chronicle, a name they chant because fuck, did you see how he took the ball and passed it so razor sharp to Kirkby it can only be called pure science. Is it too much to hope for that? Recognition of a job well done?

Steve doggedly gets up every time he's worked to the ground, tries to fight them off. It hurts, but he's had worse. He isn't afraid to use his body; he's not unfamiliar with its working and with the discomfort that comes with using it in a way that's perhaps ill-advised. If this doesn't stop very soon, he's in risk of tearing several muscles. And at his age and in this line of work a position in the starting Eleven is easily lost. But more than that, he doesn't want to confront Daniël with bruises on his body and face when they see each other again. How does a grown man manage to get in this kind of trouble during a walk in a city that at worst shrugs off his existence as just one of the many, but mostly has shown so much affection?

One of the men boots him hard enough at the back of his knees to make him hit the ground so violently it knocks the wind out of him. His head whips so hard against the pavement it makes him swoon. Even though a less trained man would fall even worse than he does, he soon realises this is the point where he no longer is able to get up. He keeps trying though, because blind instinct goes on long after the sane mind has drawn its conclusion.

He shouldn't have forgotten his mobile phone. Daniël has teased him often enough that he seems to prefer carrier pigeons instead of modern means of communication. If he hadn't misplaced the stupid thing … but, honestly, what does it matter now? The next match will be played without him, no matter how many phones he might have been holding in his hand.

He tries to look them in the face. They have to know he's human. They have to be reminded of their own humanity. But the smile he sees on the faces of every single one of them makes him strangely relieved, grateful even, that Daniël is at home, safely in bed, hopefully having a nice dream about the next time they'll see each other.

They now start to make serious work of venting their frustration about whatever is bothering them about life in general and him in particular. Something inside him wishes that later, when he sits in front of a nice and understanding (they have special training, he's almost certain of that) police officer (no man or woman these days, it's called officer) he can say that it all went so fast, that he hardly was aware of what happened. Or that he's able to witness his own suffering from a safe distance, like he once read in a magazine article during the flight to an away game. But his brain refuses to work like that; it doesn't subtract even one second from any of the agonizing minutes. The pain isn't lovingly covered up by endorphins.

"He shouldn't have come here. Not to this park or this city or our club."

Kick in his stomach.

"I hate it when they pretend to be normal."

Kick at his left side.

"You guys think this piece of Irish shit is the only poof in our club?"

Kick against his right hipbone.

"Kirkby?"

Kick in his crotch.

"Hey, no one talks shite about the skipper."

Kick in his back.

"Sorry."

Kick against his left hipbone.

"Levee? Only joking, boys, only joking."

Kick against his breastbone.

"Not funny. But, seriously: any of the other foreign lads, perhaps?"

Kick against his right shoulder.

"Can hardly believe that Moreschi really is a man."

Kick at his lower back.

"He's the best striker we had in ages. Would be a shame."

Kick in his belly.

"Dominguez?"

Kick right in the middle of his spine.

"Don't be daft."

Kick against his left shoulder.

"Any of the French guys?"

Kick against his buttocks.

"Nah …"

Kick against his ribcage.

They must not say Daniël's name. They must not even think his name.

Kick …

"Daniël Borghart?"

The sound he makes stops the kicking for a second. Even he hears how different it sounds from the grunts and groans that follow every time one of their iron-nosed boots and his body make contact.

Don't you dare touch him, he wants to say: not with your eyes, not with your words, not even with your thoughts. Don't you dare to make him as dirty as your vile hearts. Hearing them say Daniël's name hurt something inside him their boots hadn't been able to touch. It is not theirs to defile, not theirs to even know about. It should have been loving parents, a respected coach, close friends. Not them.

"So you get it up for Borghart? And does he like the idea you're a bleedin' bumfucker?"

"I don't think so, or else why are you here, getting touched up by fairies?"

"Nobody's stupid enough to open his mouth about stuff like that to his mates. They can say whatever they want about it being normal, but I don't want any poofs even looking at me and I know for sure that's the same for the Kinbridge Town boys."

"Did you come here to get sucked off? Would have thought Kinbridge pays enough to order a rent boy. Keep it discreet and all. Did we spoil your fun?"

"It would make Borghart sick if he knew you think of him when you're playing with your bloody prick. I bet there's going to be a photo in the Chronicle of that boy being spotted with a nice local girl in less than a month."

They are like one man in their resolve to save their Kinbridge Town Football Club, the club they claim is as important to them as their mother and first born, from him. A misplaced kind of affection that has just as much the power of its own conviction as any form of love. Had he been the praying kind, he would pray for their indifference.

"Not sure about you, boys, but I don't want to see him on the pitch ever again. Filth doesn't belong on Chestnut Road."

The others mutter their agreement.

The tibia of his left leg snaps with a sound that's not as dry as he thought it would be, and right after that the fibula. Soon after the same bones in his right leg follow. He has forgotten about the number of bones in his feet, and though he doesn't hear them breaking, the sound of his own voice tells him at least some of them are no longer whole. It's no use to cry out his agony when two of them, in an act of bizarre choreography, stamp their full, substantial weight at the same time on both his ankles. He's just helpless to stop it.

One heavy boot resting on his upper leg and one on his shin to make sure his left leg stays motionless. His kneecap cracks. The same procedure happens for the right one. Steve hears it right through his own screams and his attackers' laboured breathing. Breaking down the body of a sportsman who takes care of his health and condition proves to be more work than they likely imagined.

He's almost certain the femur of the fit, adult male, the strongest bone in the human body, and protected by regularly used muscles in his case, can't be broken by human force alone. He will never again underestimate the power of love turned into hate.

They can stop now. If it's the spilling of blood they're after, they can rest in the knowledge to have done a satisfactory job. There are enough broken bones in both his legs, enough torn muscle to keep him in hospital and out of Chestnut Road Stadium, even as an spectator, for weeks, if not months to come. If it's about hurting him so much he's forgetting what it feels not to hurt, then the sounds he makes must be a reliable indication of their success. Likely he'll never see the training pitch at The Three Graces Park again. If he'll ever be fit enough to do anything with a ball, it will be as a last reserve of a low ranking non-league club when everybody is out with the flu. Miracles do happen, and he has borne witness to them, but not with guys past a certain age. Not the goodbye he imagined for himself. He'll live, though.

It doesn't stop. If there was a moment they could have walked away, happy with the result of their intervention, they have missed it. If anything, they raise their effort. Their boots take turns, but never rest at the same time. They appear to have found their rhythm.

He no longer wants to look into their eyes. And why would they want to look into his?

Fear grows stronger than pain, even if it's for only a few seconds. He's willing to beg, to grovel at their feet. They want him to lick his own blood off their boots? No problem. Say out loud that's he's a fucking queer and he deserves everything they did to him? Why not? He'd even try his best to sound genuine, if so required. If it gives him the chance to see Daniël again, he will do it all. Football is just a game. His life is reduced to a fast dwindling list of essential items, and dignity is no longer among them.

"Please …"

He doesn't trust they even hear him. But perhaps the way they silently, simultaneously use their boots on him must be considered their answer. He starts to tremble, though he feels it's not fear as such, terrified as he might be, that's causing his body to shake uncontrollably, but something mainly physical. And still he tries to crawl away, the need to get to Daniël and be safe in his arms greater than the logical conclusion that a wrecked body won't get him very far. Something, hard and heavy like a branch, hits him on the side of his head. He hopes it will be enough to be knocked out, if only for a short moment, to give him some respite from the agony. It's not. He does however hear a strange murmur in his left ear and involuntarily he shakes his head.

"What? You don't like it here, with us? We're not good enough for you? Don't fancy us, real men? You want to be some place else? Perhaps getting fucked by that tall Dutchman? Does it hurt your poor little heart that he doesn't go for poofs?" The man uses his boot to stamp Steve's left hand into the ground. "Do you use this hand to wank when you're thinking 'bout him?" He switches to Steve's right hand. "Or this one? Oops, I guess you're not getting any action any time soon."

He doesn't understand why they are still talking. Do they think their words somehow add to the hurt? That there's some dignity left that can only be killed off by verbal abuse?

A thick branch is shoved under his nose. "You must have taken a peek when you're under the shower, after the match. He's got a big one? Like this?"

Sometimes, when they're totally sated with their lovemaking and still hovering a bit between being awake and asleep, Steve oh-so-gently cradles Daniël's spent cock in his hand and waits until dreams find him. His attackers will never know this beauty. He doesn't pity them for it.

He's just as surprised as they are that he's able to whisper a few words that are halfway understandable. "You … will … never … have … him …."

The toe of a boot makes his words taste like blood.

"Get his jeans off; I'm going to stick this thing so deep inside those rotten guts of his he can bite on the other end with whatever teeth he's got left."

"He might even get off on it."

Their laughter drowns out the rest of the words. Steve only knows both his ankles are taken into iron grips and he's dragged away. Pain, once again, gets a new meaning. He screams with wide open mouth, the sound lost and small.

The tiring shivers finally stop, only to be replaced by violent, irregular convulsions.

His bladder and sphincter muscles give out.

He knows he's dying. He feels rather than hears his own pitiful, soft whimpering. He's a hunted animal, offering its throat to the beast, unable to flee, past the will to fight.

His left hand is under my head.
His right hand embraces me.

He is no longer aware of the individual kicks. Muscles continue to tear, bones to break and blood to mingle with blood. He stares blindly at something he's no longer able to see. His ears still pick up sounds, but are not able to give useful meaning to any of them. Pain blossoms into the fullness of its potential. None of it matters.

My beloved is mine and I am his.

He just wishes he wasn't so tired.

I adjure you, daughters of Jerusalem,
If you find my beloved
That you tell him that I am faint with love.

His collapsed lungs try their best against cracked ribs. His heart is as brave as ever, but sometimes all the courage in the world isn't enough. There's so much love in every fibre of his being, it lights the darkness of the deepest night and it is strong as life itself, but like all living things, it too must bow its head for death. Hadn't he kissed the words on his beloved's upper arm? Smiling because … god … so young his treasured boy … *Mors vincit omnia* – Death conquers all …

I am my beloved's.
His desire is toward me.

He's grateful he said goodbye to Daniël with a smile and a kiss. Not a bad word between them. He has been blessed with the joy of friendship and love.

This is my beloved, and this is my friend …

A calm sadness is all that's left.

Chapter 3

Everything is as usual and yet everything is somehow slightly off. The match is a match, with a pitch and a referee and linesmen and the sound of fans, but he has no idea against which club they're playing. He's acutely aware of them being there, and yet every time he thinks he's able to take a glimpse at one of them, they turn out to be as invisible as the saints and angels his nan told him about when he was young enough to know he could actually see them if only he tried hard enough.

He's absolutely everywhere. No sooner has he prevented a player of the rival team (A new guy he never played against before? Why didn't Degaré tell him?) from scoring or he's at the other end and he makes a goal that will be shown on TV over and over again. It's such a beauty he knows Daniël will be joining in with the others to make him disappear in a celebratory huddle. Before that happens however he's already somewhere else, assisting in the next goal. He hears the crowd.

Steve Gavan, he flies without wings,
Steve Gavan, defender of Kings.

But before he gets the chance to celebrate with his mates, with Danny, he's right in the middle of the next action. He plays like an angel, like the devil gone mad. He runs and takes the ball from opponents he still doesn't recognise. He knows Daniël and the others must be there. Someone plays him the ball, so he can score and score again. And if he doesn't kick the ball in the net, someone else does from his passes that are so sharp and accurate there's no way the net could have been missed. The Kinbridge Kings have never been louder. No matter how fast he is, they follow him with their song.

Steve Gavan, he flies without wings,
Steve Gavan, defender of Kings.

He knows that some referees don't like the players to make a full blown orgy out of a goal celebration, but this one is extremely tight on the schedule. A chummy slap on his back from his captain would be the least he deserves. Possibly a little hand-touching with Danny? Not even Moreschi or Jensen or Kirkby make goals like this on a weekly basis, let alone a full back like him.

Perhaps this is just a friendly, merely something to use as practice for when it really matters. But then, why doesn't the crowd feel like it's mainly for fun? He can always hear the difference between being comfortably in the lead against an opponent they know through and through, and the almost desperate faith they had in their team, during the relegation match the first season he played for Kinbridge Town.

> *Steve Gavan, he flies without wings,*
> *Steve Gavan, defender of Kings.*

He keeps running, playing magic tricks with the ball. No one can touch him. He used to dream as a little boy that one day he would play like this. This was when he was not yet aware that football is team sport. That players remain in relatively fixed positions. That a lot of dull work is needed to make those few brilliant moments even possible. That there's a reason defenders seldom score. Or even that he will become that quiet guy whose main role it is to stop a certain thing from happening.

He slides through the opponent's defences. Alone. But he's not alone. They're all there. He recites their names in his head. Kirkby, Moreschi, Levee … The ones who always play unless they're injured. Jensen, Jaworski, Dominguez … The ones who get a regular chance. Miller, Lain, Kowalski … The ones who get at least as far as the bench. Portland, Celan … Even the ones who know they will be in the transfer window at the next opportunity. Laporte, Devries … He knows they're all there. They must be all there. But he isn't even sure who's on the pitch with him, who's on the bench and who's sitting on the terraces.

> *Steve Gavan, he flies without wings,*
> *Steve Gavan, defender of Kings.*

Out of the corner of his eyes, he sees Daniël. He wants to jog in his direction, perhaps make a little joke about the strictest referee in the history of football. But he's already forced to make sure their lead, although he has no idea about the score, stays as comfortable as it's likely to be. Why this frantic running for the ball? The first half surely is almost over and they can't possibly lose unless they walk out of the pitch, all eleven of them, and keep the goal open for whoever wants it. It must be humiliating for the other team and their fans. Not that he even hears any of their singing and chanting. Did they show up at all to support their team?

Steve Gavan, he flies without wings,
Steve Gavan, defender of Kings.

He's getting tired. Forty-five, or even ninety minutes can't be that long. The days when he was twenty and could go on forever and ever have long gone. Games at this level, no matter how much he loves to play, will soon cost more than he's able to pay, as willing as he might be. The physical aspect is not the most important element, even accounting for injuries and the fact that it takes more time to recuperate from a match. Real decline goes much slower than that. No, the will to compete – to show who's the best, to prove beyond all doubt who's worthy to lead, to mate, to become one of the stories told around the fire during cold, dark winter's nights – can only be the main driving force for a limited amount of years.

Steve Gavan, he flies without wings,

He starts wondering why he's running all over the place. Are there no mid-fielders to make the game? No strikers to finish off the attack? No other defenders to keep the goalie from having to make a dive for the ball? Some new tactic Degaré's giving a try? The manager is known for his fondness of experiments, for trying out unusual player combinations, to let them experience how it feels to play in a different position. Nah, what's happening here is not how this game is played.

Steve Gavan, defender of Kings.

Talking about the gaffer: why doesn't he remind the ref time's up? Or at least, why isn't he using any of the substitutes? It near to never happens that the starting Eleven is identical to the finishing one, as far as Steve's experience goes. Not at this level. Doesn't the gaffer see he can't go on much longer? Are his team-mates blind? Can't the skipper do something? Anything? He can't believe Daniël's ignoring his desperate attempt to be taken out of the game, but why are the others ignoring Daniël?

> *Steve Gavan, Gavan ... without wings,*
> *Gavan, Gavan ...*

He no longer wants to be there. His body is aching, the wires in his brains are in overload, his lungs are burning and his heart goes much too slow after having beaten much too fast. He's reduced to a machine shutting down. And still they sing and chant; for no one else but him.

◆

All of a sudden, he knows where to look and he sees him. Sees it, more correctly. For Death is neither man nor woman. Neither young nor old. Neither man nor beast. Neither angel nor devil.

"Take me with you," Steve hears himself saying. "Take me from here, because I'm so tired. I know you have stolen intensely wished for children from their mothers' wombs as matter-of-factly as you have ignored the prayers of old men until they had used up their bodies to bitter decline. You are not impressed by kings and their armies. Money is of no help. Sometimes you pick up healthy men during a match and you change everything for the ones around them. You make us wonder: am I next? What makes me so different, so lucky, that I was not taken?

"You took my mother not long after I finally had the money to say to her, 'Sit down, you've worked long and hard enough. Now it's my turn to take care of you.' And I thank you for that, because she welcomed you as her liberator, even if it broke my nan's heart."

Then insight dawns upon him. "I'm not on the pitch, am I? There is no referee, there are no linesmen. No one is singing for me in the stands. There's no other team. There's no our team. It's just you and me. You have come to fulfil your task and show me your mercy. I'm at peace with that and I surrender myself into your hands."

Death doesn't move.

"What's keeping you? There's so little left of me. I promise not to fight you."

Death still doesn't move. No, there is in fact a slight motion, but not in Steve's direction.

Steve looks. Daniël is standing next to him. He doesn't look back at his dying lover but stares intently at Death, and he is a terrible sight to behold. The madness of a man gone berserk shines from his bloodshot eyes. He's baring his teeth like a ferocious animal. His face is distorted in rage. He's bloodlessly pale.

"Don't you dare to take him from me. If you want him, you'll have to go through me. You can have me too, I don't care. I know what's inked in my skin. Not the one that says you have the last word. The other one. The Heart or Death. I made my choice, now I shall live it. Even if it means I'll have to die by it. The two of us or the deal is off." Daniël's threatening whisper is the softest sound Steve has ever heard and yet to him it's easily distinguishable between the noises that have no meaning to him. "He's in unbearable pain and he's beyond exhaustion. Some of the more serious damage to his body, to his brain, may well be permanent. I know that. And I shield him from the only thing that can free him from his suffering. What I do is cruel, I know that too. Consider me love's ugly face.

"You can try and scatter his bones all over this earth. Know that I will find them one by one. If you take him to the underworld, I will come to reclaim him. And I will not look back, even if his decaying flesh touches mine. Someday I will have to let him go, and I shall take his hand for the last time in mine and say to him that, yes, he is going to leave me for you. *Mors vincit omnia*. But today is not that day.

"I, Daniël Borghart, stake my claim on Steve Gavan." He stands as tall as his body is able, his head high and defiant. "Because he is my beloved and my friend."

Death makes a move, swift as the hunter it can be. Daniël still moves faster. He dives on Steve's bed, covering him with his body. Shielding him.

"My sweet boy, you have to let me go."

"No."

"Your love weighs so heavy on me."

"If love is weaker than death, if it's as light as a feather, what's its use?"

"There is no shame in bowing your head for the only true justice in this life."

"If you're no longer able to fight, I will defend you. As long as you're in my arms, you're safe. I am yours and you are mine."

"Together."

Death crushes down on them with scorching fire, with the claws of the beast and the gentleness of the welcoming earth.

Chapter 4

There is nothing, absolutely nothing. No light. No darkness. Not even time, because there is no beginning and no end. There are no answers, because there's not a single question left. And there is no word for nothing. There are no words. No thoughts. Nothing.

Then, slowly, Nothingness makes place for the peaceful, instinctive knowledge that he's somewhere safe. No longer is he imprisoned inside the boundaries of his physical existence. He's as small as a single atom and as vast as the universe. Travelling among the stars is as easy as exploring the depths of the deepest ocean. He remembers everything that is ever forgotten and foresees everything that is yet unknown. He sees how all that is begins and there is no doubt in his mind how it will all end. It's nothing he hadn't already known, because it's ingrained knowledge to all that comes from the same source: he just hadn't been aware of it.

And yet, among this perfection there is the tender beginning of doubt. At first not more than a small seed, an almost too easy to ignore feeling that he is not where he's supposed to be. But it grows. And with it time starts, however feebly. And memory that is his, and his alone, takes form. He's assumed to have words for everything so he can say what needs to be said to the one who needs to hear those words from his mouth. He's supposed to have hands to touch the one who needs to be touched by him. To have eyes because there's someone in need of being noticed by him. To have a body so his beloved can hold him. He cannot be limitless, without fixed boundaries.

He has to return to his body. Even if it means losing the ability to touch the sun without burning and witness how life moves forwards with death so close in its footsteps they are like lovers unable to be without each other. His beloved needs him. It all comes down to this simple, unavoidable truth. What's the use of having all the knowledge in the world and being without any physical boundaries when he's unable to hold the one human being who truly matters in his arms, or when he doesn't even have the words to tell him that everything will be as it should be? He is at peace with himself and with the end of his existence, he embraces Death as a liberator, a friend even, but he has to go back to the all-too fragile flesh and bones. Time will no longer be without beginning or end. The darkness will be no longer be absolute, the light not all-embracing. His brain will no longer allow him to remember the terrible violent beauty of the birth of all life. His heart will mourn that loss bitterly. He will have to give up his final wisdom for love. If love is the one thing that rules above everything else, then it is at times a harsh and unforgiving monarch. But it has to be done.

So he looks and immediately looks away.

But already it's too late.

This has to be a mistake. If this is a joke, then he isn't laughing. How can he return to this ruin? He hadn't just lived inside this dwelling; it had always been far more than merely a vessel for his mind, or his soul, if you like to call it that. He had lived by its laws and needs and talents. He had learned by it. Discovered the world by it. His body's ability to do something so many little boys dream about and so few men see actually coming true, had granted him the rare privilege of earning a more than comfortable living doing something he would do anyway, even if he'd have to pay for it out of his own pocket and work some mind-numbing job in an office.

His had always been a good body, dutiful and functioning as it was supposed to, most of the time. A source of many pleasures. Injuries had been part of the job, but everything healed fully with adequate treatment and the right combination of rest and exercise.

Love, or perhaps he should be more blunt about it and call it sex, hadn't been all that special, but at least good enough to keep serious complaints, both his own and his partners, to a bare minimum. He knew himself to be gentle and caring enough to at least try his best for whoever landed in bed with him, but also too reserved to make a lasting impression.

When he no longer reckoned with it, love did found him in its most physical form. A tall boy, bordering on skinny if it wasn't for the muscles formed by hard work, a freckled face, blue-grey eyes, and wise sayings tattooed on his arms that should have stayed mere words for many years to come, had been introduced to him during training. Not much had happened then. The world hadn't come to a grinding halt. His life hadn't changed all of a sudden. His body and soul hadn't recognised their mate.

Or perhaps they had and it was he – or more precisely the rational, thinking part of his brain – who had been too cautious, too weak in his faith.

Not that he had been a virgin when Daniël kissed him for the first time. Far from it. He's old enough to be able to genuinely smile at the memories of the awkward discovery of what it could mean to be no longer an innocent child with an equally almost too young boy and the long self-forgiven shame of not being able to control himself with a girl far too beautiful for his inexperienced fumbling. There were the more mature encounters. Mostly pleasurable, almost none of them memorable.

Daniël's touch had burnt traces in his heart and memories in his brain. The boy's unassuming inquisitiveness, his generosity as well as the vocal expressions of his love for Steve and his body, had changed a man who thought himself set in his habits. Danny had made him aware he had found something he didn't even know was missing.

Whatever it is lying there is not his body. There's nothing familiar about it. It is broken, damaged beyond recognition. A condemned house; uninhabitable. No longer safe. And yet his beloved sits beside a bed in a room that looks somewhat familiar, although he has no recollection of how or why he, or rather the body he ought to call his own, came to be lying on that bed, connected to so many tubes and wires. Daniël sits there and, with heart-breaking tenderness, touches a small patch of skin on the inside of the right forearm. As far as Steve can see it's the only part of the body that isn't hideously bruised.

His beloved moves his body slightly forward and bows his head deeply, and then he places his lips against that patch of intact skin, kisses it. His beloved talks to him, but he can't understand the words. He can't even hear the sound of his voice.

Steve yearns to feel those lips, those fingers. He belongs in those arms. The mysteries of the universe, of life itself, have been unravelled before his eyes, but what's the point if he can't hear the voice of the one he loves? But it can only be if he accepts his body as it is.

So he makes the journey home.

Too much. Too much. Pain and pain and pain. Screaming in his ears. Clawing white heat of light behind his eyes. Shredding his skin to pieces.

Mauling the flesh off his bones. Gnawing at his bones to get to the nutritious marrow. Devouring him and spitting him out to start once more.

Daniël's voice, as clear and real as the pain, cuts through it all. "Steve."

He flees, shocked to the core of his being. His instinct tells him to get away as far as possible. He then stops abruptly. He has to think, has to be rational about it. He knows he has to go back to his physical existence and he believes he's ready for it. But his body definitely isn't ready for him.

Perhaps an ever greater shock than the avalanche of pain has been Daniël's voice. Not a memory, a vision or a beautiful dream, but the real voice of the real man, saying one word: Steve's name. His lover sits with him and watches over him. This is the absolute truth.

He accepts the journey back will take longer than he reckoned with, but he knows now for certain there is a home waiting for him.

Chapter 5

All is quiet. His senses are at rest. He's aware of Daniël being with him, he doesn't need proof to know. Death also is still there. Not doing much. It's like a presence, observing Steve from a distance, almost as if it's curious to see what happens next. Steve has no illusions: Death will do its job if it gets the chance. He doesn't take it personally.

The monster called Pain, that's a different story. Steve fears it deeply, although he knows the only way to get back to Daniël is to face the terror and either defeat it or make peace with it. Or most likely, defeat it by making peace with it. He doesn't want that. He's like a little boy in this, wishing he could make it go away by closing his eyes very tightly and counting to ten. He wishes Daniël would chase it away, like he fended off Death for Steve, though he realises even love big enough to stop Death in its tracks won't make the monster disappear. He knows, however, exactly what his beloved would say to Pain.

"If you have to hurt someone, because that's your purpose in this world, do it to me. I don't fear you. My body is strong. My love is stronger than my body. I can take it." And he would take Steve in his arms, with a tenderness that would move the monster to tears, but it still wouldn't stop the pain. He might be able, to a certain point, to trade his life for Steve's, but pain, by its very nature, has to be carried alone.

Daniël will be with him, every step of the way, but he has to be the one smiling his acceptance at pain, without ever forgetting this isn't how it's supposed to be. It had to be a wise man who said that you have to make peace with the enemy, not with your closest friend.

For now he hardly dares looking in its direction. Daniël is touching him, is touching the one small part that doesn't hurt, but he can't feel it without feeling the pain of the rest of his body. So he keeps himself from feeling anything. That hurts too, but it can't be avoided for the moment.

It's hardly a conscious decision when the part of his brain responsible for smell kicks into action. The first impression is disappointing. It's not really bad or even frightening in its overwhelming complexity, it's just something he knows he smelled before and he didn't like it then either.

And it certainly isn't Daniël. But he has patience, accepts the facts for what they are. Disinfectants. Soap, but not one of the nicer ones. Blood. Some traces of human waste. A handful of people coming and going; the females somewhat sweeter than the males, but all with the same undertone, like they have something very essential in common.

It's there. It's really there. Daniël's scent. He smells of not enough fresh air, of coffee and takeaway meals, of needing to change his clothes. He smells of Daniël. He smells of home. The scent fills Steve with sweet memories. It gives him the courage to look at the monster called Pain, even if it's only for a few seconds out of the corner of his eyes. It's enough to make him tremble with fear. So he forces himself to look exactly one second longer than he dares. But then he's forced to look away.

He rewards himself by concentrating fully on Daniël's scent. With a bit of trial and error, he even succeeds in blocking out all other impressions for a few precious seconds. It's almost as if he's close enough to his beloved to be actually capable of touching him. In a way, he is. In fact, he is not.

He ignores Death and the monster, he even ignores his own craving to feel Daniël's touch on that small part of his arm, to hear his voice, and he concentrates on the memories brought on by the scent of his lover. Them doing their laps at the start of training and them being on the pitch during that away match against Liverpool, he on the right, Danny at the centre, both of them concentrating on their job as defenders, waiting for the signal …

No, too early for that. Much too early. He sees the monster stir, getting ready to pounce. Even Death looks more interested.

This is better. Last summer, June to be more precise, and it had been raining for days. The boy was going mad, desperate for air and exercise. Steve, going mad from Dan's restlessness, had pushed him out of his apartment for a long walk, with the instruction to stay away until he had run off all excess energy. Obviously having sex a dozen times during the last 24 hours hadn't done the job.

Daniël returned wet to the skin and with a glow to his face that would have made Steve fall for him then and there, hadn't he been up to his ears in love with the man already.

Steve had taken him in his arms, not caring about getting wet himself, and he had pushed his nose against his lover's neck and inhaled deeply. "I can still smell myself on you."

He smiles at the memory of summer and rain and Daniël's scent being indefinable and yet the one thing he will be able to recognise blindly from millions of other scents for the rest of eternity. He knows it like a mother knows her child. He knows it by head and by heart. It will never stop being a part of him. Elements are ever changing, depending on a wide range of food, activities, the brands Daniël's using for his personal hygiene, his health. The ground note however is solid. Despite everything that seems to happen around them, this is what anchors him to his physical existence.

He holds on to it. Sometimes, it seems to be gone. At such moments the beast stirs, licking its fiery tongue so close to Steve's skin he feels how the burn finds its way to the marrow of his bones. It is then that Death shows a renewed interest.

Daniël always returns before the monster delivers Steve into Death's arms. But it still exhausts him, makes him want to retreat more fully. He doesn't. Because of Daniël. And because of something he can't put into words, but is there all the same.

So he's more than grateful when he discovers that at a certain moment, Daniël's scent is still there with him, even if his beloved seems to be gone for a short time. The scent is stable and very close by. A shirt worn by Danny, carefully placed on the pillow, close to his face? Such a clever boy.

It makes Steve look at the monster called Pain long enough to realise he's ready for the next step: he's going to find Daniël's voice. He knows now what to expect and it all happens in such overwhelming abundance that he has to try several times before he's even able to accept any sound at all.

If the scents and smells were too much to take in all at once in the beginning, the noise is so much worse. There's beeping and rattling and voices, voices, voices. There are things he doesn't even know the name of producing sounds he has no idea how to describe.

It takes an enormous effort from Steve before he's able to sift through the sounds. There are routine sounds, mechanical things that are just there all the time, stable and perhaps irritating, but not indicating imminent danger. He recognises footsteps. Sometimes of individuals, fast and slow.

Sometimes of whole groups. There are voices. He has no idea what they're talking about, or even what language they are using, but at least he knows they are human voices. It's never fully quiet. How do they think his damaged body is supposed to heal with such a racket?

He needs to hear Daniël's voice, so why can't they all shut up? It's difficult enough as it is: making sure his beloved's scent isn't drowned out by disinfectants and coffee and a dozen other smells he has no use for. The vile mixture of sounds only makes it so much, much worse.

He's prepared for the monster. He thinks he is. Of course, he's mistaken and pays the full price. And still he refuses to let go of that filmy thread connecting him physically to Daniël. He knows beauty and peace await him as soon as he decides to let go, and he wants to let go so desperately all he can do is hang on and let the monster do its job.

When he thinks the hellish noise is finally going to drive him truly insane and the pain makes him want to take refuge in Death's embrace, a sound so small he shouldn't be able to hear it, finds him. The monster called Pain retreats. Death lets its welcoming arms drop by its sides. He doesn't recognise the sounds as words, doesn't even recognise the language, although he realises Daniël must be talking to someone. For now, it doesn't matter: as long as the boy talks. He wants to drown in the beautiful familiar sound of his voice, in the small laughter and reassuring whispers. Together with Danny's scent, it lulls him into a state of near perfect bliss.

If only he would be able to see him, feel him …

He can't stay in this dream-like state, however appealing it may be. He has to concentrate. Daniël is talking. His beloved uses words. Words have meaning. Understanding the meaning of those words is essential. Steve has no idea why, he just knows. So he concentrates instead of letting the gorgeous sound rock him into oblivion.

Funny though, he hears Daniël talk, but no answer from the person he's talking to. No duet of voices, no back-and-forth, no question and answer. An interesting riddle Steve doesn't have time to solve because another person enters the room. That person, a man according to the timbre of his voice, says a few words to Daniël. Daniël answers and the change of tone is so clear and abrupt, Steve can't help but wonder what it could mean. Danny doesn't sound angry or upset, or any less beautiful, just different.

For a moment, he just listens to the two men talking. He hears concern, a hint of anger, but not directed at Daniël, who sounds like he trusts the other man, like he knows him very well, but not like he knows and trusts Steve. They are friends, not family, and definitely not lovers. And if Daniël and the man who isn't Daniël are friends, then that man could be friends with him as well, Steve realises.

Matthew? Captain?

Daniël is not alone in this. Matthew Kirkby is standing right beside him, showing friendship and support. That's good.

Another person enters the room. Another voice. This time he gets it almost right away: Gael Dominguez. A sign perhaps his consciousness is seriously starting to work again? Still no meaning to the words, but that's a matter of time, he expects.

Again: friendship and concern. And he's not sure how or why, but both Matthew and Gael sound distinguishably different when they specifically talk to each other. It's subtle enough to make him realise he wouldn't hear it if he could have concentrated on the content of their conversation, but since the sound is the only thing he seems to be capable of processing, he's sensitive to exactly these easy-to-miss distinctions.

Every now and then, Daniël's voice gets this special warmth that goes straight to Steve's heart. Like a soft blanket, his lover wraps around him and gives him at least the illusion he's somewhat protected from the monster. The realisation that Daniël talks to him, offering him words that are made of love, no matter their meaning, makes Steve strong enough to look at Pain longer than ever before. He's still crippled with fear, but he looks and he doesn't look away until after what feels like an impossibly long time.

When Matthew and Gael are gone, Daniël is still with him; sometimes talking, sometimes silent, but nearly always there, with his scent of coffee and different kinds of food and that hard to define something. With his gentle fingers against the few centimetres unmarred skin, even if Steve can't feel it, he knows. And he leaves the shirt with his scent on the pillow when he isn't beside the bed.

The words come so gradually, Steve even misses the beginning. He just hears Danny singing: very, very softly, and almost shyly.

"'t Is in de kamer zo stil, zo stil ...
Zijn de kinderen al naar bed,
of lopen ze nog buiten?
Zijn de kinderen al naar bed,
of lopen ze nog buiten?"

(It's quiet in the room, so quiet
Have the children gone to bed,
or are they still outside?
Have the children gone to bed,
or are they still outside?)

He wishes he could see this: his beloved blushing and carefully touching the man he loves and singing a lullaby for him, perhaps to remind him he's safe and unconditionally loved.

Daniël no longer sings.

"Alsjeblieft Steve, wordt wakker. Laat me je mooie bruine ogen zien."

(Please, Steve, wake up. Show me your beautiful brown eyes.)

A soft sigh.

"Wat zal er van ons worden?"

(What will become of us?)

Silence.

"Vergeef me. Ik kan het niet helpen dat ik ongeduldig ben."

(Forgive me. I can't help being impatient.)

More silence.

"Ik laat je niet in de steek. Ik hou van je."

(I won't abandon you. I love you.)

Steve looks at Death, looks at the monster called Pain and acknowledges them with a smile. He allows the last remains of the perfect peace and wisdom he knows to be there, to slip through his fingers. It's time to open his eyes.

Chapter 6

Steve thinks that by simply envisioning opening his eyes he will be able to look at Daniël's radiant smile, hear him say something sweet and tender with that lovely accent, feel him touch his face with careful fingers, feel his lips, dry and boyish, on his own.

That's not how it happens. There's still a long distance to go between a heartfelt wish and taking that one step. A step that he somehow knows – although he's still a long way off from the how and why – is both a last and a first. Waking up and looking at Daniël is his most important goal for the moment: he even imagines it being more important than making sure Death simply leaves and Pain no longer terrorises him. But it will not be the end of his journey, no matter that he has absolutely no vision of what awaits him after that first welcome back smile.

He pushes the question of why he is in this situation, why the need to fight for his life, why he's trying so very hard, and quite literally, to get back to his senses, to the far background of his mind. There are monsters even more terrifying than the one he's already facing.

For the moment, he's enjoying the re-found ability to understand human speech. Most of the time, he's at a loss as to why people are saying what they're saying or who those people are, but he remembers having heard most of the words before, and it will have to suffice until he's able to ask questions. Able to truly remember.

"He's stable at the moment …"

"His blood pressure is still much too low …"

"He needs more fluids …"

"The infection should have been contained by now …"

"He's had a relatively quiet night …"

"His temperature has gone up again …"

"We'll need to do a brain scan to know more …"

"More morphine? Too much of a risk, I'm afraid …"

"What keeps him here? Honestly? I guess about half of it is our work. The other half? Depends on whether you're a religious person or a romantic …"

He accepts the voices of strangers as being non-threatening. Daniël would never let him come to harm. In fact, his lover often talks to those strangers and those strangers talk to him. He guesses they are the ones trying to help him, help his damaged body. He still prefers it when those strangers are not there with him and Daniël: just the two of them, with Dan talking quietly to him, sometimes reading out loud.

Weather reports from the morning paper. "They're promising rain again. Just like yesterday and the day before that. What's new?"

The results from the latest match. "At least we walked away with a point against Fulham after that disaster against the Gunners last Saturday. Dag made the equaliser in the 86th minute. Not the prettiest he ever scored, but it counted. Perfect assist from Gael, by the way."

A poem by E. E. Cummings.

> "here is the deepest secret nobody knows
> (here is the root of the root and the bud of the bud
> and the sky of the sky of a tree called life; which grows
> higher than the soul can hope or mind can hide)
> and this is the wonder that's keeping the stars apart)
> i carry your heart (i carry it in my heart.)"

And the menu of a take away pizza restaurant. "Thinking about asking Kurt if he can drop by at the pizzeria, there's a good one two blocks from here, for a quattro stagioni before he visits us. Could do with a bit of decent junk food."

Sometimes he is so full of joy to be able to hear Daniël talk for minutes on end, to hear his voice among all the noise without the monster attacking him, without Death even looking at his direction, that he forgets to listen to the actual words. He allows himself to flow on the waves of Daniël's sounds and scents.

◆

Daniël is talking, but not to him, and Steve doesn't hear anyone answer. Silly how long it takes him to work out the obvious: the boy's talking into a phone; Daniël's line to his family and friends in Holland. To his friends in England, who can't be with him all the time.

Sometimes, Daniël speaks in his own tongue. To him. To someone else. Not the same thing. In a single word, the tone of his voice changes. He listens to the words, separates them from each other, even though he knows he lacks the knowledge to understand them. A few expressions, some to do with love, some with anger he does understand, but apart from those all too rare exceptions, the words mean Daniël's talking and are, as such, worth his full attention. But most of the time he talks in English, as if he's beyond any doubt Steve is able to hear him.

"You should have seen the rain yesterday. I ran outside to feel it and ran back again because I missed you more than the rain."

"I miss you so much."

"I miss you more than the colour of the sky or the feel of the grass when I sit down to listen to the gaffer."

"I miss you more than waiting for the toss so the match can finally start."

"I miss you more than listening to really loud music."

"I miss you more than driving a very fast classic car on an empty road."

"I miss you more than my dad and mum and Naomi."

"Come back to me …"

◆

He remembers lying in Daniël's arms one Sunday morning, still in bed after the private celebration for the much-needed win against Blackburn, awake but not ready yet to start the new day, asking him to talk to him in Dutch. It didn't matter about what, just the sound of his lover's voice made him feel truly at home. He once asked if his lover didn't feel any homesickness, talking his own language in a strange country. Daniël hadn't understood the question.

He appreciates it when Dan has visitors, people who tell him about the world outside, or who simply listen to his silence. They visit Daniël in pairs and they visit him alone. They speak English with French, Spanish, Danish and half a dozen other accents. Some stutter and fall silent, others cry, most curse, but none of them stay away.

"The bastards …"

"They should lock them up and throw away the key …"

"They should leave scum like that to us; one at a time against a bunch of us to make it fair …"

"Absolutely fucking nothing can be used as an excuse for this …"

"Bloody animals …"

"Animals would never behave like those kinds of beasts …"

"Who needs the devil when there are people like that walking around …"

"Rest your eye full of mercy on this man and his beloved and do not forsake them in their hour of need …"

"Bloody hell …"

"Poor sod …"

"I think I don't even want to understand this …"

What are they talking about? They are his mates, they shouldn't say such things, even if they mean well. Aren't they aware of the horrors they are setting free? And now it's too late to shut his hearing down on time. Too late to keep the monster from attacking him. A monster with changing faces but all with similar distorted expressions of hate. The stench of leather and beer. The biting of metal into his vulnerable flesh. The monster mocks him, tells him it knows about Daniël. Tells him Daniël is disgusted by him. Tells him everyone is disgusted by him. The monster, who had been silent until now, speaks with the voices of those Steve wishes never to meet again. He needs to warn his beloved, needs to protect him, but he has forgotten how to use his voice, and his body is too broken to fight.

When he thinks he can take no more, a calm voice cuts through it all. "You know we will not leave you alone in this, boy. Both of you are part of this team, never doubt that."

Steve guesses Arnaud Degaré has visited Daniël before, even prior to his ability to recognise voices again. Time passes between his words, indicating a series of visits. He sounds concerned, fatherly, when he talks to Daniël. He sits longer with him than most others, like he has a special status. He is the gaffer; that should count for something.

"I know that, coach, but …" Daniël's voice falters.

Steve knows Degaré will put a gentle hand on Danny's shoulder and he's grateful for that. Still, it's his duty and privilege to comfort Daniël, to cheer him up. He looks at Death, who's standing far enough away to give him the illusion, if only for a short moment, that the war has been won. Then he looks at the monster and remembers there's still a long way to go before he can take Daniël in his arms and tell him they will face together whatever they'll meet on their journey through life.

And Death is no longer as far away as it looked a short moment before.

◆

"… I was so scared. I wanted my heart to stop beating when your heart stopped. Forgive me for being selfish, but the thought of having to go on for fifty or sixty or even more years without you is unbearable."

Steve imagines Daniël's lips on his arm.

"*Alsjeblieft* … Please …"

No, this is definitely not his imagination. He feels the dry lips so gently against the inside of his right forearm that it's easy to believe it's just a beautiful dream. But it's as real and true as Daniël's voice, as his scent, as his existence.

Steve opens his eyes. He looks into his beloved's eyes. And his beloved looks into his eyes. It is then that he knows with absolute certainty that he has made the right decision. He doesn't need any prophetic gifts to predict that what awaits him for a long time to come will be unimaginably hard. Yet he's prepared to go through every stage of hell, knowing he has been the source of the joy he sees on Daniël's face.

There is no need for him to close his eyes to know Death has retreated. Pain will be with him, in all possible variations, during most steps of the way, and while he refuses to befriend it, he will try to accept it for what it is. It's no longer a monster to him.

He feels pain because he's alive.

Because Daniël doesn't have to mourn him.

Because he made it home.

Chapter 7

"Mr Gavan? Can you hear me? Mr Gavan? Steve?" The voice, clearly belonging to a female, sounds professional, but doesn't lack human warmth. The kind of voice he usually hears when he has an injury bad enough to need treatment in a hospital.

"Please stay with us a little longer, Mr Gavan. You're in a safe place. No one will hurt you. I know that you can't talk, but that's because of the tube that helps you to breathe …"

Shut the fuck up. Just keep your trap shut. You're not Daniël, so there can't be a reason in the world why you should even say one word to me.

"Mr Gavan, the doctor will be with you very soon. I promise you, everything will be explained. This must be an overwhelming experience, but you are in good hands."

Who cares? He doesn't. He isn't sick, didn't tear a muscle during a nasty foul, he's pretty sure there wasn't even a match, so what's the talk about a doctor? He just needs Daniël. And he needs his voice back so he can tell her to go away. He didn't come all this way to be pestered by someone he doesn't even know. If Daniël's out for a few minutes to get a cup of coffee or something, he's happy to listen to the gaffer, or the captain, or Gael or Gabrysz or any other of the boys … see, he's not that unreasonable.

"Hey gorgeous, I see you're awake." The kiss on his cheek feels new and familiar and absolutely wonderful. There are so many brilliant things. Like being able to smile as a reaction to what Daniël tells him. Or even move his head a bit. It's almost like talking again, even though it's not. But it makes Danny so happy when Steve gives any kind of reaction, so he keeps on trying to get the message across.

Now that Daniël is finally back from his break, they can have a few moments on their own. Now shoo, whoever she is, so can he enjoy his lover's presence in peace. He smells so wonderfully of having been outside. He'll have stories to tell, about how the winds felt against his face and how the rain finally did stop and there was something that almost looked like sunshine. He'll tell him about who visited them when Steve was asleep.

He remembers having seen Matthew for a few seconds. At least, he's pretty sure he has. His captain's face all wrinkled up like he was trying to find the solution to a problem he couldn't share with anyone. A familiar voice, laced with a heavy Spanish accent, greeted everyone present at that moment and the gloomy face became boyish and happy.

The gaffer was there, telling him about Match of the Day. Steve likes it when someone talks to him about nice and normal things, like what's on the telly, or who's most likely to win the PlayStation competition. Degaré talks to him like he's really there, like he's part of the conversation and not just a motionless silent body.

He misses most of the visits of the others, but Daniël always keeps him up to date about who was there, what they said and how long they stayed.

It's an art in itself to keep track of his waking moments, sparse as they might be. The pain, though still a steady companion, is no longer all-encompassing, and somehow that makes him feel all the more how tired he is. He tries to integrate Daniël's scent and sounds and how he looks, how his fingers feel on his arm, but so much is still missing and so most of the time he's happy with whatever he can get. Too much is not quite what it's supposed to be, is lost in this elusive dream he finds himself in, to complain about the all too rare gift when he can watch his lover's face. When he can enjoy his smile and hear him whisper sweet nothings; when gentle fingers softly touch the inside of his arm, right where it feels so good, he has nothing left to wish for.

"You're getting a little more alert each day, aren't you? I can see it in your eyes and perhaps very soon, you'll tell me ..." Daniël stops talking for a few moments. "I know you will talk to me again. To all of us again. We just have to be patient."

He pauses again, like he notices something. "Are you tired?"

Steve discovers he can move his head just enough to indicate that yes, he is tired.

"You want me to stop talking?"

He indicates that no, he doesn't want Daniël to stop talking.

"I'll tell you about how I made my first goal as a pro. Totally by accident, too. You like that?"

Steve nods, letting himself wrap snugly in the warm safety of Daniël's voice.

"Well, you have to know there was this midfielder, Spakenburg, a bit older guy, very experienced, but he had that weird habit of …"

◆

Suddenly, Daniël smells differently, like he has just taken a shower with an unfamiliar brand of shampoo. Steve blinks in unconcerned surprise.

"Good afternoon, sleepyhead. The doctor will be here in a minute. Shall we wait for him together? It's only one, this time. There's almost always a bunch of them. You don't like that, lots of people you don't know around. I wouldn't like it either." He kisses Steve's cheek. "If only it were just you and me."

He sees a lot, his Daniël …

◆

A quartet of doctors (more than one? Has he slept again?) talking in a language that sounds like English, but isn't quite the same thing. They talk about him in big words that seem to excite them. They are important people and they know it. Some are more important than others. They talk the least, like they recognise their words carry so much weight that using too many of them would disturb a fragile balance. They talk to him, too, but he's not under the illusion they actually expect a reaction from him. Still, it's fairly easy to understand at least part of what they're saying. The words, that is, and their meaning as to be found in any dictionary, but why they're telling him about ventilation and brain scans and healing and not healing fractures and drips with pain medication is something he's not quite sure about.

He knows he only has to allow the memories to fill him and every word the doctors and nurses say will be clear. But he's terrified the monster with the many faces and the many voices will return to tear the flesh from his bones, to break his bones, to taunt him. To take Daniël's name in its foul muzzle and defile it. So he doesn't remember.

◆

"Good morning Mr Gavan." She's a good woman, he knows. Her voice is filled with the kind of compassion that can't be bought by any kind of salary. She's the bringer of all things good and merciful.

Could she please leave him and Daniël alone?

"I have very good news for you. Doctor Nisha will remove the tube so you can breathe on your own. Just follow her instructions and it will be over in seconds."

A petite woman, the doctor, Steve assumes, talks with Daniël. He sounds a bit excited, but in a positive way. Like something good is going to happen. That's all he needs to know.

"Give yourself a few moments to get used to the sensations. Don't fight it." Her small hands seem to fiddle with something that apparently needs fiddling with.

Daniël's touching him.

"You're ready?" the doctor asks. Out of politeness, he's sure.

He nods. Also out of politeness.

"Welcome back, Mr Gavan."

The hard part is over as soon as he realises there is a hard part. To be honest, very honest, he feels like shit. The tube, at least the one down his throat, is gone, but it still feels like something nasty is halfway stuck and no amount of coughing is able to get it either up or down. But there's also the radiant happiness on Daniël's face, like when they managed between them to prevent Manchester United from scoring the winning goal in the very last minute of the match and they walked away from Old Trafford with a point, and a feeling that can't be expressed in any of the languages they speak with some fluency.

He's breathing on his own. Despite the huge chunks missing from his memory, the magnitude of simply letting his lungs do their job feels like a milestone. He sees it in Daniël's huge smile, feels it in the way he touches his face, hears it in the way he says, "Oh Steve."

It makes him more aware of the other things that make his body feel it's no longer his own. There's a big needle in his forearm, but it doesn't bother him all that much. He hates the tube in his penis, for obvious reasons, but he accepts it. Not much to be done about that at the moment. There's more, but what's the use of trying to check his whole body for things that weren't there before.

Before what?

Not being able to touch Daniël, even if it's only moving a finger over the back of his lover's hand, is unbearable. He doesn't care about the pain it will cost or how exhausted it will make him, but he will lift his hand and place it, gently, against the most beautiful face he has ever known, and Daniël will rest a moment against Steve's hand and no words will be needed.

He still wants to talk, though. Daniël may be clever at interpreting his nods and smiles and stares, but there are questions he needs to ask and those he needs to answer. He wants Daniël to experience the joy of hearing his name coming from the mouth of his lover. Isn't that the reason he came back from somewhere better than where he is now in the first place?

His list of things to achieve is growing. There are already two things he wants to accomplish: touching Daniël's face and saying his name. Strange how he was never aware how complicated talking, saying even one single word, one name, actually is.

The sound he produces is at least halfway human, but that's about the only positive thing he's able to make of it. It reminds him of … he doesn't want to be reminded. So he falls silent again. It doesn't prevent Daniël from having that big, happy smile on his face, from bending over and kissing their special patch on Steve's arm. Even though there's a lot more now that can be touched and kissed, those few centimetres of skin are still favoured.

"One day, you will lie in my arms again and you will say my name. You have taught me that I'm much more patient than I ever thought. I guess you have taught me how to stop looking at the clock."

It's then that Steve notices Daniël isn't wearing his watch.

Chapter 8

He makes sounds. He forms them, again and again, with great dedication and dogged perseverance. It is a conscious act, an act of will, not the by-product of unimaginable distress. He wants to make those sounds, even if they are still not real words. At least he has the choice. Perhaps the doctors have some plan in mind about when and how his rehabilitation is going to happen. But he refuses to wait. He has waited long enough. And if practising vocalisation is the only thing he has any influence on at the moment, then that's exactly what he's going to do. Daniël, too, has been patient long enough. Even without his watch to look at every few minutes, time still eats up his youth. He discovers certain sounds make syllables, then very short words, then short words. Whenever he's alone and awake, he practises. His jaw feels heavy, his face not like before … before that thing he remembers not to remember. Then suddenly, when he wakes up and finds his lover not with him, he says Daniël's name. He says it again and again, just to be sure. He keeps repeating it until the sound fades away into the sounds of the room he's in.

It's not often he's alone. There's almost always Daniël. He has no way of being sure about it, but he has the impression the amount of time he's awake and aware of his surroundings is slowly increasing. And so the time he can actually spend with his beloved gets longer by the day. Sometimes Daniël just sits next to the bed, quietly looking at Steve. Not saying a word. Someone has brought him his laptop from his apartment and almost every day, he's reading and writing. Steve sees him smile and frown and read some more, write some more.

"Does it bother you when I'm typing?" Daniël asks.

It doesn't. Daniël believes him, not asking again to be really sure that Steve isn't just being polite. They're not ready yet for politeness.

Far too often, there are nurses and doctors. They try not to hurt him, and he believes them, but they do so anyway. It's nothing personal, he understands that. They give him "something for the pain" but that makes him drowsy, which means he has less time to enjoy with Daniël. They do explain to him what they are doing and why, but it never really registers.

He's familiar enough with his body to know that it takes whatever time it takes. He's been relatively lucky with injuries for most of his career but once or twice, some problems with his left knee kept him off the pitch for months on end. It never did him any good to feel sorry for himself, to get impatient. This time is no different than all the previous ones. The medical staff do their job. One day, most likely sooner than he prefers, he will remember why he finds himself in this room, in this bed, and he will understand why so many doctors and nurses walk in and out of this room and talk about him, to him, do things to his body.

He's truly thankful, though, when he's deemed ready to take sips of fluid. Water first and very little of it, but once he has proven he doesn't choke with the first drops, he gets promoted to juice. The taste of apple on his tongue. The liquid coolness sliding down his throat. Daniël's delighted smile while he watches Steve sip on a flexible straw. It's not the single best taste in the world, obviously, but it comes damn close.

No, he isn't very often alone and awake. But when he is, he thinks of words to say and he says them. Bit by bit, the old familiarity of using language returns. His throat feels almost normal. His jaw doesn't. He knows he no longer has a complete set of teeth, but chooses to ignore it. Some words probably sound funny when he pronounces them, but what can he do?

His mind thinks Daniël and his mouth says Daniël almost instantly. The ever-moving boy who learned to sit still for him. Who talks Dutch through his mobile to his parents and little sister and reads the weather forecast from English newspapers, like he and Steve are planning on taking a trip this very afternoon. Who cheers like he had just watched his lover scoring a goal because Steve moves his fingers a little. Who isn't a saint by far (the red card he got for that trick he pulled during the away match against Wigan last season had been totally deserved), but who has a heart full of love and compassion like few others.

It's time to surprise his lover.

"Daniël?" he simply says it. No huge drama, no waiting for the perfect moment.

And Daniël turns in his direction. "You want to tell me something, love?" He sits down next to Steve's bed, touching his hand.

Steve nods, out of words.

"You said the one thing I needed to hear so much. That's what you wanted to tell me, isn't it? My name. You came back to say my name."

"Daniël." Steve says it again. "Daniël, my Daniël."

"Your Daniël. You said that right." He kisses Steve's lips.

The warm, intimate silence that follows is all too short.

"Good morning, gentlemen. Are you ready for your sponge bath, Mr Gavan? We're sure you'll also appreciate nice clean sheets and some fresh dressing. It gives us a perfect opportunity to check on that infection. It did look good, yesterday, so I'm optimistic."

It's not a real question. It's not a real attempt to start a conversation. They, two nurses as usual for this procedure, are going to increase the amount of morphine via the drip in his arm until he's gone enough to be almost indifferent to the pain.

◆

"Good to see you awake." Degaré gently touches his shoulder for a few seconds and smiles at Steve.

Steve smiles back. At least, he hopes that's what he's doing. "Daniël …" he says. He just has to say it.

"I know, he told me." The gaffer understands. "He just went outside for few minutes. I told him to get some fresh air. Stretch his legs for a bit."

"Good."

And it is good. Fresh air makes Daniël's eyes shine, his voice cheerful. Makes him smell so wonderful all Steve can do is close his eyes and enjoy the sensation.

"The boys ask if it's okay to visit you again. They were here when you …"

"I know."

If the manager is surprised, he doesn't show it.

They don't talk about it, whatever it is they don't talk about. Still, the silence between them is not unpleasant. Everything has changed and will not change back to what it was before.

Before …

No, they don't talk about it. Degaré tells about his four daughters and one grandson. About madame Degaré. A few anecdotes. A sentimental memory. Enough to give Steve a reminder of the normal world outside the room he's in, not enough to make him feel the desperation that's lurking from every corner.

"You're getting tired, non? Is it okay for me to talk to Daniël about who's going to visit you during the next days?"

Steve is strangely touched, not only by Degaré assuming the damaged man in the bed still has a will of his own, but also how he involves Daniël in this decision in such a matter of fact way. It's only later that Steve realises what the manager's words actually implied.

◆

By twos, they visit him. Never longer than a few minutes. Daniël is strict about that, even without a watch. He simply looks at Steve's face and a short, "Guys …" is enough. Steve enjoys those minutes. Even if he reacts with hardly more than nods and smiles, their grumbles about the ref and the linesman seeing it wrong because Gael was so totally not offside when he scored that goal, fill the room with something akin to normality.

Francesco brings roses of an almost modest red, and from the expression on his face Steve knows the boy thinks it's silly to do such a thing. "The girl in the flower shop said they have an extra nice smell. Dan told me, well you know, so I thought …"

Steve simply closes his eyes and for a few seconds, he sits outside in a garden and feels the sun on his face.

Ray's tall body and short, short hair make him look boyishly clumsy while he tries to find a safe way of giving Steve a hug.

"Thank you," Steve says, and Ray blushes.

Niko shows the latest pictures of his sons and daughter. Flaxen heads and blue eyes: all three of them. Nope, no question about who's the daddy.

"Juice. Stacy bought it from this organic thingie shop. Don't ask me," Anthony says.

Gabrysz hands Daniël a booklet. "Poems. To read."

They all bring him something beyond shy smiles and awkward attempts at normality. They bring him friendship that knows how to remember the questions, but also to realise this isn't the time to ask them. They may have their opinions about certain things, but they keep them safely hidden in a place where they can't hurt their team-mate. Of course, there are words that are not being said, even if they are omnipresent. Instead they make jokes about the cute nurses and express their, and it's honest too, admiration when Daniël tells them Steve has eaten half a cup of chicken broth. And they all want to see how he moves the fingers of his left hand.

"Must have taken a lot of practice, from what I hear they did to …"

Etienne's words are cut in half by a nervous-sounding Alexandre saying that "Steve must be very tired by now."

"Good afternoon, Mr Gavan, Mr Borghart." A nod to the visitors. "Gentlemen …"

The reading of the stats. Temperature, blood pressure, what more? The changing of the bags with fluids and medicines. The changing of the urine bag. The questions about pain and other discomfort. Sacred routine between nurse and patient.

Steve's knows now he can hide for the rest of his life and still the monsters will find him.

"Tell me about you when I was away. Tell me about me."

The typing on the laptop stops.

"Tell me."

"Shall I get a doctor to explain it all to you?" Daniël tries, helplessness shining from his eyes.

"Tell me your story." Steve insists.

"I will tell the wrong things in the wrong way. I will hurt you. And you've been hurt enough."

"Please, Danny?"

"The doctors and the nurses have been working so hard. You are doing so well." Daniël sighs. "You have no idea."

"Then tell me."

"You're exhausted."

"Tell me."

Steve's voice is hardly a whisper, but Daniël bows his head to it.

"Go to sleep. When you wake up and still want me to tell what I have seen, I will." Daniël gently touches Steve's face. "I love you so much."

Steve stares defiantly at the monster with the many voices, which are somehow one voice, lurking behind his beloved. This will hurt no less than learning to breathe on his own again, swallow again, talk again, and move his fingers again. He accepts it. Knowing that it will be hard for Daniël to tell what he knows is less easy to be complacent about. But hadn't he already learned that love is a harsh ruler at times?

Chapter 9

Daniël sits next to the bed. He talks. His voice is soft, falters every few words, but he talks.

Steve listens, not asking questions, not commenting on anything Daniël says.

"The gaffer called me. I had such a nice dream about you. Then the dream changed and the gaffer called and mum told me I couldn't drive so I called a taxi. I think I did.

"When we were having dinner I couldn't stop thinking about you and about what we had done the night before. Mum and dad even asked me where my thoughts were hiding. I wanted to tell them so much about you, but I didn't want to spoil your chances with other clubs if Kinbridge Town had told you they would have to let you go after the season.

"I was afraid it would destroy my career. Us being together. Us being found out. That's the truth of it, isn't it? Is to keep totally silent about something, someone, really all that different from telling a lie?

"I kept seeing your face, like it was right after we had made love, while we were having dinner and mum talked about family and dad asked about the upcoming match.

"And then I couldn't remember your lovely face, I could only see that other face.

"I didn't know you kept that passport photo of me in your wallet. A bit hidden away, I bet. You sometimes looked at it? When we couldn't be together? They're always a bit stupid, those kinds of photos, huh? It's how Degaré guessed about us. The police found that photograph. They asked him if he had any idea what it meant and he called me. Never asked me one wrong question.

"They knew who you were. They didn't recognise you. Not even when they found your I.D.

"I was faster than any of them. Smarter too. They couldn't keep an eye on me all the time. I stood in the corner, not moving, not making a sound because I was afraid they would send me away. They were too busy working on you to notice me. I wasn't supposed to see you like that.

"Why didn't they notice me and send me away?

"I couldn't find you at first. You were hidden behind all those doctors and nurses doing things to you that were meant to keep you alive but looked so much like violence. They fought like an army and your body served as their battleground.

"I can't say how you looked when I finally saw you. I try to say it, but I don't have the words. Not in English. Not even in Dutch. I can talk about broken bones and bruised skin and blood, blood, blood and more bruises, bruises and more broken bones and your legs twisted and your hands like claws and your beautiful face that was no longer your face or even a face and the sound you made and the silence that was even worse than that sound …

"But they're not the right words. There are no right words.

"I had never smelled blood before and still I recognised it.

"I remember how bitter the bile in my mouth tasted. How my own blood tasted because I had bitten my tongue.

"I didn't make a sound. Not even to say your name.

"I forgot you. I tried so hard to remember you, but I couldn't. You had been inside my body so many times. I had been in yours for the first time only hours before. I had touched you with my hands, with my whole body, kissed you. I had looked at you while you were eating, reading the paper, watching TV, sleeping, running with the ball at your feet. I couldn't remember how you looked. I couldn't remember anything about us.

"There was nothing left.

"I saw death. Not seeing it like it was a real person. But I still saw it. I knew death was there, trying to touch you, to lure you away from me. It had been sent to liberate you, because your body was too damaged. I couldn't let that happen.

"I claimed you as mine.

"You remember the first time we kissed? When we both thought the other wanted 'Cesco? I was so sure no one and nothing in the whole world could have separated us. Don't laugh; I was even thinking up ways to stay together when one of us, or perhaps both, would be sold off to another club. I was selfish enough to hope you would perhaps end your career as a professional player a few years early, so you could find a job near where I would be playing. Start your own business. Do a bit of coaching. Something like that.

"You see, I'm not such a perfect guy. I wanted it all, playing football and having you. Keeping it all out of the press, so we wouldn't be bothered.

"Did your hands itch too, like when we were training and I just had to touch you?

"If I had been a braver person, I would have told mum and dad and you would have been with us and not in that park. You belonged with us, having dinner. Mum and dad. You and me. The four of us.

"I told myself it was all for the better to keep quiet about you. It's private they all say. But it's fucking not private. It never is.

"I saw them, trying to get tubes and needles in you, trying to get your heart to beat again. Trying over and over again. But there was nothing left to put needles in, to put tubes in.

"And I stood there. Death would have been kinder to you than I was, but I fought it off. I couldn't let you go. Not even when I saw you lying there.

"You were blood and bruises and broken bones and I stood there and watched. Not once I looked away. My eyes were wide open.

"Strange, isn't it, all that time I knew I wasn't dreaming, I wasn't having a nightmare. It was you lying there, it was me standing there.

"They were hurting you. You were dying and they wouldn't stop with their needles and instruments, like you weren't even there. Like you didn't matter. But they were the only ones who could do anything for you. They made sure your heart kept beating long enough so your body could start fighting for itself. They kept you alive long enough to get you into the operation room to repair the most dangerous damage that would have killed you for sure.

"So strange, such a tiny woman, she didn't even reach my shoulders and she was wearing shoes with high heels, telling me what they had found when they admitted you to the hospital. I couldn't believe hearing someone so small and fragile using those words.

"I saw them leaving with you. I didn't stop them to say goodbye. I was stupid enough to believe, to know, I would see you again and you would see me again.

"I couldn't stand mum's touch, or dad's. I didn't want to be touched if it wasn't by you. Not my family, not the gaffer, not any of the boys. Just you. But they wouldn't leave me alone. Not until you were in intensive care and I could be with you.

"Mum didn't understand why I hadn't told her and dad. I think she was a little bit upset with me, like I didn't trust them. Like they hadn't given me the right upbringing, or something. They would have welcomed you into the family, after asking a lot of questions, of course. She was always worried I would fall in love with someone who wasn't really interested in me, Daniël, but in someone who's a bit famous and with money. You have made a name of your own, have your own money.

"They stayed a bit longer than they had planned, but they had to go home. They have phoned every single day. Naomi too. I wish she would tease me and make jokes about you and me, because then I'll know everything is all right. They're all so nice and caring.

"What the doctor told me? Yeah, right, I tried to forget that, but I can't. She looked so perfect, with shiny black hair and tiny hands. She never used medical language that doesn't mean a thing to me. She tried to explain to me why you would die without actually saying it.

"Cranial bleeding. Swelling of the brain. Fractured cheekbones. Fractured eye socket. Fractured upper jaw. Fractured lower jaw. Several teeth missing. Bruising and swelling.

"Several fractured ribs. Fractured collarbone. Fractured bones in both left and right hands. Fractured wrist on the left side. Fractured bones in both left and right under arms. Fractured right upper arm. Bruises covering most of the torso and the arms. Bruises covering almost all of the back, several overlapping. Ruptured spleen. Damage to the stomach, liver and kidneys. Severe internal bleeding. Damage to the spinal column.

"Complicated open fractures in both legs. Fractured ankles. Fractured kneecaps. Fractured bones in both feet. Severe bruising of both legs.

"Bleeding wounds all over the body. Grazes. Bruises.

"You were in a shock because of the blood loss and the pain. You went into cardiac arrest twice during the time they tried to get you into the operating theatre, once more in the theatre itself.

"They only worked on the life threatening injuries, leaving most of the fractures and cuts and bruises for later.

"You were kept in an artificial coma. I guess they were surprised you came out of the theatre alive and they wanted to give you the chance to die in peace. You know, going slowly from here to whatever there is. Perhaps that's why they let me stay in the beginning. It would be over soon, they must have thought. Give the boy a few hours to get used to the idea.

"But you didn't die. Not that day, not the day after that, not the week after that or the month after that. They suggested I could go home after a day. To get some rest.

"I thought: as long as I'm with you, in the same room, death doesn't stand a chance. Yeah, I know, stupid me.

"I've haven't left the hospital for even half an hour since that day. The head nurse made me solemnly promise to never get into their way and let them do their job. Sometimes the gaffer or the captain and the other boys bring club shirts, signed and all, to hand out to the kids. The nurses even put up a bed on the other end, so I don't have to sleep sitting on a chair.

"I didn't leave the room for the first week, not even if they had to take care of your wounds and infections or when they cleaned the mucus out of your lungs. I couldn't take the risk.

"There was that tiny patch on your arm that was just undamaged skin. I started touching that. One finger first. Just touching, because I had to know there was still something left of you. And I began to remember you. How you tried to look inconspicuous while you were watching me reading a book. How you forgot to eat sometimes to watch me eating. How you couldn't take your eyes off of me when you fucked me. How you had given me the most wonderful six months of my life.

"It wasn't like what you see in medical series, on TV. You lying there, all pale and still and not making a sound, and then, suddenly, opening your eyes and be all awake and present again.

"It wasn't like that.

"Sometimes your lips moved, but there wasn't a sound. Or your eyelids fluttered. There were those little spasms and twitches. A few times it looked like you tried to move your hand, but of course you couldn't.

"Sometimes you moaned. They said you couldn't be aware of the pain. I wish I could believe them. I was selfish for letting you suffer because I didn't want to live without you.

"I sat and watched and wondered where you were. Would you come back to me?

"I touched that small piece of your arm, and then I kissed it. I started talking to you, because it was impossible not to talk to you.

"The first time you looked into my eyes again it was almost five weeks after …

"After …

"It's now more than three weeks since you opened your eyes. And you've done so well. You can stay awake for nearly five hours a day, though not all on end yet. You can sip juice and broth. You can move your fingers. And most wonderful of all, you can talk. It's perhaps a bit slow and you need a bit of time to remember some words, but I know that will be much better with practice."

"They couldn't make you leave me. But I will not talk of them."

"You're tired." Daniël bows his head to kiss Steve's arm. "*Ik hou van je.*"

"Two months …

"You …

"With me …

"Two months …"

Steve falls silent with the realisation of Daniël's words.

Chapter 10

It can't be avoided. A crime has been committed and he's the only one, apart from the perpetrators, who's able to tell what actually happened. After what Daniël told him, Steve understands the need for justice, for society to know who did this and punish them according to the law. Sounds great and all but the thing is, it's about him and he doesn't want to let the monster come this close. As long as it's safely cowering in the far corner of the room, he can pretend he's able to deal with it. But as soon as the two officers, or rather detectives, one young man and one not-so-young woman, enter the room and greet him and Daniël, he starts to shake. It's the most peculiar feeling, the chattering of his teeth, the tremors that make his body move in a way he couldn't accomplish voluntarily.

The police officers simply wait, not commenting on anything, not trying to make him feel more at ease. They stand aside and let Daniël touch Steve, let him whisper calming words until he's able to at least hear and understand their introduction.

The woman talks in a friendly, compassionate tone, but also in matter-of-fact words. She and her colleague are here to do a job.

It's been days since Daniël told his story. Steve can only try to guess the price in nightmares his lover must be paying for his courage to sit and talk. He doesn't mention it, since some things are not meant to be seen, not be talked about, and what time but in his dreams to store such terrible knowledge in a safer place? They don't need to speak about it to see guilt move between them, thick and tangible. Steve knows it's no use telling Daniël it happened for no other reason than that it happened. The risk to their careers of being indiscreet had been a very real one. The thing that actually came to pass was hardly imaginable.

He wants to see the guilt gone from the eyes of his boy. They both had taken the most logical decision, no matter that they could have placed their feet on another road and just taken the risk to see if their fear of total rejection had indeed been justified. Who knows, they might actually have been pleasantly surprised. But behind the guilt, there's something so much worse. They are both still far too brittle to face the stark truth that every human at some point has to come to terms with: knowing that one is truly empty-handed when it matters most.

Daniël has spoken the words, has given him a terrible gift at a price that's very nearly too costly to himself. Now it's his turn. Daniël didn't ask for it and will not ask for it, but Steve knows it cannot be avoided forever for reasons that go far beyond the need for justice.

So when the police officer asks him to talk with them to try and answer some of the questions they have and thus give as much information as he's able to, he nods his consent. If not for all the reasons of justice and the need to both restore balance and prevent blind revenge – even though he knows the guys are more than willing to skip the whole process of careful investigation and a fair and honest judicial process – then because of Daniël. The why may never be answered, but at least he will know how.

Steve knows he's not ready yet for feelings of anger and blind revenge. He spares no thoughts for the ones behind the monster. They are insignificant at this moment. He prefers to revel in the knowledge that only yesterday a nurse finally took this tube from his prick and allowed him to piss like a human being. Like a man. Hurt like a bitch the first few times, but God, give him pain like that any time of the day. He spends precious minutes remembering words and saying them aloud so he has proof he can actually say them. Other minutes are for moving his fingers until he's able to form something that looks like a grip and finally he can make an almost fist, be it a weak one. He even lifts his arms a few centimetres and for a few short seconds. But it's a start as good as any other. Concentrating on wiggling his toes is endlessly more important than spending precious energy on detailed and bloody fantasies about revenge. If only because of Daniël's radiant smile when Steve shows him what old, yet new, things he's able to do almost every single day.

If the police officers had waited a week or so longer, he might have been able to shake their hands. He doesn't want to shake their hands. He doesn't want them here, asking questions he doesn't need to hear because they force him to think about answers. He wants to lift his arms and wiggle his toes and move his head from side to side and taste the strawberry ice cream the gaffer brought for him. They want him to invite the monster, to describe it in such detail it will no longer be a monster and return to its original, much more frightening form.

The shaking has stopped.

"Sir? You can interrupt us and stop this statement at any time when you're tired or it's too much for you. We can continue at a later moment if so needed. We will record your words, so there will be no misunderstanding in the future. Your partner is free to be with you at all times. It's most likely we will ask you very specific questions about details of your story in a later phase of the investigation. For now, we only ask you to tell us as much as you are able to remember." The male officer nods to his colleague, who places a small audio recorder on the bedside table. "When you're ready?"

He hasn't forgotten a thing. At least he remembers enough to be able to tell a coherent story. But when it forms in his head, ready to be told, part of him refuses to believe. The facts are what they are: he's been in hospital for the past two months. He had very nearly died. Despite his perseverance, he's nowhere near the point where he's able to do something like sit upright without aid, let alone stand on his two feet, eat a full meal, be awake from morning until night, hold Danny in his arms. That only proves that Daniël told the truth about how bad it was. But he would never doubt his lover's honesty and truthfulness anyway. That still doesn't mean the words and pictures forming in his mind are what actually happened. Perhaps he made it all up, while he was so far away he all but forgot how to find his way home. His mind could have done some pretty weird imagining.

"Mr Gavan?" the female detective interrupts.

He looks at her, then at Daniël. He feels he has nothing to say of any importance.

"Even if you can't believe the things you are about to tell us, we would still like to hear your story."

How does she know his thoughts? He studies her face for a moment. How often had she asked questions that wanted answers like knives and fists? She must have been long enough in her line of work to know that people sometimes are truly incapable of believing their own memories.

There's still one thing he isn't sure of. The police officer had used the word partner when referring to Daniël. Do they know? Or just assume? It's no longer their own sweet little secret, Dan's story made that sufficiently clear, but that's still about family and team-mates, who proved to be as good as family. The hospital hadn't sent Daniël away and the staff treated him in no way different than they would have done with a female common law spouse.

He had overheard, half groggy from painkillers, the two nurses happily blabbering while swiftly working through the daily routine of caring for his still nowhere nearly-healed body.

"Don't you think Mr Gavan's boyfriend …?" one started.

"We're not supposed to talk about patients and especially not …"

"I wasn't going to say anything nasty. Just that I think he's a cute one and so devoted. I mean every single day and night he's here. He's always so sweet and caring to Mr Gavan. Never a wrong word to any of us either. I always thought people like him, I mean famous people with loads of money, treat everybody, well, you know how."

"I know. When Mr Gavan was still so poorly and we all thought he wouldn't make it, Mr Borghart sat right next to the bed and touched him somewhere it wouldn't hurt and talked to him. Can't understand a word of Dutch, but it sounded all nice and sweet."

"He said 'I love you' a lot. That he wouldn't leave him. I had a bit of a fling with a guy from Holland on a holiday in Amsterdam a couple of years ago."

"I want a Mr Borghart all of my own."

"Don't we all, girl, don't we all?"

Of course the police know. Naive of him to think they hadn't already done a lot of work before they even showed up at his bedside. They have previously talked with Daniël about his habits and routines, about what had been different that day. About the fact that he has no close relatives, unless a handful of cousins in Ireland he hasn't seen in years count as such. About his status as a single man. No wife or girlfriend, no children. He watches the crime serials, too. Just never thought he would be part of one.

He's trying to buy time; to spare his beloved and to give himself viable reasons to live with the monster and forget the truth behind it.

With his right hand safely in both of Daniël's hands, he starts to talk.

He keeps the words clean and neutral. He feels the dizziness of being in love and thus loving everything in and on this world deep in the pit of his stomach, but what he says is: "After I'd shared one or two pints with a couple of old football mates, I felt like taking a bit of a walk before heading home."

Daniël's hands warm around his right hand. This isn't what the boy deserves for his courage.

"Walking makes it easier for me to think. About the kind of job we do, about …"

"The police know about us, we talked when you, well, you know. There's this anti-hate-crime policy. That's also for people like us. So you don't have to pay attention to your words all of the time. I'm holding your hand, right? Don't see Kirkby doing that and he visits you twice on most weeks."

"I guessed as much. Still, old habits and all." Steve once again feels the pavement under his feet and the wind in his face. "I was having a bit of a daydream about how we could be together and still be playing for the club. Perhaps stay in the same region when they couldn't use me any more in a year or so, with me being past thirty and with the influx of young talent at defence."

Don't the police officers hear that strange whistling sound when he talks? Or are they too polite to tell him he's almost unintelligible? Daniël understands him … but Daniël is Daniël. Should he ask for a drink of water?

"If Daniël had wanted that, me staying in Kinbridge and finding a job, I would have done it. Or gone with him to no matter where, if he changed clubs. I can imagine some really big clubs wanting him in a few years. Making it look all unsuspicious. But I would have left him, if he thought the risk would be too much for his career. Couldn't ask him to give it all up for me. Not when he's still that young and has so much to give to the sport."

Daniël makes a small noise, but doesn't say a word.

Steve sips on a glass of water the female officer hands him. "I wasn't paying attention to where I was going. Just walking and thinking about Daniël. You already know, of course, he had his parents over. They don't know … didn't know about us. I was thinking about that, too. I was thinking so much. Not paying attention. Just walking and thinking about Daniël and me."

He drinks more water, but it doesn't really do much good. He hears himself babbling. He knows he has to get into that park. The park has a name; he knows it since yesterday, because he had asked Matthew about it. Queen Elizabeth Park. He must have heard about it during the five years he's been living in Kinbridge. Doesn't ring a bell. He doesn't want to set another foot there, even if it's in thought, in words. Let them figure out what happened. They're the police, it's their job. He's probably going to say the wrong things, anyway. Making them look in the wrong direction, perhaps even getting perfectly innocent fans into trouble. They should be doing those DNA things you see in what's that series called? The doctor had told Danny about the swelling of his brain. Must be bad for remembering things correctly.

His right hand in Daniël's hands.

"I'm so very sorry. I know I shouldn't have done it. But I just had to." Shame and embarrassment creeps up his face in a flaming heat. "I didn't realise there would still be other people there. Seeing what I did. Some fine example I've been setting."

Then he sees the hurt look in his lover's eyes. It's gone almost as fast as it came, but he didn't miss it. "Stupid, isn't it, me making such a fuss about having to pee and not being able to find a decent place to do it. Like it's the end of the world. Must be my nan's influence to always be a gentleman." It still doesn't make him feel any less embarrassed. "Of course I'll pay the fine."

He looks at the policewoman. She knows what he's trying to do, but doesn't fall for it. She's so patient. Why is she so patient? They both are, she and the younger man. As if they don't even care how much time he needs to tell his story.

"You're still okay?" The male officer asks.

Steve nods. It doesn't matter, does it? He sips water and continues to talk.

Why were they doing that? What kind of place had he landed in? What was that man thinking?

"There was this man, trying to touch me when I was done zipping up. He kept looking at me. He even told me he was married, that he had a family. Said he understood me. I should have pushed him away, tell him to get lost. Tell all of them to get lost. Tell all those men standing there and watching. I heard them, breathing so heavily like they were …

"I should have told them to do that somewhere else. I wasn't interested. Why would I do something like that? What reason could I possibly have? Cheating on Daniël with a complete stranger in a park? They didn't know about him. No one did.

"Suddenly, they were all gone. All of them. That man too.

"No one warned me. Not one of them."

Daniël's hands warm and safe.

"There must have been half a dozen or so of them. Big blokes. Smelled of beer and chips. Their boots made those scraping noises. They were KTFC fans, so they recognised me. I thought …"

He's silent for seconds, then what must be minutes, but neither Daniël nor the detectives say anything to encourage him to speak of what happened.

Then he talks again. He says the words that speak of pushes and shoves, of trying to fight back and trying to get away. Of being kicked until he's no longer able to get up again. He hears himself tell about the kicking and the speculations about who else might be a bloody poof too.

They say Daniël's name. They say: "Daniël Borghart," in his voice.

They break the bones of his legs. As calmly as the voice that tells about them breaking fibula and tibia and anklebone and kneecap.

They talk and talk and kick their heavy nailed boots against skin and muscle. Against his soft belly and muscled back. They say Daniël's name, he says: "You can't have him" and his mouth bleeds, his skull cracks. They make jokes while his fingers break and his hands turn to pulp. He speaks their obscenities while they try how much of his body they can hit at the same time.

He says: "You make him sick."

They drag him some place else. No longer talking or joking while they kick until already broken bones break again, already bleeding skin bleeds even more.

When he's dying, they are no longer part of his thoughts.

"Daniël."

The boy is ashen.

What else can he do than lift his arm and, gently, place his hand against his beloved's cheek?

"How can human beings do this to another human being?" Daniël whispers. He closes his eyes, his voice soft against Steve's wrist. "I wasn't there for you."

"They weren't with me during my last moments. You were, my sweet, beautiful boy."

The recording device clicks off.

Chapter 11

He sleeps through most of the day following the visit of the police and giving his statement. He knows that because after he wakes up, nurse smiles at him and makes a little joke about him sleeping like a baby for more than twelve hours.

"Mr Dominguez and Mr Kirkby were here to visit you, but they didn't want to wake you up. Would you like a cup of tea? Perhaps you would like me to brush your teeth? A quick wash?" She's the chipper nurse who only seems to exists in chick flicks. Steve has seen her before. A good woman, who combines efficient professionalism with a warm and outgoing personality.

"I appreciate that. Thank you."

While brushing his teeth, another thing on his list he wants to learn to do for himself again, like the grown up that he is, the nurse happily babbles on. "Mr Borghart's gone for a walk. It's lovely outside. I hope it keeps that way; I have to do a bit of shopping tomorrow with my friends. I've been invited to the wedding of a colleague, next month. Good excuse for a new dress, don't you think? Oh, but you could do with a shave I see. I was thinking about another hairdo. A bit more layered, makes it looks fuller, my mum says. Here you are, wet cloth to freshen up your face a bit. Get a comb through your hair so you look your best for your fella. You're nice and clean now. With a bit of time, you'll get to visit the dentist and you'd be surprised what they can do these days. Cologne? Trust me; guys love it when you smell nice and sexy." She turns her head towards the door. "Hey, there's Mr Borghart, too."

"Thank you." He's looking forward to the day he can take care of his personal hygiene himself, but he's able to say thank you and that's something.

Daniël kisses him. "Hi there, gorgeous. Hello nurse Rich."

"Good afternoon Mr Borghart." Her smile warms the whole room. "I'll leave you gentlemen alone now."

When nurse is gone, Daniël sits at Steve's bed, as close as his chair allows. "You okay?"

"Bring me a mirror, please Dan? I haven't seen my own face in more than two months."

"You're sure you don't want to wait till a doctor's here? Or a nurse?"

"Just you and me."

Daniël gets a shaving mirror, places it in Steve's hands.

The bruises and swelling are gone, as to be expected after all those weeks. He's pale, but not in a healthy, attractive way like Francesco or Niko. He smiles, in the knowledge what he's going to see. A big gap at the front.

"Gorgeous? You call me gorgeous?"

"Because that's what you are. You don't see what I see, sweetheart. You never did, not even when we had just fallen in love."

Steve looks again. It's still his face: noticeably, but not as bad as it could have been, off balance as a result of the broken but almost fully healed bones, plus a few scars and in obvious need for some serious dental work. Practically nothing that time and a good dental surgeon couldn't deal with. His eyes have changed though, and that change cannot be undone. Because what they have seen cannot be undone.

Daniël puts the mirror aside. He takes Steve's face between his hands with such tenderness it silences everything inside Steve's head. Then he kisses him. It's a soft and gentle kiss, but unmistakably the kiss of a lover. The tip of Dan's tongue glides over Steve's lips, as if he's shy, like a young boy asking for his first real kiss.

By allowing Daniël in, he gives himself permission to feel human again. He's being loved as a man, not just being comforted as a victim who has gone through unimaginable suffering. He shudders when he feels how his lover's tongue touches, explores even, the gap where his teeth are no longer there, to travel on like the imperfection is just a fact, to tease his palate and the teeth that are still there, to caress Steve's tongue with his own.

He's more passive than he would have been, no longer sure how to react to something that was, not even that long ago, part of his daily life for six months, before it had been taken away from them with blinding cruelty. And now Daniël kisses him like he always does: warm and tender, tasting like coffee with milk and sugar.

It shakes him off balance. But he doesn't retreat, because he hasn't got the heart to reject Daniël. Because somehow this kiss, unexpected for both as it may be, is even more important than being able to wiggle his toes or move his fingers until they form a fist.

When the boy breaks the kiss, he looks Steve right in the eye and blushes.

"I got carried away a little, I guess." Daniël uses his thumb to stroke a cheek. "I can't help needing to touch you. Kiss you. It's always there. Always. I never stopped needing you. Needing this."

Steve doesn't know what to think, let alone what to say. He understands what Daniël is trying to say, or perhaps what he's not trying to say, at least he thinks he does, but guilt has a way of messing up thoughts, both his and Dan's, and so he says nothing.

"It's too much, isn't it? Did I hurt you?" Daniël is becoming worried about Steve's silence.

"Of course you didn't." Steve smiles reassuringly, even now he knows how his smile looks, and kisses Daniël for good measure.

"Well, at least we don't have to be careful and discreet any more," Daniël says with a light-hearted note in his voice.

Steve needs a few moments for the words to sink in. "Who exactly knows?" Perhaps disaster can still be avoided. Perhaps Daniël can save his career at both Kinbridge Town and the Dutch national team.

Family, the gaffer, team-mates, hospital staff, the police: dozens of people. All of them good and trustworthy individuals, but also very human and some of them might, without intention, have given away more than they should.

"Everyone with a TV or internet access, I guess." Daniël shrugs like his words are of no consequence.

Steve has no illusions about his own future, but did they put Daniël and him together? He had always assumed Degaré had found some plausible excuse for why Daniël had been missing from both training and matches for such a long time when he had left his most recent match in perfect health. Naïve perhaps, after so many weeks, but it's not the first time a player disappears for weeks, even months, with some semi-transparent declaration about a persistent injury. "I don't understand. Someone talked to the press? They sold us out? That must have been a nice sum, too."

"I gave us away. For free."

"I still don't understand what you're trying to say. They were waiting for you, the paparazzi and TV crews, when you went for a bit of fresh air? With the boys and the gaffer coming in and out every day, there must have been a few of them at least. Perhaps they saw you stepping outside for a few moments but never really leaving." Steve feels how panic digs a hole in his stomach. "I wouldn't have blamed you for denying there's anything more between us than friendship. Perhaps you're in the hospital for your own reasons. You should have told them that. We all tell the press the odd white lies, you know that just as well as I do."

"I'm not telling lies about you. About us. And keeping my mouth shut is lying too." Daniël sounds indignant, like Steve said something that really bothers him. "After this? No more."

His lover's almost-anger, though not directed at him, makes it hard for Steve to formulate his thoughts. They had never talked about it in detail. What was there to talk about? The stark contrast between their behaviour in public and in the privacy of either of their homes had been accepted by both of them as simply how things were. It had been a choice, just like anything else, but that didn't mean it had been a conscious one, taken after long and heart-breaking talks. No other couple in professional football had done it before them and they weren't going to be one of the first.

"They knew where you had been found. The police and the hospital knew, and of course the press. No idea how, but they did. Almost immediately the rumours started on the internet, the accusations, then the filth spread around so fast there was no way of keeping track of it. It was ugly.

"I had no idea why you had been in that park that night and I didn't care. I just wanted all of them to keep their filthy paws off my man. I trusted you would tell me what had happened as soon as you'd be able to. And you did.

"I couldn't keep my mouth shut any longer. I told the gaffer and the skipper what I was about to do. Told Degaré I assumed he would inform the owners of the club. Seemed like the decent thing, inform them about my plan. Not to ask permission. No one in this world could have shut me up for any reason. No threats and no pleas. I would accepted it if they had wanted to get rid of me."

Daniël beams. "They both sat right next to me when I gave the press conference. I'm happy to say: with the full support of Mr and Mrs Goldman."

Then, finally, he stops talking and looks at Steve with concern in his eyes. "*Lieverd*? Is something the matter, sweetheart?"

Words tumble through Steve's head and he isn't able to even catch one of them. He tries to understand what Daniël has just said, to understand the meaning and implications, but all he can do is stare blankly at the boy, who's looking more miserable with every passing second.

Why didn't he save himself? That's how it's always done, when a player did something unbelievably stupid and the press got hold of it: ignore it, fend off any questions with the same old "no comment" and let the storm pass. Within days, weeks if it's very spectacular, the bloodhounds have found another victim. And always be careful with doing vanity searches on the internet because you will find things you might not want to know.

"Is it still on the net? The press conference, that is," he finally asks, knowing very well nothing fully disappears once it's been uploaded.

"Of course, it's been one of the most downloaded vids for a while. It kept spreading and spreading." Daniël gets his laptop. "I have it on my hard drive anyway. Is it uncomfortable if I rest it on your lap?"

"No problem."

"You never complain, but I know you still hurt." Daniël places a pillow on Steve's lap, the laptop on top of that and opens it. "Comfortable?"

Steve smiles.

Daniël moves to open the document, but Steve stops him. "I do love you."

Dan kisses him. "That's what I told them. Just watch."

The first time Steve sees the footage all that registers is Daniël's face. All the expressions, from sad to smiling, from angry to proud: he's so mesmerised by it, that almost nothing of the questions and answers reaches his ears. There's so much pain in that lovely face, such deep sorrow, that it twists his insides into a dozen knots. Such pale face, lines written by fatigue and shock layered over unmistakable youth. How can anyone so achingly young carry this heavy burden? But there's also love and pride and hope in rich abundance.

"I wasn't there for you," is the first thing he says when the video reaches the end.

"You were fighting for your life. And believe me, you were there." Daniël touches Steve's arm because he understands that Steve needs to be touched. "Watch it again?"

This time, he concentrates on what's being said. Perhaps he doesn't get every single word, but it's enough to understand that any remaining hope of life going back to normal for Daniël has proven to be a grand illusion.

There is a sad smile on Daniël's face. "I want to end all the speculation about Steve Gavan and me. There are a lot of lies spreading around, but this part is true: we are in a relationship and have been for the past six months."

He sees how pale Daniël gets when he says, "Steve's in a coma at the moment. I understand he is kept under heavy sedation to make sure he moves as little as possible to give his body a chance to heal. Against the pain. But the doctors are able to tell you more about that later ... the men who did this? You have to ask the police. I'm sorry."

Arnaud Degaré saying a few words. "The club won't make any decisions concerning either Steve or Daniël until a more appropriate moment. Of course, Daniël will be given full opportunity to be with his partner as long as he needs to be. Even if it would mean he won't be available for any match during the rest of the season. Of course, they will get their payment in full. Both of them, yes. They are part of this team, let there be no mistake about that. Kinbridge Town is a club that takes care of its people. With full blessing of the owners, I might add. I have visited Steve, yes. I am deeply shocked. This is not the Kinbridge I have come to know and appreciate."

He sees Daniël whispering to Matthew before the captain gives answer to the question of what he thinks of recent events. "It's simple, really. I see no excuse for anyone to go around and beat one of my team to a bloody pulp ... No, I didn't know about them. It had been their decision to keep their privacy. Would it have made a difference? That's private, too. I'd just like to say that all the lads are behind them one hundred per cent. We got word from other teams, managers and players, too. Both national and international. The message is clear: this isn't what football is about. I know the fans, the true fans, will be right behind us during the coming match against Manchester City. We need your support now more than ever at Chestnut Road."

Daniël is now frowning. "I have no idea why he was in that park at that moment. He's a grown man; he can walk wherever he pleases, whenever he pleases. I trust he will tell me everything. Why? Because he loves me. Believe me, I know. How do I know? How do you show your wife – you do have a wife? Or a boyfriend? – you love her? I don't like your insinuations. As I said, I can imagine him being lost, not paying attention to where he was going. Just because you walk in a park, does that mean you know what some men are using that same park for? It's not like they have road signs for such places."

His lips are one tight line while he listens to the next question. "It's not about a professional footy player being caught in a gay cruising area with his pants down, it's about a human being brutally beaten and left for dead. *Ik ben er zeker van die hij niets verkeerds deed* … I'm sorry, I mean to say I know he did nothing wrong."

Daniël's smiling. "We just fell in love. It happens, you know. We were quiet about it, but that doesn't mean our relationship was any less serious. I hoped Steve and I would be able to share our lives after his retirement from football. I still do."

His eyes are now wide in anger. "I don't speak for any organisation or movement or anything. I didn't want to come out to the wider public, at least not as long as we were both playing as professionals. This isn't about politics. I don't care what other people would do. I respect their choices, but that's all. I'm here because I won't accept that the man I love is getting dragged through the mud while fighting for his life. I defend him because he can't."

Followed by quiet sadness. "*Waarom zou iemand zo'n schat van een man überhaupt iets willen aandoen?* I mean, why would anyone want to hurt him? He's such a sweetheart of a man. He has never said one wrong word to any of his fans. What reason could they have had?"

Cocking his head. "What I plan on doing now? Stay with him until he wakes up. Stay with him after he wakes up. That's what I wanted a week ago. That's what I still intend to do. *Ik heb mijn besluit genomen.* Yes, I made my decision."

Daniël takes the laptop and puts it aside. Then he sits on the chair next to Steve's bed. Neither of them says anything while Daniël takes his lover's hands in his own and kisses them with slow tenderness.

Chapter 12

The police officers return with questions, which he answers to the best of his abilities. They tell him there have been several arrests. They show him photos. He looks at them, and remembers the nipper with the shirt and the school team and the poster that, he's certain, will no longer be above his bed. He remembers the derisive laughter as if he said something funny by stating in a civil manner that he wanted to continue his walk. He remembers the voices, the heavy breathing brought about by performing a physically demanding job that asked as much of them as playing the full 90 minutes did of him when he was still competition fit.

He had tried to make a habit out of looking at his fans' faces, even if just for a split second; perhaps as a reminder of their individuality beyond the chants and waving mass of black and red shirts and flags, of their need to be noticed for what they are. He remembers the men in the park because he had looked at them. Not one of them a monster. Just plain English working-class faces, reminding him of the streets of his youth. The faces of the dads and uncles of his friends, of neighbours. The faces he smiled at and who had smiled at him when he signed autographs on shirts and pieces of paper. The photos tell him nothing new. But when Daniël talks about this with Matthew and Gael, relief and bloody revenge in their voices, he closes his eyes and pretends not to hear.

Life, such as it is, moves along. He's able to eat a light meal without assistance. He no longer falls asleep several times a day, exhausted after being simply awake for more than two hours, although he still needs a long nap in the afternoon. He can hold a cup, though not if it's full with a hot drink. He's able to move his legs somewhat while sitting in bed, but he has no idea if they'll ever take his weight again. He believes he remembers pretty much all the words he knew before, but he isn't certain, because they come more slowly than he was accustomed to and sometimes, in the middle of a sentence, he wonders if he might have lost a few of them after all.

He's taken out of the room, fully conscious this time, for a scan. He's had those before, no big deal. No need for knocking him out. He holds out for an eternity before he starts to shake and whimper his distress. And he doesn't even know what he's afraid of.

"It will be kinder to give you a mild sedative, so you can sleep through it all. Three minutes was exceptionally brave of you but we need you to lie still for almost an hour," the doctor says.

Later, Doctor Nisha tells him his bones are healed, though several of them have suffered from the compromise needed to keep him alive and perfectly set bones were not the main priority. But bones are not the most complex element of a human body.

"The internal organs work as well as we might expect or even hope. That's a huge plus considering the facts. We had feared for your kidneys but you are one lucky man in this aspect, Mr Gavan. And not just in this."

Steve nods. "Daniël told me."

"Your body has used up much of its muscles in the effort to heal itself. A special diet and therapy will help you to build up strength. Just like your brain will have to work hard to compensate for the damage caused by … well, we all know what happened and the weeks you were in coma. Your body had to fight on so many fronts at the same time; one could say it had to make some tough choices. It will take months, perhaps even years, before anyone will be able to draw the final conclusions. But there's no reason to assume you won't get better than you are now.

"If you'll ever walk again? I don't know. Nobody knows. With injuries of this extent, there is no way of predicting the future in such detail. But we're going to try our best to give you at least a chance to stand on your own two feet again."

When the doctor has left again, Daniël sits closely to Steve and takes his lover's hands in his own. His smile is radiant; his kisses are warm and eager. "You're doing so well. It takes a brave man to point out their photos and give information, so the judge has more than enough reasons to put them away for years and years. It was on the news, too. Mrs Goldman said a few words to the press. Told them she and Mr Goldman are of one mind with the manager about how he deals with what's happening with the club right now. That she's very proud that KTFC is at ninth position at the moment. But knowing the gaffer, it's not going to end there. You don't remember her visiting us, do you?"

"I might, without knowing."

"It's okay. You know her dad used to play for the Kinbridge Town youth team before the family immigrated to the US, back in the early fifties? That's why she loves football and this club in particular."

Steve smiles. "I read it in … can't remember, when they bought the club. They brought Degaré with them. Seems they were friends from way back. I was one of their first new acquisitions."

"Stupid of me … anyway … fans have been sending so many emails and get well cards and little presents and requests for information that the club had to hire two part-time secretaries to deal with it. There were thousands of reactions from players and fans from other clubs as well. And it's not just England, or even Europe. But of course I've also thanked everyone on my blog, and more than once, too. They will be so happy to read about your progress. By the way, has Matthew told you they already made a banner for us? Right from the first match after the press conference. And it's there every single home game."

Daniël sighs. "I'm just talking and talking. I wish I could make it all go away. All the pain and the destruction and the fear. Just make it go away. But it's not like on TV, now is it? All problems solved in less than an hour."

He's so full of life, his Daniël. Not even months of being surrounded by hospital walls, unable to fully stretch his wings, has changed that. A bit paler perhaps, his freckles less defined, definitely thinner, but still with that special light shining in his eyes.

"And the boys are going to be so happy to hear about the scan. They already know about the arrests. If they had any say in this, there wouldn't be a trial. I think it's the first time I've heard Gabrysz say anything really nasty. But they'll tell you themselves, with their next visit."

"I won't come back." Steve didn't expect the words leaving his mouth, nor the matter-of-fact tone of his voice.

"I know." Daniël doesn't try to soften his reaction, doesn't show him the many wonderful things he'll still be able to do once the healing process is as complete as possible. Steve already knows football is of limited importance during the best of times; no need for Daniël to tell him that. He won't miss it, not even on days when missing it will hurt like hell.

"When they were kicking the life out of me in that park, there was this precise moment I knew I would never play football again. I knew it for a fact. I didn't care. Funny, perhaps less than half an hour before I had been thinking about how I could find another club, if Kinbridge Town was going to put me up for sale, and still be with you. And all of a sudden, it didn't matter any more. It only matters that the gaffer was there for you when I couldn't be, that Matthew and Gael and all the others never skip a day to make sure you're never totally alone, that so many fans tell you they still want you in their club. But during that one moment in Queen Elizabeth park, I said goodbye to what I believed was more than just a job to me."

"Do you also remember when you said goodbye to me?"

"At the very end, when everything else was gone." Steve brings Daniël's hands close to his face and kisses the long, slender fingers. "Thank you for the press conference."

"If I had done it sooner, you wouldn't have walked in that park at that moment."

"Those men who left me for dead could have walked away instead of attacking me. They could have made hate chants about me for the next match and started an online campaign with other fans to pressure the owners and the manager to get rid of me. It's not something that gets talked about a lot, but it wouldn't be the first time it happened. The men running away because they knew the sort of bastards that were approaching could have warned me or even turned around, and together we would have had a fighting chance. But hey, then they would have run the risk of having to tell their wives and families and colleagues and friends about what they were really doing during 'overtime' or 'the night out with the lads.' They'll have to deal with their consciences in their own way. You heard the policewoman telling us there had been exactly one anonymous phone call from that group. Two days later. That I was found more or less by accident, because there had been a bar fight at a nightclub, not even a ten minute walk away, and a couple of policemen were on their way to assist their colleagues."

So many slow words. So much silence between the words. So much patience from Daniël.

"I know it was their choice to attack you until they were pretty much certain you were dead, of the others to run away from you and leave you at the mercy of those bastards." Daniël sighs. "Sometimes I wish I was guilty of something, at least then I could try to pay for my shortcomings. This is so … I just wish I knew …"

"Without you, there was no chance I would have made it. When I was so far gone I didn't know how to find my way back, I still remembered I had to return to you."

For a few moments they sit in silence, their fingers enlaced. Then hospital reality takes over and Steve is once more reminded that eating a small plate of mashed potatoes and white fish is a task that takes all of the skills he recently mastered. His coordination is still shaky at best and by the time he's halfway through even this moderate amount of food, he's exhausted. He's thankful when Daniël holds the beaker with the protein shake so he just has to sip it through a thick straw.

◆

When Arnaud Degaré visits that night, together with Gael and Francesco, Steve uses the time Daniël needs to get some coffee for the visitors to ask him for a favour.

The manager smiles his agreement. "Of course I'll be happy to see Daniël during the next training. The boys will be thrilled. And I can see for myself that he certainly could use a bit of real exercise instead of a walk around the hospital and doing stretches between the beds. I'll make sure there won't be any press to bother him."

But when Daniël hears about the plans for him, he simply shakes his head. "I'm not leaving you alone. Not for hours on end."

"You need it. Please, Danny, just try it? Fresh air, running and kicking the ball …"

Being among healthy people …

"No." Daniël doesn't give in that easily.

"If I stay with Steve, would that be all right?" Gael offers spontaneously. "You agree, gaffer?"

"Now you see, sweetheart, you're out-numbered." Steve pulls on Daniël's shirt sleeve to get him closer and whispers in his ear, "I bet you'll smell all nice when you get back after training."

"Hey guys, get a room," Francesco blurts out. He grins from ear to ear, hiding his blush behind a curtain of deep black hair.

"You're just jealous," Daniël teases and he gives Steve a short, sweet kiss.

Francesco pouts. And once again, Steve wonders why Dan has chosen him over the heartbreakingly beautiful Spanish-Italian boy, even though Francesco has been dating his girlfriend for over a year now. But, he guesses, such are the strange and mysterious ways of love.

◆

As expected, Gael proves to be pleasant company. He's not above a bit of innocent gossip about the club when Steve asks him how things are going in general, but when the conversation stops he simply sits next to be the bed, takes out his book and reads. Now and again, he looks at the other man, smiles, then returns to reading again. Handing Steve a glass of water when he asks for it. Asking questions about his hand and arm exercises.

Would he do for Matthew what Daniël did for him? Leaving everything and everyone behind to sit quietly next to a hospital bed for weeks on end, with just a sliver of hope to hold on to? Of course, he will never ask this question. There's no need; it doesn't take that much of his imagination to know that both Gael and Matthew have not only thought about it, but most likely have even spoken about it.

What would I do ...? What would you do ...?

Hidden under that, there's the real question. *What if it had been you?*

Gael reads, sometimes looks up and smiles. Says a few words and reads again.

The doctor said months, years. And even then it's not certain if all the endlessly complicated connections between instruction and execution will ever work as seemingly effortlessly as they used to. Once again, he can't help but notice how young Daniël is, how full of life and promises for the future. He is born to do things, to move, to compete, to have fun. He has a body that is clearly made to be used to its full potential. Not meant to adapt to a slowed down existence far too many years before old age. He's a man, with needs that shouldn't be put on hold just because they're not convenient at the moment, and won't be for an unforeseeable time in the future. There is nothing but love and devotion in his lover's eyes. His touches are gentle, his kisses speak of patience. But he's still only human.

When Daniël returns from training, he glows with health and joy. He smells of grass and fresh air. Steve wants to drink it in, close to tears because of the beauty of it all. His kiss is definitely that of a lover, full of longing and lust. His hands, unobtrusive as they might be on Steve's arms, tell the same story as his lips. He's full of brand new stories and stupid jokes to tell. Such a change from the too quiet, too pale boy who has given up so much to be with him.

"Oh Steve, it was so great to dribble the ball, do a five-a-side, run until I was out of breath, hit the back of the net, even though I saw that Kurt was distracting Gabrysz on purpose. Thank you so much for asking the gaffer." He looks at Gael, who's still waiting at the door to say his goodbyes and who seems mostly amused by the can't-stop-moving boy. "Thanks for being here."

Then he turns to Steve again, to cradle his face between his hands.

"I loved it so much being on that pitch."

Steve feels soft lips on his forehead.

"The first contact with a ball in months."

The lips travel, kiss by kiss, to his right cheek.

"I'm so going to feel my muscles tomorrow."

More kisses until the other cheek has been reached, with a short stop at his chin.

"Being tackled and feeling the grass under me."

The softest of kisses on his lips.

"And still I'd leave it all behind to be with you. Rather be with you than winning every single trophy available in Europe."

More kisses.

"It lost so much of its meaning without you. I loved the exercise, trying out to see if my skills are still any good, having a laugh with the guys, but I guess in a way I said goodbye."

Steve has to ask to be sure. "You're thinking about leaving football? Or has anyone said anything to you? There's still a place for you, isn't there?"

"No idea. Don't care. I can play football without being paid for it. Or run just because I love it. I'll see what happens when you're home again." He seems to think Steve still looks too worried. "And no one suggested anything about me leaving the club or leaving the game. They missed you, too, and I could see they meant it. They don't want me gone but it's not up to them. Not all of it."

"It's your career, dear boy, and so much more than that." Steve kisses Daniël on the cheek because he hopes he can still taste a bit of the world outside. "You have ten or more years on this level ahead of you. I think you still don't realise how incredibly talented you actually are. I've been wondering how much longer Kinbridge Town can hold on to you, before one of the big clubs snatches you away. That's not something you carelessly shove aside."

"I'm not worried about it." Daniël smiles at Steve. "I love football but I really love you."

Steve knows what he has to say next, but it takes him more than a day to actually say it.

Chapter 13

"Daniël?"

The boy looks up from his laptop.

"Can we talk?"

The smiling face becomes cautious. The dear soul feels a storm is brewing. Steve knows he must be strong now. No use in stalling the inevitable. Facing the truth and dealing with it isn't cruel. Absolutely painful, perhaps even harsh, but also in a way, the kindest thing he could possibly do.

Daniël sets his laptop aside and takes Steve's hands in his own. "Something's bothering you? Something the doctor said? Are you worried you're not going to get better?"

He has to say the words. They need to be said. Not just in his head, but out loud so his beloved can hear them and, in a way, he can hear them himself. He needs the reality of the sound of his own voice.

"I love you. You know that, don't you?" He feels the truth of these words in the marrow of his bones, in the very core of his heart, but it's not how he planned this talk.

Daniël leans forward to kiss him. "Silly man, as if I would ever doubt that."

Steve smiles, despite the panic forming in his head and limbs. He almost hopes the police come in to ask about the most gruesome details, again. Or that the doctors have to do some time-consuming and somewhat painful tests.

He's honest enough with himself to admit he doesn't want this. He'd be perfectly happy holding Daniël's hands and sharing a few kisses and talking about nothing in particular. But that would be selfish, and Daniël deserves more than that. He deserves to hear the words lingering in Steve's mind. "Please, you will let me finish what I have to say, even if you don't like it at first, or if it perhaps confuses you?"

Daniël frowns. "One of the doctors told you something that scared you? Has it something to do with your recovery? When I was at the Graces, training? I knew I shouldn't have gone."

"Listen, please?"

Daniël nods, finally agreeing to Steve's request.

"I understand the doctor perfectly well. It will take months to get me as healthy and mobile as possible. I'm brain damaged and I'll never again be the man I was. My days as a footballer are over; a bit early, but at my age, that's something I can live with." Steve pauses, thankful that Daniël doesn't protest at the first opportunity. The grip of his fingers around Steve's hand is telling enough, though. "You still have a chance. You're young, healthy. Perhaps a bit out of practice, but a few weeks of training should take care of that. If Kinbridge Town can't keep you, I'm sure there are still clubs who'll be more than eager to contract you, once the storm quiets down a bit."

Daniël starts to laugh. "That's it? You're still worried about my career? You know I was set to go to university before Kinbridge offered me a contract. I can still do that."

"Look at me, Danny, really look at me. You have your whole life ahead of you. I'm not saying that it won't hurt me, or hurt you, but the pain will heal in time. You will give so many people the joy of your talent. You will find love. Don't throw it all away."

The laughter dies. Daniël shakes his head in furious denial; his eyes wide and dark in a ghostly pale face. He's still clutching Steve's hands.

"You gave me a reason to live when all that beckoned me was death. You were with me at my darkest hour. You didn't abandon me when the monsters were tearing me apart. Now let me give you your life back. Please, Daniël, this is the only gift of any value I have to give to you. There is so little left of me." His voice is reduced to a whisper, he's close to begging. "I'll give a press conference to declare that this is my idea, that it is me asking you to leave. That you were and are a loyal friend, but it's time to …"

Abruptly, Daniël stands up, not accepting another word. For a second, he stands tall and with a rage able to stop Death in its tracks. Then the expression of his face changes and his legs give out.

The sadness of the boy is unbearable to watch. He huddles on the floor against the bed where he's been sleeping every night for the last few months. His face hidden against his knees, his shoulders shaking violently with the sobs that seem to crush him like a tidal wave.

Instinctively, Steve stretches his hand out as far as he's able to, but he can't reach his distressed lover. He sees how his gift, the sacrifice of letting Daniël go in order to make sure his beloved can lead a normal life, turns out to be the very source of such deep sorrow. These are not the tears of a regretted but unavoidable goodbye. Daniël isn't trying to hold back what has to be accepted in the end. He isn't mourning for all that has been lost, what has been taken from him and can never be given back in full.

In all his good intentions, Steve had failed to see the truth for what it is: he's trying to spare himself, not the man he claims to love. What worth has a sacrifice that hasn't been asked for? Why does he consider the brooding in his own head, about being too much of a burden for the younger man, of more value than the look in his lover's eyes? No one, no matter how strong and motivated and healthy, can stay in this environment for so many weeks on end, and still be the person he was. The few moments outside during the day, if he can avoid the press and the fans, are not enough to let Daniël keep a healthy colour. The lack of regular exercise results in a decline of muscle definition, like his body retreats to the boyish lankiness of its youth. Tiredness creeps in. A certain sadness. And yet, every single time he looks into Daniël's eyes, he sees light and warmth and the sheer pleasure that comes from being with someone whose company gives him nothing but joy. Of being exactly where he wants to be. Many look at him with compassion, admiration, quite a few with genuine friendship, but Daniël is the only one who sees him through the eyes of a lover.

Perhaps it was for that very reason he told the boy to go. For he no longer can fool himself into believing it's all because of Daniël's needs. How much can love endure before it slowly caves in under the pressure? Before its fire is no longer even a smouldering ember? Before the light dies and bitter duty takes its place?

The boy sobs his heart out because he sees his love, given from a transparent heart and without asking more in return than Steve is able to give, thrown back at him for reasons that are altruistic at most on the outside. Honest love is being met with paternalism disguised as concern.

Being confronted with the stark reality of the limits of his body, with little hope of becoming fully independent again in all aspects as is normally expected from a grown man, he can't imagine Daniël seeing that same body and accepting it for what it is. They are in an extremely physical profession. Injuries or even simply being past 30, 35, will be enough to be forced to look somewhere else. Another club, lower in the hierarchy. Another job altogether. The time between being a promise for the future and being past absolute prime isn't much more than a handful of years for most. And what happened to him surpassed everything that still could count as 'he's getting a bit older' or 'he went never really back to his old form after that broken ankle.' So how can Daniël look at the ruins of the healthy, able bodied man to whom he said "See you in two days" and still want it above everyone and everything else?

"I'm not even able to hold you." By whatever undeserved mercies, the words that leave his mouth this time are the right ones. The desperation revealed by that handful of simple words is as honest as the truth of them.

Daniël looks up and rubs his eyes. His face is blotched, with snot running from his nose. He gets on his feet again, takes a towel still lying on the bed from a few hours ago when he had washed his hair, and uses it to clean his face provisionally. Then he grabs a couple of pillows and turns to Steve.

He kicks off his shoes. "But I'm able to hold you."

With infinite care, he helps Steve to turn on his side, arranging the pillows so they support his back, and gets on the bed. He uses one arm to support his lover's head and neck, while the other embraces him. Their bodies are touching from head to feet.

"I missed holding you in my arms so much," Daniël whispers. "You're comfortable?"

Steve nestles himself against Daniël's slightly taller body. "Is nice, this." He feels himself calm down, like he finally, after a long journey, has arrived at the place where he belongs. His muscles relax; his breathing becomes more free and easy. Daniël's heartbeat is like a song that he can't get enough of. The steady rising of his lover's chest, the slight weight of his arm, the subtle pressure of his lips against Steve's forehead make it possible for him to say: "I wasn't thinking. I was thinking too much. Can you forgive me?"

"Say that I'm very lucky, and there's still a club willing to pay me a good salary to play for them. Perhaps Kinbridge Town, perhaps another one. Doesn't matter. Assume I'll be active as professional football player for another ten, fifteen years. That makes me not even forty. Who knows, maybe I'll die when I'm past eighty. You tell me that I should give up half a century of being with the man I love, for most likely hardly more than ten years of getting paid for a hobby I happen to be fairly good at? I'm still young, but I already know that's not how I want to look back on my life.

"Any player, who would make the next game more important than his brutally attacked wife when she needs him the most, would be spit out by the fans and the media. Why should I treat our love with any less care than would be expected of me if you had been a woman? If that's what it takes to be a high level professional player, if that's what clubs, sponsors and fans expect of me, simply because you and I are both men, then I have no business being a footballer." Daniël pauses for a moment. He glides his hand over Steve's side and back as if to tell himself this is really happening.

Then he continues, his words a fast flow he can't seem to stop any more than the tears ten minutes earlier. "You did nothing worse than what was taught to us: to be second class people with second class relationships. Oh, it's perfectly normal nowadays, society has become all modern and open; it's just not me or any other footballer. If we're really clever, we make some cryptic remarks during interviews and hope a few get the message, because hiding your true nature hurts so fucking much. And if they confront us, we can always say it was a joke. I did the same thing before that night. Of course we kept silent, of course we were discreet. It's all private, isn't it? They don't tell us the intimate details of their sex lives, so why should I kiss you goodbye at the airport when we have international duty?

"You tried to send me away out of love, because you thought it was for the best. But at least you could have asked me about my biggest fear. Or were you afraid I wouldn't tell you the truth out of pity?"

"Will you walk out of the door when it is time for you to go?" Steve has to ask.

"Unless you start having an affair with that cute male nurse who gave you your sponge bath yesterday, why should I? I'm not here because I think it's my duty. If I had been your best friend, I would have visited you once, perhaps twice a week, but I would not have bribed the hospital to let me stay. I'm in love with you, Steve. You know, in love, as in sexually attracted, wanting to be romantically involved? Set up a home with you? Share my life with you? Grow old with you?"

Daniël's kiss leaves nothing to the imagination about what he wants to express. And Steve leans happily into that kiss, perhaps not fully understanding why this beautiful, inside and out, young man wants him this much, but for once accepting it without question.

"The programme to get you more mobile starts tomorrow. I'm so looking forward to that," Daniël says. "Getting you out of this room."

"I guess we could both use a bit of air and exercise," Steve acknowledges, although for the moment he's perfectly happy where he is.

Daniël's hand roams Steve's body as far as he can reach.

"Changed a lot, didn't it?"

Daniël nods, while continuing his exploration over, and then, so very shyly, under Steve's pyjama top. The hand feels warm and safe.

"Thank god you're wiser than I am," Steve sighs. "I can't bear to think about if you had done what I told you and walked out of …." Then, mid-sentence: "Set up a home with me? Grow old with me? Are you trying to …?"

"Well, as a matter of fact, I guess I am."

Some decisions are too important to waste time and thought over. "Yes. I'll marry you."

"Good. Since I'm not planning to go anywhere ever again without you, we might just as well make it official." And Daniël kisses him, while taking him even more tightly in his arms.

"Uh, boys, you could perhaps wait till the actual wedding night? You know, the night after the wedding?"

They look up, startled.

Matthew grins, Gael right behind him with the same silly smile.

"I'm just sampling the goods," Daniël jokes. But he still gets out of the bed, making sure Steve is returned to the most comfortable position. Then he turns to the other two men and says, "Did we tell you already this hot piece of man isn't only freshly engaged to the luckiest guy in the world, he's also going to start rehabilitation therapy?"

Steve hears the three of them talk and talk and talk. Too exhausted from the storm of emotions, he isn't able to contribute much, so he simply lets himself be wrapped in the warmth of their presence and gentle words.

His hand safely in Daniël's.

Chapter 14

Within three days, all the guys (including the reserves) have been paying a visit to ask, "Is the skipper pulling our legs, the two of you engaged to be married and all?"

To be honest, Steve needs a bit of time to get used to the idea. One moment he's desperately trying to set Daniël free and the next he's almost casually saying yes to a between-the-lines marriage proposal. But what if it was all a misunderstanding? Perhaps Daniël was just trying to reassure Steve he still loved him after what had happened? Was he being too nice, too decent, to admit he didn't actually mean to say he wanted to formalise their bond? Did he not want to embarrass Steve in front of Matthew and Gael when they entered the room and heard what they heard?

But as soon as the other two are gone Daniël gets his mobile out. "Mum and dad just have to hear this. They will be over the moon for us."

It's too fast, but he understands Dan's need to share the big news with his family before they read it in the paper, and so he nods and smiles and thinks it's okay, really. If the man he loves always talks with such warmth and affection about his parents, then they can't be anything else but be good people.

And it is okay. He hears a lot of Dutch words, with his own name as a familiar sound laced between them. With his free hand, Daniël fiddles with the sleeve of Steve's pyjama top. Then, suddenly, the phone is pressed against his ear. "They want to say hi."

A female voice, heavily accented and speaking in high-school English, greets him. "Congratulations Steve. I'm so happy for the both of you. Daniël told so much about you in the last months; it is as if I already know you. But I am sure we will meet in person before the wedding."

After her a male voice with the same accent came on the line. "Be good to my boy, that's all I'm asking of you."

He says something polite in return. Are they really okay with their eldest child, their only son, sharing his life, and his bed, with a man? A man who was picked up by an ambulance in a park … cruising … he hadn't been cruising … but the press … the internet …

He's too tired to keep his thoughts in line. Sleep comes easily enough, but with a fitful edge and when he wakes up with a shock Daniël has to reassure him that he's just having a bad dream.

Not long after the morning rituals of having a wash and eating breakfast, a mountain of a man enters the room with (Steve soon learns) hands that make him feel muscles he can't remember he ever possessed, and make them all better again, almost within the same touch.

"This is just preparation for the real work. Your work. For now, your muscles have to wake up to their task or else we do more harm than good. So I'll start with giving you a daily massage. I will also give you instructions for some light exercises you can perform while staying in bed. Just as important, your brain needs to learn to do its job again. Restore the connections where possible. Work around the damage if there's no other choice. And they will. Trust me, they will."

The big, big hands feel their way over muscles and tendons and joints.

"I can only do so much. You are familiar with your own body ..."

Steve shakes his head. "I was."

"You will be again. You have my word on that."

Steve knows this is true, but he's not certain he wants it to be true. He will learn the difference between the pain that is simply always there, and the out of the ordinary signal that something is acutely wrong. He will remember that he could perform certain tasks that he'll never be able to do in quite the same way. And still he will perform them. It makes him wonder if there was an exact moment when he said good-bye to his old body, or if that moment is still to come.

Later that day, Arnaud Degaré visits him, before all others, as is right and proper, since Matthew obviously couldn't keep his mouth shut. Daniël is out for a cup of coffee and so Steve has the chance to ask the gaffer, once again, for a favour.

"He's very welcome at the training. No need to ask. Anthony Levee has a slight problem with the tendon of his left knee. I'm sure he's happy to stay with you for a few hours. And Daniël will get used to leaving you for a few hours in the hands of the hospital staff. We'll just have to give him a bit of time, oui?"

"I sent him away, gaffer, yesterday."

"To save him." It's not a question. "And, was he grateful?" This is a question and a good one too.

"No." Not much more to say about that.

"Why did you try it?" The mild, non-judgemental tone of the voice almost breaks him.

"They still want him with the club?" He has to ask it.

Degaré smiles. "It seems our young Daniël discovered his main priority. It's not easy, is it, knowing you are that priority?"

Steve blushes warm enough to feel the heat on his skin, a reaction he can't quite explain to himself.

Degaré stands up from his chair, bows lightly towards Steve, and gives him a peck on the forehead. "Don't try to give him what he doesn't need."

◆

Later still, he does his exercises. They will decide the rhythm of his day for the coming weeks and months. Since life has been given back to him, since Daniël thinks he's worth the risk of a sea of time unimaginable for someone hardly in his twenties, it's the least he can do. He has to make his best effort to be a husband who's as healthy and mobile as possible; anything less would be unacceptable. There is no debt between them, Steve knows that all too well, but in the end, love weighs so much heavier than duty.

So he sets his first goal: get into that wheelchair. That's easy enough. Takes him a day's worth of energy, lasts all of five minutes, but what glorious minutes. Getting on his feet will be, doubtless, a whole different story. But he's been out of bed, and he's got to start somewhere. His lover's smile is worth every single painful step on the long road he has to travel. If he never walks again, it's because he's truly defeated.

Talking Daniël into going to training again isn't as hard as Steve feared.

"Anthony and you will have so much to talk about." Daniël leans his face very closely against Steve's. "You love it, don't you, when I get back and smell all nice and sweaty. If you promise to do the exercises for your legs, I promise to skip the shower after training."

He kisses Steve's lips. "God, I miss it so." There's a hint of sadness and shame in his voice. "Sorry, didn't mean to ...."

"What, sweetheart, what didn't you mean?"

"You know, put pressure on you."

"You don't think I miss it too? Miss holding you and touching you and being touched by you? It meant so much to me, when you got into bed with me. It's what I needed more than anything."

"Your skin under my hands feels all warm and dry. Or sometimes cool and wet when you come out of the rain. Your lips and tongue are making a trail from my neck to my tail-bone. I'm falling asleep with my face against your belly; your face against my belly. In the early morning, we wake up in the same position and continue where we left off."

"I'm so sorry." Steve breathes the words against Daniël's mouth.

"Don't even think it. You were no longer in immediate danger, but still so very far away from me. I didn't know what to do with myself, with my hands. There was so little I could touch, except for this tiny part of your arm." Daniël kisses Steve's arm before he continues. "Sometimes I was so desperate for any kind of contact that I would get my face really close to you without actually touching, so I could get as much as possible of your scent. I had to know it was still you, under the stink of disinfectants and infections."

Steve starts to stroke Daniël's hair. *Melkboerenhondehaar* the boy calls it, hair of a milkman's dog. Too dark to be blond, too light to be brown and very comb-resistant. How could he not love it?

The boy leans into the touch. "I'm not a saint, you know."

Steve tries to keep his voice calm and accepting. "I won't blame you if you might have found distraction, comfort perhaps, in the arms of someone else. I can imagine, with you being here all the time, and some of the pretty nurses, or perhaps a visitor ..."

"What are you talking about? You're the one for me and that's that. I didn't ask you to marry me because I think it's romantic. It's just that at night, when I hear you softly breathing and it's all quiet and I know you're in the other bed and I can't even touch you and at such moments, I get so fed up with my own hand. I sometimes feel so impatient and needy and goddamn horny and I'm so sorry."

Steve doesn't know what to say, because he doesn't know what to think. The words he hears are precious, like the one saying them, but he has a hard time getting his head around them. Being loved by this generous soul is something he can understand, even if he thinks it has mostly to do with the way Daniël simply is and not as much with being deserving of that kind of boundless affection. But being desired on such a physical level by someone attractive enough to have all the choice in the world is a whole different tale. It's not that he doubts the sincerity of his lover's feelings, but it's just so easy to imagine it could have been someone a lot more handsome.

"Anthony will be here in a few minutes. You go and have fun. And I'll do my exercises." He can't help but notice Daniël's watch still lying on the table ever since he took it off, because time pretty much lost all meaning.

Daniël sees the direction of his stare. "You leaving this hospital will be the moment I'm going to wear my watch again."

A head peeks around the corner. "I'm here, lads. So keep yer hands above the blankets." Anthony smiles brightly. "I need coffee. Oh, and Dan, is it alright if I use yer laptop?"

"Good morning to you, too. There's a Thermos of coffee on that table. One of the nurses brought it specially from home, and it's halfway decent. And yes, you can use my laptop. There's a guest account, so go ahead." Daniël turns to Steve again and kisses him with unhurried tenderness. "See you in a couple of hours."

"Don't forget what you promised."

Daniël looks back from the door, "About skipping the shower? I won't." He gives a wink, and is gone.

Anthony pours some coffee, sits down and clears his throat. "How did it happen? You and Dan, I mean. I didn't know we had men like yer two in our club. In any club, for that matter." The question is blunt in its honest curiosity.

"I fell in love with him. He fell in love with me. We somehow managed to get the message across. And if you're very curious, he kissed me first."

"Now that doesn't surprise me one bit, with yer being quiet and invisible most of the time," Anthony reacts. "But with Dan being all skinny and boyish, don't yer miss curves and, yer know, girly bits?"

"Don't you miss hard muscles and, well, boy bits?"

Anthony breaks out in roaring laughter. "Point taken."

"Sorry you had to hear it this way, like we didn't trust you and the others."

"With the jokes we made in the dressing room and the chants from the stands, it's not like we were exactly giving you and Dan the idea it would be okay to hold hands during half-time break." Anthony takes a swig of his coffee. "I read what Dan wrote in his blog about what happened in that park, that yer were just walking there, not to you know what …"

Steve feels himself getting silent and withdrawn. Anthony seems to notice the change and hastens to say: "Those fuckers had no right, even if yer had been trying to pick up some guy. And I believe yer that yer were just walking there. I might have been in that same park meself a couple of times as a kid. I had no idea the Queen Elizabeth's that sort of place. Hell, if they would do the same thing to every player in the league who's cheating on his wife … Yer know what I mean to say. Yer don't go around beating people halfway to their graves because yer don't like what they're doing with their pricks."

Steve feels pity for the man trapped in his own good intentions that are somehow going all wrong. "It's alright. Really, it is."

"Just want yer to know I'm happy for you and Dan. True gold that boy. Makes yer wonder how many of the wives and girlfriends would do the same thing if it happened to one of us."

"Surely …" Steve tries, but Anthony cuts him short.

"There are some good, solid marriages, make no mistake about that, but how many of the pretty birds would even look twice at us if we had been on the dole or with a dead end job?"

Steve nods. There's no denying the facts.

"I saw him, when all of us had a hard time believing yer would stay alive. Sorry about that. I hoped you were in some sort of better place. But that boy … It broke me heart, it did. The gaffer made sure every day there was one or two of us checking on the two of you. He sat there, talking to yer. Like yer could hear it."

"I could. Not at first, and for a while I only recognised his voice, but nothing of what he actually said, not even what language he spoke."

"Can't even imagine what happened to yer."

"You think I can?"

"I guess not."

Silence moves between them in a quiet, not unpleasant way. Steve leaves Anthony with his own thoughts for a while. He's starting to comprehend there are others, too, who somehow have to learn to live in a world that isn't quite the same any more. Some might hang onto the illusion that it couldn't happen to them, because they are not 'like that'. Others might feel hurt for being kept out of the secret. Some might feel aversion, and in turn feel guilty about that. All will have to deal with a theoretical question that has become reality. No longer are they talking about some imaginary guys who might not even be there. Now it's about two of their own. Blokes they trained with. Shared the highs and the lows of the season with. Shared dirty jokes with. Shared a changing room with. And it would be terribly naive to think it stops at Kinbridge Town Football Club. Somewhere, in clubs no one would ever guess at, some fully inconspicuous men are very, very scared.

Should he have said something to Gael, the last time Daniël went training? But how do you put into words the lost ability to hear between sounds that had absolutely no meaning other than simply being human? About how something in Matthew's voice and Gael's voice changed when they talked to each other? How he thinks it still happens, but no longer is able to hear it because language has come back to him? Are they even aware of it themselves?

Anthony's voice shakes up his thoughts. "Didn't Daniël say something about exercise?"

He's grateful that for ten or fifteen minutes, he can fully concentrate on putting his leg muscles to work. It looks like nearly nothing, those small movements, but it's just as necessary as the more spectacular job waiting for him in the physio room.

A nurse brings a healthy snack. Every few hours, he's supposed to eat or drink something to get enough proteins inside his body to make the hard job of growing muscle and being mobile again possible at all. His body is starving, but that doesn't mean he feels like eating. Still, spoon after spoon, the custard with added vitamins gets eaten.

After that, he's so tired that half of what Anthony tells him doesn't even register.

"I guess I'll leave yer in peace for a bit." He opens Daniël's laptop. "I'll keep meself busy."

As always, Steve isn't aware he moves from being drowsy to actually falling asleep. But a sharp, angry voice wakes him up.

"Don't they have a fuckin' heart? Bleedin' pictures …"

Fear creeps in. "Daniël?"

A gentle hand on his shoulder. "It's nothing, lad. Just me getting a bit worked up. Yer fella's back in a good hour or so. Yer need a nurse or somethin'?"

Steve shakes his head. "No, I'm alright. You said something about pictures?"

"Yer know … the usual paparazzi stuff." Anthony closes the laptop just a fraction too hastily. He's as close to blushing as Steve has ever seen him. Steve knows he's lying, but doesn't say anything about it.

It's time for another cup of whatever it is he's supposed to drink. After that, he tries for a few more minutes of exercising his leg muscles.

"Yer set a date already for the wedding?" Anthony asks while Steve stretches and relaxes his feet.

"From what I understand, Dan needs to do a bit of paperwork, because we can only get legally married in Holland and officially he lives here, in England," Steve explains. "But he's a Dutch citizen and for me EU rules apply, so it should technically be okay. Recognition in England is another matter, but we'll deal with that later."

"You're right about wanting the real thing and not some stupid compromise to keep the religious people happy." Anthony doesn't need two seconds to have his reaction ready.

Steve appreciates it deeply. "We haven't really talked it over yet in detail. It was kind of unexpected for both of us."

"Yer just get out of hospital first. I can imagine yer not being up for some huge party."

Steve doesn't care either way at this point. He just knows he wants to be with Daniël. A short ceremony in front of a civil servant, putting their signatures on the dotted line and going to their shared home. Unnoticed by everyone. But that's probably not quite how it's going to happen. Not with their relationship no longer being their own private business.

Daniël steps into the room with a bright smile and warm kisses. He smells so wonderfully of fresh air and grass, Steve can't stop himself from pressing his nose right into the crook of his beloved's neck.

"Now yer behave, lads, till I'm gone." Anthony's eyes have those little lights that tell he's actually having fun with the whole situation. "Before I forget, Neil and Dag are planning on visiting you tomorrow after training. They're asking if yer want them to bring something specific with them."

"They told me, yeah." Daniël nods.

"And, thanks," Steve adds.

"For what?" The other man looks sincerely puzzled.

"Everything."

Anthony shrugs, obviously not sure how to react. "I'll see yer both next week or so. Oh, and Dan? We could do with another defender. Heard yer any good, so yer available by chance?"

"Liverpool gave you a thrashing last Wednesday. Four against one? Painful."

"Don't remind me …" And he's gone.

The door hasn't even closed when Daniël kicks his shoes off and gets in with Steve. They snuggle close together, finding places for arms and legs, their bodies heavy with desire.

"You smell so nice," Steve whispers, tasting the salty clean sweat.

The kisses Daniël gives him taste better than any food ever could. He decides to stop worrying, at least for today, about the gap where teeth should be, about bones sticking out or about how there are enough scars to form a language of their own. Instead, he concentrates on the velvety glide of his lover's tongue over his lips. The soft puffs of Dan's breath against his cheek. The soft moan when he answers his kisses.

It gets all warm and fuzzy in his belly, and feelings that are not forgotten – never that, but perhaps he should say they are 'stored away' – start bubbling up again. The way Daniël's breathing changes, the way he moves against him, tells him it's exactly the same with his lover.

"Time for your snack Mr Gav … oops, excuse me." The nurse carefully places the plate with pieces of diced fruit and some yoghurt on the bedside table.

"Oh god, I'm so sorry. Please, we didn't mean to …" Steve tries. A fear that he doesn't quite understand is tightening his chest.

Daniël seems to notice something is wrong, because instead of getting up at lightning speed, he wraps his arm more tightly around Steve's body in a gesture of protection, like he's shielding him. He's totally focussed on his lover, all but ignoring the nurse.

"You're not the first patient who needs a good cuddle, and I'm sure you won't be the last. But perhaps it's best when either you or Mr Borghart give a word to one of us, so we can give you a bit of privacy whenever you want to talk or something. We need to be able to do our work, of course, and we appreciate common decency, but there's nothing to be afraid of. The first of the nursing staff saying anything bad about or to you for showing affection has some answering to do." She smiles in reassurance and is gone.

Daniël keeps close to Steve for a few more minutes before he gets off the bed again. "You're okay?"

Steve nods, while tasting the first piece of fruit his lover offers him with his fingers. Tinned pineapple. Quite nice, actually, both the fruit and the way he gets to eat it.

"Is it okay if I take that shower now?" Daniël asks and fifteen minutes later, he sits nice and clean next to Steve's bed. "I bet you and Anthony had a lot to gossip about."

Their hands find each other on instinct while they talk about the day. It's all relaxed and calm, almost like they're sitting in their own living room, simply enjoying an hour of each other's company before it's time to go to sleep.

Steve has no idea why he says what he says; he only knows he doesn't stop himself. "Anthony said something about pictures on the net. I heard it when I was half asleep. He sounded so angry. I asked him what made him upset and he lied to me about it."

Daniël weighs his words carefully; Steve sees it in his face. "I don't want to lie about it, too, even though I understand why he did. But I don't want to talk about it right now. Please, wait until tomorrow?"

Steve thinks he already might have an idea about what Daniël is going to say, about what he's going to see. Yes, it can wait until tomorrow.

Chapter 15

Tomorrow becomes another day and then another. Days full of hard work. Work outside the walls of the room he's been dying in, living in, for weeks, months on end. It's not as scary as he had feared it might be, sitting in the wheelchair and being wheeled through the corridors. He has been in hospitals before. But behind this, there's outside and for the first time since that night, outside becomes more than a vague dream about the future. Outside also visits him in the form of a man who, with practised ease, gets a camera in front of his face and snaps a few shots of Steve in his wheelchair and Daniël walking next to him. The man doesn't wait until he's thrown out by security.

"I'm so sorry, Mr Gavan, Mr Borghart," the nurse accompanying them says, visibly embarrassed by what happened. "We're trying so hard to keep those people out. I shall report this immediately to the head of security."

"At least you're wearing that nice new dressing gown I gave you two days ago," Daniël jokes, although his eyes are flashing with anger. "But you're okay?"

Steve shrugs. It's unavoidable. This will be the first published photo of them as a couple. No doubt with an article that's a handful of speculation, based on a more than generous interpretation of the truth. And faster than you can say 'cheese', scans of the article will be spread all over the internet. So much for trying to live an unobtrusive life.

For a fleeting moment, he's reminded of the pictures that made Anthony curse and Daniël look so unhappy, then all of his concentration and energy is taken up by the daunting task of making his body his own again.

He feels like a stranger to himself. All the things he did because he simply did them, because his mum and nan had taught him to, because teachers and coaches told him so, because only months ago he had still been wired to do so, have to be relearned. He knows about injuries and being ill and having off days, but this is not like all those times his mind and body weren't quite on the same page. This is learning a language that he used to speak fluently, but has all but forgotten, all over again. At an age that most professional players at his level, however reluctantly, start contemplating how to slowly wind down their career, he has to start at first principles.

One day, he'll watch the videos made during dozens of matches and see with his own eyes the man he used to be, and still the memory of his body will be no more than the words from Daniël's mouth, the look in his eyes. He knows he's the man running there, trying for the net, passing the ball to a team-mate with better chance of scoring, tackling an opponent, arguing with the ref, going down and getting up again. That's in another part of his brain, which has no knowledge of the memory of his body. It's like looking at photographs of his first baby steps. He knows it's him, but it's just from hearsay. Daniël will tell him how it was, and those words will have meaning.

Daniël once said, "You have your own special kind of walk. Whenever I see that shuffle, I know it's you, even when you're a tiny moving figure on a TV screen and I can't see your face or shirt number."

Steve also remembers how Daniël, during one of the training sessions, was standing next to a goalpost, observing him for minutes on end. Not saying anything, not even pretending he wasn't watching. When Steve, in the privacy of his home, asked him what he had been doing, the boy smiled and said, "Enjoying the view."

He wants to get up, take his beloved by the hand and walk out of the hospital, like nothing bad ever happened. But if it ever comes to that, them walking out of the hospital, holding hands like a couple of teenagers in love, it will be exactly because something bad has happened to them. Honestly, would they have had the courage, the imagination otherwise? Or would they have waited until later, later, later … only to see their love slip away, with the next transfer window as the deathblow? But he still wants it, holding Daniël's hand and walking out of the hospital, and that's a feeling he's not willing to let go of any time soon. It makes him work harder, try one time more than he thinks his body is capable of.

It also makes him extremely grateful for sitting on his bed again, leaning into the pillows, sipping on yet another protein- and vitamin-spiked shake.

Daniël opens his laptop. "If it's all right with you, I'm going to write in my blog for a bit. Your fans have to know how hard you're working. When you're a bit less tired and you feel like it, it might be fun to take a look at some of the things they've written about us, and to us. You know they even made a few songvids? I usually pretend it doesn't exist, but Ray Portland told me a few days back there's some really nice stuff around. Must be, if it's got you in it. Some are a bit sentimental and sweet enough to break the enamel of your teeth, but … yeah … they mean well, other people. Perhaps not all of them, that would be a bit much to ask, but so many more than we feared seem to be genuinely accepting we are a couple."

"That's good to hear. Perhaps, in time, it'll be a bit easier for others. So a handful of guys can stop pretending being happy with a trophy wife."

Steve remembers Anthony's anger, Daniël's promise. "And those other pictures? What are they about? Something from inside the hospital? That's it, isn't it? Someone has taken photos of you right after Degaré called you. When you were in distress. Of me when they brought me in with the ambulance. How did they even know it was me? Police radio?"

Daniël's hopeless shrug gives Steve an indication it's even worse than that. An idea forms inside his head, but he dismisses it as nearly impossible. "I don't remember seeing anyone using their phone to take pictures. They were too busy breaking my bones and … well you know."

Daniël takes a deep breath. "They did take pictures. A few minutes of video too. At the very end, when you were no longer able to …" His voice wavers. "I assume they wanted to watch their happy memories together and be proud of their hard work. And if they uploaded it on the net, other people could also enjoy the results of their efforts. Although several of the guys told me there were a few discussions on message boards and blogs if it might be a very clever hoax. Some elaborate sick prank."

The boy pauses for a few seconds before he continues. "After making their masterpiece they went away, leaving you for dead. I'm trying to understand the way such people think. Did one of them simply take out his mobile phone and take pictures? Or did someone suggest they all should use their camera, like, for fun and keepsakes? I'm willing to believe they kept on kicking you out of blind rage, long after you were down. Because they smelled blood. Pack frenzy, or whatever it's called. But what possessed them to look at a suffering human being and take photos, even make a video of it? They're good quality pictures too, so there were no shaking hands and they were not in a hurry. The one with the camera in his hands even took care to make sure not even the nose of one single boot got on a picture by accident."

Daniël looks so helpless in his effort to comprehend the incomprehensible. He talks and talks because he doesn't seem to know what else to do. But his face betrays that he doesn't understand his own words.

Steve reaches out to take his beloved's hand. "That must have been so hard for you, being confronted with such images. And poor Anthony. Who else has seen it?"

"You should rather ask who else hasn't seen it. They tried to get it banned, the Kinbridge Town lawyers, but it's impossible. If it had stayed local it might have worked, but the pictures and the video were spread all over the net before we even realised what was happening." Daniël pauses again. "The days after the photos and the video became widely known, the mailboxes of the club crashed. It was all over the news. Everywhere. There were Dutch and Irish journalists coming over to ask the gaffer and Matthew about their opinion on what had happened. Mum, dad and Naomi could hardly get a foot outside home without being pestered. I heard from the others every football forum, fan group and what-have-you went crazy. As if they finally understood it was real pain happening to a real person, not some horrible story they could choose to play down. Matthew and Degaré made an appeal to our fans to please no longer make those pictures available. From what I heard, the fans of most other clubs spread the word as well. Same goes for the national teams. It worked somewhat, but Anthony saw it had been uploaded again on yet another site. Server could be anywhere in the world. He got so angry about that. And you know Anthony Levee when he gets worked up about something …"

"Can you show me those pictures and video, please?"

Daniël shakes his head, his eyes pleading with Steve. "I don't want you to look at them. They will hurt you as much as they hurt me. And I want to keep you from hurting as much as I can. Isn't it enough knowing they exist?"

"You shouldn't have to carry this alone. Besides, what's the alternative? Never read another paper or magazine for the rest of my life, because of what they might have published? Not using the internet ever again because you'll never know what might be behind the next link? I tried so hard to stay invisible and you can see what good it did to me, to us."

The first things he notices are his shoes. Specks of blood on them, but still the shoes he wore when he took that walk through the city. The jeans are torn, dark wet with blood, as are the jacket and shirt. Bruised flesh on display. The man, and on a rational level he knows he is that man, is lying on his back, limbs spread out in grotesque disorder. There are several photographs from different angles. All being variations on the same theme.

Daniël's hand trembles when he tries to click on the link to the video. So Steve takes the hand into his own, brings it to his lips and kisses the fingers one by one until the trembling stops.

The obscenity of what his eyes see is beyond his imagination. Or perhaps it's not even the image itself, though it defies description, but the knowledge that the ones causing the suffering chose to calmly, perhaps even with some naive curiosity, observe his last moments. Chose to record the image of their dying victim in order to be able to share it with the rest of the world. In anonymity, for sure, but it still had been a human being making those images.

"Brain damage," he whispers his recognition when he sees the shocks and tremors.

The eyes wide, but no longer seeing. Breaking. The mouth gaping in agony. The laboured gasping for breath. Pink froth on the lips. White dots of what remains of his teeth. Clotted blood, so dark it looks almost black, matting the hair.

The camera phone must have been held mere inches from his face at that moment.

Such utter loneliness.

He sees himself dying, like the one holding that mobile phone must have seen it. Like the others present in the Queen Elizabeth Park at that time must have seen it. Like anyone with access to an internet connection is able to see it. Like Daniël sees it.

Without a word he closes the laptop and sets it aside. Daniël gets on the bed and this time, it is Steve holding him.

◆

For more than a week, his days are filled with him doggedly trying to get on his feet. He's finally starting to get ready for his anger. A small flame yet, but it's enough. The pictures are never mentioned. There's no need.

He wants to stand next to his man when they make their pledge to each other. He feels a joy and pride in his being asked to share his life with this beautiful human being that's almost too much for his body to contain. So he moves weights and kicks water to test the limits of his endurance.

His nights are filled with dark dreams. He greets them in the same way he smiles his welcome at the pain when he's doing his exercises, because they both fulfil a purpose. And Daniël is always there, holding his hand and whispering his love until he's able to sleep again.

He tries and fails. He tries a dozen times and fails. He tries a hundred times and fails.

With his hands firmly gripping the bars and his arms rigid, he stands upright. His feet are carrying most of his weight for the first time since what seems like an eternity. He takes one single step. It's not even long enough to be able to count a full second, but time can be measured in much smaller units.

That night, his sleep is peaceful.

Chapter 16

That one step proves to be the first of many. There are numerous skills he learns to master with some confidence. Not as before, but what a pleasure to brush his own teeth and comb his hair without having to thank a nurse for his or her trouble. To be able to finish a meal and the only reason Dan is feeding him a few bites is because it's such fun. He marvels at the sheer luxury of taking a shower and washing his own hair, even if it's sitting down on a plastic stool. Getting dressed in normal clothes, even if the jeans and shirts Gael gets from Steve's apartment are at least two, and possibly three, sizes too large. His hands are not stable enough to shave himself, but having Daniël doing it for him is something he can live with. The quiet morning ritual, so intimate in its simplicity, grows on him. On both of them he guesses, judging from the expression on his lover's face.

He no longer spends the majority of his time in bed, even if it means investing a big part of his energy and concentration on simply staying upright. He sleeps no more than nine hours, with an extra hour after lunch.

He knows not to dwell on the thought that almost all has been taken from him and is being given back incompletely and slowly. And it's not even a free gift, because he has to work for it. Hard work, that's often painful and tedious. For a short few days, he had somehow hoped it would be more or less like recovering from an extremely serious football-related injury, as far as getting to walk again is concerned. Perhaps taking a bit longer, but certainly not so much different and harder he might just as well have no experience at all at getting mobile again.

Day after day, he finds himself taking careful, hesitating steps behind the Zimmer frame, willing an unwilling body to follow orders from a brain that has, and he knows it with absolute certainty, changed forever. No neurologist needs to tell him otherwise.

The anger stays within firm boundaries. It's there, he acknowledges it, no longer afraid to look at it, but he lacks the need to feel it rushing through his veins. It might look good in the movies, blind rage, but he doesn't know how to set it free without hurting Daniël. Mourning is a slow trickle, a mild sadness that isn't bad enough to hurt but unstoppable in time, and Steve dreads the day it will have grown into an ocean of tears. There will be no way to rationalise his way out of this; no words of consolation, pointing out to him how much worse it could have been, that he came out of his ordeal alive, will be enough.

He's in no way prepared, however, for the shock of having lost the written word. The possibility had never even entered his mind during all those weeks and months of slow, imperfect, recovery. He's able to form coherent thoughts in his head; he's able to express those thoughts adequately enough to be understood by others. Whatever speed he had, and he was never a fast talker to begin with, has been lost, but the hesitation between thought and uttered sound doesn't prevent him from saying anything he wants or needs to say. Or to understand what others are saying to him. He assumes, not without good reason, that if he feels like it, he can take a newspaper, open a website, and read it.

So when Daniël works on his blog to jot down the proud achievements of his soon to be husband during that day and Steve gets curious, it's easy enough for Dan to turn the laptop in Steve's direction. " Read it yourself, if you want to." It's also a perfect excuse to steal a kiss.

Great kisser, that boy, and he is getting even better at it with each new day.

Steve smiles contentedly. He has worked incredibly hard today. Performed the aqua exercises in the small pool beyond what was asked of him and he really made that Zimmer frame see every corner of the physio room. Perhaps not all that impressive for the average 80 year old but considering all he had been through, every single tiny step counts for something.

"Danny? You're writing your blog in Dutch?"

Confusion on Daniël's face.

Steve laughs, still assuming this is some sort of misunderstanding. "I don't recognise any of this. I'm not as clever as you are, I'm afraid. *Alsjeblieft, dank je wel, ja, nee, ik hou van jou* and a few dirty words. That's about the extent of my fluency in Dutch."

"I'm sorry, but what do you mean? It's all in your language. The English guys swore to me it's pretty good English too, with only a few mistakes." Daniël looks at the screen. "You want me to enlarge the text? Would that help?"

Steve shakes his head. It's a real effort to keep the rising panic under control. "I can see everything on the screen clear as anything. No blur. I know those are letters and words and I know it's language, but it doesn't mean anything."

"I'll read a few sentences, perhaps you'll recognise something. You keep looking at the screen too, okay?" Daniël clutches at straws, but Steve hasn't got the heart to tell him that.

Daniël reads slowly and articulates every syllable, like he wants to spoon feed the words to Steve's mind.

"Steve showed us he's the master of the Zimmer frame. Looks damn sexy too, him getting around. I sneak a look now and again while I work on the bike or do my stretches. The last couple of months haven't been much good to my condition or muscles and I want to get back in shape before the wedding. (No date set, but it can't be soon enough for me.) He works harder on learning to walk again than any of us ever did to win a match or to get back into the first team after being out with injury. I know in how much pain he still is and how exhausted he gets. But he never complains about it. How can I look at this man and not fall in love, over and over again?"

Steve understands every single word Daniël says. And even now they make him smile and blush a little. But the lines and dots on the screen are just that: lines and dots.

"Hieroglyphs …" he murmurs.

Tears are welling up in Daniël's eyes. "This is so unfair."

Steve can't remember he has ever heard the word *unfair* used in all of his years as a professional player. Or perhaps he has, but so infrequently that the word never really settled. Bad luck and shit and fucked up and the ref should get his eyes fixed and the gaffer mostly knows what he's doing but not this time … oh yes, that and so much more, but unfair is too much part of the sport, and their privileged position within this game, to even mention it. So many boys, equally talented, just as eager, left behind. Countless careers that have been broken because of injuries, done to them and by them, or because a new manager has fresh ideas about the composition of a team. Chances never even given. Or not taken for reasons long forgotten. Always someone else being better, if not now, then in a few years.

"I don't know how to deal with this," Steve confesses. Even with his rational mind telling him it took him time to be able to recognise and understand speech again, to say Daniël's name, to learn to properly speak again, and he's aware he still sounds slightly impaired; he feels desperation filling every hidden corner of his body. His lover used the only words meaning anything at all.

It's not fair.

Steve realises if he doesn't find a way to restore his ability to read and write he might be able to stand next to his man when they take their vows, but he won't be able to sign his own name and understand what he's signing, or read his husband's name on the contract. The endless stream of paperwork, dealing with the aftermath of what happened in that park, dealing with anything having to do with insurance and retirement matters, the contract with the club, will have to be read to him. Like to an uneducated person, a small child, a mentally handicapped person. Always depending on others.

Newspapers and magazines and e-mails and labels on jars and handwritten letters from eight year old fans and signs in the street and lettering on windows of shops and user manuals and subs with foreign movies and instructions for appliances and medications and …

It's not fair.

Daniël sets the laptop aside. Other than that he doesn't move, doesn't say a thing. His hands don't find Steve's. He hardly even dares to glance in Steve's direction. He looks so helpless, at a loss for any kind of comfort to offer, or to receive.

"It's too much, Daniël, simply too much."

It takes Steve an eternity to find voice for his most urgent need.

"Could you please get on the bed with me and hold me?"

Daniël slowly lifts his head, like he's waking up from a dream, and walks to the door. "Just telling the nurses." He's back before Steve even notices he's gone, and closes the door. Then he helps Steve to get settled on the bed and gets on himself.

Steve hides his face against his beloved's neck, safe in strong arms.

They are not ready yet to face this new challenge. This too will pass, in one way or the other. Time will do its job, showing both cruelty and mercy that cannot be quite foreseen by either of them. But this night, they give themselves to the simple, honest truth of their bodies.

They share kisses that are gentle, but slowly grow in urgency. Hands find their way over and then under shirts. Finally buttons and zippers are loosened and fabric gets pushed out of the way. Warm skin meeting warm skin. The few words that are spoken are used to express love and affection, but not concern or reassurance.

Daniël doesn't apologise when his body reacts in the way the body of a young, healthy man is bound to react when he's being kissed and caressed by his lover. He does however ask if Steve is okay with him staying on the bed instead of retreating discreetly to the bathroom.

Steve doesn't believe the question is even asked, although in some way he can understand it. No matter how much Daniël tries to control the movement of his hand, the rawness of need – expressed in panting breaths and the fierce concentration on his face, the pupils of the grey-blue eyes widening in lust, the blush covering most of his body – is overwhelming in a way Steve nearly had forgotten about. During all this, he touches Daniël's body, a gentler counterpoint to the faster, more and more aggressive pulls and jerks of his lover's hand.

"God, so beautiful," he whispers in his lover's ear while the boy rests in his arms.

Daniël, too much out of breath to say anything, kisses him and it's by far the most perfect reaction he could come up with. It is then that Steve, almost timidly, takes Daniël's hand and brings it to his filling cock. And Daniël looks at his own fingers around the shaft, looks at his own hand moving, his own thumb stroking the head. Wonder in his eyes. "I have missed this so much, touching you like this. Having sex with you," he sighs. "Let me taste you, please?"

His lover's mouth is warm and welcoming, so patient and tender the tongue that explores deeply familiar and yet somehow new territory.

Finally, Daniël takes him as deeply as he's able to, humming around his cock. Pleasure mixes with sorrow until he no longer feels the difference. Something has been taken from him and something has been given back to him. His orgasm and his tears happen at the same time. Finally, he's resting in Daniël's arms, the few tears being kissed from his face. "I don't know how to say what this means to me. What you mean to me."

The next day he asks Daniël to take a piece of paper and a pen.

"Please write your name, so I can learn it again."

D A N I Ë L.

The key to all other words ever written.

His scent.

The sound of his voice.

The meaning of his words.

His touch.

Steve smiles because he no longer doubts this too will come back to him.

Chapter 17

Steve is, on an intellectual level, able to interpret the struggle of a beaten down man getting on his feet again as somewhat heroic, even if he thinks it's a bit presumptuous to think about himself in such terms. It certainly doesn't look like much, him counting the steps from the physio room to his own room, still struggling to keep his balance with the crutches. Grateful for the short ride with the lift, but refusing to sit in the wheelchair the nurse brings along. At least he made the promotion from Zimmer frame to crutches. He wonders why he's still so unstable on his feet, even with all the practising he does and the experience he had before with work related injuries. But there's no denying it, progress it is.

Sounding out letters like a five year old, his index finger firmly on the page of the small Reading Tree book, to learn how to read IAM like three separate sounds until something clicks and he actually understands what he is saying, is asking more of him than he's willing to admit to the endlessly patient and encouraging therapist. Or to the neurologist who explained to him, after another scan, which part of his brain is responsible for this, and how it's possible to be able to use and understand spoken language and still be blind to the written word. What does it help him, knowing they are different functions of different parts of his brain? Does it make it any less humiliating? Does that lessen the pain in Daniël's eyes? Does that feed the hopeless hope when he asks if there's medication that might help, or even some technical device? Or, the word never spoken out loud, an operation? The brave smile when they're alone again nearly breaks Steve's heart.

He's a grown man. He used to read the paper every morning. He used to read magazines about his sport, his profession. He used to read books, real ones, with hundreds of pages and small print and words with easily six or more letters. He did all that without ever giving it a second thought. Leaving notes for Daniël not to worry about dinner because he ordered some take-away. Read Dan's message on his cell phone. 'I'm parking the car now. Get naked.' Easy like that.

IA - M

"I am …"

He's what?

No longer a little boy discovering something so unbelievably wonderful he can't wait to learn more, even if it's the most difficult thing he's ever learnt; even more difficult than tying his own shoelaces. Those days of innocent wonder and discovery can't be re-created. This is work. He refuses to call it anything else. He knows why he's doing it and he sees no reason to complain about it, but it is what it is. The only way to regain at least some of what has been lost is by doing his exercises. Over and over again, until his head has found a way around the problems. Learning to walk properly and learning to read again to feel like an independent adult are not so different in that aspect.

"You call your fiancé Dan for short sometimes, Mr Gavan?" the therapist asks.

Steve nods, unable to hide his smile. And why should he? "He's making a round at the children's ward with some of the other guys. He should be back in an hour."

"Then let's see if we can surprise him."

She writes three bold black letters.

D - A - N

He knows what the combination of letters means, because he looks at Daniël's name so many times a day it's like it's engraved in his retina, but that's not the same thing as being able to actually read and write it.

"Why is it so hard to do something this simple?"

"It takes most children, and I'm talking about healthy, intelligent children at the right age to learn to read, often days before they're able to really understand the first few words. And their little heads are made to learn. It's not simple for them. Your task in comparison is daunting."

She's right, but somehow that doesn't really help. He'll do his work alright, and he will be standing next to his man, signing his name next to Daniël's. And no price will be too high, no exertion too much.

And still …

Doesn't matter. Self-pity won't get him anywhere.

D – A – N

D – A – N

His finger taps the letters one by one. He vocalises the sounds.

D - A – N

The sounds, separate at first and slow, get speed. Become one.

"Dan."

He grins. "If I were called Dan, I could read 'I am Dan'. Now I have to learn to read 'I am Steve'. Just my luck."

Writing the letters down from memory is relatively easy after that. He even gets his own name done just before Daniël gets back, although that's mostly from learning by heart. It still looks good, though.

DANSTEVE

Daniël is as proud as anything when Steve shows him what he has learned during his absence. They share stories about their hour and a half without each other. Words lovingly wrapped in eager kisses and roaming hands.

Days on end are filled with work. And in the hours between, Degaré and Matthew and Gael and Francesco and Anthony and Ray and Niko and Kurt and Dag and the others come to say hello and admire his progress. Come to tell stories about the world outside.

"I swear those two can read each other's minds. Downright spooky, I call it. I mean, Matthew wasn't even looking in Gael's direction ... sweet goal, though. The Everton keeper never knew what hit him."

"Dag didn't tell you he crashed his car into a tree? Nah, not a scratch on the boy ... his Audi, however ... poor thing, and only after such a short life ..."

"Is it okay for me to hide here? Nat has her girls over for a fashion party. You have no idea how lucky you are...But now I come to think of it, why aren't you boys interested in fashion? You're doing something very wrong on the queer front ... ow, that hurts ..."

◆

The only day he doesn't go for physio is when he's in the dental surgeon's chair as a first step to getting his teeth repaired. Stopping his body from trembling, fear bordering on panic a constant companion as soon as the chair gets into the reclining position, is more exhausting than any kind of exercise. The device to keep his mouth wide open, so the doctor can actually work inside Steve's mouth, doesn't exactly help.

He's told it will be a lengthy process because so much needs to be done; that the surgeon waited this long because his jaw had to be healed fully and he had to be strong enough to undergo the complete procedure, including several hours of anaesthesia.

The days before the operation to restore his teeth, the implants have to be made first, are filled with yet more walking and reading lessons.

Steve stops wondering if walking will ever be possible without pain and the feeling he could stumble at any moment. It takes him a good week to master the very basics of reading. After that, it slows down a bit, but that doesn't mean he slows down. He even tries to skip his afternoon nap, but the nurses and Daniël are adamant about that one. They are right, and only he fully appreciates how much, but still Steve tries to smuggle in a few extra exercises.

He thinks about going home. He knows it can't be long now. The thought excites and scares him. He tells Daniël, so they can be excited and scared together. They talk about their marriage and confess to each other it's easy enough to see the years ahead of them, of simply being together. But making plans for the actual day? He just learned to write his own name again, so can't they just bring the papers so he can sign them? His name and Daniël's, next to each other, they say "yes, I do" to a registrar and really, what more could they possibly need?

"After they patch up my teeth, how long will it be before they discharge me from hospital? But what's left of me, Danny, to send home?"

Daniël becomes quiet, almost withdrawn. His eyes are still filled with love when he looks at Steve, his smile no less genuine. He's not stingy with his kisses. His hands hardly ever stop touching his lover. But when Steve does his exercises to train his sense of balance, he can't help but notice the way Daniël bends over the bike, pedalling with furious aggression, his face set in full concentration. Steve would even go as far and call it over-concentration, like his lover is trying to get away from something as fast as he's able to, without getting anywhere. There's no fun, and certainly no joy, to be found in the way he works his body to the point of exhaustion. His breathing becomes fast and panting; sweat staining his shirt.

The physiotherapist notices it, too, but doesn't comment on it. He reminds Steve to concentrate on his own work, but that's it. No questions, no concerned look, like Daniël's uncontrolled explosion of physical activity isn't something he's seeing for the first time.

Daniël needs longer than usual to take his shower and Steve knows all too well why. The lingering musky smell of sex, of overpowering masculinity, is impossible to ignore. Steve feels he's not ready for this kind of aggressive sexuality, this blind need to take, to conquer. That doesn't seeing the loneliness in his beloved's eyes hurt any less.

"I'm sorry …"

What else can he say?

Daniël makes a helpless gesture. "I feel so … angry and helpless and frustrated. You work your arse off, and what's your reward? Getting around on crutches, reading books about a magic key, or what's it called. It took you so much courage to stay on that dentist chair. And I couldn't even hold your hand to help you, because I would have been in their way. And now I hurt you again by pleasing myself under the shower. It feels like I'm cheapening you and your love for me."

"Look at me, Danny. You can't make the impossible happen. No one can. That's why it's called the impossible. But without you, I don't know if I would have the strength and the faith to do even what is possible."

Daniël gets up and starts to walk up and down the room before he sits again. "Now you're trying to cheer me up like you always do. What about you? How much more can you take?"

Steve looks at Daniël for seconds without saying a word. He can't help asking himself the same question again: will love be enough in the end? Or will love, however humanly inadequate, be their only chance? Will it be the one thing that will always be there, when everything else fails and crumbles apart, because it's the one thing strong enough to carry the burden?

"I don't want to know how close I am to desperation because that's a truth I can't face at the moment." His voice is flat and expressionless. But his hands are safe in Daniël's.

"You're with me. I'm with you. All the rest I can learn to deal with, somehow." Daniël bows his head, like he has done dozens and dozens of times, and kisses Steve's arm.

"What if I'll never learn to walk again like I used to? What if I can never again read at normal speed? What if my speech stays this slow? What if …"

Ghosts of years before them, when finally both of them realise things won't be better in time. Healing has stopped. Miracles come at a price.

Daniël shrugs. "Then I'm married to a guy who needs a bit of extra time for certain things. I can live with that. But seeing you unhappy because you're afraid I might find you less intelligent for not being able to read like other adults, or scared during medical treatment, or think what your body has to offer is no longer enough for me, that makes me so bloody sad and angry."

"We're never really alone, here. They're good people, all of them, but this is not our home ground. I think it's time for us to go home and get married. I know I'm not finished with all the therapies and I'm scared as hell, but do you think the doctors will be okay with us going after I'm recovered from the operation?" Steve hears the hesitation but also the longing in his own voice.

Daniël smiles brightly. "I bet you're not half as scared as I am. There's so much we need to do. We need a house, with things we both like. That's what mum told me on the phone a few days ago; make sure you start your married life in a house that really belongs to the both of you. Make a home." He pauses. "Am I going too fast?"

"Much too fast, but I like hearing you talking about a house that's going to be our home."

"Don't forget a bed. One that's comfortable and huge. You bet we're going to spend an awful lot of time in the bedroom, and lots of it won't be for sleep." Daniël's eyes light up; he even blushes.

Steve isn't aware of it, but from Daniël's sudden change of mood, he concludes something must be wrong with the expression on his own face. "What is it, Danny? You doubt I want exactly the same thing?"

"I thought I was perhaps frightening you with my need and, you know, the reason why I jerked myself off under the shower, an hour ago."

Steve stops him with a kiss. "Never apologise for being a young, healthy man with matching needs. And I'll try not to apologise for being less strong and having far less stamina than before. We both know you can give me everything I need from a lover, but I can't do the same thing for you."

"I need a good, hard fuck. I miss the feeling of your fat cock up my arse like mad. On some days, I miss it so much it actually hurts. I'm honest with you about that. But I need you."

"What about the other way around?" Steve has to ask, even if he's uncertain about his own feelings at this very moment.

"Is that even a question?" Daniël's head a bit tilted, surprised. "I guess it is."

"Tomorrow's the operation. Will you sleep in my bed, with your arms around me? I'm so bloody nervous."

Daniël grins. "Not even half a dozen registered nurses and their fearsome matron will be able to stop me."

"Thank you. Oh, and another thing ..."

"Yes?"

"The next time you give yourself a little, you know, personal attention, warn me, so I can watch and enjoy the view."

Chapter 18

Daniël holding his hand while he falls asleep on the dentist chair is without a doubt the best medicine to keep blind panic far enough at bay to pretend it's not even there. And Daniël is holding his hand when he wakes up again, if only for a few moments. The rest of the day is more or less lost in painkiller sleep.

The first time he looks into a mirror, he sees a familiar face, but also more of a stranger than he had anticipated.

"I don't know, Danny …" Steve struggles for words.

Daniël, just as helpless, gently touches his lover's face. "It's you, believe me, it's you."

"What if I'll never be the man I was when I walked into that park, even if I start looking like him again?" He takes another look in the mirror.

Daniël cradles Steve's face between his hands. "Still you, always you," and kisses him.

Initially the kiss is chaste, but no more than a few seconds. Daniël is as curious as the first time he kissed him with his teeth still in ruins. As curious as the very first time he kissed Steve. His tongue teasing, exploring.

Finally they stop kissing; blushing a little, panting a bit.

"To me you couldn't be unsexy if you tried," Daniël whispers, "And believe me, what I'm seeing now is sexy as hell. Those eyes and cheekbones and lips and … I wasn't surprised when mum told me all her friends are jealous she's got such a handsome son-in-law. I would say, more than ninety per cent is you being you, and the rest is added by a surgeon doing a pretty good job."

Steve wonders if what he sees in the mirror will ever again be roughly the same as what he sees in his mind. But he doesn't doubt Daniël's words.

Two days later, the petite doctor he remembers is called Nisha tells Steve he's ready to be discharged from hospital.

"Am I ready to go home?" he asks Daniël. "Do I have a home to go to?"

"We have to decide if we're going to stay at your place or mine for the time being. I'm sure we'll find a good house before we get married. I was thinking about a nice little place with a garden." Daniël happily talks. Then he seems to realise something. "You're not talking about where we're going to live."

Steve shakes his head.

"I think your apartment is a bit more comfortable, and you definitely have a bigger and better bed. Because after tomorrow, there's no way I'm ever going to sleep in a bed that hasn't got you in it. Okay, with the exception of tournaments and matches."

"And the night before the wedding," Steve adds.

"Why?"

"Tradition."

"Love it, an old fashioned man with principles. It's definitely one of your charms. Like those old cars dad restores. He used to let me watch when he worked on them. On the rare days I wasn't learning new tricks with a ball, that is. He told me if you treat those beauties with respect and kindness, they will never let you down."

"Hey …"

"You know how I think about cars, and especially classic ones. I'm so looking forward to marrying you. And that's not because of the wedding. Although, the wedding night …"

They kiss, because talking about the big day makes them somehow want to kiss. And when they kiss, they don't have to talk, or even think, about how they will have to deal with things they can imagine, and things they don't want to imagine and that will happen anyway.

◆

Neither of them reckons that even leaving the hospital will be a complicated task in its own right.

"There's going to be lots of press waiting for you when you get out of hospital. No idea how they'll know, but they'll know. So we're going to spread a false rumour about the exact time. A few of the boys and I are going to visit you, then we go out again. Answer some questions. Distract them as much as we can while the two of you get smuggled out by a nurse. There'll be a car, with a driver, waiting for you. We can't fool them all, so be prepared for a few pictures in the tabloids and on the net, but it should at least be manageable. I talked it all though with the gaffer and Anthony and with Gael of course, because he's very clever with those things and you guys have enough on your plates anyway." Matthew explains the plan of action like the captain of a warship.

He reaches out and almost touches Steve's mouth. "By the way, looks good."

Daniël smiles even more brightly than Steve himself. "I know. And thanks for the help."

"Don't mention it. You know what the gaffer's like when we seem to forget certain principles. And as far as I'm concerned, you're both part of the team I've been captain of for nearly five years. Make no mistake about that."

Daniël nods. "If you don't like working in a team, you might consider taking up another sport. And of course there's also his famous: we're not friends; we're family, so we don't have to like each other to take care of one another. And eh, I appreciate what you just said."

"I mean every word. Anyway, we'll make sure both of your stuff gets to Steve's, so you don't have to worry about that," Matthew says.

So Daniël starts collecting clothes and everything else he and Steve can well miss for a bit more than 24 hours and stuffs it into whatever bags are available. Somehow seeing him doing that, while still talking with Matthew about all the things that need to be done to make the transition from hospital to home as easy and pleasant as possible for Steve, makes it all so real it knocks the air out of Steve's lungs.

He sees himself kissing Daniël. "See you in two days, have fun with your folks."

He sees himself walking through the city with a smile as big as the world on his face and a spring in his step, the scent of his lover on his skin.

Getting confused about what the hell is going on in that park.

Finding refuge in his beloved's arms so he didn't have to die alone.

Crawling his way back to Daniël, away from perfect beauty and final wisdom, because there was no other path to follow.

Learning everything anew, like a child, knowing he isn't one.

Having no illusions whatsoever that some things are lost forever and still not being quite able to accept the plain facts.

"I went for a bit of a walk. It took me months to get home," he says.

Daniël stands there, a plastic shopping bag half filled with shirts and a pair of jeans. Silent.

"You done a bloody miracle," Matthew's words explode from his mouth like fireworks. Then, much softer: "But lad, you paid an awfully high price."

Steve refuses to say that it could have been much worse.

"Both of you have."

Daniël looks at the man who's still his captain. He puts his hand on Steve's shoulder. "Perhaps." Not a trace of self-pity in his voice.

After Matthew's gone with a few bags of clothes – not too many because that would attract attention – and with the promise a couple of the other guys will come in a few hours to get the rest of what needs to be moved to Steve's place, both men sit on the edge of the bed, holding each other's hands. Like two lost children.

That's how they stay when Doctor Nisha visits Steve to ask some questions, give some last pieces of advice, say goodbye, or rather until later, because the surgical team agreed there's perhaps still progress to be made in the operating theatre.

Nurses and other members of the staff, who don't have a shift until after Steve's gone home, say their goodbyes. Smiles and hands outstretched in more than just professional courtesy. There's so much to be said, and so little is actually spoken.

The next day they look around in a room brought back to the essentials. Just a hospital room, except for cleaning all set for the next patient. The last thing Daniël does before they leave the room is putt on his watch. He smiles at Steve. "Ready to go home?"

◆

Steve still can't walk without his crutches but when he steps out of the hospital, Daniël takes one crutch in his right hand. Hand in hand, they walk the few steps to the waiting car. There are no tears in Daniël's or his own eyes and they don't say a word about it. They just walk outside, in the morning sun, holding each other's hand.

Expecting a hired chauffeur, Steve's a bit surprised to see Anthony Levee opening the door for them.

"Not going to let yer be brought home by some stranger."

Matthew was right, there are hardly more than a few handfuls of photographers. A couple of mostly female fans stand in silent awe. A young woman with a microphone asks a question Steve ignores and Daniël answers with a polite but short, "More information will soon be available through the club, thank you."

When the photographers threaten to get too close, Anthony tells them off with words that leaves little to the imagination.

"At least now they got something to write about." He grins while he helps Steve inside.

Before he sets the car in motion, he makes a short call. "I got it under control, Matthew, we're on our way."

Steve looks through the window. The world is still the same, he didn't expect anything else. But somehow it all looks different to him. No longer the same streets and houses. No longer the same people.

Daniël steals a quick kiss. Anthony jokes about it in a good-natured way. Then he spends a few words on how traffic is murderous, even at this time of the day, but that at least the sun is shining. "Specially ordered for you."

Steve smiles his gratitude. "Thank you."

Anthony weaves smoothly in and out of the traffic, humming along with the radio. Steve has to admit he actually enjoys the relatively short drive.

"Nice to see a bit of the world again?" Daniël asks, caressing the back of Steve's hand with his thumb.

"Yeah." And it is.

"We're here," Anthony says. "We got yer home."

Steve does the polite thing and asks their friend in, but the man refuses. "Nah, I bet you guys could do with a moment for yerselves. I'll just make sure yer safely in and I'm on my way. Oh, and Dan, we made a few deals with the gentlemen of the press, so at least yer two should be left in peace for the weekend. After that all bets are off, I'm afraid."

With the help of Daniël Steve manages to get out of the car with reasonably ease. They ignore the lonely photographer who snaps a few shots and is gone again, and walk to the door of what will be their apartment for the time being, though strictly speaking it's still Steve's place.

Then, suddenly: "I don't have the key."

"But I have." Daniël places it in Steve's hand. And Steve tries not to wonder what this simple gesture means.

His hand doesn't shake when he opens the front door. He doesn't cry when he walks from room to room. Whatever this was before, after he closed the door behind him and said "See you in two days" to Daniël, it no longer is.

Make no mistake about it, he's happy to be back after so many weeks and he smiles when he sees his belongings, exactly because they are his and as such, he cares about their history and their practical and aesthetic value. He notices how everything has been cleaned and tidied and, even without opening any cupboard or the fridge, he knows there's plenty of food and something nice to drink as well. His bed has been freshly made. There are flowers on the table. He is grateful for those gestures of friendship. But whatever home means to him, it is standing right next to him, looking him intently in the face. The apartment is just a place to stay. Things are things, nothing more. He only needs to pack some very personal items, like photos of his mother and grandmother, part of his CD and DVD collection, books and gifts from friends, in particular from Daniël, and he's ready to go again.

"Daniël?" He places his crutches carefully against a chair and wraps his arms around the other man. "Promise me something?"

"Anything"

"Find a real home for us."

"Just say where you want to live and I'll follow you. I can work anywhere. If no club wants me, I'll simply do something else." Daniël kisses him. "What about you sit down, I'll make a cup of coffee, perhaps a few sandwiches and we'll talk about it?"

They're sitting as close together as possible while still being able to drink their coffee and eat their sandwiches. For a while, they don't say anything. There's just the joy, slowly seeping in, of being there, together, on that couch, touching, drinking coffee.

"You want to leave Kinbridge?" Daniël begins.

"Someday, perhaps. The club's hinting at wanting to sell you during the next transfer window? You're thinking about finding another club?" He's not even surprised how calm his voice sounds.

Or Daniël's voice, when he answers, "Not that I know of. I'm happy to stay for a while longer. I promised Degaré to start training after the weekend, to see if I can fight my way back. Who knows, he might give me a chance with the first team as substitute. If that doesn't work out, I'll look around. Lots of clubs won't touch me with a ten foot pole, despite all the public declarations. Good chance my market value has gone down a few million, and not because I'm a bit out of practice. On the other hand, that makes me perhaps interesting for some less wealthy clubs, if I insist on playing football. I only know I'm not going anywhere without you."

He leans his head against Steve's. "First I'm going to find a place for the two of us. And of course, we have to decide a date for the wedding. "

"Perhaps we could rent for a while. At least until we know if you stay here for the next season. It doesn't have to be anything big or fancy."

"I'm afraid we'll have to deal with the media attention, or we can never go anywhere without being pestered. I'm not going back into hiding, but I also want you to feel safe and free to go wherever you want to go." Daniël bites his lower lip in a nervous gesture. "I don't want to be too afraid to leave you alone for even half an hour, or to let you go out of the house without me. I didn't want to think about it, back at the hospital, but I'm afraid. Not for me, I don't care what they sing about me in the stands, but I can't live with the thought that someone might even say something hateful against you, let alone the rest."

"If we lie on the couch I can hold you in my arms," Steve says. "Like before …"

It's a bit narrow, they remember that all too well, but love doesn't need a lot of space.

"Being discreet to the point of making ourselves invisible didn't help. I guess some people will be nasty for a while. But how long will it take before they'll find something more interesting to make a fuss about? Weeks? Months?"

Daniël looks at Steve, kisses him. "Why are you so calm?"

Steve kisses Daniël back. "I'm not, it just takes a while for me to understand how goddamn scared I am. But somehow I don't care. Perhaps

I will tomorrow, or next week, but not today. I got out of hospital alive. I'm holding my boy in my arms. We're talking about our future. I can live with a bit of fear."

Saying the words somehow makes their significance clear. It's not just a matter of being able to go anywhere as a couple or to openly share an apartment, and not needing a girlfriend as prevention against certain questions. It all goes far beyond that. They have entered the world of the grown-ups, the adults; willing to sign a contract with the promise to take care of each other in sickness and health. They're a couple, setting up a household, instead of pretending it's actually fun to sneak in and out of each other's homes, or to arrive at the training grounds in separate cars. They no longer hide behind the childish lies about their love being a private matter.

He regrets the possible consequences for Daniël's career, but doesn't feel guilty about it. If Daniël had chosen to ignore Degaré's phone call and stay away from the hospital, he would have accepted that and not laid any blame. But his lover has made a clear choice as an adult, as a man, and he isn't going to cheapen that by guilt. He had tried that, with the best of intentions, and he wasn't exactly proud of the outcome.

"So nice, having you here. Not having to warn the nurses. Not being distur –" Before Daniël can finish his sentence the ringtone he uses for his mother's mobile sounds. "I told her you'd come home today."

Steve listens to him talking in fast Dutch. Nodding and humming and sounding so full of joy it makes his heart leap in his chest.

"Here, she wants to talk to you too." Daniël pushes the phone against Steve's ear.

"Just saying hi. You must be so happy to be home again. I said to Daniël he should take good care of you and not let you do anything." She talks for a few minutes more and Steve nods and tries to get a few words in until Daniël takes the phone from his ear, says something in Dutch and then it's quiet again.

"She asked how you're doing and if we had any trouble with paparazzi. I told her we're going to look for a place after the weekend and we'll decide a date for the wedding very soon." Daniël presses his lips against Steve's temple. "Say that's okay. Please?"

"That's very much okay. We'll keep it small and simple, so there won't be a lot of organising to do." Steve suspects it won't be quite that simple, but for the moment he's happy to bask in the illusion they're just like any engaged couple planning for their special day.

Daniël starts kissing him in earnest, his hands roaming wherever they can reach, his breathing speeding up. "Can you feel what you're doing to me?" He moves his crotch none too subtly against Steve's belly.

"I can feel it yes, the big little boy is getting even bigger." Steve can't stop himself from teasing his lover.

"The poor thing can't help wanting you."

"I'm more than happy to give it a lot of loving attention." Steve ghosts his fingers over the prominent bulge. "But I'm afraid this couch is going to kill me in about two minutes."

"I'm so sorry, I should have …" Daniël almost falls on the floor in his haste to get up and help Steve in a sitting position again.

"Hey, it's no problem. It's just so good with you, I kind of forgot. My body reminded me of a certain fact." Steve smiles through his pain.

"You're in pain. I mean, more than usual. You need something for that?" Daniël looks positively guilty now.

"You, me, a bed and a nice massage, that would be perfect." Steve leans heavily on Daniël, suddenly feeling more tired than he had been aware of moments before.

They walk slowly to the bedroom, where Daniël helps Steve to undress.

"What about you?" Steve pushes the hem of Dan's shirt upwards and licks his lips when he sees the strip of naked skin. He's tired, yes, but his eyes are working perfectly fine. "Besides, I know the big one feels much better when he has a bit of breathing space."

"You're a saint. Not a selfish bone in your body." Daniël grins, but undresses quickly.

When they lie on the bed, side by side, touching, in each other's arms, against each other's naked skin, touching and touching all over, they are silent with the wonder of it. They take their time, or perhaps, Steve thinks, they allow time to happen. They don't do anything of great importance, or say anything of great importance. There is so much they want to do and are going to do, but not right at this moment. And all the words that are

126

going to be said, just like all the things that are going to be done, just have to wait a bit longer.

Then, just as naturally, Daniël breaks the silence and kisses Steve on his lips. "I owe you a massage."

Steve has no idea if there's still some suitable oil in the bathroom, but Dan obviously does know, because soon enough his hands find all the kinks and just-not-right places on Steve's body and make it all so wonderfully, perfectly right.

Steve closes his eyes and enjoys that for as long as it is given to him, his body is just his body. No pain, no things slightly off, no things almost working and yet not as he remembered. Although his memories of what was are slowly replaced by what simply is.

Ever so gradually, Daniël mixes touches purely meant to relax sore muscles with touches to arouse. Those touches get intermingled with deep, hungry kisses. Once again they lie side by side. Steve touches Daniël in all the places he knows his lover likes to get touched, kisses him with the clear message that yes, sex is very much on the menu.

Daniël gently scrapes his teeth over Steve's shoulder and with his right hand, he grips Steve's left.

"You want to ask me something?" Steve teases, his free hand cupped around his lover's scrotum, enjoying the warm weight. Daniël's untouched cock throbbing in envious need.

"Your fingers in me," Daniël blurts out. Then, hastily, like he wants to correct himself before Steve even has a chance of misunderstanding him, "I know we're not ready for a good, hard fuck, but that's not the main reason. I just …"

Steve, as gently as possible, places his hand over Daniël's mouth. "I haven't forgotten. Hand me that massage oil, please?"

There's still the logistics of it all. Steve knows he can't stay on his knees for more than a very short time without being in serious pain. He hopes that will get better in time, but for now it's something he simply has to deal with. But he also doesn't want to lie on his back, with Dan on top of him. He isn't sure why not, he just doesn't. And side by side, be it face-to-face or in a spooning position, has its own practical problems, with his hands in an awkward position and Daniël not really being able to move freely.

"Let's try this," Daniël says, after he collects all the pillows on the bed and even walks to the wardrobe to find one more. "You just sit upright," he continues and at the same time shoves the pillows behind Steve's back. "Comfy?"

Steve nods. "Very comfy. Feel free to offer me a massage any time of the day."

Daniël gives a nice, deep kiss before he continues. "Now you spread your legs as far as feels comfortable. You'll be honest with me on this, promise?"

Steve nods again. "I'm so sorry we can't just have sex in any position we feel like. Not very spontaneous and not much variation in what I have on offer at the moment."

Daniël kneels between Steve's legs, and then lowers himself enough to be able to look his lover in the face. "You have you on offer. I can't think of anything better. I want both of us to have a good time. And I'm not having a good time if the man I love is in pain or feels scared." He takes one of Steve's hands and brings it to his fully formed erection. "What do you think this is? I'm so fucking hard for you."

"Perhaps spontaneity is somewhat overrated in sex." Steve admits with a wry smile.

"But love isn't." Daniël rests his forehead against Steve's. Then he turns and kneels away from the sitting man, his legs wide open, offering his back to his lover. "Please."

It's been so desperately long since Steve has touched his beloved boy in this way, it makes his hand shake a little, but he doesn't mind too much because he notices the slight tremble in Daniël's limbs. The trembling stops when he gently caresses as much of Daniël's body as he can reach without having to stretch himself. His hands become steady.

One oil slicked digit is accepted very easily, two with hardly more effort. The deep sigh of sheer pleasure that comes from deep within Daniël is a reminder to Steve that his fingers are not a poor substitute for his cock, but are welcomed and loved in their own right.

"Oh god, I love this," Daniël whispers. "Always have and always will."

Steve twists and turns his fingers inside his lover, opening him up, knowing from the reaction he gets he's doing something very right because

Daniël starts to moan, thrusting his body against the pattern of Steve's small, teasing stabs.

"Fuck yes, oh fuck yes." Daniël hides his head between his hands on the bed, but there's no shame of shyness in his full surrender to the pleasure Steve brings him.

His cock almost aches with the need to be touched, so Steve wraps his fingers around the shaft and tries to find a rhythm that takes off the worst of the pressure, but doesn't let him come this very moment.

He removes his fingers from Daniël's arse. "On your back, please."

Daniël turns as quickly as he's likely being able to.

"Use your hands to support your legs, so you can really open up." Steve presses two fingers against Daniël's relaxed opening, going in with one smooth move, spreading out a little bit to make room for the third one. His lover had told him over and over how he enjoyed the feeling of being stretched. Showed him many times more.

Steve, fully concentrated on the needs of his lover by now and no longer touching his own erection, watches Daniël's face until he sees the expression that tells him pleasure is so close to pain, the boundary between the two becomes translucent like a membrane.

"Please, let me come. I need to come," Daniël moans and he tries to spread his thighs even more, yielding himself; his eyes staring into Steve's. There are no secrets, no pretences, no lies. He tries to push himself further against Steve's hand. Sweat dripping from his brow. His cock is now a deep red, throbbing in need. His testicles look full to the bursting. But he keeps his hands where they are. "Tell me to come. Please, Steve, let me come for you."

For a split second, Steve wants to reach out with his free hand, knowing that a few strokes will be enough. He would be mad not to want it, but he doesn't give in to it.

"Then come for me." Four simple words.

It's all Daniël needs.

He grimaces and tenses up and shudders and trembles and moans and gags and grinds his teeth and drools and cries and comes and comes and comes and …

To Steve, there could not be a more beautiful sight in the world.

He can't blame himself for touching his cock and bring out his own orgasm. Thick strands of come land between Daniël's still widespread thighs.

Somehow, he finds himself in Daniël's arms, cleaned up, warm and safe.

A smile. A soft kiss on his lips. Nothing more.

Chapter 19

"You think there are paparazzi outside?" Steve asks while resting in the circle of Daniël's arms.

"I guess there's always a few, temporary ceasefire with the club or not. Why? You're planning to go out? I mean, if you want to …"

"Not particularly."

"Good, because I want to spend the next two days spoiling you rotten in every way possible before we have to deal with everything we have to deal with."

Steve snuggles even closer, inhaling the scent of his lover. "Spunk and sweat. Didn't realise how much I missed it until now."

"I know I could do with a shower, I smell pretty rank," Daniël admits shamelessly.

Steve knows Dan's right, but he doesn't care.

"Care to join me?" The suggestive undertone in Dan's voice is unmistakable.

Of course Steve would love to, but he isn't sure how long he's able to stand without support and what if the floor is too slippery and what good would he be to …

Realistically, Daniël isn't really able to read Steve's mind, but he comes pretty close because he gets up and says, "I've got something to show you."

The change is in the details, but those details make Steve's eyes wet with tears while at the same time he can't stop smiling. The floor has been made non-slippery, there are some strategically placed handles so he has a firm grip no matter where he stands, a simple but comfortable stool in the shower stall: it all speaks of well-thought out care.

"They did a great job, didn't they?" Daniël beams. "I asked Matthew to hire someone who knows about these sorts of things so it will be good and safe for you when you take a shower."

Steve can only nod and smile and not cry.

"Want me to wash your back?" Daniël asks, standing very close to Steve even though there's room enough for him not to. But then, why shouldn't he?

"Thank you."

Steve has said 'thank you' a lot of times in recent weeks, and many of those times it was in situations he wasn't really thankful for, although he always appreciated that someone was kind, or at least professional enough to perform any particular task for him. But this thank you is as real as the man tactfully supporting him so Steve's able to keep standing on his feet just a little longer. And those few minutes are sufficient for Daniël to get a good feel of Steve's body while getting him nice and clean. The sheer luxury of time and privacy is something he doesn't want to get complacent about, but he also knows he's all too human in his tendency to forget to count the small blessings.

"Tired?" Daniël asks.

"Lost in thought but yes, also a bit tired."

Daniël helps him on the stool. "I'll finish quickly and perhaps you can rest a bit while I prepare dinner. Sounds good?"

"Good? Sounds perfect."

There is something to be said about sitting comfortably in a well heated shower stall while watching your gorgeous lover washing himself, Steve muses. Good strong erection too on the boy, or perhaps man would be a better word in this case.

Daniël notices the direction of his gaze and gives his cock a bit of extra attention while, with mixed success, trying to keep a wicked grin from his face. "You'd like me to jerk myself off while you're watching?" He cradles his scrotum in one hand, forms a fist with the other one and pumps up and down a few times.

Steve's voice isn't really as stable as it sounds; he's just very good at pretending. "Since when do you need to ask me that?"

"So hot, your eyes on me," Daniël breathes. "Fuck, so hot."

"Show me what you usually do … did … in the hospital shower … Please, Danny …"

Daniël closes his eyes, but Steve knows it's not to shut him out. It even gives him a chance to study the face of his beloved, so concentrated in lust it makes the boy grimace in a way that would almost be comical if not for it being so honest and bare in its vulnerability.

This is no longer a show or a kinky fantasy. Daniël is standing in that hospital shower, fucking his own hand in equal lust and frustration; biting his lip close to bleeding to keep himself from making any noise. Steve knows this beyond any doubt.

"Daniël, please look at me."

The boy opens his eyes.

Even in his orgasm he's silent.

"I'm sorry … I'm so sorry …" The words stumble over his tongue. "I was back in the hospital and I watched you die and I couldn't let that happen. So it didn't happen. I wanted to touch you, but there was almost nothing left unbroken and I tried to imagine it was you touching me, and that didn't work either. So I jerked myself off out of frustration and missing you so much I thought I was going to throw up with it. And all I wanted was giving you a bit of real life porn to look at."

Steve gets up, praising the cleverly-placed handles once more, and takes him in his arms; the boy sighs like a lost child finding home again. "I asked you, remember. What fantasy could be more beautiful than the truth on your face?" Steve places a gentle hand against Dan's cheek.

After a few moments, Daniël reaches for a big, fluffy towel and wraps it around Steve. "Do you wonder too how long it will take us before we've left the hospital for real?" He dries himself methodically and puts on his clothes before he helps Steve.

"Yes."

"Not much we can do about that now. I guess it takes time. What about we leave it for now, and concentrate on dinner in say an hour or two? Is that enough for you to get rested?"

"It depends on what you have planned for the rest of the evening," Steve jokes.

"I'm all for a little improvisation. No nurses, no visitors, no nothing but you and me and this whole weekend to do whatever we please."

"There is something I would perhaps like to try. But, after dinner." Steve hears in his own slowing voice how tired he is.

"A surprise? I love surprises, especially from you."

Steve almost regrets having said anything. "Would you be very disappointed if it doesn't work out the way I hope?"

"Stop worrying. You've already given me you. The rest is icing on the cake." Daniël offers Steve his arm. "Ready for your nap and then ready for dinner?"

He doesn't do much napping, but Steve still feels he definitely needs the rest. It's nice hearing Daniël doing whatever he's doing in the kitchen and living room, humming as he went. It starts to smell nice, too, after a while.

◆

A soft kiss on his lips. "Wake up, sleepy head."

He must have fallen asleep, even if he thought he hadn't.

Daniël joins him on the bed for a few moments, giving him time to get his body and mind in motion again. Then Steve takes his crutches, walks to the bathroom and washes his face. On Daniël's suggestion, they both change into their best clothes. Having both lost a lot of weight, they look like children playing in their dad's suit.

"If I may invite you to join me at the table?" His lover offers him his arm and accompanies him to the living room.

Steve has no trouble being speechless: the distance between the fluency of words in his head and the slowness of his tongue is more than adequate for that, but in this case, he would be speechless no matter his eloquence.

There's the perfectly set table, with damask, crystal, china and silver. There are candles and music. There's even champagne in the cooler.

"You like it? It's not too much, not too sickly romantic or anything?"

Before Daniël is able to continue on the path of ever growing insecurity, Steve kisses him right on the mouth. "It's beautiful. Thank you."

He feels genuinely spoiled by the detailed care that's been put into this meal. He knows Daniël didn't have the opportunity to shop for all this, but it's his idea and he managed to get it across to the others, who did more than their best to make sure the initial idea and the final result were a perfect match.

"Gael helped me a lot with this. He even prepared some of the dishes, so I only had to put them in the oven," Daniël explains with unconcerned honesty. "It was fun talking about your favourite foods and champagne and how we could make you feel extra special. He wrote down for me exactly how much time everything would take, so it would all be just right."

Steve knows the best compliment to this wonderful display of love and friendship is enjoying the meal. And he does. Slowly and with all the attention it so highly deserves.

Savoury and salty and sweet and smooth and crispy and hot and cold and creamy and … It's all there and often as a surprise. He had almost forgotten food could be like this. Not just prime ingredients, but also love and care and, an often forgotten ingredient, time. Seafood can be fresh, chicken doesn't have to be dull, potatoes do come in various qualities and vegetables are not just cultivated as a weapon for mothers to pester their children.

"This is so good. I can't imagine the amount of work put into this."

By the time they're enjoying their gourmet coffee with a small drop of brandy, Daniël beams like he just won everything there is to win in the football world. He quickly clears the table, but leaves the candles and the champagne.

Steve will never know, and neither does he care, if it's the candles or the champagne and that drop of brandy, or simply the way Daniël looks at him, all beautiful and smiling and so, so much in love, but he simply can't stop the words flowing from his mouth.

"I don't know if I'm truly ready for this and I'm not even sure how we can make this work, technically speaking, but please can I try and …"

"You're saying what I think you're saying? Yes, please?" Daniël gets up from his chair and kneels down in front of Steve. He rests his head against his lover's thighs, letting out a happy sigh when Steve starts to stroke his hair.

"As much as I want to do it with you on your back or you on all fours and me kneeling behind you, it's impossible at this moment. My knees … and besides that, I can't support my weight, or what's left of it, with my arms. I wish I knew why, but even thinking about lying flat on my back with anyone on top of me makes me blind with panic."

Daniël looks up. "I think I understand why."

"But it's you. This is so painful for both of us and I feel so embarrassed by it."

"You were robbed of even a last chance to defend yourself, to protect yourself. You must have fought so hard before you could fight no more."

Steve feels himself drown in an ocean of sadness. "You gave me this perfect dinner and I want to make love to you, and now I'm fighting monsters again."

"When you were still so bad and all I could do was sit and watch, some of the nurses took a few minutes to talk with me while they washed you and made sure your lungs were clear of mucus. Every single one of them told me how important time is. They said it's more important than talks and therapy and anything. It was only yesterday you were released from hospital, after having spent months in that room. After having seen death."

"This will be part of the rest of our lives." It hurts even saying the words.

"I know, and I'm at peace with that if that's the price I have to pay for still having you in my life." He tries, oh how the boy tries. Courageous, stubborn soul. Daniël gets on his feet to be able to kiss Steve. "Absolutely nothing life throws at me can be even remotely as bad as losing you. All the rest, I'll deal with." He almost sits on Steve's lap, making sure as little as possible of his weight rests on his lover.

"This could work," Steve says, all too aware what he's doing. "This could actually work."

The sadness will return but for now, he deliberately turns his back to it.

"What ..." then Daniël understands. "You clever man. You sexy clever man." He gets up again. "I'm going to get some stuff."

Halfway he stops as if changing his mind. "I want you to be comfortable and feeling in control. If it would help, I'd happily let you tie me to the bed but that's not what you need at the moment, is it?"

It's not really a question but still, Steve shakes his head. "I wouldn't know what to do."

"Okay, pillows, lube, something else?" Daniël takes the few steps to Steve to kiss him once again. "You know, this planning to get laid is actually growing on me. Doing things knowing it's all to get that big, fat cock up my arse."

His lover's words find their way straight through Steve's body.

"Gets you hot too, I bet," Daniël whispers in his ear while he cops a feel of Steve's beginning-to-form bulge. "Is all of this for me?"

"Go get the pillows and the lube, please Danny," Steve urges him.

"My man is getting seriously horny." Daniël gives him one long, deep kiss before he, for the second time, goes off to get the stuff they need.

Anticipation makes his fingers itch in need, but he wills himself to wait until his lover has returned, which is pretty soon, much to Steve's relief. He gets himself on his feet, making sure he's standing as stably as possible.

"You have to help me get undressed." He accepts he has to ask Daniël this because while he might have found adequate strength in his legs again to be able to stand for several minutes, his sense of balance is still shaky at best. Besides that, getting buttons through a small buttonhole, especially with excitement shaking his hands, will take half an hour. And that's not a manner of speaking.

"Eager much?" Daniël teases him while he makes short work of buttons and buckle.

Steve nods. "Nervous too."

"You're okay?" Daniël takes him in his arms. "Does it bother you that I feel the need to protect you?"

"I'm fine. And no, it doesn't bother me. I guess I feel the same about you. Does it bother you?" Steve caresses Dan's long, strong back.

"Why would it? You're my man; of course you want to protect me. Not everything has changed." Daniël kisses Steve's lips. "I approve of where your hand is going."

Steve grins. "I approve of your approval." And he takes a buttock full in his hand.

"You can stand a few moments longer?"

Steve nods. With one hand leaning on the table, he's fine. It feels wonderful to stand there, palming his pretty much fully-formed erection, watching Daniël put one pillow on the seat of the chair and one against the back rest.

And it makes Daniël even more interested, because one of his hands joins Steve's for a moment before he manoeuvres Steve on the chair. "You're sitting a bit higher now, and a bit more to the front, to make it easier for both of us when I ride you."

The words make Steve's cock twitch in anticipation. "Hand me the lube, please? I want to prepare you."

It takes a bit of trial and error, but they laugh through it all and in the end Daniël is very much relaxed, sufficiently opened up and ready for action.

Steve feels how his nerves calm down, how his heart loses the hasty beat and how his breathing becomes easy and free. There is not a trace of fear in his mind or body when Daniël straddles him and, with steady slowness, lowers himself until Steve's cock is fully seated inside him.

Warm ...

"God, Steve," Daniël's voice breaks in fragile syllables.

"You ... oh ... Steve ... you ... Steve ... Steve ... Steve ... Steve ... Steve ... Steve ..."

He frames the face of the trembling boy between his hands, covers it with butterfly kisses.

"You.

Are.

Inside.

Me."

It sounds to Steve as if every single word needs to be said as precisely as possible, because they have to carry such heavy load of significance beyond the simple fact.

You didn't die.

I didn't lose you.

You didn't die.

I didn't lose you.

"My Danny."

Because, what else is there for him to say? What words are there when there are no words?

Slowly, Daniël rocks himself to completion, helped by Steve's fingers stroking his cock.

Every second of every minute, Steve focuses his gaze on his beloved's face.

To know and to remember.

His own orgasm is hardly more than a shiver, a sigh. It's enough for Daniël to close his eyes and rest his head against Steve's. Warm fluid fills the palm of Steve's hand.

Daniël takes the hand into his own and brings it to Steve's mouth.

Steve licks the palm of his own hand clean, tasting his lover's essence.

"God ..." he whispers.

Chapter 20

He can't remember how he landed in bed and doubts Daniël remembers much more. But when he wakes up in the morning, Dan's not with him in bed. It doesn't alarm him. He would know if Daniël weren't close by. He doesn't even need to hear or see him for this.

And soon enough, the bedroom door is pushed open and Dan enters, balancing a tray with coffee, freshly baked rolls, boiled eggs, strawberry jam and some already peeled oranges. And, of course, the unavoidable protein-spiked shake. He sets the tray on the chair so he can then help Steve sit upright.

A quick kiss. "Ready for some breakfast?"

Steve nods, too busy smiling to be able to say much.

"We make this a nice, quiet Sunday. Lazing around a bit …"

"Having sex a bit," Steve teases before he takes a bite of the roll with butter and jam.

"Oh yes." Impressive how Daniël doesn't spill a drop of his coffee while he turns his face sideways to give Steve another long kiss on the lips. "Breakfast first, because you need some meat on that skinny frame of yours. Doctor's orders, remember."

Steve doesn't feel offended by Daniël's remark. No need to hide behind pointless vanity. Just like Daniël doesn't hasten to say how sexually attractive his lover still is to him. Something that obvious doesn't ask for superfluous reassurance. And it's not a blind love either, because Daniël has seen the worst and he never once looked away.

They both eat one half of an orange.

"You'll help me shave, later?"

"Okay."

The conversation eases on, as gentle and natural as anything that could happen between them.

"We're doing it the other way around, it seems," Steve says. "Being married, I mean, and having a wedding."

"I guess we are, "Daniël chuckles. "Look at us. Old married couple. Now all we need to do is adopt a puppy."

Steve smiles at himself, at his unspectacular happiness. He finishes his roll, drinks the last of his coffee, and eats the half of another orange he shares with Daniël. They kiss and touch each other just to kiss and touch. The need is always there, sometimes demanding, often as gentle as the look he sees in Daniël's eyes, but never fully absent. Anyone who claims the love of body is inferior to the love of mind has no idea what they're talking about. This body, this healing but never fully healed remains of the home he once inhabited with such ease, is what keeps him with his beloved. And Daniël knows that too. Whatever they may wish for in their secret of secrets, it's this and nothing else.

So Steve eats everything Daniël wants him to eat with pleasure, including the shake.

In the bathroom, he sits on the stool while Daniël shaves him. It's as pleasant and important as touching each other while eating breakfast in bed; as important as all other things. And while Steve knows there will be undeniable hierarchy between things later on, for now there's nothing small and relatively insignificant.

They talk about the wedding, sitting on the couch, not yet fully into the business of how exactly they want it and when, but more concrete and factual than ever before. No fancy fuss, no exalted drama, and certainly no self-written texts to say out loud to each other in front of their gathered friends and family. Them standing there, in front of a registrar, who is making a short speech, is exactly the declaration they want to make.

And because talking about the wedding makes them itchy in a very pleasant way all over, but mostly in certain areas, they once again return to the bedroom. They lie side by side, kissing and touching; not in a hurry, but it's still as much sex as anything they've ever done. Brushing cock against cock, their hands kneading buttocks in appreciation. Then, almost at the same time, they wrap their fingers around each other's pricks.

"I totally love your hand on my cock," Daniël breathes against Steve's mouth. "Reminds me of all the times we were so hot for each other we didn't even make it past the hallway."

It's not as simple as it looks, concentrating at two equally pleasurable but still very different sensations, but Steve thinks that might exactly why it's such fun. His cock is being touched, like he's jerking himself off, but it's not by his own hand. His hand is finding the perfect rhythm around a shaft that's not his own.

"Love you," Daniël gasps while his body shudders closely against Steve's.

They lick their fingers clean, not caring which hand belongs to whom.

"I want to be able to be fucked by you on our wedding night," Steve says before he can stop himself. But he will forever be grateful for Daniël not saying, even if it would have been totally honest had he said it, that it's not that important, that love is wonderful between them no matter what form it takes.

"After your first time, I couldn't stop thinking about it. I couldn't concentrate on anything. It was all you and what you had given me. Until the gaffer called, I was hoping you had liked it enough to let me do it again. After that call, being able to touch you at all took up all of my ambitions." Daniël kisses Steve with a tenderness bordering on aggression. "You could say certain thoughts are firmly back in my head now."

"I like them being there, in your head. I want to be strong enough to be able to stay on my knees for longer than three minutes without pain. I want to be strong enough to fuck you with you facing me and your legs wrapped around me, or you doing me from behind. I want to have you on top of me, full weight and all, and not panic."

"And most of it isn't even about sex."

"No, I guess it isn't." Steve sighs when Daniël wraps him in his arms.

Then they talk further, because even if kisses are the best language, they still want to talk about everything ahead of them. Having a future, being able to express what they would like and want is still so shiny and new, and how could they not want to put that into words? Even the hard and scary things are not to be avoided, because it means they are giving themselves at least a chance to do the things that frighten them, instead of avoiding the risk.

"I can't help but want to keep you hidden from the world," Daniël says, "And I'm afraid it won't be the last time I'm telling you this. The world is no longer a safe place and I don't know how to make it right again.

"I can't help but want to hide," Steve says, "but I'm not going to. Just like I know you have to be out a lot from tomorrow on. I want to try and be with you as often as I can, but I'm afraid my days won't be half as efficient and I'm definitely not as full of energy as you are."

"We'll work around it. I took the liberty of talking it over with the manager and he says it's fine that when I do the training, you use the physio and the exercise room. And that includes any help if you need it. That is, if being at the Graces doesn't make you feel uncomfortable." Daniël looks slightly nervous; like he isn't sure he should have done what he has done.

"That's very thoughtful of you and the club. This way I can be close by to you while working my own programme." Steve nestles even more tightly into Daniël's arms. "I don't know how I'm going to feel when I'm there."

Daniël nuzzles Steve's hair. "And I don't know how I'm going to feel with you being there and not being there. Beside myself with happiness because all the while I'm training, I can be with you in two minutes; frustrated because you're not training with us."

"I might have been sold off anyway; I already did get less playing minutes the last couple of matches than during the season before ..." It's a stupid thing to say because it doesn't matter what would have happened, and Daniël is right for closing Steve's mouth with his own.

"Time for food. Doctor's orders, remember? Eat a little something every few hours. And I promised a few people I'd give them a quick call to tell them that everything is fine." Daniël stretches his tall, very relaxed body and yawns like an overgrown kitten.

"Simply watching you makes me the happiest man in the world." Steve knows there was a time he would have thought it but the words wouldn't have left his mouth. Not so any more.

Daniël turns on his side again, his head resting on his arm. "Sometimes I look at you and I have to quickly look away because it feels like my heart could burst and my body ..." He shrugs and sits upright. "Not even sure what I'm talking about."

"I think you do," Steve says quietly.

"I can't stop touching you. I want to make love to you practically all of the time. I couldn't care less if there's a match on TV or a nice movie. I don't want to update my online journal. I don't even want to phone mum and dad, or have a good giggle with Naomi. Just feeling you, just that, like we are nothing but skin and mouth and hands and cock and arse. Just that." Daniël moves his hands as if trying to get a hold on his own confusion. "Last year I wouldn't have told you this. I didn't need to. Now it's words and more words …"

"Thank you. It can't be like before, perhaps never, but thank you for telling me with words what you would have shown me with your body." Steve kisses him, consciously pushing the sadness aside. "I'm sure in a few months we'll be watching Match of the Day together and after that we'll go to bed to sleep. And only to sleep."

"You mean because we already had sex before dinner?" Daniël grins, gets up from the bed and starts to fetch his clothes. "I'm starving. What about a steak and whatever else I can find in the fridge?"

"Nice. And I already know what's for dessert."

"I bet you do." Daniël stretches his hand out. "Come on, we'll run a wet cloth over our faces, wash our hands and raid the kitchen."

Even taking their time, out of necessity and because they're really not in a hurry, it's no longer than half an hour before they sit at the table, enjoying a simple but tasty meal. After they have finished and the dishes are in the dishwasher, Daniël, as promised, phones his parents and then Degaré.

Finally he calls Matthew. "It's been great. You guys are the best. We really needed a bit of alone time. To be honest, I'm scared to think about the coming weeks and months, too. We'll manage somehow, after all we've gone through, Steve and I and all of you …"

After Daniël ends the final call, he turns to Steve and says, "They asked how you're doing, the first days home. But it hasn't even started, has it?" Daniël takes Steve's hand and holds it for a while before he gets up to make coffee.

"Even if we both know we have to face the world again, this is still important, us here, being together, without others. We needed this more than anything and they made it possible." Steve keeps talking, while he walks with Daniël to the kitchen, trying to see if he can manage the short distance with one crutch. It's feasible, but he's still a long way from being able to walk through his own home without needing any support.

"Don't I know it. They did all the grocery shopping for us and even put it away in the fridge and cupboards. They somehow managed to keep the press away from us. By the way, we have to talk about that and make a few decisions."

Steve leans against the sink, watching Danny make coffee, letting him talk. He knows some seriously difficult times will be waiting for them but at this very moment he's happy and fulfilled.

"The press," Daniël starts once they are comfortable on the couch, "can't be ignored. What happened to you, to us, stopped being private right from the moment that man tried to feel you up because he recognised you. No, it started even before that. I told you the club have hired two people just to deal with the stream of letters, mails, gossip, anything having to do with us, haven't I? I've seen a fraction of it. It's both far better and far worse than we could have imagined when we fell in love. And it's not just here in England, it's in Holland and Ireland, but also in every country with any kind of football culture. All over the world, there are items in sport shows and news shows and god knows what shows. Every dog and its owner have an opinion about us. It looked like it died down a bit, but now you're out of hospital and we're planning to get married, it's starting all over again."

Steve wishes it could be simply them and a few friends, the club, Dan's family, but he knows better. They can try and turn their backs to the world, and still the world is going to watch them.

"If we give in to every request for interviews, we'd be busy every single day for at least a month, if not more, and that's just for TV. Not going to happen." Daniël pauses. "You're okay?"

Steve nods. "It can't be avoided forever, can it?"

"Please, say no if you're not up to it, but I think giving a press conference within a relatively short time would help at least a bit. The press wants to see you, have some news directly from our mouths, and be able to ask questions. If we do it, Degaré will be there, and Matthew, but I'm not going to let you do something that makes you very unhappy. I know I can talk for us, and they'll have to wait if and until you're ready to tell your story."

Steve takes his lover's hand, twining their fingers. "Most likely, I will feel a bit scared, definitely nervous, but there won't be a prouder man than I sitting next to you."

"We could perhaps do a long interview with a quality journalist right before we get married. I wish I could say they'll leave us in peace after that, but well …"

Steve finishes his coffee. "Then they get the same story over and over again, until they understand we are the most boringly happy couple in the country."

"It would be a tiny bit easier if a few others would open their mouths as well. But I don't expect a lot of professional players to stand up and declare their love for their fellow men. Or do you think Gael and Matthew …"

Steve knows what he's hearing, but it takes a few seconds to actually hear it. "You've seen it, too?"

"Poor bastards, scared as hell after what happened to you and no one but each other to talk to about it, because they hope no one has any idea what's happening right under their noses."

"I knew what was going on but only on an instinctive level, when I heard them talk while I was still halfway waking up, but could already distinguish voices. When they talked to each other, they sounded like when you talk to me."

"To me, it was in their eyes. Never noticed it before; they were at least as good at hiding as we were, but suddenly I knew for certain what I was seeing. And what do we do now?"

"We do nothing. Support them by example. They are family men; they have to deal with this in their own way. Believe me; what they don't want is us telling them how obvious they are to us. It won't help them, or their families."

"You believe they should live a lie?"

"We lived a lie before I walked into that park. A beautiful, beautiful lie, but still a lie. The truth started when you came to the hospital and stayed at my side, when you declared your love for everyone to see and hear, even though you didn't know yet if I would ever wake up again to confirm your belief in me had been justified." Steve can only hope his voice sounds as gentle as he means it to sound.

Daniël stays absolutely silent for a moment.

Steve gives him his time, before asking, "Did I upset you?"

"Yes. It's still true, isn't it?"

"But you also hear what I say about you turning a lie into the truth?"

"I love you. What else is there to say?" Daniël puts his arm around Steve. "It was the easiest choice I ever had to make. I belong at your side. And once I decided my priority, the rest became so simple."

"Come to bed, please?" Steve asks. "I have to feel you as close as possible."

"Yeah," Daniël says. "It's too much, talking about this."

His support is enough for Steve to get to the bedroom without his crutches, although Steve leans so heavily on him it must feel like he's carrying half his lover's weight.

"It's my head," Steve mutters, "my head more than my muscles or my bones."

"Remember what they told us in hospital? Exercise your muscles and perhaps your brain will remember." Daniël kisses him while they land safely on the bed. "Indulge me? Let me undress you?"

"That sounds more like you indulging me." Steve spreads himself out as much as he's able to. "Well, have fun."

Daniël starts with loosening one button of Steve's shirt. "Feels like opening a gift for my birthday and knowing it's exactly what I asked for."

The rest of the buttons follow. A kiss for a button and a button for a kiss.

Steve shivers in undiluted pleasure when his lover's tongue swipes over the right nipple, then the left, and continues over the surrounding skin. Daniël skips, an impish grin on his face, to the still clothed crotch to tease the bulge with his lips, but doesn't stay there because before Steve is used to one sensation, he's being kissed on his mouth. Wet and warm and oh, how it takes his breath away.

Suddenly, it stops.

"You make me so fucking greedy for you," Daniël says, face flustered and eyes bright, while he starts undressing himself. "I wish I could just ..." His shirt off, he seems to decide he needs to touch his lover again and skates his hand over Steve's belly, only to return to unfastening the belt of his own jeans.

Steve waits patiently, watching his beloved boy trying to do three things at the same time and hardly managing one. After a few minutes, he decides to intervene. "Why don't you start with getting yourself naked, then me?"

"You're eager to feel me all over?" Daniël finally manages to get himself free of the last stitch of clothing, his erection a proud declaration of want and need.

Steve stretches his hand out to make Daniël sit on the bed. "More than I perhaps realise."

Daniël doesn't forget to undress Steve while he talks. His gestures form a moving combination of eagerness and care. "Would you allow me to be on top of you for a very short moment? I won't even rest my full weight on you. Perhaps you'd like to be on top of me first? Sorry. I'm asking too much too soon. Sorry."

"I'm not afraid of you, I'm afraid of the monsters in my own head."

Daniël stretches himself out on his back, and opens his legs to create a comfortable space for Steve. "Please?"

And Steve settles himself on top of his beloved, relaxing into the safe embrace.

"Good," Daniël sighs and he kisses Steve.

"Perfect," Steve sighs and he kisses Daniël.

Carefully, making sure there isn't even the slightest chance to startle his lover – Steve has no other way of interpreting the way Daniël's hands glide over his back – Daniël explores Steve's body as far as he can reach, taking extra care with the many scars. Instead of avoiding them, he familiarises himself further with them.

"It's like getting to know you all over again," Daniël whispers against Steve's ear. Then, almost like an apology: "Will you have patience with me?"

"Patience?"

"When I want things to go faster than is possible. When I ask you for things you're not ready for. I can see in your eyes you're aware I'm holding back because I'm afraid to hurt you, to overwhelm you. God, Steve, what more have they taken from us?"

Steve touches Daniël's face. "Something in me will always want things to be like before, but without the secrecy. Even if I'm not ready for what you so obviously need, that doesn't mean I'm not just as eager for it as you are. That I don't want you so very, very much."

"So it's okay I can hardly wait till our wedding night?" Daniël almost sounds like a combination of a naughty boy and a blushing virgin, and Steve can't help but laugh.

When Daniël licks the very last drop of come from Steve's spent cock, and Steve slowly, longingly, retracts the two fingers from Daniël's opening, and when they have cleaned themselves provisionally with a damp cloth, finding rest and safety in each other's arms, both men smile and know they are ready to face the world again.

Chapter 21

In the warm embrace of a still half-asleep Daniël, the shy light of early morning gradually gaining strength, Steve whispers, "Remember what you asked last night?"

A lazy kiss on his forehead. "What, sweetheart? What do you want me to remember?"

"You asked if you could be on top of me for a moment."

Daniël looks very much awake now, and more than a little alarmed.

"Would you do this for me? Please? At this moment I need feeling your strength more than I fear the monsters in my head. Than realising how defenceless I am." He hides his face against the crook of Daniël's neck. "I want to feel I can face other people again, but I'm still so scared."

Daniël doesn't say a word but just holds him a bit tighter.

"Thank you for not saying I'm able to defend myself or that you would never let me come to harm ever again. I know, like I know few other things, you would have died defending me in that park, and it still won't change the truth."

"But then you would at least have had someone fighting beside you." Daniël presses his lips against Steve's forehead. "How can I live knowing you were dying alone?"

"I wasn't alone. I was never in doubt about your love, no matter what foul language they used." Steve looks at Daniël. "And still the monsters are there. And the knowledge of how empty-handed we sometimes feel is there. Hush, boy, without you I wouldn't even be able to talk about facing the monsters."

He turns on his back, taking Daniël with him. Fully aware he's only able to do that because his lover doesn't resist him. His tall body is now covering him, though with most of its weight not resting on him.

"You're shivering," Daniël whispers.

"We both are."

Steve looks at Daniël's dear face and Daniël never averts his eyes from Steve. They stay as they are for a while. Not talking, not moving. Not even kissing. Just being there: together.

"I think I'm ready to start the day," Steve finally says.

"Then I'm ready too." Dan kisses him as a way to say thank you and gets up.

Steve feels strangely calm while they get through what is fast becoming a treasured routine of taking a shower, brushing teeth, shaving, getting dressed, preparing and eating breakfast.

Of course, he notices Dan's almost erection when the boy's taking a shower and feels excited by it, although he doesn't know how to initiate any kind of sex at the moment.

"When I get near you, I get hard." Daniël continues to wash.

"If you want to …"

"Would you like me to?"

"Yes, please."

This time Daniël doesn't close his eyes, isn't transported back to the hospital shower, frustrated and angry. He looks at Steve, nothing but happiness on his face. The blush spreading over part of his body is clearly from excitement, not shyness.

"You look so … I'm not sure what word to use, alive I guess. It does you good, being out of the hospital." Steve sits on the stool, no longer able to stand without discomfort. "You're the most beautiful thing in my life. Second to none."

"I am?" There's nothing feigned in Daniël's question.

"Utterly. And before you start, I am aware of your imperfections. In fact, I've kissed them so often I know every single one of them by heart."

"And my cock, you like my cock too?" Daniël moves his hand up and down, covering the head with the foreskin, then baring it again.

"Like it so much. I like looking at it and touching it and smelling it and taking it in my mouth to taste it …"

Little puffs of air are leaving Daniël's lips while he thrusts into his own hand.

"I remember how you felt inside me. How your cock felt inside me. But most of all, I remember your eyes. And when I walked through the city, I knew I had to see that look in your eyes again. You want me as much as I want you?"

"Oh yes, fuck yes …"

Yes to all and everything, Steve thinks and he knows Daniël thinks it as well, even when Daniël is no longer able to make any sound except for the soft moan announcing his almost silent pleasure.

As soon as his lover stumbles from the shower cabin, Steve gets up and catches him in his arms, appreciative that Daniël doesn't actually lean his full weight on him.

"You manage to have sex with me without even touching me." Daniël leans into Steve, kissing him. "Can't wait till tonight."

"Even if it would mean me falling asleep because I'm so tired?"

"You would fall asleep in my arms. You bet I can't wait for that. But first, there's a whole day ahead of us. We could do with a bit of food. And coffee. I need coffee."

"Makes you sleepy, huh, getting off?" Steve smiles while he watches Dan getting dressed.

"Wouldn't mind going back to bed, cuddling up against you, sleep a bit, have sex again … But I'll be a good boy. So, coffee it is."

And it is coffee and toast and Daniël with a pen in his hand, a note pad before him.

But Steve's not quite ready to make lists and decide priorities.

"I remember how much I loved it, having you on top of me. So much of you, covering all of me. You doing whatever you felt like when we were alone, because you knew I could take it all. Because I wanted it as much as you did. I want it back."

Daniël puts the pen down to take Steve's hand. "You were shivering under me, but you didn't panic and you didn't push me away."

"I'm not pushing you away." Steve chuckles. "I do sound indignant, don't I?"

"A bit. I could see it when I looked into your eyes, how much more you love me than you fear the monsters. And you fear them so much."

"They're as human as you and me, the ones attacking me and the ones running away to save themselves, not even stopping to see what was happening, not realising it until they saw it on the news. And I have to make peace with knowing what they are. Because I don't want them looming over our marriage." Steve shrugs. "Time will take care of that."

"Does it help, me saying how much I love you?"

"I know you love me, even if you would never tell me again in so many words. I don't think it, or hope it, or believe it, I know it. But, yeah, I love hearing it."

Daniël smiles, takes the pen in his hand, writes something in bold, strong letters.

"Read this."

The basics of reading have been mastered; the automatic skill is still a long way off. And he wants to read it, not give a, most likely correct, guess.

"DANIËL ...

"LOVES ...

"STEVE ..."

Daniël carefully folds the piece of paper. "Keep it with you. And if it wears out and tears, I'll make another one."

The next half hour is spent with deciding what needs to be done first, what can be delegated, what's for them both to do, what's for Daniël, what's for Steve and how to prevent themselves from drowning.

"I'll start making a few calls; going to ask a housing agent to make a short-list of houses that are suitable for us. Degaré invited us for training after lunch. Just saying hi to the guys, more like. We both start regular training later this week. Your hospital visit isn't for another month or so, so that's off the list for now. And we have to get a few things like fresh bread, something for tea. Most importantly, I think we should make some decisions about our wedding sometime this week: an approximate date and a few rough ideas about what we want, who we want with us and where we want it, so I can hire someone to organise it."

Steve knows it's not all that much, but his head has to battle to get it all in. Getting out of the apartment, going to the Three Graces Park, meeting the others: there's enough to make him clutch the piece of paper in his hand to remember what it is all about.

"Too much?" Daniël asks.

Steve nods. "It doesn't matter. I know you'll do the calls, so I shouldn't be worried about that and we'll go by car when we go anywhere but ..."

"Too much."

"As I said, it doesn't matter. Just because it's difficult and scary doesn't mean I can't do it. As long as you're with me, I'm fine."

It gets him through the day, even if it means knowing once again his photo has been taken in an intimate moment of vulnerability, when he gets out of the car at the Three Graces Park and for a moment stands in the circle of Daniël's arms before he's ready to get his crutches and walk inside the training ground.

"Mr Gavan, care to say a few words to us?"

"Steve you believe you will return to the club?"

"Mister Gavan, what exactly happened that night?"

"Daniël, you perhaps …?"

Then, salvation in the form of Gabrysz' smiling face and wide open arms. "Wonderful to see you again, Steve, Daniël. Come quickly, you've been missed."

And then to the press: "Come on boys, give them a bit of privacy and breathing space. They'll tell their story when they're ready, okay?"

The greetings vary from reserved politeness to overenthusiastic cries of welcome, and from a genuinely warm embrace to a matter of fact but well-meant, "Hey, you're back."

Steve smiles and shakes hands and he thinks he says something, but the only thing he's sure of is Daniël's hand on his shoulder. He's glad nobody's asking him how he feels being back, because he honestly has no idea.

Is he back at all?

But he recognises happiness for what it is when he sees Daniël running over the turf, trying to stop Francesco from scoring, grinning in triumph when he tackles the striker who counts as one of the fastest runners in the English competition.

Degaré sits next to him while they both watch Daniël in a struggle for the ball with Dag and Neil. "He's a fighter. I wouldn't want to lose him for the club or for the sport in general. On some days, I still can't believe one of the bigger clubs with a much bigger bag of money wasn't there before me when he was still in his teens. Although, meeting his parents when he signed the contract and later in hospital explained a lot. The Borgharts are a very down-to-earth family with healthy ethics about the sport and the money. They refused to have his youth taken from him. But I'm sure Daniël has already told you that. I'm aware of my reputation for breaking players' egos and reputations to win a match, and I don't regret any of that, but I still think this club, this sport, needs people like him."

"Then give him a chance. And I'll make sure he's going to be there every training. I have to pick up my own programme. There's still so much that needs work."

"You're both ready for that?"

"Does it matter? We didn't ask for any of this. None of us did. It must have been tough on the boys too. I bet there's some ugly chanting and singing on the stands, especially with the away games. And what about our own fans? Don't tell me there's love all around."

"Ugly has been part of the game since the first boy decided to kick a pig's bladder. As for the fans, a few dozen season tickets being returned to the club, an internet petition to get rid of Dan with less than 500 signatures. A few fights before and after games. Some pub brawls. Nothing we hadn't anticipated." Degaré looks at Steve and smiles. "We mustn't forget who the real culprits here are. I saw that passport photo the police showed me and there was only one thing I could do. I appreciate that you two have been discreet all those months, even if it would have been wrong to expect it from you. It made life easier for everyone, except for you, of course. But nothing would have been easier for you, just differently hard at best, I assume. It's high time this sport and its fans enter the twenty-first century."

"You talked about it with other managers?"

"Of course I have. You and Daniël …" Degaré waves about. "Everyone's eager to hear your part of the story."

"Daniël suggested a press conference."

Degaré nods. "You're up to it?"

"Yes, I am." Steve knows it's the truth up to a certain point, but it's all he has to offer himself and the man next to him for the time being.

"When's the club officially going to let me go?" The question has to be asked.

"It's early in the season still. Hardly autumn. Let's give Daniël some time to work on his comeback, the two of you on all the other things. Professional football, certainly on this level, is a ruthless business. I give Daniël a chance because of his talent and fighting spirit. If I see I can't use him by the time the next window opens, he will be just like any of the other players. No privileges, other than earned by talent, hard work and usefulness for the club. As for you, sometimes doing things the logical way is doing them the wrong way."

"It's more than I can ask for. Thank you."

"The owners and the board do realise the club has a name to win or lose. Good PR is worth a man's soul." Degaré pats Steve on the shoulder. "We're a long way from paradise yet."

Then he's off to shout instructions to a group of the younger guys who seem to be having a bit too much fun.

Daniël looks positively radiant after the more than hour-long training session. "I'm going to take a shower and change back real quick." He kisses Steve on the cheek. "You had a good talk with the gaffer?" And he's off.

Matthew, in his capacity as captain, takes a few minutes to talk to him. They both try their best to strike up a conversation that at least sounds normal and meaningful, but it's still too early for either the mundane or the real questions and so they're left with talk about the weather and if the paparazzi have been much of a bother.

Steve knows he will be at the training ground several times a week for the coming months, and nothing is going to convince him he's still somehow part of this all. Daniël, however, is, and he's thankful his lover has been accepted back so readily. He's one of them. Still one of them.

◆

That night, he lies next to Daniël in bed. After tea and talk about the day, after Daniël doing the last of the planned calls while Steve takes a much needed rest, there's quietness and touches and kisses.

"It was beautiful, seeing you running on the turf with the others," Steve whispers, while Daniël nibbles on his ear.

"And it was beautiful, seeing you sitting next to the gaffer, talking to him," Daniël whispers while Steve takes his fingers to his mouth and starts to slowly suck and lick. "Are you trying to …?"

"What does it look like?" Steve glides his tongue between the fingers.

"You're trying to make me crazy with your mouth, that's what it looks like."

Wrapping his fingers around Daniël's cock, Steve teases, "I wouldn't mind having a taste of this too."

Pre-come forms in thick opaque drops.

"On our sides would be the most comfortable for me until ..." Before Steve's able to finish his sentence, Daniël changes positions, so he's head-to-toes with his lover, and takes a first lick of Steve's cock.

"I'm afraid my poor old brain doesn't allow me to concentrate on two equally exciting things at the same time and I hunger for your cock. Please, Danny?"

"I'm all yours." There's proud surrender in his lover's voice, next to all-out need and want.

Leaning on his side, Steve takes his time to look, just look, taking in the details of nuances of colours and veins and the dripping down of pre-come; the slit widening to a tiny circle. When his eyes have had their fill, he uses the tip of one finger to touch, slowly following the line of a vein, the journey of a sticky drop. He's close enough to be fully aware of the scent: this wondrous, delicate balance between the best and the worst.

Only then does he allow himself a first taste.

Daniël makes an almost startled sound. But he doesn't move a muscle.

He takes the head in his mouth, sucking as gently as he's able to.

Daniël doesn't tell him what to do, even though the tension in his body crackles the air with electricity, his fingers clawing the rumpled sheets. Sweet, caring boy; trying not to intimidate his lover with the force of his sexual need.

Steve retracts, then moves down, down until he can't go any lower even when he's willing to. He goes up again, his lips and his tongue savouring every slow second.

He used to do this with wild abandon; sloppy and aggressive. He used to do this with aching tenderness. He used to do this with methodical precision. He used to do this so often the taste became the taste of almost every day. He tried to make it the start of the day, the end of the day.

The taste of his lover and the scent of his lover. Lingering through the days.

Falling on his knees in the kitchen. "Keep doing whatever you're doing." Afterwards, the taste of food and the taste of his lover on his tongue.

He brings two of his fingers in the direction of Daniël's mouth. The boy understands and starts to lick and suck. He even changes the position of his legs slightly to give better access without Steve having to ask him.

Steve places the fingers against Daniël's opening, presses them in, while at the same time he starts sucking the head with as much force as he's able to.

Daniël tastes like sweet memories, like salty tears, like bitter anger.

And Steve drinks it all.

Chapter 22

The morning of the press conference, right after waking up, Steve manoeuvres Daniël gently on top of him. Daniël is more than happy to oblige and for a few minutes, they enjoy lazy kisses and brave smiles.

They don't feel an urgent need to talk about their nervousness of the upcoming event, but neither do they have any reason to avoid the subject while drinking coffee and eating rolls with strawberry jam.

"We don't have to say anything we don't want to say. But we can't stop them from asking questions that will hurt you," Daniël says. "And to think it's not their business anyway."

"At least I can look them in the face, give my honest answer, and have you and the gaffer and the skipper sitting next to me. I can't make anyone believe me, but that's not really my concern." Steve knows he sounds much calmer than he actually feels because in some way, he does want those others to believe him. He doesn't want anyone, not even those whose opinion he doesn't particularly value, to doubt or dirty his love for Daniël or his unwillingness to hurt his boy for some meaningless pleasure.

"They will try to make you remember. To talk about the men who did this to you. About the way you talk, about how you still can't walk properly. About the matches you'll never play again. About the players who feel embarrassed by us, the managers who'll have to deal with it. About the fans: the many who stand by us, defending us, and about the other ones. Hell, almost any gay man in the world thinking we can mean something for them, and to be honest, I don't want us to be anyone's spokesperson. Right now, I can't even pretend I care. It's not our battle because we have our own to fight."

"I get reminded every day. I don't even have to think about it." Steve takes Daniël's hand in his own. "I just wish it could be just the two of us. But, who knows, after a while people might get less curious about us."

"I'm sure it will help if I'll end my professional career," Daniël offers sincerely.

Steve shakes his head. "Please, no. I saw you running, having fun with the others, trying to see if you're still good enough for a place in the first team. It made me so happy. Degaré is eager to give you a chance. He knows a good thing when he sees it and he wants to keep it for as long as possible."

Daniël stands up from his chair and kneels at Steve's feet. Resting his head against his lover's thigh, he starts to talk. "I can't help wanting to see how good I still am. I don't want to walk away without having tried. Even if I don't care all that much any more if this club, or any club for that matter, is still interested in me. Even though I know I'll have to work twice as hard as the other guys to be seen as half as good, I want to play football."

Almost without thought, but aware of the tenderness seeping from the tips of his fingers, Steve caresses Daniël's hair. "Then give yourself that chance." He sighs. "Perhaps they have a right to their questions; all of them, in their own way. It must be important for people to hear certain things from me, from us. The lads took some horrible flak for what happened. I bet Arnaud Degaré didn't even tell half of it to spare me. Nothing to do with them, but you know how these things work. As long as we keep in mind in the end, it's you and me. Just love. That's the simple truth of it."

Daniël gets up from his knees. "Can we make love before we go? We still have a few hours. I guess enough to have sex, give you about an hour of rest, take a shower and get to the Graces in time."

Steve agrees that all the words in the dictionary will do nothing for them at this moment. There's no need to agree on every single thing they'll say at the press conference. They won't agree on every single thing and they're free to do so. There are no secrets to hide, just private things they like to keep private. But a smile and a joke should be enough for that. Painful, embarrassed silences are no longer part of their vocabulary.

So Daniël supports Steve to the bedroom to undress him and then undress himself. For as long as he feels like, he kisses and touches every nook and cranny of his lover's body. Steve understands all too well how the boy is rediscovering over and over again what is still so much a miracle to both of them.

Steve moans when Daniël takes his cock in his mouth and swirls the head with his tongue.

"This feels so good; I'm not sure how much longer I can stop myself from coming."

One last, lingering lick and Daniël looks up. "We could try it sideways, with you behind me. It's easy and gentle too. Not totally sure about having to bend one of your legs, though. We never used this position when we still … did we?"

"Don't think so. Any other time, I would love to try, but not right now. I need to see your face, your eyes, when I'm inside you. I want to remember how you looked at me when they'll be asking their questions."

Daniël nods his understanding, gets lube and pillows. He makes sure Steve is sitting comfortably and prepares himself.

"Like we did on that chair."

"Yes." Daniël positions himself, holding Steve's erection at the base, stabilising it enough to be able to lower his body and breach his opening.

The first tight grip makes Steve gasp. He loves this moment of invasion, of feeling how his lover's body gives up its last resistance and allows him in. How close this could be to violence, and is still such a tender, careful act. Then the head is in and a slow, smooth glide follows.

They kiss hungrily when Steve's cock is fully inside Daniël, tasting the traces of strawberry jam and coffee.

"God, I'm such a lucky bastard," Daniël moans against Steve's mouth.

"You are? I thought we had an agreement I am the lucky bastard in this relationship." Steve curls his fingers around Daniël's hips to keep him from moving just a little bit longer. He grins wickedly.

"You wish. Not only am I getting married to the sweetest, bravest and let's not forget sexiest man I've ever met, he also happens to be the owner of a fat, juicy cock and right now I can feel every glorious centimetre inside me. I totally get off on how it stretches me and fills me. No one else could be this perfect for me. On moments like this, it feels like I was actually made for you; like I was intended to be with you. And yes, I know how that sounds. And you know what? I don't care how I sound, as long as you get to hear it."

"I don't know what to say. I …"

Daniël puts a finger on Steve's lips. "Simply accept that I love you? That I couldn't ask for more and don't long for anything to be different?"

He starts to move. Small, controlled. Finally he leads Steve's right hand to his cock. "Please …"

There is an aching tenderness in their lovemaking, an almost disbelief this is happening to them, this is what they are doing. This is them, together. Still together.

Steve has to look at Daniël's face. It's impossible to close his eyes for even a fraction of a second. All the details get, once again, etched into his memories: the brows furrowed in concentration, the teeth worrying the lower lip, the drops of sweat, the pupils dilating until only a small rim of the iris is visible, the vulnerably exposed throat, the inked words on his upper arms, the freckles.

"What do you see? Tell me, what is it that you see?" Daniël asks.

"Everything." Steve struggles to even say those few words. "You."

Steve allows himself to reach his climax first. He sees the marvel in Daniël's smile. A few more strokes are enough to give his lover his own pleasure.

They both sigh in regret when Steve slips his spent cock out of Daniël.

"Please, your fingers …" Daniël mutters when they lie side by side, close enough to breathe each other's breath. He smiles contently when Steve reaches around, gently touches the closed but still very relaxed rim and slides two fingers in.

"Like this?" Steve moves the middle and index fingers a bit.

"Yeah. I missed it so much all those months. Tried it with my own a few times, but it's just not the same. It has to be yours."

Minutes pass in gentle half-sleep.

"I'm perfectly happy like this, but I'm afraid I have to rest for a bit. The press conference …" Steve retracts his fingers again, but kisses Daniël's lips to make up for it.

"Can't we tell Degaré and Matthew to give that press conference without us? Hey, Matthew might even declare his undying love for Gael. Now that would really be something for the tabloids and it would give us a bit of peace and quiet," Daniël half jokes.

Steve feels too drowsy to give any kind of reaction but a faint smile. He can't even get his thoughts in a straight line, let alone say anything that would make any sense.

Then a kiss on his forehead. "Steve? *Lieverd*? I let you sleep for as long as possible, but I'm afraid you have to shower and get dressed so we get to the Graces on time. Before I forget, there's some letter addressed to you. It looks like it was personally delivered because it has no stamp on it. You want me to read it to you? I haven't opened it, of course."

Steve nods, but soon he's too busy to remember it. The letter simply has to wait until after the press conference. If it's important, it would have been sent to the Three Graces Park anyway.

◆

Less than half an hour later, they're on their way. They don't talk much in the car. Partly because they're too nervous but also, what's the use of repeating the same things over and over again? Steve expects the journalists to be curious but not overly hostile. He knows his words, and those of Daniël's, will be interpreted freely and even be twisted beyond recognition, but there's not much he can do about that. He will be asked to consider answering questions he doesn't want to hear, and he will answer them in some way or form. What's the use in him being there otherwise?

They are greeted by Arnaud Degaré and Matthew Kirkby.

"Remember, you have full freedom to speak your mind, or to refuse to answer any question you don't like," Degaré says. "When it gets too much for you, we can stop. Oh, and Daniël? There are some gentlemen from the Dutch press. They'd appreciate it if you could answer a few questions in your own language."

Daniël nods. "No problem."

Then, to Steve, "You're okay?"

Steve takes his crutches from Daniël and smiles. "I'm fine. You're with me, the manager's with us and the captain. The best support anyone could hope for."

"We have a pretty full house too. About fifty of them … no, must be at least a dozen more. I guess nearly half from abroad," Matthew says. "It's enough to make even me nervous."

The words are an invitation, and Steve appreciates his captain's (still his captain, mostly because of Daniël, he knows all too well) gesture. "He sat there for me, all those months ago, when I couldn't defend myself. He trusted me implicitly. And you and Degaré were at his side. How can I not do this?"

Matthew nods. Steve doesn't miss the quiet sadness in his eyes, the almost-suggestion of jealousy, but there is nothing he can do or say to make it better.

The press room is packed to a point that several journalists have to stand. It's not easy to ignore the rising panic for Steve, but Daniël touches his shoulder in a gesture of support. He doubts he will be able to say anything coherent in the next hour. Staying on his feet until he's ready to manoeuvre himself on to his chair is hard enough as it is.

"Could have been at least twice as many, with the amount of requests we received," Matthew whispers in his ear. "But that's not really helping you, is it?"

Steve can't help but smile.

He hears Degaré cracking a few jokes with some familiar faces to break the ice; to distract them. He never liked being the centre of attention, and he managed to avoid it with a certain aptitude but this time, most eyes will be concentrated on his face, even if one of the others is actually doing the talking.

He feels Daniël's face very close to his own, their foreheads touching, and his lover's hand gently resting on his arm. And for a few blessed seconds there's no one in the room but them. Whatever happens over the next hour, he knows what does and doesn't matter.

Like always, the questions are asked in polite voices. They're professionals, doing a job.

First it's Arnaud Degaré and Matthew Kirkby talking, giving Steve an opportunity to gather his thoughts. The usual and well-meant words, he has to admit, are a palatable mixture of club politics and friendship.

Mr Degaré, you're reconsidering Daniël Borghart's future with the club?

"Any consideration has to do with his performances during training and matches. I expect him to be available for the first team in a few weeks. We have very strong and motivated defenders, and he's definitely one of them."

What about the reactions from the stands?

"The same rules apply like always. Football is a sport with … how shall we put it … its own unique character and we accept that, but only up to a certain point. You might have noticed the continuous support from many Kinbridge Town supporters for Daniël and Steve. And by far, not all fans from our opponents express themselves in an inappropriate manner regarding this subject."

There has been a remarkable progress in the club's performances during the past five years, you're not afraid that might come to a sudden halt after this?

"Why should it? KTFC has now established itself firmly at the top half of the table and we're hungry for more. You gentlemen and ladies might have noticed that we are part of a very strong competition. And we play to win."

Mr Kirkby, a word about Daniël Borghart from the captain?

"A hard worker, nice lad, too. Great talent. We're looking forward to his full return."

You know what we're really asking. Now that you know, does it make a difference?

"I assume you're referring to the dressing room? Steve has been part of our team for five years, and none of us had any idea about him. You know him, quiet sort of guy. Sweetest bloke ever, but quiet. I had no idea about Dan either. They never gave us any reason to suspect anything. Why should we get nervous all of a sudden? With permission, but I don't think Dan's very interested in our naked behinds. During training, he's almost too fanatical. Totally focussed on the job. I mean, that boy really wants to return to work. Afterwards, he's behaving like a lovesick puppy who can't wait to get to his fiancé. You bet we make fun of him about that. But seriously, during the months when Steve was recovering from the attack, we saw a side of Dan we don't see too often with anyone. He made a huge impression on all of us. Both of them did."

Mr Degaré, you were the first to be informed about what had happened to Steve?

"I was, yes. It was a moment I will never forget. Some things you hope you never have to deal with. I have given it much thought, talked about it with madame Degaré, with friends and colleagues and I still don't understand it. Why this murderous aggression towards a loyal servant of the club from those who claimed to be fans? Everyone who has seen him play know he gave nothing but his best for Kinbridge Town; a self-sacrificing defender who always played with the interest of the team in mind, and a gentleman to his fans. Surprise, perhaps even shock, that's to be expected. I'm aware we would have been dealing with some potential problems once you guys would have found out about Steve and Daniël, but this? I think I can guess what the next question might be. The answer is no, without the passport photo in Steve's wallet, I wouldn't have known about them. They were both nothing but professional in their conduct on and off the pitch. But when that photo was shown to me, there wasn't a doubt in my mind what I had to do."

Mr Gavan, what happened that night?

What happened?

"I ... don't know ..."

Daniël's hand resting on his. "I'm here."

The cameras will show him saying the words, will show their hands. The sound will be recorded. The words will be jotted down too (in case the recorders fail). Strangers will watch and judge. Will pity them. Will not understand. Will cry. Will curse. Will still have doubts. Will deny. Will believe they are somehow part of this, of them. This is the price he and Daniël have to pay for an illusion of peace.

He talks. The words are like lumps in his throat, no water pitcher can ever be filled enough to drink it all away. But he talks.

A long, long time ago, so long it can't be measured with any instrument, though some will say it's hardly more than half a year, a man, not very young and not very old, went for a walk. That man, you have to know, was so very much in love with a younger man from a faraway country that he could see nothing but beauty in everything around him ...

"Daniël was spending a few days with his parents, who came over from Holland. I wanted to think about my future. I wondered if it could be our future. So I decided to take a walk before I went home. I didn't pay attention to where I was going."

But not everything was beautiful and some ugly monsters, no, the facts are what they are, human beings, just like the man who was in love, didn't want to believe that love ...

He had just been at the wrong place at the wrong time. That's the bitter truth of it. It wasn't about what he was, about whom he loved, but all about what they thought he was doing.

"I wasn't aware of what was happening in that park, what kind of place it was, until it was too late. It's not for me to judge others, but ... sorry ... not my thing. I'm too old-fashioned I guess. I didn't run away because I couldn't believe anyone would think I had anything to do with those cruising men. I still have trouble understanding why anyone would even want to … sorry … I guess I'm a bit naive in these matters … sorry …"

And those men? They weren't there for the first time it seems.

"They were out to beat people up, the men with their nailed boots. But they were used to everyone always running away. That's what I heard them say. And then someone didn't run away. Someone they recognised and admired. How could I have known?"

Does his hand tremble? Or is it Daniël's?

Daniël spoke as he squeezed his hand, "All of you must have seen the pictures, the video. What more do you expect him to say?"

What are your plans for the future, Mr Gavan?

Next question. Next. Next. There must be plans, things to do, to achieve. They've already seen death on his face by simply downloading a video from the internet; that has to be so much more interesting than anything he could possibly tell.

"Getting married, doing my exercises, having a few more operations, learning to read and write again as well as I can."

If we can return to the men who ran away without warning you? What are your thoughts about them?

"I have no thoughts about them; none at all."

And the men …

Daniël sounded like he tried to hide his irritation as he spoke again: "Honestly, what do you expect him to say? Or me?"

What do you feel will be the effects of your coming out on professional football?

This one, too, is for Daniël to answer.

"I didn't come out. Neither of us did."

Disbelieving laughter from the journalists.

"Do you come out as heterosexual when you defend your wife or girlfriend against the vilest slander? When you hold her hand to show support and affection?"

But you have to admit …

"I speak for me, for us, and for no one else. We're nobody's role models, or how do you call it. And we never will be. But we're no longer being so-called discreet, like we're talking about some embarrassing disease or a dirty secret. We're as private with our private lives as the captain or the manager, or any of you. Nothing less, nothing more. It's really simple. I love Steve, Steve loves me. As long as a club wants me, I'll play football. If it comes down to there's no place for someone like me in high-level professional football, like it has always been said, I'll find something else to support myself and my husband."

Do you know of other gay players in the league?

"You all remember the one that got destroyed by it, more than ten years ago. Or you should. It went pretty much silent after that, didn't it? Perhaps I do, perhaps you do, without being aware of it. Let people decide for themselves."

Mr Degaré, will things change now there's an openly gay couple?

"There will be football and matches to be won. Simple, non?"

Mr Kirkby, your opinion on this?

"After what happened to Steve, it all changed, didn't it? The whole discussion became a bit obsolete if you ask me. I want players with me on the pitch who do their job, talented men who care about the game and the club. Why should I give a shit, pardon me, about the colour of their skin, the gender of their spouses or the kind of music they prefer?"

And the fans? The sponsors?

Degaré answered this one and to Steve he sounded almost tired, like it wasn't the first time he had said those words, "I firmly believe true fans support the players for their talent and their work for the club. And in most cases, I know I'm right about that. The others shouldn't call themselves supporters. Any sponsor who loves their money will keep a sharp eye on the fans. I understand there's been a sharp increase in the sales of Borghart shirts. There've even been special requests for Gavan ones."

Still, there have been season ticket holders of many years sending back their cards. Fights with rival clubs. Wasn't there a petition …?

It's Matthew's turn again. "I heard about it, of course, and it makes me angry and disappointed. Some people can't deal with reality and some of those people are, sadly enough, football fans."

More answers follow more questions about the police, the hospital, the whatever.

Steve feels his face tense up in a forced smile.

Mr Gavan, will you miss football?

He had been willing, less than a year ago, to give up the love of his life for, when all is said and done, a game. He had been giving up his boy without even trying to put up a fight.

"I'm going to be Daniël's biggest fan when he gets into the selection again. Okay, apart from his mother, perhaps. Support the other lads too. So I guess I don't have to miss football."

The Dutch press get their opportunity. Steve can guess their questions and Dan's answers.

Finally, it's over. His muscles tremble in fatigue. His limbs refuse to obey his overloading brain. Everything hurts. Even his bones ache with gnawing pain.

"I don't know how I'm … please, help me Danny." Leaning heavily on his lover, he makes it to the car. He wants to get away, to get home.

◆

A letter from the lawyer is waiting for him, and he asks Daniël to read it aloud.

"It says that the trial is getting near and they will call you a day or so before it actually starts. I guess that's good, in a way."

"I can't deal with it right now. I'm so tired."

Daniël helps him to bed without saying more than a few words, kissing him on the forehead. "Rest a bit."

"In your arms? Please, Danny?" Why such fear in his voice?

"Right where you belong." Daniël settles next to him, making sure Steve rests as comfortably as possible against his shielding body.

That same day, after they've had tea, Daniël downloads the press conference on his laptop.

Staring at the screen Steve feels a shock at what he's actually seeing. Is he that slow-speaking man? The man who sounds like he has trouble even formulating the simplest answers, dragging the words from an unwilling brain with a sluggish tongue? The man whose eyes seem to have trouble focusing? The man clutching his beloved's hand? His beautiful, young, healthy, so full of life and talent boy? The man who's almost unable to stand from his chair and can't leave the press room without assistance?

Is he the pitiful shadow of what less than a year ago was a healthy man in his prime?

Is this what people are seeing?

Is this what Daniël loves?

Steve hides his face against Daniël's body and cries his heart out.

Chapter 23

Even tears that seem to fall without end have to dry up at some point. After that, there's pure empty nothingness. No relief or remaining sadness. Nothing. Not even exhaustion. Daniël holds him through it all, not trying to soothe him or show him there are other, more helpful ways of interpreting his situation; offering his body as an anchor against the storm. He thinks at some point he falls asleep, but there's too little difference between sleeping and waking to be sure. He knows, however, Daniël is with him, every second of every minute of every hour. And just like he used that knowledge to leave perfect peace and joy behind, because making sure his beloved didn't have to lose him was more important than any version of paradise, he uses it again to slowly wake up from this almost catatonic state.

Daniël kisses him on his lips. "I'll make tea and something to eat. Perhaps you'd like a shower later."

Steve lets it all happen. He doesn't have the illusion that a good cry will make everything okay somehow, but for now he accepts the quiet resignation before there will be some long, hard talking to do. He has seen himself through the impartial eyes of the stranger and if his marriage to Daniël is to have any sort of chance, they'll have to come face to face with it, one way or the other. Even Daniël's love, that can't be measured or perhaps fully understood, won't be enough to prevent them from having to walk a different path at times to arrive at the same point; and if it does turn out they were on the same road all along, their steps won't be matching.

"First tea and sandwiches, then a shower, and if you don't need to rest by then, we'll talk." Daniël smiles when he puts the tray on the table, but Steve can hear in his voice he means business.

They sit on the couch, touching as much of each other as possible while drinking tea and eating ham and cheese sandwiches.

"Nice," Daniël sighs and he kisses Steve's cheek.

Steve's in awe at how Daniël is able to fully enjoy this simple moment, no matter what's behind him or what's still waiting for him. If he's worried about Steve's moment of deep mourning, and Steve can't imagine he isn't, it doesn't keep him from sitting next to his lover, drinking tea, kissing his cheek and saying, "Nice."

After a long, hot shower Steve, doesn't have enough energy left to even pretend he's up for some serious talking.

If he dreams, he doesn't remember.

He must have been sleeping for more hours than usual because by the time he's awake, it's fully light and Daniël is up and dressed.

"I just got an e-mail from the estate agent about some houses we might want to take a look at. Relax; it's only photos and descriptions. I have afternoon training. So do you. And we mustn't forget to get something for supper. I'm thinking of omelettes." Daniël talks while he shaves Steve in the bathroom. "There's another letter too. I guess from a fan. The handwriting looks the same as the first one. Shall I open them?"

"I don't feel like reading letters from fans right now. I know it sounds rude and unthankful, but ... perhaps later?"

"Everyone knows by now that any mail to you should go through the club. Not our fault if there's always a few who won't listen. By the way, Matthew messaged me; there are some very nice reactions to the press conference. You mind if I get a few newspapers?"

Steve knows Daniël doesn't expect a real answer, or even a reaction, it's just him starting the day in a pleasant manner. He also isn't trying to evade the hard subjects; there will be time for those, too. But it would be unbearable to talk about the truth that stared him in the face when he watched the press conference without knowing Daniël is seriously training again, without the everyday stuff.

After breakfast, Daniël goes for a quick round of shopping, while Steve gets his books, notebook and pen out to work on his reading and writing. Only when Daniël has closed the door behind him does he become fully conscious that he's alone in what is still his own apartment, for the first time since he came back from hospital. He shrugs it off as something of minor importance, although he guesses it's not as easy for his lover. Leaving him alone in the house, even if it's just for an hour, is something the boy must have lost quite a bit of sleep over. But he's a brave, sensible spouse and so he does what he has to do.

Steve smiles while he reads, syllable for syllable, words of growing complexity.

Hedgehog comes snuffling in his prickly coat ...

He has to remind himself that it wasn't long ago since he discovered words had changed into unreadable hieroglyphs, because he's so very ready for anything that isn't cute and inoffensive. Then he reads on. Any practice is good practice and after lunch, it's time to do his physical exercises to strengthen his muscles. If he works hard and luck smiles upon him, he should be able to give Daniël a really nice surprise very soon.

Something close to pride stretches its warm fingers out over all of his body. No matter how sad he still feels about what he has seen about himself, he still wants to be as healthy and as strong as possible for Daniël. Because he will not again offer his boy something he didn't ask for. That sadness is something he truly can't bear a second time.

The sound of the key opening the front door startles him for a minor fraction of a second, and then he recognizes Dan's footsteps and smiles. No doubt this is going to become one of his favourite sounds.

"Hey gorgeous," Daniël kisses him. "Sorry, took me a bit longer than I planned. They're good people and mean well, but I can't spend the rest of the day talking with fans and giving out autographs when I have to prepare lunch for the sexy beast who happens to be my fiancé."

"No one said anything hateful?"

"I think I heard a couple of boys shouting something, but I bet they were having some kind of bet." Daniël starts to laugh. "You should have seen the groups of giggling, blushing girls and their mums. 'You two looked so cute together in the papers. You're the most romantic things ever.' I'm glad there was at least the guy behind me at the check-out who wanted to know when Degaré planned on letting me start again."

"Must have been nice, talking footy for a bit." Steve sets the books aside.

"It was." Daniël puts the groceries away and stacks the papers he bought on the table. "They asked how you're doing, and if you're getting used being home again, if you're still in a lot of pain and if the doctors think everything will be alright."

"And what did you tell them?" Steve uses his crutches to follow Daniël around.

"That you are doing wonderfully and work very hard, but still have a long way to go. They seem to genuinely care. I couldn't just ignore them like with the paparazzi. Not after all the cards and mails and little gifts. Is that okay?"

"Why wouldn't it be okay?" Steve leans against the kitchen sink while Daniël gets out the eggs for lunch.

"I don't know. It's private?"

Steve can see he's half serious about this.

"We'll be friendly and polite to the friendly and polite, and we'll ignore the rude and nasty as much as possible. All the rest is a matter of behaving like normal, decent human beings. I can't think of a better way to get as much privacy as possible."

Daniël nods. "That comes down to us just being ourselves. I like that idea, not having to pretend and making sure we behave in such way we don't even have to lie because no one's going to even ask that one question. You want mushrooms with your omelette? Ham too?"

They happily chatter through the meal about their plans for the rest of the day. Daniël doesn't make a secret of how much he enjoys training again. Steve accepts doing his exercises is not his favourite hobby, but he sees no reason to make a tragedy out of it.

The crushing sadness of yesterday takes on an almost surreal quality. Or perhaps it's just being ignored for the time being, like the unread papers and the envelopes that are still unopened. Because while Daniël might be wearing his watch again and there are moments during the day they have to follow the rules of time, he has learned in the past months that things don't go away if you put them aside for a bit.

And so, after training and after tea, Daniël opens the newspapers one by one and grins and frowns and chuckles and reads parts of it to Steve. There are some screaming headlines, but the words are nice enough. There are fair and to the point reports about what each of them said. There are sharp and insightful background articles. There are some interviews with managers and players of other clubs, but also with a spokesperson from a GLTB pressure group and a handful of gay football fans.

And okay, there's still the condescending undertone in the choice of words in the tabloids, but in comparison to the usual tone about this subject, it's a miracle of decency.

"I guess even for them it's no fun kicking a man who looked into his own grave and came back alive," Daniël comments.

Steve shrugs. "I doubt if they really believe me that I truly didn't know."

"You care?"

"What those sorts of people think? No."

"This is interesting. Want to hear?" When Steve nods, he reads aloud, "'The question has been asked many times: is there a place for openly gay professional footballers? The answer given in variations on the same theme: football isn't ready for it. The clubs. The players. The fans. No one is ready for it. And yet it happened. And it happened in a city not exactly known for its glamour. It happened in a club slowly climbing out from years of mismanagement, financial troubles and players who had lost nearly all confidence in themselves and pleasure in their sport. It happened, and now the world is watching.'"

Steve nods, unsure of what to say.

"Feels like it's not really about us, doesn't it?" Daniël gives him a small smile, full of understanding. "There's so much, going to take me days to work it through. Here, some guy doing a psychological analysis about what's happening around us. That's almost a full page. I quote: 'It's hard not to speculate about the group of men attacking Steve Gavan. The sheer brutality of their act defies imagination. And yet the pictures tell a stark and undeniable truth. How much hate is needed to cause such violence? And perhaps, a more profound question: how much love? Bitter and twisted love, desperate in its ugliness, but love nonetheless. Sometimes a man can only pray for indifference.'"

Daniël falls silent.

"You're okay?"

"And you?"

"Honestly? I don't know." Daniël shrugs. "I can't deal with it now. New subject. I bet Francesco and Gael have already seen the Spanish papers, Etienne and Alexandre the French ones, Kurt the German ones and so on and so on. And I know mum bought every Dutch paper she could get her hands on and puts the clippings in a scrapbook."

"They wrote something about the gaffer as well? They must have." Steve looks at the columns of text to see if he recognises Degaré's name.

"I bet he'll love this one. 'The Frenchman welcomed with an even less than lacklustre enthusiasm by a team of players who were close to giving themselves up to relegation, soon became a familiar sight during matches:

short, overweight and with a temper. Managing Kinbridge Town mainly out of friendship for the new owners, he didn't promise to perform an overnight miracle. Being a man with vision, Arnaud Degaré was able to envision the future. He promised that future would be bright, and he delivered. But then something happened even he couldn't have predicted. And he rose to this challenge as well, staying true to his word about building a team eager to win instead of a bunch of individuals afraid to lose. After the unimaginable attack on right back Steve Gavan, Degaré's first acquisition for the club, he didn't allow even one single day to pass without a member of the Kinbridge Town family visiting their two team-mates, with captain Matthew Kirkby setting a new standard for leadership and, above all, true friendship. There are persistent rumours about players wanting to leave when the next transfer window opens, but no one stayed away when it mattered most. Anyone taking a close look at this club can't be surprised about their current eighth position in the league.'"

"Yeah, that's the gaffer and the skipper all right." He kisses Dan's cheek. "Thanks for reading. And now I want to hear about you."

Daniël blushes. "That's embarrassing …"

"So they have written something really nice? Point it out to me, I want to try and read it for myself. Please?"

"Well, okay, but don't say I didn't warn you …"

Letter for letters and then word for words, Steve, with a bit of help from Daniël, slowly reads, "In a time of cheap thrills and fast sex, a man who looks like a boy barely old enough to be away from home without his mum and dad, is showing us all a lesson about love, trust and faith.'"

"Told you, embarrassing …"

Steve closes his boy's mouth with a kiss, but doesn't say a word.

He stares a moment at the photos of him and Daniël. Their heads close together. Holding hands while standing in the parking spot, talking with Degaré and Matthew.

"What do you see?"

"Us?"

"Here's what one of the gay fans says about the press conference," Daniël points at a section of one of the papers. A big bloke in his thirties with a round face, wearing the Kinbridge Town red-and-black home shirt is smiling directly at the readers.

Daniël starts to read aloud, "'I've been a Kinbridge Town fan since my dad took me to my first match when I was seven. I don't just watch for the pretty boys. Although, we do have some fit players. Hey, I'm only human. But I do love the game, support the team no matter what and I can talk with the best of them about strategies. Never miss a home game. All my mates know about me. Not one of them ever said anything nasty about that. But I've also felt an outsider for as long as I can remember. Of course I miss that there's never even one openly gay player in the whole premier league, but that's not even the main problem. The lads have to decide that for themselves. But the ones higher up saying fans wouldn't accept it. Now that hurts, because of what it says about my mates and me. Like all straight fans are the same and gay fans don't even exist. I saw the press conference. Is this what everybody has been so afraid of? Two guys in love? Daniël and especially Steve paid a horrible price for a minority of scumbags who don't want to be confronted with the so-called 'our kind', and a majority who doesn't stand up to them.'"

"It sounds like it means a lot to that man, us telling our story," Steve says.

"I can sympathise with that. But this other guy, telling that it's a pity we are not more political and should become part of a campaign … I just want to live in peace with my man, be a professional player for the next ten years and that's it. They already know our faces, our names; they've seen us holding hands in public. I've written how I feel about you in my blog. What more do they want?" Daniël puts the papers aside. It has been enough for one day.

Steve takes his lover's face between his hands and kisses him on the lips. "Make an official declaration, be at the centre of something much bigger than you and me simply having fallen in love. It's not important what they want. Not for us. Not at this moment. I want you to train hard and do the things you're born to do."

Daniël smiles and kisses Steve back. "Making love to you at least once a day?"

"You won't hear me complaining about that." Steve licks a trace over Daniël's lips.

"I'll make some fresh tea with a small, snack just like the doctor ordered."

Minutes later, they sit on the couch, enjoying their tea and a good helping of fresh fruit pie.

When they're done, Steve lets himself be surrounded by Daniël's arms. He listens.

"I don't know if I'll ever be able to understand what's been taken from you. You were so sad and devastated when you saw a video of yourself during that press conference."

"How can love be this blind?" Steve can't help the question.

"It isn't. I'm not. I see the damage. Believe me; I have seen the very worst of it. Day after day, I see the struggle, the pain and the exhaustion, the results that seem so small for all the work you've done, the setbacks. I see how much time you need to get the words from your brain to your mouth."

Steve listens with his full attention.

"I remember the man I fell in love with on the training pitch of Kinbridge Town. And I will keep on loving him until the day I die, even though I know he's gone forever. But I also remember the man surrendering to death, but who didn't die. I remember the man who woke up, who's fighting so hard to learn to talk again, and walk again. I love that man so much. That is what I saw when I watched that video yesterday."

Words like a fortress, protecting his beloved from an enemy that will likely never cease to attack him; nothing but love and paper-thin words against fear and doubt and frustration.

"Promise me to walk away when your love changes into pity."

Daniël doesn't sound shocked in the least; his stronghold is still standing. "There isn't a chance in hell of that ever happening. You bet I'll be frustrated sometimes when I'm out for a run and I know you can't run with me. I'll be sad when I play my next match and you won't be there with me on the pitch, and never will be. Who knows, I might even be pissed off with you just because I'm in a pissed off mood and feel like taking it out on you. But pity?"

"But you promise me? Please, Danny?"

"If it should come to that, what good would it do me to walk away?"

"You don't know the meaning of the word quitting, now do you?" It's impossible for Steve to hide his smile.

"When it comes to you? No way." Daniël holds Steve a bit tighter in his arms. "And before you start thinking I'm not only ready for sainthood, I'm also unbelievably wise for my age, it's nothing like that at all. I had a lot of time, sitting next to your bed or walking around in the corridors to get coffee or whatever. People talked to me. People like nurses, doctors, the gaffer, mum and dad, old folks who walked in and out of the hospital to visit their husbands or wives and saw me. And if an eighty year old lady with a marriage of over 50 years is giving me some good advice, you bet I'm smart enough to listen."

"It did hurt so much seeing myself. To know this is what you love." Steve's voice is barely audible. He doesn't expect Daniël to make it better for him, but still the words have to leave his mouth. They have to be spoken and heard.

Daniël holds him in his arms, not saying anything for minutes.

Then, finally: "Don't ever again ask me to leave you."

Chapter 24

"So we're agreed there are two houses in Hollycroft we'd like to take a look at, we're getting married in November so we need to hire a planner and someone who can deal with the press, but that has to be coordinated with the club and we're getting a bit low on the protein shake …" Daniël talks while he pours a second cup of coffee. "There's some administration I have to deal with so we can actually get married. We can get a marriage licence via the embassy, so we have to make the trip to Holland just once."

Steve nods, being content to leave it all to Daniël for the moment. The world is still a big place and life is dauntingly complicated. He does what he has to do, earning any sort of progress with sweat and toil. But the biggest part of the job, which is to get them married and into their shared home, is simply beyond him. He doesn't like it and feels his contribution is below what it should be, but he accepts it, happy enough that Daniël never takes any action without talking it through with him.

"I really need to start and sort out these newspapers and magazines. Stupid how busy you'll get with nothing, really." Daniël grins. "I'm excited about the houses and getting nearer the wedding. And I don't even care about the whole fuss people make of it."

"You mean you just can't wait for the wedding night," Steve teases him.

Daniël takes Steve's hand and kisses it quickly. "You never get to guess again." He thumbs through the pile of pile of newspapers and frowns.

"Something the matter, Danny?"

Daniël shows him two envelopes. "Not really, I had forgotten all about them. I don't understand why they didn't send these letters to the Graces. It's clearly stated on the club's official website and on my personal blog and I know most online football communities have mentioned it at least once. That's hard to miss, isn't it? Anyway, it's not like you can keep your private address a secret for long anyway, with those burglaries recently at players' homes and all. Last week it was Kurt, before that, Kevin. They were seriously pissed off about it. What shithead takes another man's school team trophy?"

Then he seems to realise what he's implying. "Sorry, it just slipped out."

"I'm not worried about it. It's just stuff. And what happened to me, well, you know …"

"I know. I think."

"It's probably something Jane and Emma know perfectly how to deal with. Perhaps we can drop the letters off with the girls before training?"

The girls, being middle aged women with a reputation of having an uncanny talent for sifting through letters, cards, e-mails and any written material in high speed without ever blushing or getting into something that remotely looks like panic, have their own system of dealing with the stream of reactions to anything concerning the whole matter. Even foreign language e-mails and post are being dealt with, and with the same firm but friendly efficiency.

A few days ago, they explained it all to Steve in a fast stream of Kinbridge brogue that would silence local boy and chatterbox Anthony Levee. The vast majority of the mail is easily answered with a mention on the KTFC site or on Daniël's blog: thank you so much for the continuing well-wishes and heart-warming interest in Steve's health and progress. If opportune, i.e. the question is asked, either Matthew or Degaré mention it in their talks to the press. Small gifts go, if ever possible, to different charities. Expressions of creativity get lovingly stored in the huge club archive. Work of children always gets a little personal thank you note. A relatively small percentage of mail goes straight to the police. And then there are, as to be expected, the mails and letters that are so personal that a personal answer, if possible, is the only correct answer.

There are the few handfuls of young boys hoping they can become professional players without having to acquire a wag, the closeted gay amateur players who suddenly don't know what to do any more, the 'I haven't told this to anyone before' fans. They all get a friendly word from either Jane or Emma and, if need be, addresses to get help and advice.

Daniël's voice breaks gently through his thoughts. "Okay if I take a quick look at those letters before we decide to hand them over to the girls? I'm getting a bit curious."

"What? Oh yes, of course. Sorry, I seem to be a bit absent-minded."

"You need more rest during the day? Am I pushing you to hard? Or perhaps I should be asking: are you pushing yourself too hard?" Daniël takes a pocketknife and opens an envelope. "I think this was the first one."

"I'm fine, Danny. I was thinking about all those fans sending mails and gifts. I know it's because of what happened, but when I try to understand what it all means … I'm starting to see it's more than you and me being visible as a couple. Think about those young lads hoping they have a chance in five or ten years' time because you're still training with the club, and the manager and the owners declared in public they're okay with it. I'm thankful that we can mean something to others by simply being ourselves, but …"

But he doesn't get the chance to finish his sentence.

"What a fucker. He's got some fucking guts to do this to us …" Daniël stares at the letters, his face pale and his hands visibly trembling.

"What is it, Daniël? Please talk to me. You're scaring me." Steve hasn't seen the boy this upset in a long time and he doesn't know how to deal with it. The ground is shaking under his feet and the one keeping him safe looks like he's in need of help himself.

Daniël clutches Steve's hand. "Please sit on the couch with me, I need to hold you."

Steve feels how all the muscles in his beloved's body are tensed up, like he's an animal ready to attack. His arms feel like fierce protection, instead of the loving embrace when they quietly sit together for an hour before they decide it's time to go to bed.

"Sweetheart, you do understand I have to know what's in that letter if it makes you this upset. I'm not sure if I'm able to read it all myself, but I'm willing to try. Is the handwriting difficult to read?" He talks as gently as he's able to, but Daniël has to know Steve refuses to let him carry this alone. "Is it something for the police? Hate mail?"

"Not hate mail. I'm so sorry for scaring you. I just didn't expect this. I'll make a fresh cup of tea for us and I'll read the letters to you." He kisses Steve in a gesture of apology before he gets up and walks to the kitchen, but turns at the door and looks at Steve like he wants to say something but isn't sure what exactly, then is out of the room.

A few minutes later, he returns with two mugs of tea. He takes both letters from where he had left them on the table and joins Steve on the couch again.

With one arm around Steve's shoulder and the letter in his free hand, he starts to read aloud.

"*Dear Mr Gavan,*

I have restarted this letter so many times over the past months I lost count. And I still don't know how to begin.

First of all, please excuse me for delivering this letter personally to your home. But I hope you'll understand my reasons after reading.

My name is Mark Smith and I assure you, that is my real name. I'm in my mid-forties, and I was married until recently. My daughters are 18 and 14 years old. The oldest just started her studies at the University of Manchester, the youngest lives with her mother. I used to work as a sales manager for an insurance company in the city, but I'm unemployed at the moment.

Forgive me for being this blunt, but I am the man who tried to touch you up in that park. I thought at that moment I saw in you a kindred spirit, a lonely man seeking release, however superficial and imperfect. I have to admit I was wrong.

I was also one of the men who left you in the hands of those bashers. I know none of us had this intention, because we all assumed you would be familiar with the unwritten rules and risks of this meeting place and that you would run away with the rest of us. Those thugs, I used to think they were mostly ridiculous in their behaviour, more of a nuisance than a real danger, had been bothering cruising men for months. I guess we got used to them. I, at least, had long been resigned that it was simply an unavoidable risk of this particular activity. The noise they produced had always been enough warning to get away unharmed. I never even contemplated going to the police to bring this to their attention.

Now I have to live with a guilt that is unbearable and yet has to be carried for the rest of my life.

For months, I've tried to give myself reasons and excuses, but I have found none. I've tried to blame my upbringing, society, the pressure to conform, loneliness and the need for human, or rather, male touch, but they are all cheap pretexts.

I'm not writing this letter because I'm hoping that you will forgive, perhaps even understand me. Even if one day you would grant me this precious gift, I still wouldn't be able to forgive myself.

I saw the news the next day after our meeting in the Queen Elizabeth Park and while it didn't happen immediately, my life changed. But I'm not going to bother you with that.

182

I just want to tell you and Mr Borghart how much I regret my lack of common humanity and courage that night. My silence of the past months has not been one of indifference, but of shame and confusion.

I'm willing to accept any consequences, legal or otherwise, concerning you following from that particular night."

Daniël drops the letter on the floor. He sighs and pulls Steve closer. "What does that man want from you? Pity? Attention?"

"There's another one from the same person? Read that one too, please?" Perhaps then he will feel something, anything, more than this bone-eating indifference. Anger, or compassion, or even the beginning of understanding. All that he's able to feel is geared towards Daniël, with nothing to spare for this stranger. Indeed, what does the man expect from him?

Daniël gets the letter out of the envelope. "This one is longer."

"We have time before training? That's after lunch, isn't it?"

"Next week, I'll start in the mornings, too." Daniël drinks his now lukewarm tea. He tries to get as much as possible of Steve in the curve of his left arm.

"Dear Mr Gavan,

Please forgive me for writing you a second letter, but I just watched the press conference you and Mr Borghart gave and, against my better judgement, I cannot keep silent.

Although I didn't tell a single lie in my first letter, I didn't tell the truth in its full honesty. I have to admit, though, I'm still in the middle of finding out the truth for myself.

I'm not proud of it, but I had my doubts about the reasons you were in that park even after that first press conference Mr Borghart gave, when you were still in a coma and it was very much unsure if you would survive. I even kept my reservations after I read the true reasons in his blog, when you were able to tell them. I had become that cynical and mistrustful. I had learned to lie with an honest face and expected nothing better from the men I met for one particular reason only.

It was easy enough to place all the blame outside myself. To focus on the superficiality of so much of the most visible gay lifestyle, the lack of healthy role models, the obsession with often extreme and unhealthy sexual practices. I was keenly aware of social and legal discrimination and, until recently, almost no support for or acknowledgement of gay relationships. But I was also blind to the committed couples, the friendships and the available support.

In the end, it all came down to a lack of courage to face myself, accept my true nature and look in the right places for a potential mate to share my life and love with.

I married my wife nearly twenty years ago, knowing what I was. But I thought I was wise in trading a meaningless life filled with empty sexual meetings with strangers for the adult responsibilities of starting a family. My sexual attraction to men was just that, sexual attraction. Nothing stable or worthwhile could ever come off it. Or so I told myself.

How wrong I was. My wife and daughters gave me something I so very much craved, but they couldn't lessen the other need. So after the birth of my youngest daughter, I started to visit the anonymous meeting places again. Telling myself it was just to get the tension out of my body and that my family was my true love. My real life.

Then that night happened. I hope I don't offend you, or especially Mr Borghart, but I've always found you an attractive man. You certainly got my attention when you started to play for Kinbridge Town. And I don't even care for football all that much. I just had to take my chances with you. I honestly interpreted your behaviour as shyness. I thought I witnessed the moment when the need to be touched by another man grows simply too strong, even if the risks, as in your case, are enormous.

I guess I saw what I wanted to see."

Daniël pauses, takes his time to kiss Steve, caress his face with a gentle hand. He drinks the last of his tea. "Shall I continue?"

Steve nods. "Thank you for doing this for me."

"There is nothing I wouldn't do for you."

As terrifying as that statement is in its final consequences, Steve knows it to be true.

Daniël starts to read again. *"No matter how many excuses I try to use, I ran away at the first signs of danger like I always did. I felt no solidarity with, no commitment of any kind to the men I considered my potential sexual partners. And I expected no such thing from them.*

The next day, I watched the news and read the papers. I soon became aware of the rumours spreading on the internet like wildfire. I saw the press conference Mr Borghart gave and I still tried to deny the truth about myself: that my successful career, my marriage and my beautiful miracles of daughters were the result of a false choice. I saw the face of love and I hated it because I feared it and I envied it.

I also looked at the pictures and video made of you after the assault. And I wondered what made me any better than the monsters who did this to you.

I landed in a deep depression. By the time I had crawled out of its deepest pit, I had lost my marriage and my job. While I deeply regret the pain I caused my wife and daughters, in a way, it was a relief. But it also means I have to start all over again, a man in his forties. I'm more afraid than I'm able to express, but also strangely thankful.

As I said, I watched the press conference yesterday. The consequences of what I had done, or rather had neglected to do, stared me right in the face. But I also saw the immense courage and fighting spirit. If I'll be allowed to keep only one image from all this for the rest of my life, it will be this: love.

Nothing that has happened can be undone, but I can take my responsibility. I will go to the police and make a statement. I don't know what will happen, or if anything will happen at all, but I'll accept it without reservation. I know your reputation has been blemished undeservedly. I am prepared to declare to any media of your choice what I know to be the truth, if you express the wish for me to do so.

I'm not asking for any sort of personal contact between us. Be assured: I will not bother you again in any way or form. I provide my full name, address and phone number in case your lawyers need them.

Thank you for reading my words."

◆

Steve looks for a moment at the white, still empty paper before him, takes his pen in his hand and starts to write. Slowly, making sure every word is correct. He writes the difficult words on the margin of an old newspaper to ask Daniël if they're okay.

Mr Smith,

Thank you, but I'm afraid you have nothing on offer I could possibly need.

Sincerely,
Steve Gavan.

Then he shows Daniël what he has written. "Did I make any mistakes?" Daniël smiles and kisses him. "It's perfect."

Chapter 25

In the morning, he lies in Daniël's arms for a moment before the days begins for them and the question comes up without bidding. "Was I cruel in my answer to that man, Danny?"

"Cruel? You couldn't be cruel if someone paid you good money for it."

Steve sighs. "This indifference, all the emotions I'm not feeling … I don't know …"

"Well I do. Mark Smith seems to me interested in Mark Smith first, second and last. If he had really thought of you, he would have simply gone to the police and asked for help with a therapist. Isn't there some GLBT helpline? What reason did he have to bother you? Does he really think it's somehow helpful? That first letter was hardly forgivable, the second one downright shameless. Fuck it, Steve, but even the teenagers who think they might be gay and wonder if they can still become a professional footballer without having to date a girl have the decency to send their letters to the club and not to you personally."

"I'm sorry. I didn't mean to upset you." Steve tries to hide against Daniël's body. It's not often he sees his lover this angry and he doesn't know how to deal with it.

"No, I should be sorry. I wish I knew how to protect you against such people. People who want to use you for their worthy cause, their personal needs, their whatever it is they want from you. You need every bit of energy you have for physio, getting married, finding a home, and dealing with all the stuff we have to deal with. Do they even understand half of what happened to you? And you still feel guilty for not being able to feel anything much for all those people."

"It must have been hard for him too. He tried to be nice in that park; I'm willing to believe he really thought I was scared and perhaps a bit shy. When I think about it, it must have looked that way. I just wasn't able to say anything. I was absolutely tongue-tied. I was too shocked and how could I have told the truth without giving you away?"

"From what I read in those letters, he made his own choice. We all make mistakes and who knows what stupid things we would have done if nothing had happened that night except you taking a stroll in the park, but I'm not going to blame that on others."

"Would you have found a girlfriend? Started a family?"

"I'm beginning to forget what I would have done. By the time I said see you in two days and I got to the airport for my parents, I was full of clever ideas of how to keep my job with Kinbridge Town and still be with you. Those six months before everything changed had already given me my answer. It had to be you and no one else. I already loved you so much, what kind of man would I've been to misuse a woman for that? There's no excuse for that sort of behaviour. Absolutely none."

"Not even when a girl had knowingly agreed on it? Is that so wrong? People get married for lots of reasons, not just love and sexual attraction."

"And some gays still wonder why so many people look down on them? Us." Daniël takes a deep breath. "Okay, that's unfair of me, but if you don't take your own relationship, or your very nature, seriously, then what do you expect from others? Footballers might be one of the last groups to start behaving like normal human beings when it comes to this subject, but allow me the illusion that I wouldn't have given you up for anything in this world."

Steve's breath is taken away by the force of Daniël's embrace.

"I can't live with the idea we are still together because you were nearly beaten to death. And for what? If we had been working in an office …" Daniël's voice becomes soft, vulnerable. "I'm preaching against my own fear, my own cowardice. I'm just as dishonest as that man. Taking the high moral ground …"

"You're trying to protect me. I love you so much for that." Steve kisses Daniël as a lover, with deep longing.

"Morning breath?"

"Well, it's not exactly roses." And he kisses Daniël again.

"It makes you such a sweet darling of a man, the fact that you care about not caring someone who doesn't deserve that care at all, at least not from you." Daniël frowns. "You ever think about the upcoming trial? Should I even mention it?"

"That's okay. I try not to. I didn't die, so I don't think they'll be put away that long. I guess it's complicated, too, them trying to blame each other. To blame me. They're going to get a few years at most, I guess. And it's the innocent who'll pay the highest price in the end, isn't it? Us, their families ..." Steve shrugs. "It's out of our hands and I'm happy for that. I want to share my life with you, my dear boy, not with them."

"Perhaps we'll hear from Smith during the trial or via the lawyers, but other than that, can we agree to close the subject? There are people able and willing to help that man, I'm sure. As for the monsters ..." Daniël worries his lower lip with his teeth and to Steve it makes him look unbearably fragile. "It has to be about you, about our love, not about them. But God, it's so hard sometimes."

Steve snuggles his face against the crook of Daniël's neck. "I would love to make love to you right now. Not a quickie, but really taking our time. But there's training and we have to look at those houses, so please be stronger than me and help me out of bed?"

Daniël grins. "What about a date? You, me and this bed? Tonight, after tea?"

It takes Daniël some clearly visible effort but he manages to get himself into an upright position and help Steve to do the same.

"Anything special I should wear to our date?" Steve stretches his body. Ouch, exercise is going to hurt and there's no maybe about it.

"It's all fine as long as I can get you naked real fast." Daniël smiles, kisses him and is off to the bathroom.

◆

The day is full, very full, but pleasant enough. Yes, doing his exercises hurts, but there's also the feeling that for once, he's making real progress. Not in a spectacular-tearjerker-TV-movie-of-the-week way, he's not that lucky, but his hard work of the past weeks finally seems to be rewarded. The pain is the price he's willing to pay, especially when a good massage takes care of the worst of it.

At least, enough to share lunch with the others and enjoy a quiet conversation with Gael and Niko, while Daniël is busy explaining some ideas for the next training to fellow defenders Neil and Anthony. He tells them about the houses he and Daniël are going to take a look at later that afternoon.

"You're going to look at some property in Hollycroft? It's actually very nice there. A handful of our guys already live there, and with good reason," Gael says.

"You're looking forward to having a real place for the two of you?" Niko asks. It's such a simple question, and it makes Steve feel like he's genuinely welcome to show them how happy he is.

"You have no idea. My apartment is fine and there's enough of Dan's stuff around, but it's not the same, is it?"

Both Gael and Niko murmur their agreement.

Daniël turns to him. "I'm going to the gym for a good hour, after that we'll visit a few houses. You need to rest?"

"I don't think I'll manage the gym right now, not when we have more to do this afternoon, but I'll find a quiet place and work on my reading a bit. I'm curious what I'm able to understand from the KTFC magazine at this moment."

For an hour and a half he works his way, slowly but with less difficulty than he anticipated, through a short article about Arnaud Degaré's trademark managing style and an interview with local boy Levee. His finger following the lines, his lips muttering the words. Sometimes guessing, sometimes going back a few words. He remembers how he used to be able to skim texts, getting the meaning of whole sentences with one look. It doesn't bother him any more. This is where he stands today; tomorrow will be another matter. The past? The jury's still out on that.

Daniël brings him tea and enthusiastic stories about the weights he managed to lift. "I'm beginning to get some decent level of fitness again. Interesting article, by the way, that interview with Anthony. I read it yesterday. Not afraid to admit he had been wrong about certain things. Solid character. It's easy to understand why fans worship him." He starts to grin. "But don't tell him I told you that, because I wouldn't hear the end of it."

"I couldn't agree with you more." Steve nods. "You look good: no longer so pale and frightfully skinny. Let's say I'm very much looking forward to our date tonight." He puts the magazine away and tries his tea. "Hot."

"Just like you. Hot, I mean. I watched you reading for a bit. You look sexy, being all concentrated." Daniël stretches his long legs. "The plans I have for you tonight …"

Steve can't help but blush.

"You still get shy when I flirt with you. That's so sweet." Daniël takes Steve's hand, kisses it. "Ready to hunt for a home?"

◆

The first house they walk through has already been vacated by the residents; the carefully placed pieces of furniture too obviously an attempt to give it a certain ambience. Other than that, it's near perfect. Built before the Second World War, it has five rooms, a big kitchen, a huge bathroom including a bath tub easily big enough for two, two walk in closets, a pantry, more storage room in the attic, central heating, a double garage, a shed and a garden front, back and on both sides. The fact that the nearest neighbours are at shouting distance does add hugely to the appeal of the property.

"It's a bit old fashioned, but I like it," Daniël whispers into Steve's ear.

Steve stands in the middle of a room, leaning against Daniël. "So do I."

It's a quiet, one could even say modest house, not boasting its qualities, but waiting patiently for someone to discover them.

"This house somehow reminds me of you. Not sure why, it just does," Daniël says while they, for the second time, make a round through the rooms.

The second house looks like it could be used in a magazine article about modern homes, but when they look at each other's faces, they notice the attraction isn't there.

"I suggest we let it sink in for a day or so. You look tired, you feel like taking a nap while I cook tea?" Daniël asks when they're home again.

It's only then that Steve realises how exhausted he is and ready for some rest. But it's also right at that moment he knows exactly why the old house is going to be his and Daniël's first shared home.

"You noticed the light, those windows? I've never seen it quite like that."

Daniël kisses his forehead. "I know. I fell in love with it too. Now, sleep a bit and I'll wake you up in an hour or so. We'll talk about the house when we have tea."

Then Daniël kisses him again. "Had a good nap? Food's keeping warm in the oven. Take a shower, you and me?"

Steve stretches himself lazily. "But only if you promise to wash my back."

"Back, front, any part you like." Daniël grins. "Don't tell me; I'm too good for this world."

They have a very pleasant half hour.

After that, the spicy beef-vegetables-and potatoes casserole is still palatable enough, but perhaps past its prime quality. Steve nevertheless eats with gusto and he's delighted to see Daniël do the same.

"I really liked that first house," Daniël starts the conversation.

"You think it needs a lot of work?"

"You mean if it can be ready before the wedding, so we can move in right away? I don't see any reason for major renovations, just a bit of paint, new curtains, stuff like that."

Before Steve can ask the next question, Daniël continues. "I had it inspected. It's in good condition, we just need to decorate it to our own taste, get furniture we like. A few adjustments so you can get around safely. The garden can wait until after the winter."

"There are more houses we want to take a look at?"

"Why should we? We like this one, it doesn't need a lot of work, and we can afford it. There will always be better places if we search long enough, but what's the use of that?" Daniël scoops the last bit of gravy with a piece of bread. "That's what dad told me."

Steve can't deny it's a relief. He sees nothing but joy in getting married and moving to a new home with Daniël, he just isn't sure if he's up to the less than two months leading up to the happy events.

"Hey, we'll be fine. We don't have to do everything by ourselves. There are people whose job it is to organise weddings, paint houses and help us with finding the right colour of paint, too. Mum reminded me again we are privileged to have a job that pays some serious money and be part of a club that supports us in just about anything and as long as we need it. All you have to do now is say if you like something or not."

"You make it sound like it's so easy and you have everything under control." Once more, he offers the boy a chance to venture out of his sanctuary.

But Daniël chuckles the concern away. "I'm getting pretty good at pretending I actually know what I'm doing. And when I start to panic and I haven't got a clue what to do next, I just think: as long as I have my man, I can face the whole world."

"I'm sorry for …"

"Please, don't. Everything, I mean fucking everything, has been taken from you. You have to work so hard to get the things back we all take for granted. There won't be a perfect happy end, no matter what I try to tell myself about miracles happening all the time." Daniël waits for a few seconds before he continues. "You know what was hard for me? To be almost totally passive; not being able to do anything but to wait. I was always used to doing things. Training, matches, proving to the gaffer I was worth a place with the starting Eleven, undergoing therapy to recover from injuries … Suddenly all I could do was sit and wait. Sit on that chair next to your bed, watching you. Waiting. Watching how the nurses took care of your broken body. Waiting. It means so much to me, being able to do things for you. I love taking care of you. It doesn't matter how big or small the job. Does that make you feel uncomfortable?"

Steve takes Daniël's hands in his own. "If I feel threatened in my masculinity simply because the man I love helps me to shave or with more complicated matters like finding a house and getting married, what kind of man would that make me? You had the courage and the patience to wait for weeks until I was ready to wake up, not even knowing if I would stay alive. I honestly can't bring myself to make a fuss about my male identity."

"But you don't mind me making a fuss about your masculinity in the bedroom?"

"I insist on you getting all bothered by it."

Before they start giggling like schoolgirls, Daniël places his arm firmly around Steve's body and together, they stumble towards the bedroom.

They undress quickly, too eager to do it the nice and slow way. Once that bit is done, time again is of no consequence. This is their date and they can do whatever they please and take as much time as they like.

Kissing for the sake of kissing. Touching for the sake of touching. Not ignoring the sexual excitement that becomes obvious with their erections, but simply accepting and enjoying it for its own beauty.

So when Daniël takes a pillow and gestures that he wants to shove it under Steve's hips, Steve simply nods his consent. He opens his legs wide enough to give his lover easy access, but no more than feels absolutely comfortable.

Daniël's tongue doesn't surprise him, but still makes his breathing hitch for a few seconds. Such a patient tongue, talented and patient and doing things that makes Steve want to surrender his whole body and yes please yes ...

It's just one finger. One single finger. It brings tears to his eyes because ...

How to explain this journey even to himself?

Daniël's tongue; his finger.

His body has to learn all over again.

He has to learn all over again.

Daniël's finger exploring him. His mouth, oh sweet mercy, around aching flesh.

He thinks wedding night.

He thinks Daniël.

Then all thinking stops. Only to return when he's in his beloved's arms, smiling back at his smile. He notices Daniël's still very hard cock.

"I wish ..."

"We will ..." Daniël kisses him. "We have time. But for now, indulge me?"

Steve nods.

"Fuck me with two, perhaps three, of your fingers while I jerk off?" Daniël gets the lube from the bed table.

"One of our favourites." Steve holds his right hand up. "Ready when you are."

And when Daniël lies on his back, his legs spread so beautifully obscenely wide, his body open and ready for him, Steve feels his heart shatter with joy.

Chapter 26

The contract for the house gets signed and Steve can hardly believe how absolutely not concerned he is about this major decision. Having to say yes or no to colour schemes and drapes and furniture, however, is giving him a rapid succession of headaches.

"I don't know and I don't care. You're there, so what more do I need?"

He's just so tired. Days are overfull, hard work doesn't always get rewarded proportionally despite the improvement, and he starts to wonder what it will take for Degaré to give Daniël at least a chance with the substitutes during a game against a relatively easy opponent. The boy hadn't been injured, after all, he's just out of match fitness, and how is he supposed to get that back if he doesn't get to play any matches? As for his own health, the visit to the hospital showed that yes, he had made progress during the weeks after his release, but it also becomes more and more clear that most of the still-remaining damage might well be long-term or even permanent.

Somehow, the big things are not that hard. Sharing his life with Daniël, and thus getting married and buying a home, comes naturally to him. But it's all the small stuff that makes him want to hide.

"I'm sorry this is asking too much of you. Tell you what, I'll do all the talking with the designer and the contractor. What I like, I'll show you and there's no way I can't read from your face if you agree with me or not. I just have to see you smile, that's all."

Steve feels embarrassed for being so relieved and it must be plainly visible on his face because Daniël starts to laugh.

"I'm sorry. I'm useless to you at the moment."

The laughter stops immediately.

"Don't you realise you're looking at a man who half the time doesn't know what to do with himself because he's drowning in joy? My days are full of work and training and organising things and my nights are filled with holding my man. I get to take care of the man I love, counting the days until we get married and move into our first home, instead of counting the days, and then the weeks and the months and the years, since … I'm sorry, I shouldn't have started that sentence."

"You can't say in all honesty it's that easy."

The gentle invitation gets ignored.

"I don't want easy, I want you. You going through the apartment with less and less need to use your crutches. You smiling because I showed you the picture of a floor lamp we both like." Daniël kisses Steve before he continues. "Yeah, so life is complicated and sometimes I wish we were a couple of years further down the line so at least we have a bit more certainty about some things, but this is still the best thing that could ever happen to me. Because you happened to me."

"You think you can hold me for a bit so I can get those thoughts out of my head?"

They lie on the couch for a while, Daniël's arms firmly around Steve's body.

"I wanted to wait till tonight, but I just have to tell you. Degaré wants me to play next Saturday against Bolton. Well, you know the gaffer, I'll start on the bench and with a bit of luck … It's not a huge game, and he probably wants Levee or Lain rested for the one against Chelsea and Neil has a bit of a problem with his left calf muscle, but it's the chance to prove I can handle a match again."

Steve has to let the words sink in for a moment.

"It must be tough for you …" Daniël starts, but Steve gently places a finger on his lips.

"Hush, love, this is great news for both of us. You are part of it all again."

"And you're not …"

"I said my goodbyes in that park, even before I realised I wouldn't come out alive. I get to see you again at Chestnut Road where you belong, on the bench first, but perhaps even playing. Allow me my happiness." He smiles at Daniël's frown. "This isn't about fair and unfair. Not between us."

He sees Daniël's dilemma written all over his face. So he answers the question before it is being asked. "I'll be there. We will face this together. And no one will be more proud than I."

"I don't want you to get hurt. It's the first time, you and I during a match, you know what they can shout and chant and sing …"

"Most will be Kinbridge fans anyway. They'll be excited to see you playing again. And whatever will be chanted about us won't be any worse than what we hear week after week about so many players for so many reasons. No marital problem, no tragedy in the family, no wag committing a faux-pas gets unnoticed. Or else a player is too skinny or too fat, too short or too tall. Hey, it's not really a secret you and I are doing it," Steve jokes.

"Talking about doing it …" Daniël rubs his body somewhat unsubtly against Steve's.

"The big little boy is getting eager?" Steve cups his hand around the bulge. "I want this in my mouth between now and ten minutes at the most."

He considers the seven minutes it actually takes him to get up from the couch, walk to the bedroom, get naked and feel Daniël's velvety cock glide between his lips a very acceptable time.

◆

The days before the match are being in happy anticipation. Steve watches the training during the morning so he can be with Daniël when he hits the gym in the afternoon. The need to be in close proximity to his lover is too urgent to ignore and instead of wondering why this is, he simply accepts it and acts accordingly. Daniël doesn't comment on it but he does his job with total dedication, still sparing a smile and a little wave with his hand now and again for the man who looks up from his magazine and smiles back, warmly tucked away in a coat and a blanket.

"You're looking forward to Saturday?" Gabrysz asks after training and lunch.

"Mostly." Steve nods. "I don't want the fans and the Bolton players to hurt him."

"How are they supposed to hurt someone that happy, that much at peace with himself? Where would they find that kind of power?" Gabrysz smiles at Steve. "And you? How are you doing?"

"Still finding out, I guess. But I'm relieved we've found a house so soon and the gaffer is giving Dan a chance."

"We're going to be practically neighbours. Well, I wouldn't get the car out of the garage to get from our place to yours and Dan's. I'll ask Bronia to cook something typically Polish once you two have settled. If I offer my help in the kitchen, she might even say yes. Ask the whole Hollycroft KTFC bunch, wives, kids and all, and make a nice Sunday out of it." Gabrysz keeps on chattering quite happily about shops and great little restaurants while they walk to the gym.

Steve doesn't miss that the big man adjusts his pace, unobtrusively offering support.

Then he feels Daniël's hand on his shoulder.

"Hi Danny, Kurt kept you busy? Gabrysz and I were just talking about ..."

"I heard the last part of it." Daniël faces the goalie. "You're offering to be our Hollycroft touring guide?"

Gabrysz smiles brightly. "On one condition ... we get a guys only night, with beer, pizza and bad movies at your place."

"You bet." Dan chuckles. "But now we've got work to do."

After the workout, they drive to their new house to see how things are doing. Daniël shares a few words with the contractor and Steve feels safe in the knowledge that the organised chaos will be a home for them in less than six weeks.

"Things are going to plan. The few roof tiles that needed to be replaced have been taken care of. The wooden floors are freshly stained, they're almost finished with stripping the old paint from the doors and posts, and the supplier promised the tiles for the bathroom will be delivered by the end of next week," Daniël says. "I bet by the time we really start believing that everything is going perfectly, trouble will start, so let's enjoy this while it lasts."

It's all fine with Steve. As long as he has a bed to sleep in at night and Daniël to keep him company, he can't even pretend he's worried about paint and tiles and drapes that might or might not be available the week before the wedding.

◆

"I'm honestly looking forward to the match," Daniël says as he lies comfortably in Steve's arms. "But I'm also bloody nervous. It's been so long. And it's going to be a night without you. Don't like that rule at all. That takes getting used to."

"Not being allowed to sleep at your own place, even before home matches. Whoever thought up something like that? Ah well, it's all part of being a footballer's husband. You'll do fine and what is nicer than missing someone for a short while and seeing him really soon? We will have different lives, but we'll never be really apart."

It's Friday morning, the day before the match against Bolton. They had breakfast in bed, lovingly prepared by Daniël and thoroughly enjoyed by both of them. They know they will make love later but for now, lying closely together, feeling each other, skin touching skin while they softly talk, is enough.

Steve kisses his lover. "Thank you for letting me taking care of you, even if it's just by holding you in my arms."

Daniël glides his fingers through Steve's hair. "One of those old ladies back at the hospital told me it's almost never fifty-fifty in a marriage, and that's not a problem as long as you both honestly try to give what you're able to. I can live with almost anything, but not having you beside me is the one thing that would kill me."

"It scares me at times, what I mean to you, but …"

"You can accept it?"

"I'm learning to."

Their kisses grow more urgent; their touches become more to the point. Soon they thrust against each other, moaning in need.

Steve feels how his filling cock stabs against Daniël's soft underbelly. "I need … oh please, Danny … please."

"What, Steve, what do you need me to give to you?" Daniël covers Steve's face with countless feverish kisses. "There is nothing I won't do for you, but you have to tell me."

"Need to be inside you." The urge is now so strong it spins threads of steel inside his body.

"You read my mind or something? You want us on our sides, or shall I ride you?" Daniël gets the already half-empty bottle of lube. "I won't need a lot of preparation. Just want your cock inside me as quickly as possible."

"I want to try something else." Steve gets on his knees between Daniël's widespread legs.

"What … you mean?" Hope flares up in Daniël's eyes, immediately followed by concern.

"I've worked my arse off to be able to do this. I won't know what my body is capable of unless I try. Please, Daniël, give me the chance to try."

And Daniël smiles and nods his head. "Here, I'll lube your prick so you can push right in."

Carefully Steve places the head of his cock against the closed, but relaxed pucker. "Yes?"

"Oh yes."

There's the resistance of muscle, not of mind, and when he's in and can't go further, he stays still with the wonder of it all. Daniël's sweet face, looking up at him, his legs around his middle, trying not to be a burden, keeping him close and deep.

But his body has its own needs and movement starts. Tentative at first, the edge of pain simply there, but not really *there* and finally need and want and love take over and he whispers Daniël's name and he hears Daniël urging him on.

"Please …."

The boy is now begging.

"Deeper, I need your cock deeper, taking me, using me, please …" Complete surrender in his beloved's voice. "Yours, all of me, all yours …"

Pain and pleasure race through Steve's body, arriving almost simultaneously at the finish. Burning stars are shooting with blinding light behind his eyes. His body starts to tremble. Then, finally, his mind shuts down.

" … Steve … please … where does it hurt … please …?"

Everywhere, he wants to say, it hurts every-fucking-where and it's great and I love you so much if I would say the words my tongue would catch fire … but he can't, so he opens his eyes and smiles and hopes it's enough.

Daniël blushes. "I can't say I'm sorry, because I can't lie to you."

"Good hurt. I remember good hurt" is the first thing he says when he's able to say anything at all. "You helped me to remember good hurt."

Daniël massages and rubs all the aching spots until Steve's mind may remember the pain, but his body no longer feels it. There's nothing but blissful relaxation; Daniël holding him when he falls asleep and when he wakes up.

◆

It's the day of the match and Steve sits at what he knows to be his seat for the home games as long as Daniël is part of the team.

"The paparazzi gave you any trouble?" Neil asks.

Steve shakes his head. "Not more than the usual, but thanks for asking."

He understands the awkwardness of the situation. What to say that doesn't sound superfluous and cheap? How to express this mixture of overwhelming joy, simply because Daniël is sitting there, with the rest of the reserves, and grief for the loss of everything he hasn't made an inventory of yet?

Still, the sound coming from the stands when Daniël is being announced with the rest of the substitutes is more than a polite acknowledgement, and he can't quite remember if the Kinbridge Town hymn has always been sung that loudly.

He isn't ready for the match, for being there. Neil is a good lad, offering him moments of distraction and the knowledge that he is protected and welcome, but he isn't Daniël. Steve remembers the crowd could be anything, from a force driving him on to heights he never before felt were within reach, to a claustrophobia inducing human wall of hostility, but he had never felt so overwhelmed by it that he didn't even know what to feel.

"If the Bolton fans are trying to chant anything nasty about Dan, I don't think he's even able to hear them because of the noise our supporters are producing," Neil makes a joke.

But there will be away games …

Not now. He must stay in the moment; concentrate on the here and now.

In his case, it means being aware of Daniël doing his obligatory runs and stretches, conveniently in Steve's line of vision. This is his anchor, and a damn sexy one at that. The way that boy wiggles his arse is both a reminder and a promise.

From Neil's reaction, he understands when something happens on the pitch that might result in anything good or bad, but without it he wouldn't know. It's too foreign, too unfamiliar in all its familiarity. He's happy, though, when Matthew scores, and isn't oblivious to the biting disappointment when Bolton equalise three minutes before half-time.

Neil gets him a hot chocolate.

"You're okay?"

Not really, but how to explain this core of being filled with joy, surrounded by something that reminds him too much of panic to call it anything else but panic, even though he's absolutely certain it's not panic at all?

Right before the second half, Daniël sits next to him for a few moments, taking Steve's hands into his own.

"I'm cold and a bit scared and so happy to see you with the rest of the guys. I really hope you get to play this afternoon."

Daniël rubs Steve's hands warm. "Better? And I'll ask someone to bring over a blanket and cushion for you to sit on. I should have thought of that sooner."

Steve smiles in appreciation. "That's sweet of you. After a few matches, I'll be used to it. You're glad to be back?"

"I guess I am but it hasn't sunk in yet. The crowd's nice, though. The fan club brought our banner and even made another one to welcome us back: seen it? You heard them chanting your name? It makes me so proud."

A quick kiss on Steve's lips and Daniël is back in the dugout. That will be another photo in the tabloids, the football magazines, spreading around the internet, Steve realises, but the knowledge leaves him indifferent.

Within minutes, Francesco Moreschi changes the one all into a lead for Kinbridge Town. Steve can't help but grin from ear to hear when he sees the Spaniard-Italian jump up and down like a five-year-old on a sugar high while the others try to congratulate him.

Daniël is still doing his runs and stretches.

"Look," Neil says, just after another attempt to score from the Bolton striker, "Dan's being called back to the bench. It looks like the gaffer wants him in the game."

Sixty minutes, and the electronic placard goes up. Number 21 out, Number 30 in.

Daniël acknowledges Steve and touches Levee's hand in passing, making sure the referee sees him entering the game.

Steve feels his heart expand with pride and love.

Daniël gets the welcome of clapping and shouting and chanting and singing. For minutes, his name is all there is to hear. Waving through the stands it forms a sea of sound. He gets showered with affection and admiration. The love, courage and utter humanity he has shown over all those months are being rewarded in the best way the fans know how.

And they carry Steve through the remaining thirty minutes of the game.

Chapter 27

"More?" Daniël's voice is an open invitation; his middle finger teasing against Steve's prostate. "I think you're ready for two fingers. You think so, too?"

"Yes, please, yes." Steve tries to open his legs a bit wider, but Daniël stops him with a calming gesture.

"Don't do that. I want this to feel perfect for you, without even the good hurt."

Steve nods, accepting his lover's lead in this, joyfully giving over to the fingers exploring the most intimate part of his body.

Two fingers means there is some stretching, but it's ever so gentle and whatever minute hint of pain might form gets soothed away by his beloved's gentle tongue.

"I want to be ready to feel your cock inside me ..."

"I'm just as eager for the wedding, or should I say the wedding night, as you are, but I think we still need a lot of practise." Daniël has a downright mischievous grin on his face.

"You think we really should wait for that one night? I'm not a virgin, remember, although it has been more than six months since my last time ..."

"The first time you had a man inside you ..."

Almost tangible knowledge moves between them, but Steve knows neither of them is able to touch it.

"You believe I'm not ready yet to try it again?" Steve moves his body ever so slightly in a counter rhythm to that of Daniël's fingers. "God, Danny ..."

"Like it when I do this?" Daniël does something and it's so subtle Steve's not even sure it is actually something, but it makes his body quiver with pleasure.

"Does it feel this good when I fuck you with my fingers? And I still want you to answer my question."

"Honestly? I believe I'm the one not ready yet. And yes, it feels that good. Why do you think I keep asking for more?" Daniël presses his lips against the taut scrotum, retracting his fingers, but pushing them back in as soon as Steve makes a sound of disappointment.

A few moments later, he licks the come from Steve's belly, his fingers still as deeply inside his lover as possible without pressing the knuckles of his hand against the tender flesh. Then he gets out as slowly as he got in.

Steve smiles, sated and content, but not missing that his lover is still in need of completion. "Stay on your knees between my legs and jerk yourself off."

It's a softly spoken order, but it makes Daniël blush in excitement.

"You got such a beautiful cock. I love the colour and the texture. Love it when it's hard and ready, but love it just as much when it's resting against your thigh … Love the smell and the taste … I love every aspect and detail …" So rarely he finds the words, even before speaking became a slow task, too reserved as he is in the verbal expression of the sexual element of his love for Daniël. Doing is limited only by the boundaries of his body; actually saying it in great detail is a whole different ballgame.

"Gets me all horny when you talk dirty to me. I felt your eyes on me when I did my stretches. Fuck, it feels great to look good for my man." Daniël pumps his shaft a few times, his gaze never leaving Steve's face. Shameless lust burning in grey-blue eyes.

"I thought my heart would burst with pride when you walked on to the pitch to take up your position. That handsome, courageous, loyal, talented guy is mine and everyone at the Chestnut Road Stadium knows it. Everyone watching the match on TV knows it."

"They can look all they want, but there's only one who gets to touch me." Daniël keeps moving against his clenched hand, gaining speed, but not yet going for the final lap.

"Thrust your cock against the palm of your hand. Show me how you're going to fuck me on our wedding night. Don't hold back. Keep your eyes open. Keep them wide open."

The head is now wet with pre-come, peeking out from Dan's fist when he moves downwards and pulls the foreskin back. "Like this?"

Steve places his hand over Daniël's moving fist, but doesn't direct it. "Come for me."

All the muscles in Daniël's body seem to contract, his throat vulnerably exposed, his mouth open in a near silent moan. His come warm and sticky on Steve's body. But the way he crawls blindly against his lover, exhausted and spent, trusting him for safety, is perhaps an even greater gift.

◆

Sunday moves slowly and gently for them. They have a long shower, brunch with all the trappings, take a short walk through the neighbourhood to get a bit of fresh air and talk about everything and nothing. There are a few people who do look at them with a hint of recognition in their eyes, but hardly anyone bothers them. There's a complimentary remark about Daniël's return to the game, a shy request for an autograph from two wide-eyed teenage girls, but that's the extent of it.

Daniël gets a call from his family about yesterday's match. That reminds him he promised a few friends to let them know how it went. He even takes time to update his blog.

"Want to read it? I specially used a bigger font. I'll make dinner in the meantime."

Steve looks at the screen.

"It looks good to read? Oh, and there's a video of the short interview I gave after the match, too." Daniël kisses him on the cheek.

"It's perfect. Thank you."

He reads, soon discovering Daniël not only adjusted the size of the characters, but also tried to use short sentences with familiar words, without sounding childish or too simple. This is like the arm his lover offered when they took their walk in the neighbourhood. How big is a heart when it's capable of such small and gentle acts of kindness? But that, at least, is a question Steve has known the answer to for a long time.

He reads the entry, smiles.

I did a lot of running up and down the pitch. I also did a lot of stretching. Because it was cold. Because the gaffer told me to. And because Steve thinks it looks sexy.

He tells about how it feels to enter the pitch, the mixed emotions, about the knowledge that while the game was still the game, for him everything had changed.

I felt so proud because the man I love could see me play football. I felt so alone because the man I love will never play football again.

Daniël enters the room with a bowl of salad. "The potatoes and baked salmon will be done in a few minutes. I'm afraid the sauce won't be home-made."

He puts the bowl on the table and looks over Steve's shoulder. "You like what I wrote?"

Steve nods. "Strange, how we had no idea when we played our last match together. But how could we have known?"

"Everything could have been a last, but it wasn't." Daniël kisses him. "I'll be sad for a while longer about you not being there with me on the pitch. Even if we perhaps would have played for different clubs against each other next season."

Perhaps …

"You watch the video while I get the rest of our dinner ready?"

Why does he get butterflies in his belly seeing Daniël, in jeans and sweater, hair still wet from the shower, on the screen of the laptop, when the same Daniël is busy in the kitchen, half a dozen steps away?

What was going through your mind when you entered the game?

"It felt great being allowed to play again. I miss Steve terribly. He should have been with me on the pitch, defending our half, but at least he was watching the match from the stands. That's what counts more than anything."

You had expected this welcome from the Kinbridge Town fans? There was even some applause from the Bolton supporters.

"I didn't know what to expect. Of course, they lost count at the club of how many letters and emails of support they received, so I hoped for the best. This was even better."

What are your expectations for the future? As a Kinbridge Town defender, that is.

"You'll have to ask Degaré about that. I hope I can stay for a while longer, proof I'm worth the trust and support the club and the fans have put in me during the past months. I think I already showed some of that today."

He feels Daniël standing behind him, his fingers playing with his hair.

"I still have a fat Dutch accent."

"I know. Sexy as anything."

Daniël closes the laptop. "Care for some food?"

Steve's actually famished. Over the last couple of weeks, his appetite has been returning. Being active most of the day and rebuilding at least some of his muscles might have something to do with that. Daniël hadn't said much about it, but the admiring touches and looks that shamelessly speak of lust are obvious enough.

But it's more than that, more than a body, if not returning to normal, then at least functioning better; healthier than it had been for a long time. It's also that he's looking forward to their marriage and moving to the place that's going to be their first home. It's the joy of seeing his beloved boy active as a professional sportsman once more. It's finding his place in the world again, even if he has no idea yet what he will do once there's nothing left to practise, to fix or to heal. But he remembers Death being his companion all too well to be worried about what to do with his life. He's aware of the huge difference between him and Daniël in just about every aspect of their lives, but they both have to fight their own battles, even if they stand shoulder to shoulder like those warriors from ancient times.

"How's your level of energy? You need to rest?" Daniël casually asks while he takes the plates to the kitchen.

"Are you asking what I think you're asking?"

"I might be."

Steve is positively certain Daniël's shaking his jeans clad booty on purpose when he leaves the room.

"I have to admit, you did look edible during that interview." Steve follows Daniël, still luxuriating in the feeling that, with a bit of support from whatever is strong and stable enough to provide support, he's able to get around the apartment without his crutches. When Dan stoops to put the dishes in the machine, he just has to cop a feel.

"Sometimes I miss the times you pushed my jeans down and then yours and you fucked me against the kitchen sink with the help of a splash of olive oil. No planning, no talking, just two guys fucking." Daniël turns towards Steve and takes him in his arms. "Sorry I said that. I'm just being stupid. Makes me sound like I'm not grateful for what we have."

Should he be grateful? Should they?

"What about we take this to the bedroom? I know where I want your perky little arse." Steve grabs a handful of said arse, while he pushes himself suggestively against his lover.

Daniël is as close to giggling as he'll ever be. "You didn't say that … perky little …"

Steve just has to kiss him on the nose. "I didn't. You just imagined it. Now, shoo, there's a big soft bed waiting for us."

Daniël rides them to a sweet, glorious orgasm, leaving them sated and so drenched in love it fills the very heart of them.

"So perfect," Daniël mumbles, already half asleep when he finally allows Steve's now soft cock to slip out of him.

And it is.

◆

Two days later, they get a phone call informing them the trial is about to start and even though they had known for weeks, months even, that one day this call would come, it still leaves them silent for minutes.

"So this is it. Crown court the day after tomorrow. You're going to give evidence," Daniël says quietly. "And you're not allowed to refuse."

"That's how the law works. I get that." Steve feels so calm and detached he knows something must be wrong.

"There will be a cross-examination and they will force you to remember everything in detail. It will happen all over again. It's like you're entering that park again. You won't run away because you don't know. They will hurt you again. You will say goodbye to me again. I will see your broken body again. Isn't what you told the police enough? What about the medical reports? What about all those pictures? God knows what else they have, like DNA and other stuff. That should be enough to put those bastards behind bars for the rest of their lives, shouldn't it?" Daniël's hands move erratically through the air in acute panic. It's almost like he doesn't even realise Steve is with him, waiting until the stream of desperate words has come to a halt.

Steve has no thoughts concerning what is about to happen, it's simply not real enough, even with all the preparations and explanations given by the ever-friendly and patient lady of the Witness Service. Danny is upset, that message burns itself into his brain, overriding everything else.

Daniël clutches his arms around him in fierce protection. "I can't even promise you that I won't let them hurt you without lying."

There's so much hopeless pain in his voice.

"Is my love going to be enough when they drag you through hell again?"

Steve takes his lover's face between his hands and kisses him on his forehead. "It won't be easy for either of us, but remember what they explained to us, that I'm not the one on trial? That I have rights, too, and that there are people to make sure everything happens according to the rules?"

Daniël nods, but he doesn't look half convinced.

"You love me and yes, that will be enough."

Chapter 28

He has listened to the prosecution's opening speech, though he can't claim he actually heard any of the words spoken. He has gone through the ritual of promising to tell the truth and nothing but the truth. He has answered the handful of friendly questions of the prosecuting counsel about his earlier statement. It felt like he was there foremost as the physical reminder of why all this is happening in the first place. The police officers, the medical and forensic specialists will all be heard later, and the consequences of what happened to him in the Queen Elizabeth Park will be reduced to factual matter. The accused will have their turn to answer the questions, to say what they have to say in their defence. So far, it's all been like he's one of the leads in a very experimental indie film: badly acted, hardly watchable, but nothing to be overly nervous or frightened about. The cross-examination by the counsel for the defendants, the part he should fear even if there's nothing to fear because he's not on trial and he has nothing to hide or lie about, refuses to become more than a formality, something that simply has to happen. Still, as soon as he had answered the last question as a witness for the prosecution, he heard himself say, "Please, can I have a short break?"

It's twenty minutes later and only now he's able to look around, to allow the room and those who are in it to become really part of what's happening to him and Daniël.

They are there, the men who are on trial because of him, seated behind glass or perhaps Plexiglas, and Steve wonders if it's bulletproof though he can't imagine why. Six of them. Monsters in cheap suits, with ordinary faces, puffy as a result of years of binge drinking and poor diets. He doesn't believe they are much different from the men in that park. Their eyes are still the same.

They do look out of place and unhappy, but Steve guesses that's not because they're in a totally unfamiliar surroundings. They have been in similar settings before, if only because of a pub brawl, a job that wasn't as legit as their mate had told them, or some other stupidity. You know, we've all been young and stupid, before the missus set us straight.

Not this time. This is beyond their means of understanding. Why are they the ones having to defend themselves in front of a judge and jury; decent men, some with families and all, while there's this poofter holding his poofter boyfriend's hand …?

Steve stops his train of thoughts. He knows all too well what he's trying to do. As long as he pretends he has some, however speculatively, insight into their thinking, into their lives and characters, he's safe in some inexplicable manner.

They are there, seated behind a glass screen, the men who had tried to kick him to death. Six of them. Not even monsters. Not even that.

Hideous suits, ill-fitting.

His hand in Daniël's hand.

"You, me and no one else," his beloved whispers.

Steve nods. Daniël never lies to him.

There's the six of them, behind glass, in their cheap hideous suits.

And there's the man who ran away, who wrote those letters about standing up in trial. The man who kept his promise. Smith keeps his head down. In shame? In thought? He has recounted his story before Steve was asked into the courtroom, but has been allowed to stay for the rest of the trial. For one second he looks up, his eyes in Steve's direction.

"Poor man," he hears himself say.

Daniël strokes the back of his hand with his thumb. "Look," he says.

Steve looks. Matthew is there, with Gael right next to him; both smiling their acknowledgement. This is their friendship. Their support. Their penance.

There are some unknown faces too, most likely family members of the accused. Steve has no emotions of any significance about them. And there's the people doing their job. Judge, jury, prosecutor, defence lawyers, usher, clerk, police, press. All are present in this room because he had walked into a park, with a spring in his step and a silly grin on his face. He still doesn't comprehend how he got out.

He's being called to the witness box again. His hand no longer in Daniël's.

As before, the usher asks in a friendly tone if he needs assistance, handing Steve his crutches, the courtroom being too unfamiliar to trust his own legs and, perhaps more importantly, his brain.

He smiles. "I'm fine, thank you." And makes sure he's stable on his feet before he takes the few steps to the witness box. He has taken the oath about an hour ago, standing up and facing the jury but once again, he's thankful for the permission to be seated during the questioning. He's supposed to concentrate on the questions, not on how to keep his balance for as long as it takes the prosecution and defence to ask them.

"Remember what's on that piece of paper in the pocket of your jacket," Daniël had said.

DANIËL LOVES STEVE

He doesn't have to look at the writing or feel the paper between his fingers to be aware of the absolute truth of those words. He doesn't even have to put his hand in the pocket of his jacket. He knows Daniël wrote those words. He doesn't need to know more.

… The truth and nothing but the truth …

He made a promise and that promise still stands. He won't tell a deliberate lie even by remaining silent – those days are long past – but will that be the same as telling the absolute truth?

The lawyer for the defendants doing the cross-examination asks for his attention. The man wouldn't be noticed in a crowded room but Steve knows that by the time he's finished with his questions, he will be very nearly as much a part of his dreams and memories as the six men in the dock.

"As you know, I'm going to ask you some questions. Remember, if any of my questions aren't absolutely clear, I'm more than happy to repeat of rephrase them, but please don't guess just to give an answer."

"I'll do my best."

Once more he's fully part of the courtroom drama.

Mr Gavan, do I understand correctly you had been in a homosexual relationship with Mr Borghart since before the incident?

Steve knows exactly what Daniël would have asked back: "It's a bit complicated to have a heterosexual relationship with a man when you're a man yourself, wouldn't you say?"

Mr Gavan, could you answer my question, please?

"I'm sorry. Daniël and I had been together for about six months at that time."

Was there anyone aware of this relationship? Friends? Family? Colleagues?

"No one knew. Daniël's career …"

This frustrated you?

"I'm not sure if I understand your question correctly."

Mr Borghart welcomed his parents from the airport that day, didn't he?

"Yes."

And you were not invited? Hadn't both of you a day off?

"That would have been impossible."

Because you wanted to keep your relationship hidden from the world?

"We had to."

Anyone specific ordered you to do so? Was there any pressure from the club you played for at that moment?

"They didn't know about us."

Had Mr Borghart asked you to do so?

"We never really discussed this subject. It wouldn't have changed anything."

Because you were afraid it would damage Mr Borghart's reputation and possibly his market value? Your own too, perhaps?

"Wouldn't it?"

But you agree that at that time, before the incident, you were actively hiding the fact you were in a homosexual relationship with Mr Borghart? A simple yes or no will be enough.

"Yes."

This fact frustrated you?

"I guess so."

Let's go back to the night of the incident. You told the police you had been drinking?

"A few pints, yes."

But you don't remember how many?

"Two, three at the most."

Couldn't it have been more?

"I can't remember. It's been too long."

You weren't going to see Mr Borghart for the next two days, were you?

"He had his parents over."

So you went to a pub, had some beers, two, three, possibly more, while Mr Borghart had dinner with his parents. Later, but still that same night, you walked through the city when you, fully by accident you stated earlier to the police, landed in a section of the Queen Elizabeth Park that has been notorious for being a so-called cruising area for many years. There had even been repeated complaints about it by families with young children and other users of the park. I remember an article about it in the Kinbridge Chronicle hardly more than a year ago. Answer yes or no, please.

"But I didn't know …"

Yes or no, Mr Gavan.

"Yes."

Could you tell in your own words what happened then?

"This is a bit embarrassing, but I couldn't find a public toilet …"

I'm sure every man in this present company has found himself with the same problem at some time. The lawyer smiles benignly. *You just happened to open the zipper of your jeans to answer nature's call right in the middle of a meeting place for anonymous gay sex at a time that's known in certain circles as rush hour.*

Is he supposed to give a reaction to this? He can't change the truth, he promised not to.

A man touched you, didn't he?

"Yes."

You tried to actively stop him? Telling him he was mistaken?

"I …"

A simple yes or no, please. Did you try to stop that man from touching you? Or did you perhaps, on a subconscious level – I'm not here to judge you – welcome his attention? You just told us you were frustrated about certain facts in your relationship with Mr Borghart. That he was spending the evening with his parents and that you weren't welcome in his home until after his parents had gone back to Holland. That you had been drinking.

"I love Daniël. I would never hurt him on purpose. He's not just the man I'm going to marry, he's my best friend. He was my last thought when I was dying. Is nothing sacred to you? I'm very sorry, I shouldn't have …"

I can only compliment you on your loyalty to your fiancé, but this is about the truth and about justice. Did you try to stop that man?

"No … I didn't know how …"

Thank you. What happened then?

"Everyone ran away."

And you were confronted with the group of men present in this room?

"Yes. Fans of KTFC. At least that was my first thought. "

How did you know they were fans?

"They recognised me. Most people in Kinbridge know about the skipper … Matthew Kirkby, but only fans who follow the club would have recognised me. Later, when they attacked me, I knew for sure."

I bet they were happily surprised to meet a regular player of their favourite team.

"They weren't."

Perhaps because of the place you were at that moment? Could it be possible they had witnessed by accident that a man was touching you inappropriately?

"But …"

That must have been something of a shock. Group of mates, having shared a few pints at the local pub, perhaps a pint too many, heading home via a short-cut through the park and there they are confronted with one of their heroes. A player of their beloved Kinbridge Town Football Club getting touched up by another man.

"I …"

Are you absolutely sure those men are the same as the men in the dock?

"Yes. I know that for certain. I looked at their faces."

And what did you see?

"Disbelief. Horror. I think I even remember one mentioned something about his kid's football kit. I'll never forget …"

Your number, perhaps? Something like that? His little boy playing your position?

"Might be."

Thank you. I have no more questions.

Steve feels his body crumble. The shaking must be even visible to everyone present in the courtroom. It will be impossible for him to get up and leave the witness box with even a modicum of dignity.

"The prosecution has any more questions for the witness? If they are more than one or two, we should perhaps postpone those questions until after lunch." The judge informs; her voice business-like.

"The prosecution has no more questions, Your Honour."

Steve knows Daniël is looking at him, but he can't look at Daniël. He can't bear the hurt on the face of his boy. Everything screams in pain.

"Can I go home, please? Danny?"

Then, suddenly, Daniël's arms are around him, and very soon Gael's too and they help him to the car whilst Matthew talks to the press.

"You're safe now, love. We'll go home first, you rest and then we'll talk. Gael offered to drive us home, because I can't. Honestly, I can't."

"I really don't know if I could have done this even half as well without breaking down much earlier," Gael says. "Matthew? I'll take Dan and Steve home. You update the gaffer about today?"

Matthew nods. "That's fine, lad. Dan? Take the day off tomorrow. With Degaré's permission, in case you're worried about that."

On the back seat Daniël takes Steve's hand, like he has done countless times. Steve uses his free hand to touch his lover's face. "Don't cry, Danny, please don't cry."

Chapter 29

On the bed, it is Steve holding Daniël, waiting until the silent tears have fallen. It hurts seeing his beloved boy this sad, but it's good to be needed, to be able to take care of him. Several ideas flash through his mind about what exactly makes Daniël this upset, but he can only hope it isn't because Dan thinks he had been, even if only on a subconscious level, interested in the man touching him up. That Steve had, without intention, been angry because their love had to be hidden from even Dan's parents like a shameful, dirty secret.

Daniël smiles through his tears, like he's wondering about Steve's thoughts, knowing him too well to not make an educated guess.

"That lawyer was manipulating the jury. Perhaps even the judge. Public opinion. I saw what he was trying to do and I can almost understand it. The facts are what they are, he can't change that, but he can try and make you look bad. It hurt me so much, seeing how he dragged you through the mud but I knew I had to keep myself from shouting out, because that would have made it only harder on you."

Steve kisses him softly on the lips. "I remembered the words you had written on that piece of paper. Those were the only important words in that courtroom. I think we have a lot to talk about, but not before we've had something decent to eat and drink. Please, Danny, can I spoil you a little? You always take such good care of me, now it's time to try and do the same for you. I can make tea and some nice sandwiches. I believe we have a few slices of roast left over from yesterday, so I don't have to use a carving knife. Would that be something?"

"That would be great. I love doing things for you, you know that, but I don't want to keep you from becoming independent again. I'll take a quick shower and I'll see you in the lounge in, say, about half an hour?" Daniël nuzzles Steve's neck. "I was so proud knowing that courageous man standing there is going to be my husband. And when you said you loved me, for the entire courtroom to hear, I wondered if even one of them really understood how lucky I am. Matthew and Gael perhaps. Must have cost them a lot to be there, but they were. The others have sent messages, phoned me, told me during the last training session they were thinking about us. And it's not just the players: many of the people working for the club as well. The girls told me lots of fans are letting us know how much they support us in thought. You know how the gaffer hated he couldn't be with us."

"I know. It means a lot to me. I hope they understand how much." Steve kisses Dan once more before he shoos him to the bathroom and goes to the kitchen himself to make sure they can eat lunch in half an hour.

It takes a bit of looking around in what's officially still his own kitchen to find where Dan keeps everything, but it feels good being able to contribute to their little household with something more than warm smiles and lots of kisses.

He tries not to think about the trial and the cross-examination and everything that will follow, because he wants to fully enjoy this moment of having overcome another obstacle. He concentrates on putting the kettle on and placing the teabags in the mugs, on buttering the slices of bread, on putting slices of cold meat on them and finishing it with a thin layer of honey mustard. Leave the green stuff for another time.

He fully appreciates how much time and effort it takes him to perform this undemanding task, and perhaps he should be angry about this because no one in court asked him about how this feels for a grown man, who was used to having his independence. Still, no honest concern and sympathy would change a single detail of the facts.

No, better he concentrate on making sure the tea doesn't get too strong.

◆

"I'm really hungry." Daniël takes a big bite of the first sandwich. "Nice."

Steve can't help but grin from ear to ear.

They eat and drink in amicable silence, their legs touching, content with the simple food and each other's company.

"They will get their jail time, those men, and …" Daniël starts. "No matter what that lawyer tried. But I bet we won't like the numbers. You didn't die; perhaps he even influenced how long they will be put away by making you look bad. But what punishment would ever be enough for what's been done to you? To us? One at a time in a room with me and the other boys for, let's say ten minutes? Letting them rot in a hole in the ground for the rest of their miserable lives? Money? This wasn't an accident, an emotional flash in the pan. Their defence lawyer tried to sell them off as decent fans with kids, being all shocked by the behaviour of one of their heroes, but they were out to hurt people long before you set even one foot into the Queen Elizabeth Park."

Steve nods and hums his encouragement.

"I know they won't get what they deserve and I have to live with that and I don't know how. I don't want hate and obsession with revenge dirtying our marriage, but there have been dreams I'm too ashamed to tell you about, because they gave me such vile pleasure. I saw them sitting there and I wondered how these men I had those dreams about could suddenly be that insignificant. Then I realised I had you beside me. If I would be allowed, I would kill them. They don't even have to suffer; I've seen enough of that in the past months. But I'm not, and so I have to leave them behind. But how do I do that?"

"I thought I would be trembling with fear, being confronted with my attackers. Instead I felt almost indifference. I wouldn't even have minded the cross examination all that much, I know there will always be people doubting my words, but I hated how that lawyer made me say things twisted into half-truths. He made me hurt you." Steve feels how he can't stop himself from digging the fingers of his right hand into Daniël's left thigh.

"He failed. I did hurt, so much, but not because I believed for even one second what he tried to make you say. So what if you had a few pints? I can imagine you being frustrated about how we had to hide all the time. I know I was. I wanted to introduce you to mum and dad, not keep my mouth shut about you for two days. Whether or not our relationship is sexually exclusive is between you and me and no one else. And even if you had been cruising, that still wouldn't be an excuse for what they did to you. It shouldn't have been about if you are a true saint of a victim, almost inhuman in perfection, but about the fact that a human being has been so brutally attacked he almost died. The rest of our lives will be influenced by what happened in that park. And the ones responsible for that need to be put away for as many years as the law allows." Daniël frowns. "You looked so lost and lonely and I needed to be with you, because I saw how much you needed me. It felt like I was abandoning you."

"It must have been excruciating for you, sitting there, watching."

"Your words felt like poison to me. No matter what I pretend, it would have hurt like mad if you had been there to look for sex with other men. And that was exactly what that lawyer was aiming for; making everyone doubt."

Steve closes his eyes for a moment to let the panic pass through his body.

"Please, don't think I doubted your love or your integrity for even a millisecond. But it still reminded me of how close I had been to losing you. And then it wouldn't have mattered for what reason you had been there, because you wouldn't have been able to tell me. I know you are your own man, but I don't want anyone but me seeing that look in your eyes when you're inside me, or hearing that soft moan right before you come, or knowing how your spunk tastes or how hard you get when you watch me getting on my hands and knees, begging for your fingers or your cock. I don't want to share you. I'm sorry."

"It will give me nothing but joy to reserve my body, or what is left of it, exclusively for you. But would it be fair to ask the same of you?"

Daniël huffs his indignation. "It has nothing to do with fair, or with morals, for that matter. Not even sure if I can explain it, but I lost whatever interest I might have had in other men. When you were still in the danger zone, I almost forgot I had a body myself. I ate and drank because they forced me. I slept because I couldn't keep myself awake. I was dying with you. But once it was clear I wouldn't lose you and I had to be patient until you were ready to wake up, I started to feel alive again."

Steve drinks the last of his tea. He touches Daniël's hand with his own.

"Nearly every single day you were in that hospital, I masturbated under the shower. Remembering us. Wanting you. Always wanting you. Not just sex. You. I couldn't have endured the touch of another man. Still can't. If anything, it has only become stronger. More absolute."

"You need me to make love to you?" Steve asks gently.

Daniël nods silently.

"Come to the bedroom then."

This time, he is the one taking the lead, thankful that Daniël allows himself to be cared for, to be pampered.

Steve kisses his lover, letting his hands travel all over his body at leisure. No part is more important than the other. "Please Danny, ask me want you want and let me decide if I'm able to give it to you?"

"Take me from behind?"

"Seeing you offering yourself to me in that position is definitely worth a little pain." Steve takes the bottle of lubricant from the small side table. "Open your legs as wide as possible."

The instruction isn't really needed, the preparations might just as well be minimal, but they both enjoy it too much to cut any corners. Dan wraps his fingers around his own erection, stroking slowly, teasing Steve to get the goods while they're hot.

"Hand me that pillow, please? Makes it a bit easier on my knees."

"You're comfortable? I can adjust my position to whatever is best for you. No trouble at all." Daniël kisses Steve before he turns his back to him and gets on his hands and knees. "This is okay?"

"More than okay. Perfect." Steve checks one more time with his finger to confirm his lover is indeed ready and presses the head of his cock against the pucker. He pauses.

"Don't tease me. Don't make me beg for it. Please …"

He's in, tight heat gripping him, taking his breath away. Happiness almost hurting more than the unwilling muscles of his legs and back. Than the bones and tendons that might never heal to their old perfection.

Daniël curves his back deeper to give as much access as possible, presses his shoulders against the mattress in full surrender. "Please, let me feel I belong to you. Everything is too much and I just want to be your boy, offering myself to my man."

Steve places one hand against Daniël's neck as a sign of gentle, accepting dominance. "You're mine, boy. And I am yours."

Then he allows instinct to take over.

Chapter 30

Days go by. Weeks are followed by other weeks. Whatever was left of the summer is now definitely gone. But in the greyness of autumn, the house they bought is slowly turning into something Steve hopes will become their home. But he isn't worried about it, because he can't imagine being anywhere with Daniël and not calling it a home.

Daniël plays a few matches on home ground and finally plays his first away game. Songs are being sung by the fans. Chants are being chanted. Nice ones and not-so-nice ones. They both try to take it all with a bit of humour and after a while, Steve is actually able to enjoy the game without being frightened and overwhelmed. Seeing Dan happy makes him happy.

Daniël scores his first goal of the season. His index fingers pointing at his lover and his big radiant smile mean the world to Steve. This moment is between the two of them, no matter how many eyes are watching.

"This one's for Steve," he will later see the boy say during the short interview at the end of the game, "just like any other goal I'll ever score. And since I'm a defender; like any goal for the opponent that didn't happen because I prevented it. Without Steve in the stands, I wouldn't be on the pitch."

The next day, there's an article in the Kinbridge Chronicle and it is Steve who reads it out loud to his visibly shy lover, his index finger leading him slowly through the rows of printed letters that make words that make sentences that make a story.

"There was this almost shocking moment when I could have sworn I saw Gavan himself play, though not necessarily in the way Borghart moved over the field. They are too different in style to ever be mistaken for the other. Gavan: the patient gentleman, always waiting for that one moment he was truly needed. Using his talent to read the opponent's intentions to make up for the speed he lacked. A calming influence during moments of panic. Borghart: the young dog, with an overload of energy. Fast and aggressive. Eager to keep Kinbridge Town's half of the pitch clean, but also hungry for more. 'Highly talented' and 'has a promising future' were the most common phrases used to describe him. No longer so, because what I have seen during the last matches is a mature defender

who stands his ground. A man focused on the job, like the noise surrounding him doesn't even touch him. And most likely it doesn't.

"When asking the Kinbridge Town manager about a possible transfer for Borghart, the answer is an almost impatient, 'Do I look like a fool to you?'

"It was a boy who left the pitch after the 1-0 defeat against Birmingham … and the boy returned a man."

Daniël's voice is soft and brittle. "But can I still be your boy? When I really need it?"

Steve gets on his feet and takes Dan in his arms. And that's answer enough.

◆

"Seems like you're starting to find your own place in this club again. Understand what I mean? No longer one of us, although you'll always be one of us, not one of the wags of course, never just one of the supporters," Gabrysz says after morning training.

They're having lunch and before work at the gym starts Steve has plenty of time for a chat with Gabrysz and Niko. From the corner of his eyes he sees Daniël cracking jokes with Kurt and Neil. It's good to see the boy laugh out loud.

He returns his attention to Gabrysz and Niko. "It's great going to the games now I know most fans, and not just our own, behave well. And the rest?" He shrugs. "There will always be the rest."

Gabrysz finishes his coffee. "True. You already have any idea about what you're going to do after all this? You are – were – one of the most intelligent defenders I've ever played with. I bet you saw how good Dan could become before you saw that other thing."

Steve's not sure if he understands the goalie's words, even if he knows exactly what the man is saying.

"When a footballer is too old or too injured to compete on this level, he's is still a young man, with thirty, forty, fifty years ahead of him."

"You believe I'll ever work again?"

"You know about football, you're clever, experienced and Dan's going to support you in everything you want to give a try …" Gabrysz shrugs. "It's none of my business."

"That's okay. And you're right about what you say, but I guess I'm still not bored with physio and trying to read the labels on cans and jars."

"In less than a month, you're going to be a married man," Niko says, finally joining the conversation. "Nervous?"

Steve doesn't miss the grateful look in Gabrysz's eyes.

"No ... yes. It's a bit more than three weeks, actually."

"And no matter how much you start with the intention to keep it simple and intimate, you end up with dozens of guests and they all need dinner and cake and a bit of music to dance to," Gabrysz teases.

"The part that's about Danny and me signing the marriage certificate is no problem at all, but it's all the rest that makes it so complicated, to be honest. We're getting married in Holland for obvious reasons, moving everyone back to Kinbridge for the party and, hopefully, getting a bit of rest in between. You bet we gratefully accepted the offer of the Goldmans to use their private jet during two days. And that's including crew members and any costs for fuel, airport fees and what have you. Makes it all a lot easier. They're very generous people who care a lot about the club."

Both Niko and Gabrysz nod their approval.

Steve sighs. "Take it from me, without Danny I wouldn't have a clue how to even get married ... that sounds a bit weird."

"That's just nerves. I bet the press has shown interest too, to make it even more complicated. Two footballers of the same club getting married to each other and all." Gabrysz munches on a piece of bread he used to wipe up some sauce.

"If we could, we would ignore it. Had we both been with a woman, we would have gotten away with it, too. But now ..." Steve sighs. "There's going to be an interview a week before the wedding. That's being filmed at my place; makes it a bit more informal and personal. We're going to move to our new home anyway. It will be free for distribution on TV and internet, under certain conditions. And we decided to provide photos from the day but, just like with the interview, not to sell any exclusive rights. They can choose whatever photos they want and place them wherever they please. We're just asking everyone to donate whatever they can miss to a charity of their choice. We hope that will be enough. "

"Clever." Niko frowns in thought. "Pity some people have to make such a fuss about what in the end is nothing more than two people liking each other enough to say a few words, sign a contract and celebrate it with family and friends."

"I hope the two of you get some peace and quiet after that. You sure deserve it. Going on honeymoon?" Gabrysz asks.

"Gael offered the use of his family's cottage in Spain, it's got a private beach and all, but we decided to get used to our new home. We would have to travel outside Europe to get any real privacy and in the end, I just want to be with Dan."

Gabrysz grins. "I bet."

"Don't tease the poor guy," Niko laughs. "He's getting as red in the face as Levee when he's having trouble with the ref. Oh, hi Dan. Your fella just told us about how you're going to deal with the press when you get married. Sounds like a sensible solution."

Dan smiles, ruffles Steve's hair, takes a seat and joins them. "I hate it that we can't keep it as private as we would prefer. But I'm not stupid enough to pretend that it isn't what it is. At least this way we have some say in the whole matter. But I would feel dirty getting any money out of it. Or for anyone else earning even a penny because of what happened to Steve, for that matter. Wouldn't be fair on you guys, too."

"How so?" Gabrysz asks.

"The first months when I was with Steve in the hospital day and night, you had to put up with everything they were throwing at you. And it wasn't all nice."

Steve looks at Daniël, supporting him with a little nod and a smile.

Gabrysz shrugs. "Not all, no."

"You know how creative the fans can be with their chants when they think a player has done something they don't agree with. The club is sacred and they make sure you'll never forget it. But we were pleasantly surprised, too," Niko says, continuing on from Gabrysz' words. "It took them less than a week to make the first banner to support the two of you."

Daniël nods. "I remember having seen the photos on the Internet, yes. Did me good. But still, you can't tell me everyone on the stands was being nice and polite about it."

"But exactly when is there a match where everyone's nice and polite? I bet it would be a boring one, too." Gabrysz gets up. "The gaffer's getting even less smiley than usual. So I guess he wants us to get some work done. You're going to the gym, too, Steve?"

"Yeah, worked on my balance this morning with one of the guys from physio and this afternoon it's all about getting my leg muscles stronger." Steve accepts Dan's supporting hand as a matter of fact. The time anyone even looked up because they're touching each other for whatever reason has long passed.

"Still no news about the result of the trial? Does it always take this long?" Gabrysz asks while they walk to the gym.

"Perhaps it has to do with the media attention?" Daniël shakes his head. "It's not like I'll get what I want, is it? We're happy as it is Steve didn't have to testify again."

"Nasty business that must have been, from what Gael told me. Making an honest man sound like a liar by putting words in his mouth in the hope some murderous thugs get away with a slap on the wrist." Gabrysz shakes his head. "What a sad way to make your money."

"Criminals have the right to be legally represented too. But I still hope they get locked up with the keys thrown away," Niko says, giving his view on the matter.

"I'm sorry, guys, bringing it up again," Gabrysz apologises while entering the gym.

Steve puts his hand on the goalie's shoulder. "That's okay. It's not going away by pretending it isn't there."

"Still …" Gabrysz trails off and doesn't finish the rest of his sentence. "Have fun on the bike."

"First bike, then a round of treadmill for added fun," Steve pretends to complain, but he's almost okay with it. He's trying to make peace with the limitations that remind him what he has lost every single time he's doing any kind of exercise, while at the same time trying to push his body and mind a little bit further. He knows he will never be near the same level as any of the others, but it doesn't stop him from enjoying his own progress. And he certainly enjoys Daniël's flirty, admiring looks when they use two bikes next to each other.

"Going to take a look at our home later? They promised the bathroom would be finished and some furniture should have been delivered today. Please help me to remember that tomorrow we must get our suits fitted again to see if they need any final adjustments. I've told the caterer we're happy with the food she suggested. And I think I forgot to tell you the contract on my apartment expires next week, so I have to move some of the stuff to our new place and ask a charity to get the rest. I doubt I've been there even half a dozen times in the last couple of months," Daniël says while working the pedals.

"I would love to see our home. I can't wait till we live there."

"You're going to be thrilled with the main bathroom," Daniël promises.

And when he brought him to their home later that day, Steve acknowledges that Daniël was right.

"See, heated floor, non-slippery too. Handles so you don't have to be afraid of falling. Double washbasin of course. Chair. Cabinet. Extra roomy shower with corner bench. There's a shower head fitted in the ceiling and it's huge. And there are adjustable shower-heads left and right, especially for massage. I thought you might like that when you're in pain. I'm very happy with the sunken bath. Fits both of us easily." He presses his lips against Steve's, teases his tongue in.

"I'm determined that the first time we make love in this house will be on our wedding night …" Suggestion is heavy in every word.

Steve grins. "What about we take a quick look at the rest, make a trip to the take-away pizzeria and dirty the sheets at *my* apartment with pizza and sex?"

"I knew there was a reason I wanted to marry you apart from the fact that you're sexy and gorgeous and clever and … come on, I've already seen the dining room stuff and I couldn't find anything wrong with it; same with the couch and the recliner. As far as I'm concerned, we're done here and I'm totally ready for pizza and sex."

Chapter 31

"You're happy with how the interview turned out?" Steve asks Daniël after his lover has put away the remote control.

"What interview? I couldn't keep my eyes away from that good-looking fella. I mean the one with neat brown hair and gentle brown eyes and the best cheekbones ever and a smile to die for. Who also happens to be the one who's going to be my husband in less than a week?"

"So I wasn't the only one a bit distracted, though in my case it was by a pretty, freckled boy …" Steve jokes. "But seriously, did you see what I saw?"

Daniël's smile is answer enough in itself, but the words don't hurt exactly either. "We look like we're totally doing the right thing. We already know that, of course, but it's so visible. I mean, man, we're going to Holland in a few days. There's more stuff to do than we have time for, and that's without the details that make us not exactly the average marrying couple. And all I see is two guys being happy. You know what? I know exactly why. No matter what goes wrong on the day, and some things will go wrong, you'll be at my side. It's about you being with me. About you not having been taken away from me."

Steve kisses him on the cheek. "We have each other. Family and friends will be with us. Seems plenty enough for me."

Daniël takes the remote from the table. "Want to watch again? I want to hear what we were actually saying."

They sit on the couch, happily leaning against each other.

They hear the interviewer's male voice. *Love at first sight?*

Steve is the first to answer. "No. But I noticed him sure enough. Just took me a bit to notice something else about the boy except his talent and willingness to work hard and learn. Lightning never strikes with me in these matters."

"Love before first sight." Daniël, looking in Steve's direction. "Never told you that, did I? Yeah, I had a bit of a crush on you when I was a kid. I thought you were one of the best defenders in English football. Good looking guy too. Never could have dreamed …"

Was it that Steve was already playing for Kinbridge Town the reason you came to this city? Or one of the reasons?

Daniël burst out laughing. "Of course not. Arnaud Degaré asked me, he offered a decent price and what young player wouldn't want to be in a team managed by him? Being on the same pitch with players like Kirkby, Levee, Lain, Dominguez, Moreschi, Miller, Jaworski? Gavan?"

But still, it couldn't have been easy to discover you had fallen for a team-mate, the football world being what it is. What made you decide to act on those feelings? Steve?

"I didn't act on them. I felt what I felt and that was it. No reason to bother Dan with it."

So I gather you took the first step, Daniël?

"Well, yeah, someone had to do it." Daniël grins.

What about the risks?

"What risks? With Steve, the sweetest, most decent man you could ever meet? One of the most private ones as well. Nah, I knew even if he wouldn't have felt the same about me, I would still be in safe hands with him."

Obviously the feelings were reciprocated. And then the secret truly began?

They both nod in agreement.

You want to share a few words about that time with us?

"I'm not even sure there's much to tell. We never really talked about it. It was all so new and we hardly understood what was happening to us. We had just fallen in love and simply being together whenever we had the opportunity was enough. We weren't ready to talk about serious stuff. And by the time we started to think about a future that might perhaps include each other, I walked into that park. We weren't even aware yet that we both wanted the same thing." Steve shrugs. "Six months. That was all. Six months of sweet secrets and innocence. How could we have known?"

Daniël's hand seeking Steve's.

"I still can't walk any distance outside home without crutches, I'm re-learning to read and write. Some other stuff I won't bore you with. And you hear how I talk. The thinking part of my brain is mostly fine, although I need a bit more time with complex situations. Getting the words from my mind to your ears, now that's something else."

You're remarkably calm about your experiences.

"I'm trying to hang on to the remains of my human dignity, I guess." Steve smiles ruefully. "I can't talk about what happened in that park. I'm willing, but I'm not able to. I'm sorry."

I'm sure everyone understands. But Daniël was with you when you woke up, wasn't he? He never left your side at the hospital?

"He even bribed the hospital to let him stay. And we have nothing but praise for the staff. They were wonderful, without exception."

"I wasn't alone, not even when my parents had to return to Holland. Every single day, at least one of the boys or Arnaud Degaré visited us. Didn't matter that I hardly said a word to them, hardly even looked at them: they were there."

Do I understand correctly not one of the team, or the manager, actually has any problem with you two being together? About having gay team-mates?

Daniël shakes his head. "Whoever said that? People still have their opinions, their feelings about it. And why shouldn't they? It's not a popularity contest. There are a bit less than thirty first team players. You think we're all best mates?"

Still, some call it the last big taboo in professional football. There are always rumours, some make bold statements without ever naming names, but you were the first to sit at a press conference, look straight into the camera and say, "The man, who's been found nearly beaten to death, is my lover." Weren't you afraid for your career?

"Yeah, Steve was still fighting for his life while I held that press conference, so naturally my main concern was if I would still be worth a couple of million on the transfer market. Or even better: I do hope the other guys still like me now they know I'm queer. And please don't let the fans make nasty chants about me. Love is a nice bit of extra, but reputation is everything for a real man. Is that it?"

I can imagine what happened to Steve sets your priorities straight. You expected to return to active football? And you, Steve, you still had any hope at some point?

Steve shakes his head. "By the time they were done breaking the bones in both my legs, I had drawn my conclusions. But yes, I never stopped hoping Daniël would be accepted back. Someone with his talent and work ethic belongs in this sport."

Daniël says, "I can't imagine our manager being thrilled about what had happened. But there was no way around it. Suddenly, Kinbridge Town was the club with the gay couple. Degaré deserves everyone's admiration for how he dealt with the pressure. He kept us a team. And a strong one, too, if you look at the table."

Continue, please.

"It's not just about an openly gay guy playing for the Premier League, is it? About what happens in the dressing room and if you can still celebrate a goal by jumping into another man's arms, or about fans singing nasty songs. This, with us, makes everyone nervous, because most people can deal with closet cases having their dirty little secret and a trophy wife and a couple of kids so no one asks any questions. If Steve had been beaten to death in the Queen Elizabeth Park, a closeted gay man cruising for anonymous sex, it would have been easier for a lot of people, I bet. But two men in a committed relationship, planning to get married? Footballers? Professionals? On this level? And they didn't even struggle with their sexuality? How did that ever happen?"

Well, how did that happen?

"I fell in love with this man and now I can't imagine my life without him. I would have given up playing football on a professional level for him without a second thought, but it seems I'm a very lucky guy and I can have both."

I have to ask this. I'm under strict orders from the missus. Who proposed?

Steve starts to laugh. "I don't think there even was a proper one. Danny mentioned certain things, like sharing a life and growing old together, I asked him if he meant what I thought he meant and before we knew it, we were engaged."

Then there's the sound of the interviewer chuckling. *It happens to the best of men. But let us continue. How did the fans react? Not just when they heard about the upcoming wedding, but in general? You are in the middle of quite a storm. How are you experiencing it all?*

"The club's been great in this too. They even hired two very efficient ladies to deal with the thousands and thousands of reactions, most of which are very friendly and supportive. To be honest, during the first few days I was too focused on Steve to be aware of the outside world. But after a while, I started to listen to the stories the other lads told me when they visited us in the hospital. Kinbridge Town has fans to be proud of."

"And not just our own club's players and fans," Steve adds.

"So many players, fans and officials took the trouble to send us a few words of encouragement and support. There were also players and fans who told me they thought it was unwise of me to even try and continue my career as a professional footballer, but still wanted us to know that what happened to Steve was unacceptable. It reminded us there are still good people on this earth. And believe me, I really needed to be reminded of that."

Steve?

"I was worried for a long time whether Dan would still be welcome, not just with our own team, but also with our fans, with our opponents and their fans."

I can imagine the first away game being quite stressful.

"You have no idea. It felt strangely good to hear Dan getting booed because he made a brutal tackle on their striker and the ref didn't show him red. I knew then for certain he had been accepted back. They hated him for he did, not for what he is. They were right, too: it was a nasty foul."

You two talk shop often? Or is that still too painful?

"It's coming back slowly. I really enjoy watching the matches again, giving a few tips here and there, although Dan never listens …"

"Now, that's not true. He was so good at what he did, and I'm just beginning to learn."

"I'm only teasing. I'm so proud of him. He's a born defender; he belongs on the pitch, playing matches against strong teams. It would be downright wrong if fans had to miss the beauty of seeing him play for no other reason than that he loves me."

"It wouldn't mean a thing without Steve. Don't get me wrong, I love this sport and I work my arse off to earn my place in the first team, but if anyone thinks football's worth living with regret for the rest of my life …"

You sound angry.

"I am angry. The reason Steve walked into that park was perhaps worse than if he actually had been picking up men. That's simply doing something stupid for private reasons. And now, tell me, who am I going to blame for what happened to him? The six men literally trying to kick Steve to death, and almost succeeding too, appeared in a Crown court and I have enough faith in the system to believe they'll get their punishment. But who will name all the others bearing at least part of the responsibility? Who's going stand up and say: I am part of this. I allowed it to happen through my silence and my cowardice and my lack of imagination, or because it was easier to hide behind the backs of a minority of loud-mouthed bigots than to face my own demons." Daniël's lips are a straight line. "I allowed it to happen."

A complex matter …

Daniël is now looking straight at the camera. "In fact, it couldn't be simpler." Touching the part of his arm where he knows his tattoo to be, he says, "*Cor aut mors*. The heart or death."

Steve?

"I'm still here, and I know the sole reason why."

A few more questions about the wedding, the next away game against Wolves and that's the end of the interview.

"I think we did pretty well." Daniël gives his verdict.

"I think so too." Steve nods happily. He can't deny the man being interviewed isn't the man he was a year ago, but there's no denying either that he made some real progress since the press conference at the Graces. Not so much in his ability to speak like he used to, he isn't blind or deaf to the facts, but in his ability to look at himself with some sort of kindness and acceptance. Even if he will never be able to look at himself with Daniël's unconditional love, it's still progress.

But there isn't enough time to contemplate much of anything, because within a week they'll getting married and move into their new home. They started to realise how impractical their romantic idea of moving into their joint home on their wedding night had been, with having to make the journey from apartment to house over and over again during the past weeks; with stuff that should be in one place but turned out to be in the other. Even with all of the old furniture given away to charity, clothes, personal belongings and what seemed to be dozens and dozens of items, including everything Daniël had taken from his own apartment to Steve's, still had to be moved.

"I don't care about practical. Our first night in our real home will be as an official couple, even if we have to use a private jet to get from one country to the other on the day." Daniël kisses Steve, holding him in his arms. "We can sleep and have sex comfortably, eat at a table, take a bath, make tea, prepare a meal: what more could a man possibly want?"

Steve kisses him back. "Nan and mum would have loved you so much. I know I don't talk often about them, but they live in my heart, I know they're safe there."

"You miss them? And I'm not really asking a question."

"I know. And yes, I do miss them terribly. But I also know I'm not without family on my wedding day, even though none of them are related to me by blood or will be by law until we have signed the marriage certificate and spoken our vows."

"Is it strange for me to feel the same?"

"Not strange, just one of the many reasons I love you." Steve kisses Daniël again, slow and seductive. "I know we don't have much time, but …"

"What do you mean no time? We have all the time in the world."

Chapter 32

Three days before the wedding, Daniël reads the formal letter to Steve about the sentencing of the attackers. Nine years is a meaningless number. But any number would be just as meaningless. So Daniël puts the letter away and scans the papers of that morning without comment.

◆

Steve's apartment is strangely empty of most things that are personal to him and Daniël. Books, music, movies, photos, almost all their clothes, and the odds and ends: it's all moved from where they are to where they are going to be. Their house in Hollycroft looks like it's actually a place where real people might live very soon. But they still have a couch to sit on and a bed to sleep in, an electric kettle to make a cup of tea, so Steve wouldn't call it uncomfortable. Perhaps it can best be described as being a guest in your own home. His wedding suit hangs in a nearly empty closet, next to Daniël's, two pairs of shoes standing underneath it. It's one of the few items they will carefully pack for their trip to Holland. After that, he won't come back to this place because a home is waiting for him. A home and a husband.

◆

The flight to Rotterdam in the Goldman private jet the day before the wedding is extremely comfortable. Steve feels a bit awkward about this kind of extravagance until Daniël reminds him it's not polite to not enjoy this generous gift. "I can't imagine anything being too good for you. And we don't want you tired from the journey on our big day. After all, if I have any say in this, you'll never have to do this again in your life, except for our anniversaries, of course. And we'll have lots of anniversaries … just teasing you, love."

Daniël spends the night at his parents'. It's silly beyond words, considering that he left his parental home years ago, but it feels right and proper that he spend his last hours as an official bachelor in the folds of his family. He insists on Steve also not being alone, and it's Matthew who readily volunteers to stay the night at the small apartment that Daniël kept when he moved to Kinbridge because he saw little benefit in selling the debt free property and it never hurts to have something to go back to. He hasn't gone back in more than a year, obviously, and the little Dutch hideaway never got used.

Just for the fun of it, a bunch of the other guys decide to make a quick, and very loud, appearance to bemoan Steve's last night as a free man. No stag night? That's not an excuse.

They're all gone now, back to the hotel in Rotterdam to get some sleep before the big day; Francesco and Dag and Neil and Niko and Gabrysz and the others. Only Matthew and Gael have stayed behind, and Gael is standing in the doorway to get his coat too. Dallying.

"You might just as well stay the night," Steve says and he knows he has gone too far as soon as the words leave his mouth.

But Gael sits down again, without saying anything, being far too intelligent, too insightful to not understand what Steve is implying.

Matthew doesn't react at all, not even when Gael takes his mobile and calls Doncia to tell her he will spend the night at Daniël's apartment. "She's fine with it; the girls are having a chick flick night anyway. I'll have to get up early, to get to the hotel and change."

"That's okay, lad." Matthew sounds like he has said those exact words dozens of times.

For a long moment, the three of them are sitting rigidly, separated by more than actual space. In silence. Matthew and Gael are next to each other on the two seater couch, stiffened in their socially acceptable distance.

Then, suddenly, Gael smiles and stretches his hand out to Matthew to touch his arm.

Steve can't help but notice how fragile they look.

"You've known for a long time, haven't you?" Matthew asks.

Steve nods. "When I started to recognise human voices again, even before I understood what was actually being said. But it was never about what you said anyway. I would never have guessed if …"

"No one knows. Not even she does." Gael moves his fingers a few millimetres over Matthew's arm. "She knows everything about me, but not this. And so she knows nothing."

"On some days, the silence weighed so heavily it felt like it would kill all love," Steve says. "I didn't even get it on a rational level at that time. I thought it was how it was supposed to be. That love doesn't need to be recognised by others to stay alive. That it was all between Danny and me and no one else."

"And now you know the truth." Gael shrugs.

"We were afraid to express our true feelings and thoughts in words, not only to the outside world, but also to each other. To face the truth about what was happening between us. As long as we didn't talk about it, it wasn't there. And still he sat with me and waited and never left me ..." Steve's voice trails off. "You want me to ask you how long? The two of you, I mean."

Matthew frowns, and then a smile breaks through. "Right from the start. I had no idea, of course. Didn't want to know either. One day, after months, he asked me a question. One single question."

"You do realise we are in love with each other?" Gael says softly, his hand now finally touching Matthew's. "And then you said ..."

"Fuck, we're in deep shit."

"And you gave me our first kiss."

It's as if there's a veil being lifted from their faces. A mask has been taken down. He has just as few illusions as them about tomorrow, about their near future, but at least this can't be taken away from them. Their love has been witnessed.

Matthew sighs deeply. "So, that's it. You've seen it. Now you know, and Daniël, of course. No secrets between you the two of you, I understand."

"I didn't tell him, he discovered it on his own."

Matthew frowns. "We're not getting obvious, are we?"

"I doubt it. No, Daniël became very aware of the people around him because of what happened with Steve," Gael reassures him.

"It must be hard for you, tomorrow." Steve almost regrets saying the words.

"It's not about us, but about you and Dan," Matthew reacts a bit too fast. "You think this started the night you were brought into the hospital?

Or when the gaffer introduced me to Gael? I've known about that part of myself since I was a boy. I simply thought it didn't matter because only football mattered. And girls were okay, too, in a way. She's a good girl, can't blame her for doing anything wrong. I just never reckoned with love." He shrugs helplessly. "During some games I hope and pray some big defender, compensating for his lack of talent with brute force, stomps on my ankle and it's over and done with. And this sport and this club mean so much to me …"

Thus far no mentioning of his family …

"I won't ever stop being a father, that's what I'll always be. My marriage? It couldn't be saved on the wedding day itself; it won't ever be more than it is, even if I stayed with her until the day one of us dies. Even if Gael moved to another club and we never saw see each other again. Because Gael cannot be undone."

Gael's hand is now fully resting into Matthew's. "I guess I can repeat Matthew's words about always being a father and no longer being a true partner to the mother of my son. If I ever was. And yes, it will be hard tomorrow, but also wonderful and about hope and love. Without you and Dan, I'm not even sure there would still be an us."

Matthew continues. "But now, no matter how hard it gets on some days, we remember what the two of you went through and we know we can deal with whatever we have to deal with. I just wish it could be done without hurting the people we care about. But they're going to be hurt anyway. Doesn't matter what choice we make in the end."

We, Steve hears, not I, we.

"I know we're not ready yet to follow you guys' footsteps but yeah, it means a lot to us, you and Dan. We're happy to be there, tomorrow." Matthew smile is sad, but genuine. "Dan told me to make sure you got to bed early and I don't want that boy to get angry at me. He's a bit protective of you."

Gael laughs. "I bet his mum had to take away his mobile to make sure he's not going to text you every five minutes. But we'll keep you from having contact until you see each other before the registrar."

"What about I make you guys a last cup of tea? A small snack perhaps? Could one of you walk with me to the kitchen to carry the tray? I'm afraid I'll need some help tomorrow with shaving and the buttons of my shirt.

Those tiny things take me ages. Oh, and the tie as well. Complicated stuff is still, well, complicated."

"You're okay with me shaving and buttoning up this handsome guy?" Matthew jokes to Gael.

"I'm not worried one bit. That man is blind to every bloke except one."

"And there's only one for me." Matthew's lips curve upwards. "We get you dressed up in time so your fella can be all proud on the big day. And no, I won't forget the ring."

They drink tea, talking about everything and nothing. Matthew leans against Gael, smiling and looking very relaxed, like for a moment he has let his guard down. Gael looks so happy it has to hurt. They make a striking couple, Steve can't help but notice.

"Thank you, for this. For telling me to stay," Gael says.

"You could have limited the contact with Dan and me to the bare minimum. I would have understood it, and even now I think it would have been the sensible thing to do, but you proved to be true friends. You guys would be wise to avoid our home for the next two weeks or so, but after that, you're more than welcome. And I know I speak for Danny as well." Steve gets up. "The alarm is set at half past six. Is that early enough for you, Gael? The wedding starts at half past ten."

"No problem."

"You get to choose, but I'm afraid the beds in both bedrooms are a bit narrow …"

"And why exactly is that a problem?" Matthew grins dirtily at Gael.

"Good question. Dan had been planning to get a double last year … but … yeah … His mother told me the beds have been freshly made yesterday, and there are towels and all, so …"

Matthew chuckles. "You're going to get married tomorrow and you blush like a virgin."

"I'm so not going to tell you there's an unopened bottle of lube in the bathroom cupboard. That'll teach you to make fun of me." Steve winks. "You have a good night, boys and thank you again for being there for Dan, and for me, all those months."

Sleep comes easily. Waking up is a joy, knowing his beloved boy will be waiting for him in a few hours. He takes a quick shower, makes tea and coffee, makes some toast and remembers there's no way he's able to get the tray into the room, where Matthew and Gael are still sleeping, without making a terrible mess.

"Well, if breakfast can't come to the boys, the boys will have to come to the coffee and toast." And he knocks softly on the door and peeks around the corner.

Gael is clearly awake, holding a still sleeping Matthew, who's resting his head against the naked chest of his lover. The look in Matthew's eyes when he wakes up says more than all the words he could possibly say in any of the languages he speaks with reasonable fluency.

"It's time," Steve says, as gently as possible, as if he's afraid to damage something so fragile it doesn't even need to be touched to break into countless fragments.

He leaves them their privacy to start the day in the way and manner they prefer or need, and sits down for a bit with a cup of coffee and a piece of buttered toast. In less than four hours, he will stand next to Daniël and they will make their formal promise to each other, witnessed by the people who care about them. Perhaps he should be nervous and full of last minute doubts, but he isn't. He knows where he belongs and that's all he needs to know.

"Looking forward to seeing your fella?" Gael asks. He has already showered and dressed. "I'll have a cup of coffee and some toast and I'm on my way. Need to change into my best suit and all."

Less than ten minutes later, he's on his way.

"Traffic can be a bother at this hour, Dan told me, but he'll make it on time for the ceremony. I'm not going to ask if you're nervous, because I know you're not." Matthew munches on a piece of toast with Marmite. "I had no idea the Dutch eat this stuff, too. Dan hates it. Never mind. Ready for your shave, the suit and everything else?'

Steve gratefully offers himself into the tender care of his no-longer-and-yet-still captain.

Yeah, he's ready.

Chapter 33

Give up requesting me to go away from you, or to go back without you: for where you go I will go; and where you take your rest I will take my rest; your people will be my people and your God my God. Whenever death comes to you, death will come to me, and there will be my last resting-place.

The registrar talks about how they have lived through the full meaning of those words so often used in so many ceremonies of commitment, how their experiences had made it possible for them to make their promise to each other on this day. How their love had changed from an overwhelming emotion to a rule to live by. And how that love had reached beyond the closed intimacy of their own existence.

"Hey gorgeous," Daniël had greeted him half an hour before the ceremony. "You look ... I mean ... And here I am, thinking I couldn't be more in love with you than I already was."

Arm in arm they had walked over the red carpet of the wedding room in the old town hall, through rows of friends and family; slowly, but Steve without his crutches. Daniël being so breathtakingly beautiful, so radiant in his joy, that it took Steve a few moments to notice how strikingly handsome he looked in his suit. It took him even longer to become fully aware of his surroundings, with the classic dark blue and gold wallpaper and the wainscoting, the bouquet of red and white roses on the table, the chairs with blue velour seat and back, the dark purple robe of the registrar, the registrar herself, a woman with short grey hair and a kind face, and most important of all the faces of friends and family.

The registrar talks about how they had gone from a hidden life in utter silence to one that can be supported and carried by the people around them, because they are known to those who matter to them. How their love had a chance to mature and how they had an opportunity to become familiar with the everyday practice of a committed bond, with all its highs and lows.

He had seen how Matthew greeted Gael, masks fully in place again, but his lips forming soundless words. "One day, love ..."

"Steve and Daniël, we have now come to the official part. May I invite you both to stand up and take each other's right hand?"

Daniël helps him up from his chair and support him until he finds his balance.

There's a short bout of laughter when they have a bit of trouble deciding exactly which hand is their right one.

The registrar smiles brightly and gives a short nod. "Gentlemen?"

His right hand safe and warm in Daniël's.

"Daniël Borghart, *verklaart u aan te nemen tot uw wettige echtgenoot, Steve Aidan Gavan, en belooft u getrouw alle plichten te vervullen die de wet aan de huwelijkse staat verbindt? Wat is daarop uw antwoord?* "

No a wavering in his voice. Clear as anything. "*Ja.*"

"Steve Aidan Gavan, *verklaart u aan te nemen tot uw wettige echtgenoot, Daniël Borghart, en belooft u getrouw alle plichten te vervullen die de wet aan de huwelijkse staat verbindt? Wat is daarop uw antwoord?* I repeat in English, Steve Aidan Gavan, do you declare to accept as your lawful wedded spouse, Daniël Borghart, and do you promise to faithfully fulfil all duties that the marriage law asks of you? What is your answer?"

The whole universe lives in the eyes of his beloved. He didn't leave it behind when he returned from death to life. It had been there all along.

"I do. I mean, *ja.*"

"*Dan verklaar ik als ambtenaar van de Burgerlijke Stand van de gemeente Schiedam dat u door het huwelijk aan elkaar bent verbonden.* As registrar of the municipality of Schiedam I declare you joined by marriage."

On the registrar's cue, both Daniël's father and Matthew hand them each a ring. On the inside, each other's name and the date of the wedding have been engraved. On the outside of the otherwise unadorned golden ring, reads the inscription: my lover, my friend.

"May I invite the young couple and Daniël's father and Mr Kirkby to sign the register to bring the official part of this morning to a conclusion?" The registrar gestures at the table with a leather bound book and two pens.

No, the hours of hard work are not forgotten when Steve signs the single most important document of his life. There's too much joy for that.

The face of the registrar reflects their happiness. "It is both my pleasure and honour to congratulate you on your marriage. It's a good custom for a couple to share their first kiss as a married couple at this very moment."

He feels Daniël's arms around him, his lips pressing against his own, tongue teasing for a short moment.

Then there is laughter and catcalls and a teary mum and just about every female between sixteen and eighty going on about how romantic it is and how cute the grooms look.

"Welcome into the family," Daniël's father says and he embraces Steve. There's genuine acceptance in his and his wife's eyes. "One look at my son's face was all I needed to know you two made the best possible decision. Take good care of each other."

"I will do anything to make him happy because he makes me so happy," Steve promises.

"That's easy," Daniël cuts in, "He's here, with me, that's enough for me. Everything else is a nice extra."

◆

The trip back to Kinbridge gives Steve an opportunity to rest for a while. It's still several hours before dinner and the wedding party. Ample time to give their guests the chance to get there by specially chartered plane and have an opportunity to freshen up and change into evening dress in the hotel rooms reserved for them. The idea to provide photos and a video of the day and distribute them freely seems to have worked quite well. Of course, there had been around a dozen of photographers when they left the town hall, and he did see several mobile phones with a camera function being held up by curious 'wedding watchers' but he guesses that's an unavoidable sign of the times.

"Nice, isn't it, having a moment alone, with just the two of us? What a luxury, this private jet. I could actually get used to it," Daniël says with a chuckle. "Just kidding."

Steve rests his head against his husband's shoulder. He actually likes that word: husband. It has a solid, old-fashioned sound to it. It's mature and stable. Perhaps he might not be suitable boyfriend material, but being a husband works pretty well for him. "Don't laugh, but I have this feeling I did something very right today."

But Daniël does laugh. "Because that's what you did. The best thing you could ever do, in fact. You have any idea how proud I am to be married to you? If nothing good is going to happen to me ever again, I'll still maintain I'm the luckiest man in this world."

"But many good things will happen to you." Steve kisses him.

"I know, love, I know." Daniël grins like a naughty little boy.

Steve chuckles in understanding. "You're thinking about the wedding night ..."

"And you're not?" Dan teases, turning his head to steal another kiss.

◆

The rest of the day flows by like the proverbial dream. The food is near enough to perfection, the staff of the family-owned hotel they reserved for their reception and party couldn't be more helpful or friendly. The speeches are suitably embarrassing and actually almost funny. The cake is even decorated with two little grooms. "That's Dan and Steve," sixteen year old Naomi giggles. "Look, they even have different hair and the Dan doll is a little bit taller than the Steve doll. That's so cute." And Daniël winks at his little sister.

With Daniël's arms firmly around him for support Steve shuffles happily to the slowest love song the DJ could find in her collection for the first dance of the night. Then the sign is given that the floor is free for everyone to have fun. The music invites the guests to dance and so they all dance, even the ones who think they really shouldn't. But what do aesthetics and knowing the right moves matter when love and pleasure are sometimes really all you need? So when Francesco and Dag give a grinding demonstration of epic proportion, it's their girlfriends who shout the loudest encouragements. And who would hold it against Daniël's aunts when they are more than happy to give a crash course in ballroom dancing for the lovely young colleagues of their nephew? Spotty teenagers get dragged right to the middle of the dance floor. Neither do individuals above a certain age get spared. Today, all dance. Today, no one's too young, too old, too fat or too ugly.

And of course, Steve can't let the evening pass without a dance with his brand-new sister in law. That is to say, he's practically standing still and Naomi twirls around him on what she calls "the best song ever." He doesn't recognise it.

"My brother has a good taste in men," Naomi grins mischievously.

"Can't be as good as mine. But, and don't tell anyone I told you, see that handsome guy standing next to our first goalie? He's seventeen, he plays for our youth team and I heard from a reliable source he thinks you're cute."

"Really? You're not making fun of me?"

"You can ask around, and they will all tell you I'm the boring one. I never play pranks on anyone. I wouldn't know how. By the way, he's a good dancer too ..."

And off she goes, making a beeline for the cute boy.

"She adores you, you know that?" Daniël tactfully supports him towards his chair.

It makes Steve blush. "I've been that age, too."

A large part of the evening is spent talking with their guests. Thanking them for being there, for their gifts, hearing advice from the married and might- just-as-well- be-married guys, only to be told exactly the opposite from their wives and girlfriends.

"I've never seen my son this happy. I wish you had been with him when he fetched us from the airport, last year. It was all so needless. But what can I say? Life so often plays funny tricks on us all." For a moment, Daniël's mother lays her hand on Steve's arm. "You do realise you are family now? I know of course I'm not your mother, and you don't need one at your age, but ... you understand what I mean?"

"It takes a bit of time, but I'm getting there."

"Good. You have to excuse me, sweetheart, I promised a chat with Nat, Bronia and the others, over there at the girl's table. And Emma and Jane are such lovely ladies; I really should invite them for a trip to Rotterdam."

Steve sits alone for a brief moment, simply enjoying looking at the dancers.

"This chair is free?"

"For the gaffer? Always."

"You can have him all to yourself for a week. After that, I want him back in one piece, training for the next match." That's Arnaud Degaré: always on the job.

"You're definitely thinking about keeping him?"

"I have to consider the competition and the matches we have to win, the composition of rest of the team of course. I brought this club into the top half of the table, but I'm not fully happy yet because I know there is more in it for us. It would be illogical to let him go at this moment. Him and Neil, that defenders partnership could get interesting in the not too far future, when Niko is saying his goodbyes to us and Anthony might need to be rested now and again."

"Because he's good? Not out of pity?" He just has to ask it.

Degaré frowns. "When do I ever have pity for anyone as a manager?"

"That's true. I assume I will be formally released from the club at the next window?"

An affirmative nod.

"Very decent; the club kept me on the payroll all those months. They must have known pretty early on I wouldn't come back. But I had this feeling, before … before … that you would have put me in the window anyway."

Another nod.

They sit in silence for a few seconds. Then Steve looks up and smiles. "Joining us, Danny?"

Daniël sits down between the two other men. "Wanted to look see if mum and dad are all right, but mum's too busy with the girls and dad is pretending he can actually understand anything the groundsmen are talking about. Hey gaffer, thanks for sharing our day with us. I really appreciate it."

"Why so formal? I just told your husband I want you fit for training in one week." Degaré gets up. "Madame Degaré is going to do something unspeakable to me if she doesn't get at least one more dance."

Daniël takes the opportunity to get a bit closer to Steve. "You're still fine, love?"

"You have to ask me that?"

"Not really. I'm just trying to find an excuse to kidnap you to our home."

"Great wedding, guys. Don't think there's anyone not amusing themselves." Gael crashes on to the nearest chair. "Excellent food, enough to drink, great DJ and a nice mixture of likeable people. And above all, a couple who are genuinely doing this out of love and nothing else."

"This the guys' table?" Gabrysz asks and pulls up a chair.

"Must be," Matthew says, while he too sits down, "since we are here."

"Is it okay if …?" But Kevin already sits.

"Ray, we're here. No, here, you blind or something?" Kurt shouts through the room. "Etienne, here. And tell Alexandre he should stop flirting with that cute little waitress."

"Mind if I?" Dag sits down. "Anyone seen 'Cesco? Hey, pretty boy, come sit with me."

"Did I miss anything?" Niko asks. "Neil, take a chair, if you can find one and squish in."

"Wait for me." Anthony grins. "Now, who starts with the first dirty joke?"

And there're jokes and funny stories and yet another try at explaining why something is hilarious in French but not in English, and the other way around.

Steve, getting perhaps a tiny bit tired, leans happily into his husband. Daniël has his arm around him and nuzzles his hair. "Smells really nice. You, I mean, but the cologne you're using is pretty much okay, too."

"Get a room, fellas."

"Need us to tell you about the birds … make that the bees and the bees?"

"I bet Dan's too embarrassed to get up from behind the table."

"The poor lad just got married, what do you expect?"

"See that, Anthony? Steve's face is even redder than yours when you're screaming at us during a match."

"You guys think it's about time we send them on their way?"

"What do you think, Mr Gavan-Borghart, should we follow their advice?"

Steve nods and smiles. "Take me home, please."

Chapter 34

Two steps inside their new home and they start kissing. With a hunger that's as real as the love and friendship that bind them.

"Getting married gets me horny as hell," Steve hears Daniël whisper in his ear, his tongue teasing a trail. "That, and not having had any for two whole days."

"You mean …?"

"Not even under the shower. I saved it all for you. Feel like I could do it five times in one night and still having left enough for a quickie in the morning." Daniël rubs his obvious erection against Steve's belly to accentuate his words.

Steve has to admit, there's definitely something stirring down there, too … and where's the nearest comfortable surface so he doesn't have to worry about how long he'll manage to keep standing up with a semblance of dignity?

"What about we take this to the bedroom? See if that bed is as comfortable as the salesperson promised." Another kiss. Then, his hand in Daniël's, they walk slowly, carefully up the stairs. There is pain with every step, and yet so much joy is to be found in this simple act, that had been unimaginable hardly more than a year ago and physically still impossible at the beginning of autumn. Them walking up the stairs to the bedroom in their own home. Them wearing each other's rings. Them being together.

The iron bed is the undisputed centrepiece of the room. It's huge, with a handmade mattress, nice warm duvet and more than enough pillows. Egyptian cotton sheets (high thread count, of course). Soft wall-to-wall carpet on the floor.

On the table close to the window, there's a cooler with a bottle of champagne, two glasses, a huge box of expensive Belgian chocolates and a basket.

Daniël takes a look and starts to grin. "Fuckers."

"At least they have excellent taste," Steve chuckles.

The basket contains massage oils in at least half a dozen different fragrances and probably every brand of lube available in every single sex shop in and around Kinbridge, all neatly displayed.

And finally there are two red roses in a narrow, high vase with a small card standing against the crystal.

We don't want to see the two of you back until it's all used up, the boys.

"They're not just fuckers, they're sentimental fuckers."

Steve winks. "I guess we shouldn't complain; they could have barricaded the front door. Or dismantled the bed and hidden the pieces all over the place. Or ..." His words are stopped by a coffee flavoured piece of bitter chocolate, directly followed by Daniël's mouth.

"Let me taste?"

Steve opens his lips readily to receive his husband's eagerly exploring tongue. With both hands on Steve's backside, Daniël presses their body together, panting in excitement. "Tell me you want me to undress you. I really need to get you out of those clothes. Please, Steve?"

"You have to ask me that? Shall we try out the bed?"

"You're getting tired. It's been a long day and I've kept you on your feet for far too long. Now that's what I call a fine way to take care of my husband on our wedding night." Daniël helps Steve quickly to the bed, guilt written all over his face.

"It's not bad to get a bit tired on such a perfect day, certainly not when I get to be naked in the arms of the most sexy, generous, caring man who ever lived. And who will be, of course, also totally without clothes." Steve kisses Daniël's cheek to reassure him.

"I should have paid better attention."

Steve takes the boy's face between his hands and looks at him intently. "We got married today. We have a whole life ahead of us, if we're lucky perhaps even half a century. We will both make more mistakes than we dare to imagine at this moment. But right now you did nothing wrong. I want you excited and wanting me so much you're forgetting everything else. So, are you getting us naked any time soon?"

"Anything my husband desires."

Even with Daniël taking time and care to undress first Steve and then himself it's just a few minutes before they sigh in deep contentment.

"If simply holding you in my arms feels this good, I'm not sure if I'll survive making love to you," Daniël whispers in Steve's ear. "You make me so hard for you."

Carefully Steve wraps his fingers around Dan's shaft. "Want me to use a bit of lube? We've also got plenty of oil."

Quick as anything, Daniël gets up from the bed, grabs the basket, and holds it in front of Steve.

"Strawberry-flavoured lube?" Steve suggests.

"Just as long as you don't have to actually taste the vile stuff, it's pretty good." Daniël puts the basket beside the bed, opens the small bottle, squirts a bit of its contents on the palm of Steve's hand.

A few strokes, a long kiss, a deep sigh and it's done.

"Fuck, didn't even realise I was that worked up."

Steve licks the drops from his hand, swipes the rest from Daniël's belly, and licks that too. "Never let a good thing go to waste. But you're right about one thing: strawberry-flavoured lube should come with a warning: not to be used in combination with oral sex."

"What about I open the champagne? You relax a bit and I get to admire how hot you look. Or we can try out that turbo super shower. Perhaps you want to taste the champagne while in the meantime, I fill the bath." Daniël's voice trembles. He abruptly sits straight up, one eye on the champagne bottle.

But Steve stops him. "Danny?"

"Yes?" His eyes don't meet Steve's.

"It's okay to be nervous, dear boy. I've been ready for you for quite a while, and I know you're ready for me. I want to feel you inside me. So, yes, I would like to have a glass of champagne and a bit of a rest, then we take a shower and after that you're going to make love to me and it's going to be wonderful."

Daniël blushes. "Am I that obvious?"

Steve takes one of the boy's hands into his own and presses a kiss against the palm. "There's a reason I married you. A reason for the inscription on our rings."

So they sit side by side on their bed, pillows propped up behind them, agreeing the champagne has been bought by someone who actually went for taste and not necessarily for the most expensive.

"Gael," they both say at the same time, and start to laugh.

"Bet he had a sample bottle with Matthew, just to be very sure it's the right one." Daniël turns his head sideways and kisses Steve on the lips. "By the time we get under that shower I'm hard again. Never going to make it to … I'm doing it again, don't I?"

"You're not seriously worried you won't have an erection by the time you are finished preparing me, are you? You might be able to get fucked by using a bit of spit and spreading your legs, I'm definitely not. Don't look so concerned, you know how much I enjoyed having two of your fingers in me when we had sex during the last couple of weeks. You think I won't welcome your cock with at least as much joy? But, I do need a bit more, perhaps even a lot more time and preparation than you. Put your glass down, please." He takes Daniël's hand once more, but this time leads it between his legs, past his filling cock, until the fingers brush the tender skin between the cheeks.

"I want you." Daniël's fingers tremble a bit, but his voice doesn't.

"I can't help but wish opening my legs for you and a dollop of lube and your fingers will be enough. But my body has become a stranger I'm still trying to get to know, my mind a friend I hardly recognise on most days. During some moments, I can almost fool myself into believing everything is like before. But it never is."

"You see a clock anywhere in this room? Yes, I'm nervous, but even that doesn't matter all that much. Feel like giving that super deluxe shower a try?"

In the circle of Daniël's arms and under a gentle summer rain, of the kind that almost never happens in reality, Steve feels all tension slip from his body.

"You made a good home for us. Thank you."

"You're welcome." Daniël kisses Steve's forehead. "It's been a good day. Good months, too. I loved being active on the pitch more than I was ready to admit when I thought my career was over."

"It means so much to me seeing you playing regularly again, even if it was as a substitute for the last thirty minutes during about half of the matches. You're going to sign a new contract if they offer you one?"

"As long as you're happy in this house, in this city, yeah, I guess I will consider it."

"Good."

"Want to go back to bed? I'm sort of, well, getting horny again." Daniël holds Steve even closer, sliding his hand over his buttocks.

"I kind of guessed it," Steve teases. "Love your hands there."

Daniël grins. "Yes?"

"Oh yes."

Daniël towels Steve dry and helps him on the chair. "Fuck, can't even take a shower with you without getting a rampant hard-on."

"And that's a problem how?"

"It's not. But I want to concentrate on you for the next hour or so. Give a nice massage, no hurry at all, slowly opening up that sweet arse of yours."

"Spoil me a little and let me taste you?" Steve licks his lips. "I want your cock like mad. First in my hand, now in my mouth and after that you're going to fuck me so deep and good, I'll know I'm truly claimed by you."

"Bed. Now."

Kneeling on a pillow between Daniël's widespread legs, Steve closes his eyes to fully concentrate on the clean slightly musky scent of his very much aroused lover. He licks the first drops of pre-come, using one hand to retract the foreskin. Then he uses the very tip of his tongue to tease the tiny slit.

Daniël moans.

When there's enough spit and pre-come, Steve uses his thumb to touch the same area, gently, very gently, while he uses his tongue to lap the scrotum.

Daniël moans even louder.

Finally, because he knows his lover can't take much more, he takes the head in his mouth and slides down in a slow, but steady pace.

"Please, give me your fingers." Daniël fumbles with the lube, while Steve stretches out his hand. "Try three?"

The short stabbing motion of three fingers in combination with a real hard suck proves to be too much and Daniël erupts so hard and fast Steve has trouble swallowing everything.

He takes the boy, always his boy, in his arms to let him rest for a bit. He thinks Daniël even sleeps for a few minutes.

"I love you so much," he whispers.

Daniël opens his eyes at the sound of Steve's voice and kisses him lazily. "I heard that. Love you too. And not just because you give the perfect blowjob and finger fucking combination." He lets his hand travel over Steve's body. "I want to give that brave, gorgeous body of yours a lot of loving attention. Shall I use vanilla oil? It's a good one, very subtle scent. But, again, don't lick it off."

First, Steve lies on his back and enjoys the experienced hands of his lover. Daniël knows when he has to be as gentle as possible, or when to use a bit more pressure. He doesn't deny the reality of the scars, but simply integrates it into the loving treatment of his husband. He finishes with a short flick of Steve's nipples, a teasing up and down stroke of the now fully-formed erection. "Other side?"

Steve turns on his belly. And again, his muscles get treated like royalty.

"You're getting nice and relaxed; I can feel it. Can see it too." Steve feels his legs being carefully nudged wider. A pillow is being shoved under his belly. A slick finger trails between the cheeks, rests at the opening, and goes in.

He had felt it dozens of times during the last months and it still makes him forget to breathe for a split second. How can anything this simple feel this good?

Faster than any time before he's prepared to accept two fingers inside.

"You feel ready for me." The admiration in Daniël's voice can only be called endearing.

"That's because I am." Steve tries to push back on the fingers. "I need you, Danny, please don't let me wait."

"I'll make it nice and slick." Daniël works as much lube inside as possible. "I'm still nervous I'll hurt you," he admits.

"Don't be. I promise I will tell you as soon as anything happens I don't like for whatever reason. I'm not going to insult the man I gave my marriage vow to only hours ago by holding something this important back from him."

"Thank you." Daniël kisses his neck. "I want to be able to look at your face, look into your eyes. Is that too uncomfortable for you? Physically, I mean."

Steve shakes his head. "I don't think I can keep my legs up and wide for very long without support, but with a pillow or two under my lower back and perhaps resting my legs on your arms, I should be fine."

"I make sure I'm fully done preparing, myself included, so you don't have to wait too long. Oh God, I want you so much."

It suddenly dawns upon Steve how easily they talk about his needs, how they integrate the painful reminders of a history that will likely never be fully part of the past, into the reality of here and now and hopefully their future.

So he turns on his back again and together with Daniël he works out the most comfortable position. He isn't surprised in the least that Dan has a full erection for the third time in less than two hours. A shy smile plays around his mouth, his eyes filled with light.

"The last time …" Steve understands Daniël needs to say it.

"I know."

This time there's no pain at all, not even the slightest discomfort when his husband enters him. He is truly ready, body and mind. They both are.

"You feel good inside me." Steve pauses. "Thank you for fighting death for me …"

For staying at my side during the hours I was lost and couldn't reach you. For finding that one small part of my arm that could be touched when my body was untouchable. For using your voice to defend me, even when you didn't know yet I was worth your trust. For letting me work my arse off. For working your own arse off even more. For everything that is you.

Daniël kisses him. "I love you, and that's that."

Epilogue

Daniël looks at the visitor. "I had expected you much sooner."

Death doesn't react.

"I see: talkative as ever. And you still don't look like a boy or a girl and you could be any age. I bet white people see you as white and black people as black. Even though there isn't really much to see. Real clever.

"You're in a hurry? Nah, didn't think so. The work gets done, no matter what. Cancer is as good a vehicle as old age and it's not like we get much choice anyway, is it?

"It's been a while since we last met. Stupid young thing I was. Berserker. Making demands like I had any say in the matter.

"Years later, I seriously started to wonder what would have happened to me if he hadn't made it. Every possible scenario passed through my mind, from a death by overdose to being married to a woman and having a couple of kids. But then I realised I wasn't able to imagine life without him. It simply wasn't there, no matter how hard I tried and how honest I was with myself. I had managed the first 23 years without him just fine and from one moment to another, it stopped being an option. It refused to become real, even in my own head.

"Last year we celebrated our fiftieth anniversary. Or was it the year before that? It was around the time there was this documentary about us shown on TV, or whatever they call it these days. Had some footage from when we were both still playing for Kinbridge Town. We hadn't looked at any pictures from that time for years, but it didn't hurt watching it. It was sweet seeing my Steve from before. To see the other guys as well. But I had to watch a second time before I noticed anyone but him. So young, all of us ...

"We told our story between the footage. Steve was a bit shy about it. He never likes to talk much; prefers to keeps himself in the background. But for Arnaud Degaré's eldest granddaughter, he made an exception. That's perhaps because we already knew her well, her being married to an English journalist. Lovely girls, both of them. Expecting their first one any day now.

"Been quite a few years since the gaffer died. He could be harsh as a manager. Never lost any sleep over the choices he made, I bet. But to me, he would always be the man who phoned me because he understood the passport photo the police had found in Steve's wallet; who gave me a chance to fight my way back into the first team. Much later, I heard one or two individuals on the board had wanted to get rid of me. Sell me off at whatever price to any club that was willing to pay. He fought them. I played until I was past thirty. We won the Premier League once, some other trophies and silverware. I had some good matches with Oranje too. As a footballer, there was nothing left to prove for me. It was time for something else.

"She brought us to the park where it had happened, but he didn't recognise any of it. It was just a place in a city. Seeing our first house again was nice, though. Totally changed, of course, but it brought back some sweet memories. They filmed the other houses too. There weren't that many. He's never been an adventurous one, my Steve. He liked visiting our little summer home in Holland, though. He adores our nieces and nephews; and later, their children. And they, in return, adore him. Same goes for the kids of our friends. They recognised instinctively his gentle, never-judging soul. His patience that would put most saints to shame. He once made a joke about it, told me he was simply too slow for quick judgement.

"It's so much more than that. His gentleness could drive me crazy at times. How he simply waited until I was done ranting and smiled while I picked up the pieces of yet another broken plate. He made me coffee when I returned from an angry run in the pouring rain. I always told him where I was going and why. He never had to worry about me, even if I have to admit I wish I had been a kinder man during some periods of our marriage.

"There were these nightmares. I never understood why they happened to me, but never to him. Until I dragged myself to a therapist for a few talks and in the end found my own answer. He could have died, but I would have lost him.

"You understand why I had to claim him, don't you? He had to know I was there, fighting at his side, no matter how powerless I was in reality.

"It all passes somehow: time and the knowledge that we stand empty-handed in this life, the anger and the sorrow, the regrets and the victories.

He learned to live with his body. With the fact that he couldn't drive a car or ride a bike. Couldn't talk like before. Couldn't run or even walk more than short distances. Couldn't read at full speed, though that didn't prevent him from reading more than I ever did. But getting rid of his crutches was a milestone. And I learned to be patient, to stop taking tasks out of his hands because I could perform them twice as fast with less than half of the energy and effort it was costing him.

"He never missed even one of my home games and did see most of the away ones, too. I hated the nights away from home, but it was good to run out on the field for the stretches and see him sitting there. Him being a guy and having played for Kinbridge Town meant he was allowed in the dressing room after the game. He always sat quietly on one of the benches, listening to whoever needed listening to, always finding reasons to give out a compliment or two. But he left the sometimes much- needed criticism to the gaffer. I know he would have stayed out if even one of the guys had as much as hinted they didn't want him there. No one ever did, not even the new ones, who had never played with him.

"He still enjoyed the sport, followed it enthusiastically even after I stopped playing. He wrote down his thoughts about it. I had to really talk him into publishing them. But he stopped at interviews and public appearances. Still, there can't be many footy fans or players who haven't read his first book in the past 40 or so years. *The Art and the Skill* became a classic. His second and third book did very well, too.

"And then there was of course his work for charity, but he doesn't like me to talk about that, so I won't.

"It took me a while to find my niche after I stopped playing. Not having much of a talent in that direction, I decided against getting my trainer's licence. But I wanted to stay connected to the sport, so I taught myself photography. Realised my technical shortcomings and followed some courses. I discovered I wasn't one for the fast work during matches, but portraits turned out pretty fine. I had a several exhibitions, lost count of the magazines that placed my photos, published a dozen books. He wrote the text for all of them, because he understood better what I was trying to say than I did. His words gave meaning and depth to the photos I made, beyond the obvious. If I liked the idea, I did commercial work. Can't say I ever did something just for the money. That's real luxury.

"He always supported me in everything. Travelled with me, even if he didn't like it, so I avoided that as much as possible. I ended up with my own studio. He was involved in every stage of my work, from finding ideas to the selection of the final photos. I never did anything without talking it through with him. Often he sat quietly in a corner when I worked, observing. He put the boys at ease by simply being there.

"Sometimes I worked outside my studio. I'm rather proud of my *after defeat* series, not in the least because it formed such a perfect symbiosis with Steve's accompanying text. I simply told the first one to stand against the nearest wall, right after they had lost an important match. Shot a few pictures, then grabbed the next one. I did the same with every team in all the English professional football competitions and tournaments. You get the idea. It was all still there: the mud and grass, the bruises and the tears, the anger and the resignation. How much alike they all looked, and how totally different. Good boys they were, all of them.

"By that time, I was old enough to be the dad of some of the younger boys. No, I never missed having children of my own. The Borghart genes have been well taken care of, even without my personal contribution.

"We saw most of them back at our fiftieth, the boys of our team. Francesco, Dag, Neil, Ray, Kurt … They had travelled from all over the world to be with us. Of course, you remember picking up the gaffer and Niko. Soon after the reunion, you got Anthony too. He had been ill for a while, but never told anyone about it.

"Neil and I stayed good friends after we both retired. Steve and I are godparents to his youngest boy. The lad became a good defender, too. Sweet character, just like his dad. Saw quite a bit of Gabrysz as well. Heart as big as the world.

"You already know about Gael and Matthew. There had been promises they would never crash another plane for how many years now? You mean before that crash? Three more years they visited our home, to take off their masks for a few hours. Then, one day, they made their decision. This time it wasn't about an innocent man being almost beaten to death and his faithful, loving boyfriend. No, it was about the skipper, a local boy. A married man cheating on his wife with another in-all-but-name married man. Family men. They were buried under the same ugly mess as Steve and I had been a few years before that, but with a lot less goodwill.

"But when fans started to make jokes about how Matthew had broken Francesco's heart, we all knew the storm had died down. They got married, stayed the loving parents they had always been. They stopped playing soon after, neither of them wanting to end their careers at another club. Both stayed very much involved with Kinbridge Town. Matthew started training the young lads. He had some fine results with them, too. Gael became a writer and analyst.

"They grew old together and tasted the joy of becoming grandparents. They died together. And I miss them so much.

"I took a picture of my Steve on every single one of our anniversaries and one with the two of us while we're looking in a mirror. I made a book out of it, a gift for our friends and family. *Dan and Steve, A portrait*, it's called."

Daniël looks at the sleeping man beside him, and leans forwards to kiss his forehead.

"He has been the only one for me for half a century. I never even looked at another man. His body has been my home during all those years. My anchor. And I, by whatever undeserved miracle, was his all.

"Is this my final lesson, that love is what remains when all is said and done?"

Death takes a step forward and stretches its hand out.

"If you want him, you will have to go through me." Steve takes his husband in his arms, shielding him. "You can take me too; I've already been blessed beyond what I could have hoped for when he chose to love me. The two of us or the deal is off.

"He is my beloved and my friend. I stake my claim."

Death makes its move.

Author's notes

The Steve Gavan song in chapter 3 is by Joanne Morris.

Bible quotes in chapter 2 are from *The Song of Songs*; those in chapter 33 from the book of *Ruth*.

About R. A. Padmos

In case anyone wondered, yes, I'm female.

I've lived all my life in or around Rotterdam. And 30 of those years I shared with my wife. Our little family also has two sons and five cats.

I started to write stories when I was nine or ten, and haven't stopped ever since. I've published a novel and other fiction and non-fiction but the internet changed everything because I discovered there's a lot more women (and quite a few men) interested in reading and writing male/male stories. And so *Ravages* happened.

www.ingramcontent.com/pod-product-compliance
Lightning Source LLC
Chambersburg PA
CBHW072209170626
46813CB00003B/863